Templar's Acre

MICHAEL JECKS
Templar's Acre

**SIMON &
SCHUSTER**

London · New York · Sydney · Toronto · New Delhi

A CBS COMPANY

First published in Great Britain by Simon & Schuster UK Ltd, 2013
A CBS COMPANY
Copyright © Michael Jecks 2013

The right of Michael Jecks to be identified as author of this
work has been asserted in accordance with sections 77 and
78 of the Copyright, Designs and Patents Act, 1988.

1 3 5 7 9 10 8 6 4 2

Simon & Schuster UK Ltd
1st Floor
222 Gray's Inn Road
London WC1X 8HB

www.simonandschuster.co.uk

Simon & Schuster Australia, Sydney
Simon & Schuster India, New Delhi

A CIP catalogue record for this book is available from the British Library

HB ISBN: 978-0-85720-517-9
TPB ISBN: 978-0-85720-518-6
EBOOK ISBN: 978-0-85720-520-9

Typeset by Hewer Text UK Ltd, Edinburgh

Printed and bound by CPI (UK) Ltd, Croydon CR0 4YY

Neil, Lois, Emily and Izzy
(the wonderful Rowlipops)
With thanks for supporting their medievally-
challenged local writer with wine and beer.

GLOSSARY

Beaucéant   the famous banner of the Templars: white below to show the Order's kindness to friends and pilgrims, black above to symbolise their ferocity when fighting the enemies of Christ.

Bolt   short stout arrow fired from a crossbow. Also called a **quarrel**.

Bullet   small, round stone fired from a sling.

Buss   cargo vessel.

Catapult   large weapon used to hurl missiles at walls and buildings.

Deofol   devil, fool, term of opprobrium.

Falchion   heavy-bladed, single-edged sword.

Foumart   literally 'polecat', an expression of contempt.

Greek Fire   the original flame-thrower used a mixture of chemicals to create a devastating effect, like napalm.

Hoardings   wooden structures built at the top of walls,

	with trapdoors so defenders could attack the enemy from above.
Mameluk	the slave warriors of Egypt.
Mangonel	a form of catapult.
Mantelet	defensive shields on wheels, used to protect attacking forces.
Moors	a term for those who lived in Mauretania i.e. Morocco and Algeria.
Outremer	the whole of the original Crusader kingdom; included the Kingdom of Jerusalem and all the city states. Literally, 'Over the Sea'.
Quarrel	another term for **bolt**.
Saracen	ancient term for the nomadic peoples of Syria; it later came to mean Muslims.
Sequin also **zecchino**	a gold coin minted by the Venetian Republic that remained currency for 500 years.
Trebuchet	a more massive form of catapult for larger missiles.
Turcopoles	light cavalry used for reconnaissance and scouting by the Templars.
Turcopolier	head of the Turcopoles, who led the Templar sergeants into battle.
Wale	the top-most strake in a ship, the top of the hull.
Vintenary	in the military, the captain of a troop of twenty – a vintaine.

CAST OF CHARACTERS

Abu al-Fida	a Muslim merchant in Acre.
Amalric	Brother to the King of Jerusalem.
Baldwin de Furnshill	a noble-born pilgrim to the Holy Land.
Bernat	Roger de Flor's second-in-command.
Buscarel	master of a Genoese ship.
Edgar Bakere	a pilgrim seeking riches in the Holy Land.
Geoffrey de Vendac	Marshal of the Templars.
Guillaume de Beaujeu	Grand Master of the Templars.
Henry II of Jerusalem	the King of Jerusalem.
Ivo de Pynho	horse-dealer and supplier to the Templars.
Jacques d'Ivry	a Knight of the Order of St Lazarus.
Lucia	slave to Maria of Lydda.
Maria of Lydda	widow of the Count of Lydda.
Sir Otto de Grandison	commander of the English forces at Acre.
Philip Mainboeuf	a noted merchant in Acre.

Pietro	Ivo de Pynho's servant.
Roger de Flor	shipmaster of a Templar galley.
Sultan Qalawun	Mameluk ruler of Egypt.
Usmar	son to Abu al-Fida.

AUTHOR'S NOTE

Writing *Templar's Acre* has been a wonderful adventure for me – but I've mixed feelings now that it's done because sadly, it is going to be the last of the Templar series for a while.

There are many good reasons for this. The most important is that I need a change. I am absolutely convinced that for an author to interest the reading public, *he* must first be interested in, and intrigued and fascinated by his subject. As a result, I think I have become one of the worst fourteenth-century anoraks in existence.

Since embarking on the Templar series with Baldwin and Simon, I've grown exceptionally comfortable in their company. I know how they will respond to any number of influences, and I like their families and friends. More, I know their period. I am happier with their politics and politicians than I really should be. And while I do not look at those days through rose-tinted spectacles, I am equally sure that their time was better than has often been depicted.

But every author comes to a realisation that he needs to change direction once in a while, to focus on new challenges. For me, with two books written every year, and concentrating so heavily on my specific period, it has been very difficult to come up for air into the twenty-first century.

Just moving, with *Templar's Acre*, into the late thirteenth century, made writing feel more like a holiday again. Finding new, different characters to write about, a different location, and looking more to the clash of cultures than a straight crime novel, was wonderful.

I have wanted to write about Acre and this final battle for the Kingdom of Jerusalem and the Crusader States ever since my very first fan letter.

In it, so I am told (I wasn't allowed to see it), the writer listed over twenty factual inaccuracies in my book. The first was that I had mentioned that Baldwin had been at the Siege of Acre in 1291. This, the writer stated, was wrong. The siege took place in 1191, and rather than the Christians being attacked in the city, it was Saracens inside the city who were attacked by Richard the Lionheart's men.

My editor, who had only recently commissioned a complete unknown (me), was a little concerned by this list. She called me to ask if I would like to comment on a few of the points raised. The subtext, I think, was: 'Are you a complete moron who got all this detail wrong?' It wouldn't be surprising. No editor likes to think that they could have commissioned a complete turkey.

Fortunately I was able to reassure her. I vaguely recall making a throw-away comment along the lines of, 'If this fool can't even be bothered to check to see that Acre was attacked a hundred years *after* Richard took it, I don't see why I should waste more time on his questions.'

It did niggle.

So for the last seventeen years or so, I've wanted to get heavily involved in a good battle book. And this is the result.

*   *   *

Templar's Acre is a fictional prequel, but the main action and most of the characters were real.

Roger Flor was as I depicted him in the book. The only possible difference between the real man and the one I have invented, is that I have been far kinder to him than he really deserves. In later life he became a noted mercenary, until his death at the hand of an unappreciative employer in 1305.

The scenes of the end of Acre are as accurately portrayed as I can manage.

It was one of the first protracted sieges to be documented extensively. I suppose the fact that so many educated men were able to flee the city helped. Usually, when the Mameluks attacked a stronghold, it was in a place like Safed or Krak des Chevaliers, from which there could be no safe escape. Hemmed in upon all sides, the miserable victims must surrender, in which case death or slavery would inevitably result. Many, of course, chose to fight to the last, refusing to submit even when all hope was gone.

But for me, it was the glorious courage of Guillaume de Beaujeu, of the Masters of the other Orders, and of the English and other pilgrims under great leaders like Sir Otto de Grandison that tells the story.

This was a battle against overwhelming odds; nevertheless, the Christians sought to fight and defend their city. Acre was the last stronghold in Christ's Own land, and they were determined to do everything in their power to protect it. Many died under the onslaught of that terrible machine under Abu al-Fida's command, *al-Mansour*, the siege-engine of death.

The aftermath was appalling. The whole of Christianity bemoaned the fate of that city, and predictions of famine, war and disease became common. And then, in an equally shocking event for most of Europe, it was claimed that a Pope had killed his predecessor to gain the throne.

Without these cataclysmic events, it is likely that the French King Philippe would have found it a great deal more difficult to capture the Templars and break them. If they were still in Acre and the Holy Land, he would not have dared to try to rob them, as he did on Friday, 13 October 1307. With their power base in Palestine, and much of their wealth too, he would have needed a much stronger case.

For me, Acre was a critical siege. It not only evicted the Christians from their lands, it led to a fundamental rethink of the Christian faith. For, if God was so displeased by His people that He would take His lands and give them to Mameluks, that spoke volumes about His feelings for His followers.

It was a terrible time. But for a writer, the worst times are always the best!

I had great fun writing this book. I hope you get as much pleasure in reading it. However, I often receive questions about where a specific detail came from, or how I imagined a scene. Well, usually, I didn't have to. So much has been written about the end of Acre that it was quite easy to research. Whether I was looking into Philip Mainboeuf's journey to the Sultan, or into the organisation of the Templars in battle, there was always a good reference for me.

For those who are keen to read further, I would recommend:

Thomas Asbridge *The Crusades* (Simon & Schuster, 2012)
Alain Demurger *The Last Templar* (Profile Books, 2002)
David Marcombe, *Leper Knights* (Boydell Press, 2003)
John J. Robinson *Dungeon, Fire and Sword* (Michael O'Mara Books, 1991)
Steven Runciman *A History of the Crusades* (Cambridge University Press, 1954)

J. M. Upton-Ward *The Rule of the Templars* (Boydell Press, 1992)

William Urban *The Teutonic Knights* (Greenhill Books, 2003)

This is not intended to be an exhaustive list, but within each of these books are extensive references for the interested researcher to delve deeper.

As usual, any mistakes are my own. Unless they are my editor's, copy editor's, proof reader's . . .

Michael Jecks

North Dartmoor

July 2012

Acre 1291

N E S W

Templars' Ward
Tower of St Lazarus
Gate of Maupas
Hospitallers' Ward
Tower of the Countess de Blois
English Tower
Tower of King Hugh
Tower of King Henry II
St Nicholas' Tower
Tower of the Legate
Patriarch's Tower
Accursed Tower
St Anthony's Gate
Castle
Patriarchate
Montmusart
Hospital of St John
Beaches
Venetian Quarter
Genoese Quarter
Pisan Quarter
The Temple
Tower of the Flies
Mediterranean

Eastern Mediterranean 1291

N · E · S · W

Mediterranean

- Antioch
- St Simeon
- Latakia
- Tortosa
- Krak des Chevaliers
- Tripoli
- Beirut
- Sidon
- Tyre
- Chastel Neuf
- Montfort
- Safed
- Acre
- Haifa
- Castle Pilgrim
- Sea of Galilee
- Jerusalem
- Dead Sea
- Kerak
- Montreal

Templar's Acre

PROLOGUE

29 May 1291

The creaking of the ship was familiar.

As he began to come to, the sound brought back memories of his first voyage, and for one glorious moment he dreamed he was on his way there again – en route to Acre – a year ago, before the catastrophe.

Still only semi-conscious, he listened with half an ear to the thunderous crash of waves against the hull, the wind singing in the sheets, the flapping of flags, the moaning of the timbers. And then he heard the whimpers and weeping all around him, one man sobbing uncontrollably, and he remembered where he was, and his eyes snapped open at the terrible memories that flooded back. He would never sleep again in case he dreamed of them.

The broken bone in his leg hurt like hell. Each movement of the ship made it shift, and he felt the jagged edges grating. The scar at his cheek pulled, and the burns on his limbs shrieked for butter or grease, but Baldwin paid them no heed.

1

In his mind's eye he saw it all again: the flames, the shattering of buildings and bodies, the dread assaults, the devastation. He saw the corpses lining the roads, he saw his little dog, Uther, and he saw the men of whom he had grown so fond: Ivo and old Pietro, Jacques, brave Guillaume, Geoffrey of the sad eyes. All those who had endured the last hellish weeks with him – and then died. And he sobbed unaffectedly as he recalled the disaster that had overwhelmed them all. No tears would come, but he felt the grief must throttle him.

Then he saw *her* again: Lucia, his love; his mistress, with her black hair and olive skin; her calm, trusting eyes . . .

And his heart could no longer contain his desolation.

BOOK ONE

PILGRIM, MAY 1290

CHAPTER ONE

It was his first experience of battle, and for Baldwin de Furn-shill it was made all the more hideous by his sea-sickness.

The screamed alarm came while he was asleep, dozing in the sunshine with the other pilgrims on the deck, and from that first wakening, he had stood gripping the shrouds against the rolling and plunging of the ship as the two enemy vessels came on relentlessly towards them. It was like watching the hounds chasing a deer, seeing these two closing up ever nearer. As the seas rose before them, and the pilgrim ship hurtled down one wave's flank, only to bob up once more, he saw that their pursuers were now only a stone's throw away.

A whistling thrum – and he flinched. A quarrel flew past, missing his face by mere inches, only to thud into the mast. He turned and stared at it. The vicious barbs had sunk so deep, they were almost hidden in the wood. He imagined it would have passed clean through his skull, had it flown true. The thought made the hot bile rise to sear his throat, and he crouched, anxious that another might hit him.

He was not yet seventeen years old; if those galleys caught his ship, he was sure to die before his birthday. Sixteen was too young to die, he thought wildly. He didn't want to die like a coward, but he had never fought in a battle, and he stared about him in a panic, thinking there was no escape from a ship. Then another quarrel hissed past – a second narrow escape.

'Get down, you lurdan!' a man rasped behind him, and suddenly he was flat on the deck. 'Want to get yourself killed?'

Wiping at his eyes as they filled, Baldwin shook his head speechlessly. What was he doing here, in the middle of the sea, with pilgrims and crusaders? He must have been a fool to put himself in this position. But he had to pay for his crime. He prayed that God would pardon him for the murder after his pilgrimage.

If He let Baldwin live.

He shivered uncontrollably as he waited, lying under the protection of the wale.

There must have been three hundred men on board – Christians all, of course, many of them crusaders who had taken up the cross from Antwerp, from Paris or Hainault, a few like himself from England, some mere pilgrims – but they all waited with the same dread, listening to the whack of slingshots and arrows plunging into the wood. Occasionally there was a soggy sound as a missile hit a man, followed by a groan, shriek or curse. The Venetian shipmaster shouted commands as he tried to evade their pursuers, and hoarse bellows from the ships overhauling them were audible over the whine of the wind in the sheets.

All the young man knew was a paralysing terror: not of death or dying, but of failure. His failure.

He shouldn't be here, curled up like a child on this wildly rocking ship. He was the son of a knight, not some low-born bastard-whelp from the coast. His place was on a horse, winning renown and glory at the point of his lance. He ought to be riding behind his knight, a squire or sergeant, bringing a horse to aid his lord, fighting with the other men-at-arms. Instead, look at him! There was no honour in dying here. He had sworn his oath to help defend the Holy Land in hope of his own salvation, and he hadn't even reached the coast yet. These pirates were attacking while they were still on their way.

The reflection was enough to make him grab for the sheer and pull himself upright. A hand reached to drag him back down, but he shrugged it away. It was old Isaac, the pilgrim who had shared his meals from the day they first took ship. Well, Isaac could crawl and hide, but Baldwin would prefer a quick death from an arrow than a coward's end.

The other ships were close now. Even as he rose, he saw a grapnel fly through the air, and threw himself to the side to avoid its hideous barbs. It caught at the ship's wale, and he saw the sailor who had thrown it pulling hard, two of his companions grabbing the rope and helping draw the ships together. The first saw Baldwin, and he smiled – a fierce curl of his lips that sent ice into Baldwin's spine.

He tugged at the metal hooks to release the grapnel and throw it into the sea, but the weight of the men hauling at the rope meant he could make no impression on it. He stared at it, despair flooding him. And then he cursed. He wouldn't submit without a fight! Drawing his sword, he hacked at the rope. One, two, then a third blow – and there was a crack like snapping timber, and the rope parted, the loosed end lashing back. Baldwin saw it whip at the pirate's arm, and lay the man's flesh open to the bone. He screamed and fell, and Baldwin felt a savage joy. He bared his teeth and waved his sword over his head, taunting them, until a pair of arrows passed close by.

But now the pilgrims and crusaders were with him, and they were loosing their own arrows even as the two ships came closer, and Baldwin roared defiance as he saw a sailor topple, struck by a lucky shot. It was only then, as he stared at the sailors on board that ship, that he realised that they did not look like the Muslims he had expected.

These pirates weren't their enemy. With a sickening lurch, he realised that they were fellow Christians.

The flag of Genoa flew at their masts.

The man beside Baldwin fired a crossbow, swore to see it miss his target, and bent to span it again. He shoved his foot into the stirrup, catching the string on his belt's hooks, and straightened his legs until the bowstring was held on the nut. He hastily dropped a quarrel into the groove, aimed, and fired, muttering to himself as he missed again, and lowered it once more to go through the reloading sequence.

The pirates were very close to the larboard side of their ship, and he could see their grim faces: dark, bristle-bearded, savage men, with blades glittering in their fists. The men on his ship began to yell insults, screaming their contempt for the sea-raiders. Baldwin joined in, bellowing abuse with words he barely understood.

The man beside him had reloaded. At this range he couldn't help but hit a pirate, Baldwin thought – when the bowman coughed and lurched, his head striking the wale with a sickening thud. Baldwin instinctively assumed that it must have been a roll in the ship's gait that had made him lose his footing, but then he saw the fletchings of the quarrel protruding from the man's neck, and turned with shock to see that the second ship was even closer, on the starboard side. Her crew were already leaping up onto the wale-piece, and some few had landed on the deck and were hacking about them at the terrified pilgrims.

That was when saw the man with the crossbow, his eyes fixed upon Baldwin as he lifted his weapon to aim.

His bowels seemed to melt within him. All was slow as though, coming close to death, the very fabric of nature and movement of time had been slowed by God. It was punishment for his crime. God was giving him time to appreciate his destruction, as if He had chosen to demonstrate just how feeble were his own puny efforts. God was watching as this ship, full of His servants, was overrun, and Baldwin could do nothing to save himself, nor would God save him. His body was grown listless, his limbs leaden. There was no escape from a crossbow's bolt.

All was futile.

He had travelled all this way in order to reach Acre, to participate in the defence of the last enclave of Christianity in the Holy Land. It was Baldwin's task to help destroy the ungodly hordes of pagans and help drive them back whence they came. And in return, he hoped to win peace from memories of Sibilla, and the body of her lover. In those seconds, staring at the crossbow's quarrel, he remembered this. He remembered the oath taken at Exeter Cathedral, the journey to the coast at Exmouth, then the voyage to English Bordeaux, followed by an overland trip to the Mediterranean coast, where he had caught this ship. All those miles, all those leagues, only to see it end here.

The crossbow was aiming at his heart. He knew it, and in those last moments, Baldwin offered a prayer for his soul. 'Dear Father, accept this soul, undeserving as it may be, and allow me to join You in Heaven. I beg . . .'

He saw the point of the quarrel gleaming with a cold, blue wickedness, and then a man shoved him, bending to grab the crossbow from his fallen companion's hands, and in that moment a roaring sound came to Baldwin's ears. And just for a moment, he thought he was dead. For a moment.

Then the crossbow moved imperceptibly, and the man at his side gave a yelp of agony as the bolt plunged into his back, through his belly, and slammed into the timbers before him. He snarled, turning past Baldwin, and loosed his own crossbow at the ship behind him. The face of the bowman at the ship's rail suddenly gushed blood and fell back, and the man beside Baldwin sank to the deck, coughing and swearing.

And still Baldwin stood, incapable of moving, his sword useless in his hand as he stared at where the bowman had been.

He did feel, truly, as if he had already died.

Or that his soul had – and had been renewed. He felt as though all that had gone before had been taken away by that bowshot, as if it had taken his sins and foolishness with it.

CHAPTER TWO

Master Ivo de Pynho, lately man-at-arms to the Prince Edward of England, caught hold of the wale-piece of the *Falcon* as the ship wallowed in the heavy swell, nearly thrown from his feet. It was pleasant to feel the air on his face again, a cooler air, free of sand and the intrigues of Acre, or the humid odours of Cyprus. The city there stank like a midden in the heat.

He closed his eyes, revelling in the sensation.

Others weren't so comfortable. Already there were three men, one a sailor, lying and groaning down near the mast, all whey-faced as they spewed weakly. Men new to the joys of travel, he thought to himself. It was twenty years since he had first clambered aboard a ship and made his way over the seas to Outremer, the Crusader colonies, with his prince.

He had never returned home. Afterwards, the shame was too great. He had made a new life in the Holy Land. For a while – for a little while.

'Ivo, shift your arse, man! I can't see while you're standing there!'

The coarse French was the natural language of those who lived in Outremer. Ivo didn't glance towards the speaker, but waited until there was a gentle falling away sensation and the vessel began to slide down the next wave, and then walked down the sloping deck to the main mast, where he caught hold of a rope and clung on. 'That better?'

'We'll make a sailor of you yet, Ivo,' the shipmaster sneered. His father had been a German, his mother came from Brindisi. While he laughed at Ivo's Devon burr, his own speech contained an interesting combination of accents.

'You'll be in Hell long before I become a sailor,' Ivo growled with feeling.

'Me? I'll be in Heaven, man, singing and drinking! God won't punish *me*!'

'God hates all mariners, Roger,' Ivo said. 'Why else would He make the pox-ridden sons of whores so ugly?'

'Why, so that miserable runts like you, who live on land all their lives, can have a moderate chance with the women, Ivo – because otherwise, it would only be sailors who populated the world with offspring. As it is, all men who live near to port know that their women lie with sailors if they want some fun. And it is hardly surprising, man, because—'

'Yes, yes, Master. You should concentrate on the ship and the weather,' Ivo said.

'Aye,' Roger grunted. His dark eyes were watchful as he surveyed the seas before them, gripping the steering oar beneath his armpit. His sight was not very good, and he must peer hard to see all the way to the horizon. Not that the horizon was visible most of the time, Ivo thought with disgust.

Their voyage had been comfortable until today. For all his faults, and Ivo personally thought they were many, Roger Flor was a good shipmaster who understood the ways of the water about here. They had set off from Cyprus in bright, clear weather with the sea as flat as a slate, and it was only in the last day that the weather had grown more tempestuous, with the sort of winds that made Ivo glad to be up on deck with a clear view. Even *his* belly would rebel, were he down below with the horses. Their whinnying could be heard now, over the thrumming of ropes and, the creaking of timbers being tested to their limit.

'What's wrong?' he asked, watching the shipmaster.

Roger Flor was leaning forward. A tall, bearded man, almost gaunt in appearance, he had the near-black hair and deep brown eyes of a Castilian. For all that he was born a Christian a quarter-century ago, he would pass as a Saracen, were it not for the brown tunic with the red cross on the breast, and the short hair under his stained coif that marked him out as a Templar.

He called to his henchman now, a heavy-set sailor with a ragged scar on his face from nose to ear. 'Bernat, look there. What do you see?'

Following his gaze, Ivo could make out a mast on the horizon. It disappeared as their ship dropped sickeningly into the valley between two waves, and then he saw that there was not one mast alone, but two – no, three. A flag was fluttering from the top of one, and he peered in vain to see what it might be.

'You'd best make sure the horses are safe,' Roger said to Ivo, and his voice had lost all banter. It was calm and commanding as he shot a look up at the rigging, checked the sails, and turned back to the three ships. The *Falcon* lurched sideways and a fresh outbreak of equine panic came from below. 'I don't want to see the brutes lost because they haven't been tied down properly. That'd reflect as badly on me as you. Off you go.'

Ivo nodded and made his way carefully to the ladder as the ship began to tip over the crest of another great wave. When he looked at the horizon again, he could see nothing but a wall of water. It looked as though they were already pointing down to the bottom of the sea and would never rise back.

The way to the hold was a narrow ladder set against the deck, and lashed more or less securely to the hatch.

Ivo had descended this three times a day to check on his charges, a pair of strong destriers, seven rounseys and a few sumpters, along with a number of ponies, all needed by the Templars at Acre to replace their losses at Tripoli. Today, with the sea moving like a sheet of silk flapping in a gale, the passage was treacherous. Sinking down through the hatch, he felt lighter on his feet, as though there was an invisible hand plucking at him, tugging him from the rungs to fling him to the deck, but he clung on until the ship's motion changed once more . . . regained his weight and made it to the decking. He had to stand there a moment, still clutching at the ladder while he caught his breath, breathing in the odours of horse sweat, urine and shit.

Down here it was a scene from Hell. The destriers in particular were wild, lumbering and stumbling as the ship moved, kicking at the boards behind them, and Ivo could easily understand why. Down here, all noise was emphasised and enhanced. Every wave slapping against the hull made a noise like a kettle-drum, as if a giant was beating the sides of the vessel. Amidst the groaning of the timbers, the constant howl of the ropes added to the hideous din for the terrified animals.

He saw a groom sitting miserably, his head over a pool of vomit, and kicked him up. 'Go and see to the horses, unless you want me to tell the Grand Master you've been derelict, you bitch-son! If any more die, you'll be responsible.'

The man weakly muttered a curse, but rose and wandered sluggishly amongst his charges, while Ivo went to his palfrey and tried to calm him. Black as coal, he was, with a white star to the right of his brow, a strong, powerful brute. But as he patted the beast's neck and rubbed its nose, he heard bellowing up on deck. It sounded urgent, and he heard the sonorous pounding of the drum calling the sailors to. His horse whickered and jerked his head, eyes wild, but Ivo could not wait. He darted for the ladder, and was soon back on deck, relieved to be out of that noisome hole.

'Well?' Roger demanded.

'They'll live. Only two have died this passage.'

'Good.'

'Why the drum?'

'Why?' Roger asked, leaning heavily on the steering oar as he bared his teeth in a smile of wicked pleasure. 'Look up there, Ivo: Genoese, mother-swyving pirates.'

Peering ahead, Ivo gauged the distance between their vessel and the ships bound together in their battle. Shrieks and cries came to him over the water, even above the din of the massive waves. He saw three ships: two were galleys, but of different classes. The third looked to Ivo's eye to be a Venetian merchant vessel, designed for transporting high-value goods, while the galleys looked to be Genoese, as Roger Flor had said. No surprise there: the Genoese and Pisans both detested Venice.

'What will you do?'

Roger gave him a grin. 'What should a Templar ship do? I will go to the aid of our allies, Master Ivo. It is my duty!'

Ivo nodded, and clung to a rope as Roger bellowed his commands. There was a general movement of men, some clambering up the ratlines to the sails at Roger's urging, while others fetched grappling irons and boathooks, setting the tools about with careful precision. Each knew his place: these were Templar shipmen. They would fight united, as would their brothers on land.

'The Grand Master will be disappointed if his horses are harmed,' Ivo said meditatively.

'Today, the Grand Master can kiss my arse,' Roger responded, leaning heavily on the oar. The ship slowly heeled over, breasting one wave and sliding down the farther side. 'He isn't here. We have allies in the Venetians, and I won't see them boarded and robbed.' He grinned. 'Not when we could take them and keep their booty for ourselves.'

'You would rob your own grandmother.'

'That is a malicious piece of villeiny-saying!' Roger said with a hurt glance. 'I wouldn't dream of robbing her. She had nothing worth taking! But a Genoese trader, that's different. It depends what they're carrying, of course, but there could be a rich cargo on board.'

He was silent a moment, but Ivo could sense his eyes flitting towards him every so often, gauging his reaction to the news.

He had known Roger Flor some years. The shipman had gone to sea at the age of eight, and his skill as a navigator had led to his being made shipmaster after he joined the Templar Order. In those days Roger had been a callow young man of some nineteen or twenty years, and while his ability with a ship was never in doubt, it was plain that his interests lay more in the opportunities available in the Holy Land than in his duties as a Templar. And just now, he could see the potential for a good profit. At sea Ivo quite liked Roger Flor – but he didn't trust him on land.

They made good way, even with the roiling waters. At each crest, Ivo could see the ships growing closer and closer. The one in the middle appeared to be rolling to and fro violently, while the two at either side seemed more stable, and he saw that men were loosing arrows from them into the stricken ship.

Ivo knew how the crew would be served there. He had endured such battles himself, and could imagine the scene already: arrows would make the decks lethal. Bodies would be pinned to the planks beneath them, men panting and struggling for breath, while others tried to hide behind the flimsiest partitions. Screams, groans, sobs, the sounds of panic and horror.

The shame of it: Christians fighting on the open sea, when their last city, Acre, the jewel of Outremer, was desperate for aid. The other states of the crusader kingdom had been taken, and even now Muslim hordes waited at her borders, slavering with the thought of the easy prize sitting there so defenceless. Christians needed to unite to defend her, but no. Genoa, Venice and Pisa were at loggerheads as usual. And now a pair of Genoese galleys were trying to capture a Venetian cog. It made his heart weep.

But he was not by nature prepared to submit to misery. He had seen such things too often since he took up his new life in the Holy Land, and now he felt the warrior's anger again, the slow burning rage that heated the blood, as he looked at the ship. He had noticed it in the harbour, sailing off while he was seeing to the last of the horses being stowed belowdecks – a small buss, a two-masted ship of perhaps double the size of a cog from the northern waters.

Roger suddenly bawled commands, and his sailors scurried. One man paused, puked on the deck, and then carried on. The others had forgotten their sickness in anticipation of the fight to come.

'Let the flag of the Order be flown!' Roger bellowed, and the pennant, which had been stowed away two days ago when the wind began to tear at it, was hurriedly attached to the halyard and hoisted. 'Let's see what they make of that, eh?' Roger asked, his teeth shining.

The swooping, rolling motion seemed to grow in urgency, as though the ship herself was desperate to get to grips with the pirates. Ivo clung with desperation to a rope, his legs bending as the ship slammed into a great wave, hurling spray over the whole deck. There were men on the yards now, reefing the sail, while others worked with frantic haste, running hither and thither, each man knowing his position. Roger Flor was a good master, and now he kept an eye on his crew as they hurried from one point to another, depositing weapons, readying themselves and the ship for battle.

But when they were done, there was a long wait as they approached the three. It felt as though they were crawling, foot by foot, yard by yard, and Ivo was convinced that they must arrive too late to help. As it was, they must have been seen, and the two ships would be ready to beat them off.

'Bowmen, to the tops!' Roger roared, and the sailors with crossbows took their leather pots of quarrels and began to climb, bows slung over their backs. 'Men! These Genoese whoresons have tried to take a shipload of crusaders! Crusaders are here to defend our kingdom! They are here to help us! They are our friends and allies, and I mean to make these pirates pay for harming them! Do you want to let them escape with that black crime unavenged? Should we permit them to go free? I say no!'

There was a bellow of approval from the men nearest, although Ivo was sure that only a half of the crew could have heard his words over the roar of the sea and howling winds. Still, he saw from their expressions that many of them were anticipating the fight with joy in their hearts.

Typical sailors, Ivo thought to himself. Never happier than when in a brawl.

Roger looked at him. 'Soon now, Ivo. Are you ready?'

'I'm almost double your age, lad. I've seen enough fights since I came here with my prince,' Ivo said.

'Aye. That prince is King now, isn't he? And *you're* still here,' the master added pointedly.

Ivo felt his face stiffen at the reminder of his old shame. 'How long?' he muttered.

'Soon. Very soon.'

CHAPTER THREE

Baldwin de Furnshill was crippled with shame.

He was brother to Sir Reynald de Furnshill, son of a knight, a man of honour and trained in the sword, and yet he had been bested by Genoese pirates.

When the men came over the rails, he stood back to give himself room, but before he could do more than slash inexpertly at the nearest attacker, a blow from a cudgel drove him to his knees. All around, he saw pockets of resistance as pilgrims attempted to hold the Genoese at bay, but it was impossible to stand against them for long. A number of the crusaders and pilgrims allowed themselves to be driven back towards the hold, while others dropped and submitted, craving mercy of the sailors. All were spared.

Baldwin's head span, and as the deck rolled, he fell to the side, as helpless as a newborn foal. His legs were incapable of supporting him. But worse than the shocking pain was the shame. He should have died killing his enemies – that was the way for a knight's son to fight! He wanted to reach for his sword. It lay near him – but he lacked the strength to lift it.

Two sailors from his own ship continued to fight, one with a short sword and a knife, the other with a long-handled axe, and side-by-side, they held their opponents at bay. They forced one sailor to spring back, while another caught a slash from the axe across his belly that made him howl. At last two crossbowmen were brought up and ended their final stand. Their bodies fell, and were thrown overboard like carrion to feed the fishes. No Christian burial for them.

He felt himself jerked up and shoved back against the hull, and sat, his head lolling, watching as the Genoese walked amongst them, snatching at jewellery and other valuables. Any who carried purses were relieved of them. Baldwin's sword was taken, and now he felt a man yank at his purse, and there was a sudden release as the strings were cut and it was gone.

Another grabbed his hand. Baldwin looked up to find himself meeting the stare of a black-bearded man with a round face, burned the colour of oak by the sun. Baldwin tried to jerk his hand away, but the man laid a knife's edge against his knuckle and then drew the ring off. It was Baldwin's last possession given to him by his father, and he should have wept to see it taken, but he couldn't. He was without feeling. Numb.

And then the Genoese began to scurry, sensing a new danger.

There was no attempt to conceal their approach. Roger Flor aimed the *Falcon* straight at the three vessels locked together, constantly adjusting the oar under his arm as he saw the way that the three moved. There was movement on the left-most galley. A man appeared, a thick-set fellow with a black beard that was trimmed neatly. He stood on the sheer, a hand on a stay nearby, and as the *Falcon* came closer, he turned and beckoned to another. This was a crossbowman, who stood at the rail, listening to instructions from the bearded commander.

Ivo eyed them warily. He knew how accurate Genoese bowmen could be, but while they were under wind, gaining on the three ships, the bowman's ship was wallowing. He had a rolling, plunging deck to fire from. Ivo felt moderately safe.

He was right. The crossbow was raised, aimed and fired – but as the three ships breasted one wave, Ivo's plummeted down another, and the bolt flew safely overhead.

'If that prickle tries a trick like that again, I'll have his ballocks,' Ivo muttered, unnerved.

'Scared, are we, Master Ivo?' Roger Flor chuckled 'Fear a quarrel from a Genoese bow?'

A second quarrel slammed into the wale-piece directly below Roger.

'You fox-whelp whoreson!' Roger bellowed, and roared for his own bowmen to return fire. Soon three men in the forecastle joined with seven in the fighting top, trading quarrels with the other ships. 'Keeps the men busy,' he said defensively, seeing Ivo's eye upon him.

'Yes, of course,' Ivo said, and then, 'Who is it on those ships? Can you see who the master is?'

'It's that Genoese bitch-son, Buscarel.'

Just then, another quarrel flew past Ivo's belly and thumped into the wood behind him. He had a vision in his mind, just for a moment, of what that bolt could have done to him, and then he was roaring encouragement to the sailors. All were clad in their brown tunics with the red cross, apart from him. He was wearing a red linen tunic that left him cool in the summer at Tripoli, but here, about to enter a battle, he wished he had some armour: mail, a coat of plates and a helm.

He hoped and prayed he wouldn't need it.

A clatter, and another bolt fell from chains at the lateen sail overhead. It was enough to inspire his rage. He drew his sword, his head lowered, as another bolt flew past, and then there was a cheer as the bowman in the Genoese ship was hurled back, a bolt in his skull.

'A florin to that archer!' Roger shouted, and then, 'And another to the man who hits the other pirate!'

There was a loud cheer at that, but now the bolts were flying in earnest, and even Roger ducked as a pair came perilously close. 'They don't like me, Master Ivo.'

'Few men do,' Ivo said.

'True enough!' Roger said with a wide grin. Then: 'Grappling irons!'

Three men had already moved forward with their hooks, and stood measuring the distance between the ships. There was only a chain between them; a half-chain. The men grew silent with anticipation as the distance closed. Five yards, two yards, and the men swung their hooks from both ships, all hauling to pull the ships together. While the rest of the sailors weighed the weapons in their hands, the Templars crouched, ready to attack, the Genoese scowling on their lower decks, all waiting, filled with the desire to kill.

One grapnel landed in the cordage overhead, and the Templar hauled on it with determination, while the others carried on tugging at their ropes. Then the sea moved, and the gap disappeared, the *Falcon* thundering into the side of the nearer ship.

And then the peace was shattered.

'Board them!' Roger screeched at the top of his voice.

There was a clash of steel against steel, and Ivo saw three felled by arrows, all together, but the others carried on, weapons aloft, screaming battle cries as they went.

Overhead, the man with his hook in the rigging climbed up

23

the rope hand over hand, a long knife in his belt, and soon was at the yard. A Genoese saw him, and began to make his way up a stay, but the sail was already falling away, the upper fixing cut through by the knife.

'To me, men of the Order! For God and the Temple!' Roger shouted, and fixing the tiller oar with a rope, he snatched up a sword and ran at the side of the ship, leaping over and in among the Genoese.

Ivo followed, his own sword gripped in his hand, but as soon as he landed on the ship, he was overwhelmed by the sheer numbers of their enemies. All about him were Genoese sailors, and he was forced to hack and slash from side to side, keeping them away, until at last some more sailors from the *Falcon* arrived at his side and began to flail about too, forcing the Genoese back. There was a man who had a long stabbing weapon, which held them up for some time, but Ivo grabbed the point and yanked at it, thrusting forwards with his sword at the same time. It caught the man below the chin and slipped in, down into his chest, killing him quickly. A second ran at him with an axe held high, and Ivo turned, whirling with his sword as the man's blow fell, and sweeping off both wrists. The man stood staring, shrieking at the wreckage of his forearms, until Ivo reversed his blade and hacked off his head, moving forward all the time.

Suddenly he was at the ship the pirates had boarded, and he sprang down onto the deck. There were bodies all over the place, blood seeping into the boards underfoot making each step treacherous, and Ivo was cautious as he made his way onward.

A cry, and suddenly missiles were flying all about him. A shot from a sling rattled against metal, then two men nearby fell, but he managed to make his way to the far side of the ship where a lanky, black-haired youth was sprawled against the timbers, eyes almost as dull as a dead man's. Ivo threw himself down and glanced back over the deck. There were three men from the *Falcon* lying and moaning, each with an arrow pinning him, but there were more men near him, and all had weapons. The clamour of war still came to him from the other pirate ship, but now as he looked about, more men were coming to this deck. There was a bellowed order that made him give a grunt of satisfaction. The ropes binding the ships together were cut, and with a shiver, he felt the vessel shake off her attacker. With a roar of defiance and glee, the sailors of the *Falcon* lifted their arms and shook weapons still smeared with the blood of their enemies.

Ivo glanced to his side, at the young man beside him. 'You'll have a story to tell your children, anyway,' he told him.

Baldwin looked at him, and vomited weakly.

BOOK TWO

CRUSADER, JUNE–JULY 1290

CHAPTER FOUR

The view was one to fill a man's heart with wonder. Baldwin gaped: truly, this must be the Holy Land. God had preserved him to see this, to fight and protect it. He would be saved, he thought. His murder would be forgiven here.

Behind him he had left his guilt in a green, but drab England. There was little colour but grey stone, mud-daubed and white-washed houses, and grass under a gloomy grey sky.

As they approached, the vast sweep of a natural bay opened before him, and it was on the northernmost edge that the city of Acre stood. Vast, more glorious than Exeter or Limassol or any of the great French cities he had passed by and through, it took his breath away. This city gleamed as though it was clothed in perpetual sunlight: a city of gold. Terracotta made a splash of colour, and there were patches of red, blue and green that rippled in the heat: awnings to provide shade.

Stone towers ringed a fortress at the tip, overshadowing the rest of the city, and from beneath it, the wall of the harbour stretched out into the bay, where there stood another tower upon a rocky prominence. There were houses everywhere, and what looked like a monastery, with a castle behind. A double line of walls ringed it, reaching all the way to the sea, the inner wall higher than the outer so that archers could fire over the heads of men at the outer wall into enemies on the plain. More massive towers rose up along its length, while outside the walls there was a number of tents and small houses, with farmland beyond.

A city of gold, with verdant land to feed it, Baldwin thought. Yes, this was how Heaven must look. It was no wonder that men wanted to take it from Christians. Nor that Christians would fight to the last to protect it.

'That's the Temple up there at the tip,' Ivo said with a smile, seeing the direction of his eyes. 'Templars always pick the best locations. This is their headquarters, now Jerusalem is lost.'

'That's why I'm here, to help win it back,' Baldwin said with a hint of pride.

'Yes?' Ivo said, and his smile was not unkind as he looked down at Baldwin. He sounded condescending, however, and Baldwin tried not to scowl as he replied.

'I will fight for the Church to win back Jerusalem,' he said. 'My father was a knight.'

'You've much to learn, Master.'

Baldwin gave him a sharp look. He did not like to be patronised, but before he could speak, Ivo continued.

'This is the last bastion of Outremer, the "Land Over the Sea". Twenty years ago we could have taken Jerusalem, but now? We've lost the castles, we have lost Lattakieh, Tripoli, everything.'

'Those who come with pure hearts will win for God,' Baldwin asserted. 'He will not allow His land to be taken by the heathen.'

'So, of all the thousands who have come here, you think you're the first to have a pure heart?' Ivo snapped. 'Are you truly that arrogant, boy?'

'No, of course, I . . .' Baldwin faltered.

'How's your head?' Ivo asked after a moment, regretting his sudden outburst. There was no need to offend the lad. He had come in good faith to fight for the Holy Land. As had Ivo himself, all those years before.

'Better, I think,' Baldwin said, his hand at his temple. 'Why did they attack us?'

'Your flag. The Genoese hate Venice. It's always war when they meet on the seas.'

'But both are Christian.'

'Aye. That doesn't mean they like each other. They're enemies, and fight when they meet. They're so keen on trade with the Muslims that they'll draw swords against anyone rather than upset their actual enemies. That's how the Muslims have taken so much land from us.'

'It makes no sense.'

'You think I don't realise that?'

Baldwin searched his face, but Ivo gave him no further explanation. So Baldwin gazed instead at the city. 'It's beautiful.'

'Acre is the jewel of Outremer,' Ivo agreed.

'You are English?'

'Yes.'

Ivo was not forthcoming, and Baldwin turned from him. Looking at the vast port, he felt his soul shrink. The attack on the ship had terrified him, and the blow to his head had jarred his entire body, making him for the first time fully aware of the dangers of battle. He desperately wanted a friend. Home seemed so far away. He had so much to atone for: Sibilla and her man. The man Baldwin had killed. That was why he had fled. He had been right to do so, he was sure. Here he could serve God, and hopefully forget his shame. But he still dreamed of Sibilla. Her eyes, her lips, her warmth and softness.

He ought not.

Baldwin felt sure that if he told this stern fighter about his reasons for coming here, he would alienate himself. He was here to join the crusaders and win absolution, and yet seeing Acre for the first time, he realised its immensity. He dreaded being set ashore alone.

'Is there a place where crusaders go?' he asked.

'Bars and brothels, usually,' Ivo said shortly.

Baldwin felt his hackles rise. 'I am not used to such places.'

'You'll get used to them.'

Perhaps Ivo was not the man from whom he should seek aid, Baldwin thought. He was clearly brutish and ill-mannered.

'Master, I am sorry if I've offended you,' Ivo said. 'It's my own bile. I am told I have a melancholy nature. Perhaps they are right. Look, if you're sure you want to join them, you'd best go to the cathedral.' He pointed towards the monastery. 'It is there, in front of the Temple. You'll find all the help you need.'

'I thank you.'

'Aye. And godspeed. But don't expect too much honour and glory here. All you're likely to find is a coffin – if you're lucky.'

Baldwin felt terribly small as he walked the narrow streets, his pack over his shoulder. He must find the cathedral, and learn where he might acquire another sword. He needed money, too. Ivo was a kindly soul, and had given Baldwin a small leather purse and a few of the local coins so that he might buy food and drink, but it wouldn't last forever. First, he must get to this cathedral. It was called St Anna, apparently named for the mother of the Blessed Virgin Mary.

At the harbourside there were trestles with fresh fish laid out on their boards, and soon he was walking past tables filled with foods he didn't recognise: spices, nuts and berries, then cloths of a richness and colour he had never imagined.

The place was rammed with people. In the narrow streets, it was alarming to be jostled and pushed about by so many – but over his growing irritation, Baldwin was aware of a savage joy. He was near to where Jesus Himself was born. That was a wonderful thought.

Baldwin suddenly found his way blocked by a man in a cream-coloured cloak, wearing a white linen coif. Clearing his throat impatiently, Baldwin frowned at the delay. The man turned with an enquiring expression.

'My apologies, my friend,' he said pleasantly. 'Was I hampering your advance?'

Baldwin took in the red couped cross at his breast and bowed apologetically. The man had a greying beard that reached down to his chest, and that, along with the red cross, the white robes, and the sword, marked him out as a Templar.

'No, sir knight, *I* should apologise. I had no idea you were a Templar.'

'Me?' The man's eyes crinkled with amusement. 'No, I'm no Templar. Though I try to do my part. You are new to the city?'

'I have just arrived. I am here to join with the crusade.'

'Then you are doubly welcome. My name is Sir Jacques d'Ivry.'

Baldwin introduced himself, studying the man with interest. Templars were the only Order who tended to grow beards, he knew, while also shaving their heads. It was a sign of their rejection of secular life. This man had hair, he could see – but perhaps here in the Holy Land men would emulate priests and only shave their tonsure? Still, this knight had a gentle, kindly look in his blue eyes, like the vicar at Exeter's sanctuary who had blessed him and sent him on this journey.

'It is an easy mistake. I am a Knight of the Order of Saint Lazarus.'

Baldwin felt a shiver at his spine on hearing that: a Leper Knight.

He had always borne a horror of that foul disease. It was a sign of God's rejection, many said, and the victim must be uniquely foul to deserve such a mark.

Sir Jacques did not notice his revulsion. 'I joined the Order from an ambition to serve, and what better Order in which to protect the needy and defenceless? But many of my Order join us from the Templars, which is why our symbol is so similar to theirs. When a Templar learns he has leprosy, he will come to our house, and his service continues.'

He broke off. A man was proffering fruit from a bowl, and he took an orange with gratitude, bowing to the man and thanking him in a language strange to Baldwin's ears.

'What was that you spoke?'

'Arabic, my friend,' the knight said. He had a small eating knife in his hand and he cut the orange twice about the middle, so that the flesh came away like four petals of a flower. He left the skin attached to the orange, and studied it with a satisfied smile, replacing his knife in a sheath hidden under his tunic. 'So, you are new here?'

'I was told to find the cathedral.'

'It is up that road, then turn left and keep going. You are rather out of your way.'

'I am grateful.'

'It is my pleasure to be of service, my friend. I hope we shall meet again.' He pressed the orange upon Baldwin, ignoring his protestations that he could not accept it, until Baldwin took it with as good a grace as he could manage.

'Go with God, my friend. May He guide and guard you.' Sir Jacques looked over Baldwin at the market behind. 'May He guard us all,' he added quietly.

CHAPTER FIVE

Baldwin strolled in the direction Sir Jacques had indicated, eating the orange with delight. It was a rare treat for him at home, and oranges were never this sweet and juicy. As he walked, he wondered whether he was following the same paths his father had taken when he had come here.

He had often heard the story from his father's lips. Twenty years ago, he had joined the young Prince Edward and sailed here. Prince Edward had hoped to stimulate a renewed fight to win back territories overrun by the Saracens, and could have succeeded, had he brought more men with him. But with the tiny force at his command, it was impossible.

Since his departure, as Ivo had said, the Saracens had rolled back the Christians from their borders. The Hospitallers had been forced from their great fortresses at Marqab and Krak des Chevaliers, and the Teutonic Knights had lost their castle at Montfort. Now the only protection for the cities of Outremer was the ring of castles owned by the Knights Templar. This was why so many Christians from all over the world were coming here, to Acre, just like Baldwin, in order to help the people protect their city, because the dread ruler of Egypt was threatening to overrun this last enclave.

Baldwin walked past yellow stone houses. The people here wore flowing black or white robes, with strange headgear, and their dark faces had intense brown eyes that watched him without speaking, as though he was a foreigner and had no right to be here. Never before had he felt so alien, and to be here unarmed was doubly alarming.

In the alleys were buttresses with arches beneath them for men to walk along, and irregular buildings that projected into alleys, all constructed of this golden stone. To have the money and labour to set about creating a city of stone was astonishing. He knew of some buildings – castles, cathedrals, abbeys – which depended upon such materials, but not an entire city. Here even peasants must live safe behind stone.

He kept on, marvelling, until he reached a dead end, and there he stood, gazing back the way he had come. Down there, between the buildings of the twisted lane, he could see the sun glinting off the sea, and he was compelled to stand admiringly, filled with serenity, it looked so lovely. On his way back down the hill, he stopped, wondering which road might take him to the cathedral. His sense of direction, usually acute, was failing him. Surely the cathedral must be to his right, if the sea was before him?

Hearing a door slam, he saw a woman appear in the lane, and he called to her. She ignored him, so he hurried after her. When he was a matter of yards from her, she threw him an anxious look. She was tall – and slim, he thought, under flowing emerald robes – but beyond that he could see little of her. Her face was veiled, her hair hidden in a hood, but her eyes were visible. Beautiful, they were: green, and outlined in kohl.

'Mistress, I wondered if you could help me?' he began.

To his astonishment, she picked up her skirts and pelted away. Ach! There was no point in chasing her. She was fleet of foot, and he was not, after his injury. His head was pounding with pain and the heat. In any case, with the luck that had dogged him since leaving Italy, she would be unlikely to speak his language.

He stared about him dejectedly. These alleys all looked the same. After a moment's reflection, he decided that his initial thought must have been correct. The cathedral must lie to the west. He set off down the hill.

At a crossroads he turned right, hoping that the higher ground that appeared to lie this way signalled the location of the cathedral. The alley narrowed, and then he saw that up ahead it broadened into a wider thoroughfare. Yes, it definitely had the appearance of a less intimidating, less foreign area, and he was relieved as he walked on, until he entered a square and gazed about him.

At the northern edge there was a huddle of men about a table, drinking and laughing, and he gave a sigh of relief, for none looked like Saracens. Most were sailors. He walked towards them with hope bursting in his breast that he could soon be out of here and safely at the cathedral, but then his steps faltered.

The leader of the Genoese ship was among them, staring at him with hostility as he drew a long knife.

'Only three dead? You have done well,' the Marshal, Geoffrey de Vendac, said. 'Any other troubles?'

'We had to save a ship of pilgrims.'

The Marshal nodded. He was slightly older than Ivo, strong and moderately tall, with a grizzled beard and brown eyes in a square face.

Ivo knew him well, but never took advantage. The Templars were the most powerful force in Christendom, because they answered to God and the Pope, no one else. Not even the French King had an army to compare with their Knights. But the Marshal had lost much of his confidence in recent months. He had been in Tripoli during the siege, and Ivo knew he felt guilt for surviving when so many innocents had died. People like his wife Rachel and their young son Peter.

'Pirates?' the Marshal asked.

'Genoese.'

'They're a menace to all shipping,' the Marshal said, scowling. 'They plunder without thinking they harm all Christians.'

Ivo shrugged. 'It's always been the way between Venetians and Genoese.'

'It has grown worse in the last year.'

Ivo nodded at that. The Genoese blamed the Venetians for losing Tripoli, and their rivalry had once more exploded into open war at sea.

Their business concluded, Ivo was gathering his pack before leaving, when the Marshal asked quietly, 'Is there any news?'

Ivo shook his head. 'There can be none,' he said with fierce certainty. He thrust the last items into his bag and pulled the strap over his head. 'They are dead, Marshal. You know that as well as I do.'

It was more than a year ago that the Marshal himself had brought the news that Tripoli was overrun.

Ivo had not expected it. No one had. At the time, the Egyptians had seemed content. They had taken castles, towns and villages – the whole of Outremer was open to their attacks – and then they took Tripoli too.

MICHAEL JECKS

Ivo had heard much about the attacks. How massive catapults were erected and were firing their missiles within hours.
A corner tower crumbled, then a second between that and the
sea, and suddenly the whole city was open to assault.

The Venetians were blamed because it was they who pulled
out first. They grabbed their money, crammed their goods on
board their ships, and sailed away with their men-at-arms. The
Genoese, fearing the Venetians had learned of some imminent
disaster, took to their own vessels. Seeing the galleys of both
leave the harbour, it was plain that the city must fall. Women
wailed in despair, men stood shocked, watching their allies
flee.

But not for long.

Muslim soldiers scaled the rubble where the wall had
collapsed, and were over it and into the city in no time, slaugh-
tering the men, capturing women and children for slaves. Some
inhabitants managed to make it to the little island where St
Thomas's Church stood, praying for sanctuary, but the Muslim
cavalry saw them and waded out to the island.

Not a single Christian escaped that carnage.

Tripoli had been a beautiful city. Wide roads, large houses,
great churches and markets, and now, all was destroyed. The
Sultan had declared that Christians would never again live
there, and had ordered that every stone should be removed.
And as he had commanded, so had it come to pass. The city in
which beauty had reigned was a place of rubble with, here and
there, the bones of the inhabitants showing bleached white.

Ivo knew. He had seen it.

'I am sorry, Ivo,' the Marshal said. His eye held a tear. He
blinked it away.

Ivo replied stoically, 'It's nothing.'

'You have my prayers.'

'I'm grateful, but save them for the people here. Acre is his next and last target.'

'Prayers will aid those who seek to help themselves,' the Marshal said. He crossed the floor to a sideboard, filled two mazers with wine and passed one to Ivo. 'We must do all we can.'

The door opened, and Ivo turned to see Guillaume de Beaujeu, the Grand Master of the Order. He bowed deeply.

De Vendac passed his own mazer to his master, and poured a third.

'The horses are here?' asked the Grand Master.

He was a tall man, immensely powerful, with broad shoulders, the thick neck of a knight used to wearing a heavy steel helm, and a sun-bleached beard. His head was bald above his handsome, Viking face. Ivo knew him to be courageous, but also sly and shrewd when it came to politics. It was said he had spies even in the court of the Sultan at Egypt.

'We lost only a few, Grand Master,' Ivo said.

'Good. We have need of as many as we can find.'

'It is not only mounts. We need men,' the Marshal pointed out.

'We have messengers riding to the Pope and all Christian kings,' the Grand Master said, and drained his cup, adding more quietly, 'But whether they can help, I doubt me. We lost too many at Tripoli.'

Walking from the Temple's gates and out into the bright sunlight, Ivo was content to know that there would be more work for him. The weight of the coins in his purse was a comfort. There was a truth and honesty in money – and money bought wine and forgetfulness.

He kept on towards the cathedral. The Patriarch of Jerusalem had based himself here since the capture of his city. Ivo had a notion to go there and pray for his wife and son. When he had visited the ruins of Tripoli, he could not find their bodies among the piles of skeletal remains to bury them. He just hoped their deaths had been swift.

CHAPTER SIX

The moment of stillness was all too fleeting. Baldwin turned, but behind him he heard a bellow from the Genoese, and two more shipmen set off in pursuit.

There was one alley, which Baldwin might reach. He bolted for it, his boots slapping on the paved square, panting already with the exertion. The heat was not oppressive, but the humidity was, and he felt the sweat bursting out all over his back, under his arms, across his chest. He would give anything for a long draught of water from the stream at Furnshill. Just the memory of that chill, refreshing liquid was a torment. He slipped at a corner, and pelted up a second passage, narrower than the first. With no idea where he was heading, he simply kept running, his feet beating a regular tattoo.

In the shade of the alleys, he ran at full tilt, surging past traders, women, urchins and hawkers of all types. One man he butted into lost all his goods from a wicker basket, and hurled abuse after Baldwin as he raced off again, his wound pounding with each step, his head feeling that it must burst.

There was a roaring in his ears, and the hot air scalded his throat. He was using muscles that had grown moribund during his long sea-passage and did not know if he could keep running. Pain reached along the top of his thighs, and when he turned a corner and glanced back, he saw that the men were catching up. Gritting his teeth, he pounded onwards.

After another thirty yards he found himself in broad daylight in a wider thoroughfare. Ahead he saw a mass of people and was deafened by their cacophony: shouting voices, rattles and squeaks, the thunder of cartwheels and hooves. A glance behind showed his pursuers within a matter of yards, and he continued at a breakneck speed, hoping to lose them. Each breath was painful, not helped by the dust and sand in the air. Twenty yards, fifteen, and he had to leap over a boy who scrabbled in the dirt and yelped as he passed, and then he was in the street. He joined the throng, making his way past carts and donkeys, until he was in the midst of the people, and there suddenly caught sight of the magnificent church of St Anna's.

With a quick glance behind him that showed his pursuers were out of sight, he hurried on towards the cathedral.

A man stood in front of him. It was the Genoese.

He gripped his long knife, grinning, and called to his friends. Baldwin unthinkingly put his hand to his scabbard, only to remember that his sword had been taken along with his purse and his ring.

The knife moved from side to side like a serpent, and Baldwin could only stare in horrified fascination. He dared not look behind for the other men.

There was a shout as a stall-holder saw the flash of the blade, and men called to each other in some foreign tongue. The Genoese snarled something, and Baldwin had just steeled himself to try to wrest the knife from his hands, when he heard a gentle cough.

'Master Baldwin, I see you have some difficulty. May I help?'

Baldwin threw an agonised glance over his shoulder to see the white-clad knight again. Jacques d'Ivry's eyes held a menacing gleam. His thin features were set as he moved to Baldwin's side, his hands resting on his sword-belt, head jutting as he studied the Genoese.

'This man attacked our ship,' Baldwin panted. 'He killed many of the pilgrims.'

'I see,' Jacques said, without taking his eyes from the Genoese. 'Master, I think you should put away your blade before you cut yourself.'

The Genoese hesitated, but when he saw the Leper Knight's hand move to his sword-hilt, he rammed his blade back into its sheath, turned on his heel and strode away, muttering curses.

'Master Baldwin, would you object to my walking with you?'

Baldwin shook his head, unable to speak coherently for a moment. The confrontation had left him shaken, so soon after the battle at sea.

'Please, tell me how you know that gentleman,' the Leper Knight continued.

Baldwin told Sir Jacques about his journey and the attack at sea that had been driven off by the *Falcon*. 'There was a man there who lent me money – an Englishman called Ivo.'

'Ivo? Ah, I see. He would have been aboard the *Falcon* with Roger Flor. A Templar crew. That explains how you were saved from two Genoese ships,' Jacques mused. He smiled down at Baldwin, and then pointed. 'Now, master, I think you are safe enough. That rather magnificent church at the other side of the square is your destination. If you ask inside, I am sure that you will be helped. Now, once more godspeed, my friend.'

Ivo de Pynho walked to the west door of the cathedral and stepped inside the cool interior. When the Patriarch of Jerusalem had been thrown from his city by Saladin, he commanded that the Church of Santa Anna should be torn down and rebuilt as a proof that the Patriarchate would not easily be dislodged from the Holy Land.

Now Santa Anna was a memorial in stone of the oath sworn by so many knights, that they would retake Jerusalem in the name of Christ.

Ivo's head had been aching since leaving the Temple, and now he sagged with relief, dipping his fingers in the stoup by the door and crossing himself as he faced the altar. Here, in the cool nave, he could remember his wife Rachel, and little Peter, for a while. But not with an easy heart, since he had not been there when they needed him most.

The light poured through the coloured windows before him, and splashed over the floor like red, green and blue paints. It sparkled soothingly from candlesticks and the gilded icons. He walked past merchants haggling, past men gambling on the floor, a couple arguing viciously about the husband's wandering eye, to a pillar where he leaned, his eyes fixed on the statue of the Madonna. Her beautiful face was calming, but his loss was a tearing pain that would not leave him, and even She was powerless to help him. Not even Christ and all His angels could ease it.

He stared, almost expecting a miracle to strike him. Perhaps Rachel would appear, or Peter. No. If he was still in Jerusalem, maybe he might see a vision of them, but not here. Ivo sighed to himself and turned to leave the cathedral – but even as his eyes fell on the gamblers, he recognised Roger Flor, and beside him a familiar face.

Baldwin was playing at dice, and as Ivo watched, a broad grin broke out over the young fellow's face.

'Look at that! Look at that!' he exclaimed. 'I've won again!'

Ivo walked around the gamers, noting who the other men were. Two were clearly sailors; a third he recognised as Bernat, Roger Flor's henchman.

'Come, Master Baldwin, you must give us a chance to win back our losses,' Roger was saying, and Ivo saw the look he gave his companions.

Ivo knew it was hard to adhere to the Templar rules laid down by St Bernard. There were strict orders that Templars must avoid gambling. Chess and backgammon were barred, and only merrils occasionally permitted; when a game of chance was allowed, it was only for relaxation. Discs of candle-wax were used, never money, for Templars had taken the vows of poverty, as well as chastity and obedience, the same as any other monk.

Ivo sidled round and glanced at the piles of coins. Roger Flor had a small heap in front of him, and now he eagerly placed more in the middle, while Baldwin happily equalled his wager. Two sailors followed suit, and Baldwin picked up the dice and began to rattle them in his fist. When he flung them down, there was a stunned silence for a moment, and then Baldwin grinned and took the pile and scraped it to meet his other coins.

'This game looks like fun,' Ivo declared loudly, hands on his hips.

'Master Ivo,' Baldwin said, looking up at him. 'I've been really lucky. You wouldn't believe it, but I've won almost every game!'

'True, I find it very hard to believe,' Ivo said, staring at Roger.

'Something wrong, Ivo? Or do you want to join our party?' the shipmaster asked.

Ivo looked at Baldwin again. A strange feeling washed through him: a vague memory, perhaps, of the man he had been when he first arrived here by ship.

Baldwin was beaming up at him, and Ivo was suddenly reminded of his son's face. That same innocent glee, fixed in the moment, without any concern for the future – it was there in the young man's eyes. Ivo felt a shiver run down his spine as he recalled his thoughts moments before. Could this be a sign from the Blessed Virgin? On a whim, he made a decision. He would protect this fellow while he was in Acre.

'No. This has been a good game, but it's time for my young friend to come with me. Pick up your winnings, Master Baldwin.'

'Oh,' Baldwin said, crestfallen. 'I was just . . .'

'He doesn't want to go yet, Ivo,' Roger said. 'Leave him for three more games and we'll look after him.'

'No. He will come with me now,' Ivo said, stepping in front of Baldwin, who toyed with a coin but made no effort to collect the others.

'I would like to stay here a while longer,' Baldwin said. The afternoon had been enjoyable since meeting Roger Flor again. Already the memory of the pursuit through the lanes had dwindled – and gambling was a natural pastime for a knight or knight's son. 'Where do you mean to take me?'

'Yes, Ivo. What do you want with him?' Roger asked, climbing to his feet.

Ivo looked down at Baldwin. He owed the boy nothing. Baldwin was a traveller who had come here, possibly in search of money like so many of the mercenaries who arrived each year from Lombardy or Gascony. Yet there was something about him that cried out to Ivo's heart. That faint resemblance to Peter.

It was more than that alone. Looking at Baldwin, he could see a pale reflection of himself when he had landed here twenty years ago. The difference was, when he landed, Ivo had been with an army. He had not been deposited here alone, prey to the dangers that the Holy Land contained.

'Pick up your winnings, Baldwin,' he said quietly, and then, to Roger, 'You've had your fun. He's leaving.'

'Really?' Roger said with a slanting grin. 'Well, we mustn't get in your way, must we? Maybe we'll play again, Master. Soon, eh?'

Baldwin nodded, tying his purse's strings as he went. Ivo followed him, conscious with every step that Roger's eyes were on his back. It felt as though the man was aiming along a cross-bow's bolt, ready to release it with a soft depression of the trigger.

CHAPTER SEVEN

'Where is this?' Baldwin asked as they strode up to the north of the city. It still rankled that he had been dragged from his game.

'This is the Hospital. We're going to my home in the suburb of Montmusart,' Ivo said briefly.

Baldwin hefted the purse. 'I must have made six shillings, at least.'

'Think yourself lucky. They were going to take it all away from you.'

'No, they were playing well – I just kept beating them.'

'They were using loaded dice to give you plenty of rope to hang yourself. As soon as they were sure of you, they would start playing with a different set, and you'd have lost everything. All the coins you'd built up, all the spare coins, all their coins. It's a common ploy.'

Baldwin gave a low whistle. 'Are you sure?'

'I have lived here a long time.'

'I had better warn Roger, then. If those others were cheating . . .'

'Not the sailors, boy! It was Roger's dice you were playing with.'

'But he's a Templar!' Baldwin said, outraged.

'There are Templars and Templars. None are allowed to gamble. Roger Flor is a good seaman, but he's no knight.'

Baldwin eyed the fortress beside them. 'Are the Hospitallers better than the Templars?'

'They are military Orders. Neither is better nor worse than the other. Both fight for what they believe in, however, and that sometimes puts them on opposing sides.'

'How can that be? They both fight for Jerusalem, don't they?'

Ivo grunted. 'More or less. But Templars are allied to Venice; Hospitallers are more closely aligned to Genoa.'

'Still,' Baldwin said with a confused frown, 'surely their aims must meet? The Genoese and Venetians want to help Christians, don't they?'

'They want to help themselves,' Ivo said, looking at him. 'This is the last great city of Outremer. You realise that? For hundreds of years we have fought over this land. First to win Jerusalem itself, but we lost her. Since then, we've tried to encourage crusaders like you to come here and fight for our faith, but all too often the crusaders themselves have been worse than the enemy.'

'How can that be? We come to serve, that is all.'

'Aye. But serve whom? It is greed, a desire to take lands or glory that inspires most. The others are the felons: murderers and thieves who come here in expiation of their sins. Some cause more harm than good,' Ivo said with disdain.

Baldwin was silent. Ivo's words sounded like a shrewd analysis of his own journey of redemption.

'Why are you here?' Ivo said, on cue.

'I was persuaded by a priest,' Baldwin said quietly. It was no lie. As he sat by Exeter's sanctuary, it was the priest who had suggested pilgrimage to Jerusalem, there to fight and win absolution.

'I see,' Ivo continued, eyeing him askance. 'The city has to accommodate people like you.'

'Have you ever been there?'

Ivo nodded, and his face eased slightly at the memory. 'Once. I visited the Church of the Holy Sepulchre, and saw the birth-place of Christ. It made my life whole again.'

'How so?'

'None of your busines,' Ivo growled.

Baldwin glanced at him. Ivo had his own secrets too, then.

'You will find your way about the city quickly. Always look for the Towers. See, over there is the Tower of the Temple; here is the Hospital; at the top of the hill between the Venetians and Genoese is the Monastery of San Sabas with its own lands. You will need to be cautious when you are out on your own. Not all the people of the Kingdom want you here.'

'So you said,' Baldwin nodded. 'People don't like crusaders.'

'You have the arrogance of youth. Many here hate pilgrims like you. Merchants and . . .'

'The merchants don't want us?'

Ivo rolled his eyes. 'Of course they don't. Your arrival means disruption. Don't you realise? Acre is the capital of all trading between Egypt and your home. If there is a war, how will they make their money? That is what this city exists for – money. Without trade, it wouldn't exist.'

'Surely it's the centre for pilgrims too?'

'Aye. And pilgrims bring money with them,' Ivo said.

'Are we leaving the city?' Baldwin asked as a wall loomed before them.

'No. This is the old city wall. The city has grown well in the last years, so a new wall was built to enclose more land for all the people.'

'Where are we going?'

They walked under a tower in the wall, and out into a wide space.

'This is Montmusart.'

Baldwin looked about him. Before him was a garden with olives, and beyond, the land fell away slightly, towards another huge city wall. In the enclosed ground were houses and gardens, with broad roads separating each. 'It is beautiful,' he said in wonder.

'Yes,' Ivo said.

But his voice was cold. Montmusart didn't contain his wife and son.

Baldwin had suffered much from his long journey, and now he took the opportunity to rest and recover.

The city held endless fascination for him.

There were markets which specialised in silks and muslins, others which sold exotic foods, others still in which swords and armour were for sale. At one stall he found a delightful, light blade, with fabulous markings through the steel. Ivo, who was with him, sniffed at it.

'It's good in a fight without armour, but the steel is too flex-ible and light to do more than bounce from a mail shirt. For that, you need a good Christian blade formed from a bar of steel and hammered to rigidity.'

Baldwin reluctantly took his advice and invested much of the money won from Roger Flor in a two-foot-long simple blade with a broad fuller and undecorated cross. He was a knight's son, and it was unthinkable that he should walk unarmed any longer.

With his new, well-balanced riding sword, he practised every evening, and soon the weakness in his legs and the pain from his head wound left him.

When he was a boy, his father had given him his first training in swordsmanship, and when he left home at seven to learn his duties at the de Courtenay household, much of his time was spent honing his skills. With a sword in his hand, he felt comfortable. His master employed a Master of Defence, who had enhanced his tactics, and his firm stipulation was that the young Baldwin should give up time every day to practise. He had taken that advice to heart.

Ivo joined him on occasion, and they would test each other's swordsmanship. Baldwin soon learned that Ivo was a crafty old devil when it came to fighting.

Pietro, Ivo's half-deaf servant, who was both bottler and doorkeeper, would come and watch them with a sour expression on his wizened old face. He appeared to consider it his bounden duty to keep others away from Ivo so that his master might enjoy as much peace as possible. When he saw Baldwin and Ivo fight, he would glower at Baldwin, and only ever smiled or clapped his hands when Ivo got close and nicked Baldwin's arm or clothing.

'Do you resent my being here?' Baldwin asked him once, driven to irritation by the man's cackling at his latest injury – a nasty cut over his forearm. He looked at it and grimaced. The skin had pulled away from the wound, white and foul like a pig's flesh, he thought.

'Eh?' The old fellow screwed up his face and hooked a hand behind his ear, studying Baldwin speculatively. 'Resent you? Why would I do that?'

'You had a quieter time before I got here, I suppose,' Baldwin said. He held out the bleeding arm so that Pietro could wipe away the blood. He wanted to shiver, but he refused to allow Pietro to see he was concerned.

'You have no idea, do you?' Pietro muttered coldly. 'My family was in Lattakieh, and when that son of a diseased whore, Sultan Qalawun, invaded, they took my wife and children. You know what they do with women and children? My little girls will be slaves now. Ruined! And their mother, if she's lucky, she'll be kept well in a harem. If not, she'll be working her hands to the bone in the fields somewhere, or sold off for menial work. I don't know where they are, or what they do. All I know is, it was Master Ivo who saved me from life as a beggar. So if my praising him offends you, young master, so be it. I live and die for him.'

Baldwin was about to speak, when the old man turned away, and Baldwin saw the tear in his eye as he heard Pietro mutter, 'I have no one else.'

CHAPTER EIGHT

There was one sight that shocked Baldwin beyond uttering. One morning, as he strolled about Montmusart with Pietro, he suddenly encountered a man clad in strange mail, with a conical helmet, and turban encompassing it, a spike protruding from the top. He was bearded and had skin as brown as a conker. It was like meeting with a demon, and Baldwin took an involuntary step back.

His hand on his sword's hilt, the fellow swept past him with a haughty sneer that would not have looked out of place on a King's herald.

'Eh? What?' Pietro snapped when Baldwin tugged at his sleeve.

'He's a Muslim, isn't he?' Baldwin whispered, his startled eyes fixed on the man.

'So? Half the city is! There are many who prefer them as guards in any case,' Pietro grumbled, half to himself. 'Rich ladies who need protection will often have Muslims in their employ.'

'Not Christians?' Baldwin said, shocked.

'There was a woman some years ago, who inherited vast wealth when her husband died. She was kidnapped by a Christian nobleman who wanted to take her as his wife by force. When he heard about this, the Sultan sent men to demand that she be freed. From that day on, she always had a guard of Muslims provided by him. Ironic, isn't it? She felt endangered by the knights about here, but was happy enough with a bunch of heathens to protect her!'

'I must go to the Temple,' Ivo said, a day or so later. 'Will you join me?' He eyed Baldwin critically.

'Certainly!' the young man cried, wiping his face with the trailing hem of his linen shirt. He had been exercising with his sword, and in the heat had worked up quite a sweat.

'That shirt was once white, I presume?' Ivo asked drily.

Baldwin glanced down at it. 'What do you mean?'

'I mean it's filthy. You should let the maid take it to be washed.'

'I only have this one. Since the ship . . .' He had no need to continue. When he had lost all his money and weapons, his bag too had been taken, with his spare shirt.

'I should have thought,' Ivo muttered. 'We must buy some cloth for a new shirt. In the meantime,' he added as they left by the front door a short while later, 'I have been summoned to meet with the Grand Master of the Templars. Sir Guillaume de Beaujeu is the most important man in the city, no matter what anyone says, so remain respectful.'

The two set off, and soon walked under the gateway in the old city wall, on past the Hospital, and down towards the Temple.

The streets here were bustling, with hawkers of all nations bellowing out their wares, men-at-arms striding about like minor barons, servants hurrying hither and thither – and beggars. Beggars were everywhere you looked: old men pleading from the ground where their crippled legs kept them, urchins standing in the way, holding out their hands, eyes enormous with hunger as they entreated all the passers-by, younger men with limbs broken or weakened by rickets, toothless youths with sores and skin diseases.

It was the same in any street in Christendom, Baldwin knew: he had seen enough beggars in his time, and yet there was something especially poignant about these people of different races. Their eyes seemed to scorch him with their demands, and he felt ashamed to walk past them.

'You feel it too?' Ivo asked quietly. 'There was a time when I would ignore the poor, but here, I find it more difficult. There is shame in living here in the Holy Land and doing nothing for these unfortunates.'

Baldwin made no comment, but he felt their gazes on his back long after he had passed by.

The Temple was a glorious fortress, and Baldwin looked up at it in wonder as he approached. Before him were the two towers of the Temple, with a pair of smaller towers flanking each. On top of the lower ones stood a great gilded lion, as massive as an ox. In the sunshine, they were painful to look at, they gleamed so. They seemed statements of pride, power and wealth. His impression was confirmed by Ivo a moment later.

'You see those lions? They cost one thousand five hundred Saracen besants. The palace there, that is the Master's, and you see the tower over there, at the sea? That is where the Templars hold their treasure. No one would get to it there! It is said that that tower was built by the Saracen Saladin when he ruled Acre. If so, he had a good eye for a place of safety. It must be the strongest part of the entire city.'

They entered the fortress and Baldwin followed Ivo as he made his way to the Master's Palace. Two Templars in their tunics stood at the door and opened it to allow Ivo and Baldwin to pass. It was huge. The paved floor stretched away to a great dais, on which there was a table. Ivo bowed and stood in the middle of the floor. It would have been impossible to go further because of the press of people.

Looking about him, Baldwin recognised faces here and there: men he had seen in the streets, one whom he was sure he had seen on the ship on the way here, but for the most part they were rich merchants who had all the obvious signs of their wealth, with bejewelled fingers and bright, cool silks that rustled softly. Baldwin was jealous of them, standing there in his grimy shirt and old tunic.

He noticed one man in particular. He stood, tall and very strong, clad in a white Templar habit. His head was bare, show-ing the fine greyish stubble, and making his thick beard look peculiar. He had piercing eyes, heavily hooded, and a manner of jutting his head forward that was aggressive and contempla-tive at the same time. His hands were hidden in the sleeves of his habit, and Baldwin wondered whether he held a weapon in them. There was something entirely warrior-like about him, and the idea that he was unarmed seemed wrong, somehow.

Ivo pointed to him with his chin. 'Listen carefully. That is the Grand Master of the Temple, Guillaume de Beaujeu. He knows more of affairs between us here and the Egyptians than almost any man.'

'How?' Baldwin whispered.

'He has the money to pay spies,' Ivo snapped. 'Now, listen!'

De Beaujeu spoke with a calm authority that ensured silence in the crowd. On the dais, he towered over the people before him, glancing from one to another as he spoke. At one point his eye met Baldwin's, and Baldwin was surprised to see that the great leader did not look away instantly, but instead studied him as if Baldwin was as important as any other in that chamber.

'You all know that I have sent a messenger to our Father the Pope. After the fall and destruction of Tripoli, it was necessary.'

'If we don't provoke Qalawun, he will leave us alone,' a man called.

'No one provoked Qalawun, yet he attacked Lattakieh. No one provoked him, yet he attacked Tripoli. Does anyone believe that he will leave us alone here at Acre? I have heard that calls have already gone out to his people deep in the interior of Egypt, for them to gather their armies and meet him. Where is he to go? In past years, we may have thought he was making a foray into Mongol lands. But the Mongols are no threat to him. He has attacked castles. But he has Montfort, he has Krak, he has Marqab. There is only one jewel he can seek to pluck. And that jewel is Acre.'

His words rang out with simple force. No man spoke against him now.

'So, I have sent a messenger to the Pope to beg for men to defend our city, but I fear that all too few will come. There are some hundreds who are already on their way from Lombardy, I believe, and the English have promised an army, but they do not have the men to be able to protect us. So we must see to our own protection.'

Ivo had his lips pursed as he listened. Now he shook his head. 'We are too few,' he muttered. Baldwin looked back to the Master.

'The commune of Acre must invest in the walls. We must at once purchase all the timber we may, to reinforce our defences and build the hoardings. We need more machines of war, especially catapults. We need masons, to strengthen our walls . . .'

'The walls are strong already. We would have to spend prodigiously to afford all this work!' a man called.

'Very well. My walls here, at my tower, are almost thirty feet thick,' the Grand Master stated equably. '*I* shall be safe when your house is burned to the ground, with both your daughters and your wife inside it. Need I remind you how Tripoli fell? You have all heard of the violent conflagration that overwhelmed our friends there. How many of us lost friends in those massacres? Who can count the young women and children who were marched off to be sold into slavery? How many of us know women who even now are held in captivity, to suffer the shame of rape? Is that what you want for your daughters? Your wives? Do you want to die knowing that you failed to protect your families for the cost of a few ounces of silver?'

'What of the other Orders? There are only Templars here. What of the Hospitallers?' a man shouted.

Baldwin could see him. He half-expected a Templar to grab the fellow and pull him out for his rudeness, but no one made a movement.

The Grand Master nodded. 'I know you, Master Mainboeuf. You and I have worked together often enough. I will say this: I will ally myself with any man, any Order, any nation, in order to protect our city. I have asked the Hospitallers to join us here, but I fear they did not heed my invitation. I hope, and pray, that they will come to discuss this before too long. Perhaps if you, or your companions, could speak to the Grand Master, he may be persuaded to come to us and talk about how we might best defend our city.'

'You say you want wood,' a man called. 'Will you tell the Venetians to stop selling it to our enemies?'

The Grand Master allowed a wintry smile to pass over his lips. 'I already have.'

It was almost noon when the meeting was closed, and the room gradually emptied. Baldwin walked out behind Ivo, blinking and covering his eyes against the sudden glare of the sunshine.

'Those men were not very respectful,' he commented.

'Did you expect them to be?' Ivo grunted.

'I thought they would show the Grand Master respect in his own hall.'

'He was hoping to bolster confidence. Attacking his audience would not help.'

'I see.'

'So, do you feel you understand the city's position more clearly now?' Ivo asked.

Baldwin said, 'I would have been happier with the Hospitallers in the chamber with us.'

'At least it shows that the merchants appreciate the dangers at last,' Ivo said. He snorted, hawked and spat into the street. 'I don't think they realised how perilous our situation has become.'

Baldwin nodded, but as he did so, he saw a flash of emerald.

'That woman! I know her!' he cried.

'Who? Where?' Ivo asked distractedly.

Baldwin could see the gleam of her bright silken robes. Two dark-skinned warriors followed close behind her. He wondered at first whether she was a Saracen princess, until he saw her pale hand and wrist.

She passed through the crowds serenely. There was no need for gestures or threats, the people moved aside as she approached.

Ignoring Ivo, Baldwin hurried after her. He had to see what she looked like – but this time he wouldn't scare her, the way he had before. Noticing a gap in the throng before him, he forced his way through it and managed to reach her side. He caught a heady odour of sandalwood and spice as he passed, and then turned to look at her.

'My lady,' he said, and bowed.

That was as far as he got before the nearer of the two guards whipped out his sword and rested it on Baldwin's throat.

CHAPTER NINE

Baldwin smiled at her. The blade didn't worry him. Even the most determined felon would hesitate before committing murder before so many witnesses. And besides, Ivo was lumbering up nearby.

In any event, the woman was worth pausing over.

She was shorter than him, but only by an inch or so, and her body was entirely concealed beneath her flowing robes; for all that, she was arresting. Her face was hidden beneath her veil, but her eyes were wonderful. Green, unblinking and direct, she issued a challenge just by looking at him.

He bowed his head, the sword beneath his chin. 'Your beauty is captivating, my lady.'

In her eyes there was something at that, a smile, perhaps an acknowledgement of flattery, but then she averted her head. He found himself shoved aside, and she was gone, her men behind her once more, the rearmost turning and staring at Baldwin, a warning clear in his eyes.

There was something different about her this time. The

woman he had seen on the day of his arrival had eyes that were filled with terror when she saw him. This woman had the haughtiness of a princess when she glanced over him, from his scuffed boots to his uncombed hair. It was not the kind of look to inspire desire. To add to her loss of appeal, there were these guards, too. The woman he had seen in the alley had had no one to protect her.

'What are you thinking of?' Ivo demanded angrily. 'You could have been killed!'

'I wanted to see her face. I saw her before, the day I arrived here. She was in an alley near the Genoese quarter, and I scared her, I think. I called to her and she ran from me.'

'I doubt you would have scared *her*,' Ivo said. 'Lady Maria of Lydda is a very dangerous lady.'

'But who is she?'

'She was wife to the Count of Lydda, a small town over towards Jaffa. When her husband died, she came to live here in the city.'

'Why?'

Ivo shrugged. 'I reckon she didn't like it where she was. More to the point, I think she didn't like her husband, and when he died, she was keen to get away from any memories. There are even stories that she hastened his death.'

'What, you mean she hired someone to kill him?' Baldwin chuckled.

'You laugh? Why, boy, are you so well-versed in the ways of women as to think you understand them?'

Baldwin was thinking of her entrancing green eyes. 'No, but I don't think she would do something like that. She's too beautiful.'

'You didn't see her face, did you? You couldn't tell whether she was smiling or glaring.'

'She was smiling.'

'The rumour was that she poisoned his drink for him. She's too much of a lady to think of getting the servants to do it for her. Once a servant gets a taste for killing his master,' Ivo added bitterly, 'he can never be trusted again.'

Baldwin was growing accustomed to Ivo's changes of mood, and considered his companion carefully. 'So, Maria of Lydda is here because she found the town distasteful. I'm sure that there are other widows who would find that understandable.'

'Don't even dream of that woman, boy. She is as far from your reach as the moon and stars.'

Baldwin nodded and was about to speak, but then he saw a man he recognised all too well: the Genoese captain.

'There!' he cried. 'That's the viper who stole my ring and sword.'

'Where?' Ivo peered in the direction Baldwin pointed. 'I see him. Come with me! Come on, run!'

Baldwin had to make an effort to keep up with Ivo as the older man raced down one lane, up another, then along a series of narrow alleys. As they descended some steps, Baldwin saw over to the right a sudden flash of emerald, and was sure that it was the slim, silk-clad figure of Maria of Lydda. However, the instant he spotted her, she disappeared into another alley. Briefly he registered surprise that she was alone now.

Then he concentrated on following Ivo.

The horse-dealer now led Baldwin down a tatty lane, with names and graffiti carved into the old stones, and with broken and loose flags threatening their ankles at every step – until they came to a broader thoroughfare in which carts rattled noisily over the roadway.

'Master! Master Buscarel!' Ivo shouted.

Baldwin looked in both directions without seeing the man at first, but then, following Ivo's stare, he saw the Genoese approaching.

Buscarel looked Baldwin up and down, a smile on his face. 'Aha, Ivo, I heard you had taken in a waif from the streets. Perhaps this one will repay your generosity, eh?'

'He already has – I'm glad to call him my friend,' Ivo said. Then: 'I am also glad to see that you returned safely from your voyage.'

'I always do.'

'The ship you left behind was a glorious one. I am grateful for her. Roger Flor is her master now.'

'I had not known he was so fortunate.'

'It is to the glory of the Order he serves, of course.'

The Genoese sneered at that. 'Of course! I would hate to think that a man like him could seek to fill his own purse.'

Baldwin's gaze was fixed on the Genoan's finger. 'That is my ring.'

'*Your* ring?' Buscarel glanced at it. 'This is mine. It is gold. Not the sort of trinket for a penniless pilgrim, boy.'

'You stole it from me!'

'It is mine, I said. I do not give away my property so easily as some.'

'You say I gave it up easily?' Baldwin shouted, and his hand was already on his hilt when Ivo placed a hand firmly on his breast to keep him back.

'Master Buscarel, you took my friend's ring, and his money and weapons. He needs them back in order to remain here to protect you and your people. I look to you to return his property.'

'Look to me? Look to yourself! You'll have need of protection before long, fool!' He had turned and was already walking away, down the hill towards the sea.

'Let me go!' Baldwin spluttered. 'I will have my ring back!'

'Not now. If you chase him down there, you will be killed. It's the Genoese quarter. You cannot go in there and get out alive, not while threatening one of their captains. They'd cut you to pieces, lad.'

Baldwin growled a curse under his breath, but allowed Ivo to half-drag him away, and they returned the way they had come. Baldwin looked for her again as he passed that alley, but the woman in green was nowhere to be seen.

CHAPTER TEN

The following day, Baldwin was pleased to see a familiar figure enter the garden while he was practising with his sword.

'Sir Jacques!' he cried, thrusting his sword into the scabbard. 'I am pleased to see you again.'

'And I you,' the knight said.

'Do you know Ivo?'

'Very well. He asked me here. He said you have made powerful enemies already.'

'He worries too much,' Baldwin said, irritated that his business was being discussed behind his back. It made him feel like a child.

'Ivo seeks to help you defend yourself.' He indicated Baldwin's sword. 'You practise every day?'

'Yes, but I don't think I need to do it so often.'

'Oh. You have seen battle before?'

'Yes, on the ship,' Baldwin admitted grudgingly. Youthful pride made it hard to admit to his failure.

'That is good. A man learns more from defeat than from

victory,' the knight smiled gently. 'It is the way he copes with hardship that defines him.'

'I don't need to worry about my sword skills,' Baldwin said smugly.

'Oh? Good. Would you show me, then?'

Baldwin looked at him. The knight was wearing his little coif again, as he had in the street when they had first met, but meeting Sir Jacques's gaze, he saw that as well as the gentle kindness in his eyes, there was also a measure of shrewdness. Still, he was a very old man . . . He saw the knight's eyes crinkle at the edges, as though he was reading Baldwin's mind.

'Yes, of course I will show you,' he said.

Both drew, holding their swords aloft. Sir Jacques held his single-handed, almost lazily. His relaxed stance made Baldwin think he was unprepared, and he stabbed from a high guard. His sword met empty air, as the Leper Knight span about and tapped Baldwin on the shoulder with his blade, continuing his whirl away, until he was at Baldwin's side.

Baldwin frowned. 'I was always taught not to move my feet,' he protested.

'Ah, I am sorry, my friend. I have learned much from my enemies here in Outremer. They tend to fight with lighter mail, and move with great speed. It is useful, I have found, to emulate them. Please?' With his sword held in an apparently negligent grip, he beckoned Baldwin with his left hand.

It was infuriating. Baldwin took the high guard, and slashed a blow to the left, followed by a feint to the heart and a raking movement from the right, but each time, the older knight was simply not there. Once Baldwin almost caught a trailing length of tunic, but that was the nearest he came to marking his man.

'How do you do this?' Baldwin demanded. 'Whatever I try, you have moved before I strike.'

70

'I have practised my manoeuvres every day for five and twenty years,' the Leper said.

'But doesn't your disease slow you?'

'Oh! You were being kind to me, allowing for my disability?' Jacques said with a beaming smile. 'I had not realised.'

'No, I mean . . .' Baldwin was confused. He had thought Sir Jacques must be leprous to be a member of his Order, but the man moved with the rapidity of a striking snake. It was clear he was no cripple.

'I do not have leprosy, my friend. I serve my Order from compassion for others, and to repay a debt.'

'Why did you join the Lepers, if you don't have the disease?'

'I wanted to offer my life in service. If it pleases God, and I hope my efforts do, then I can die knowing my life has not been wasted. And helping a young Crusader must also give comfort to God. Or so, at least, I pray.'

Baldwin was feeling the strain. His arm was tired, and the air from the sea humid; his armpits were sweaty, his back running with moisture. He wiped his face.

'Come, Master Baldwin. Another bout?'

Again that infuriating beckon. Baldwin took his time, placing his feet carefully, thinking. Each time the Leper Knight had whirled, he had moved to the right, coming back behind Baldwin's sword hand. This time, he resolved, he would meet his opponent as he went.

His sword rose into the True Gardant, his fist above his line of sight, the swordpoint dropping down before him, aiming at the knight's belly, and then he moved. He stabbed downwards, then span, bringing the sword round to hack at the knight's thigh – but the knight wasn't there.

A sword tapped his head.

'Sorry, I thought you might try that.'

Baldwin was furious. He gritted his teeth, grasping his sword tightly, almost thinking to attack in earnest, but then he saw the smile on the knight's face grow pensive.

'My friend, I hope I have not offended you? However, if you are to survive here, you will need to practise with a Saracen I know. He can teach you much. It is not that your skills are at fault, but here men use curved blades, and a drawing cut. If you wield a sword in battle against men in armour, it is less a cutting device than a hammer. You wield a hand-and-a-half sword like a long-handled maul, because cutting through mail is not easy. Sometimes you may use it as a spear, which can work, but not always. However, in the city here you will find few wear mail. Good swordsmanship is more important. Especially against the Genoese.'

Pietro walked into the garden bearing a tray of cool drinks, and behind him was Ivo.

'I asked Sir Jacques to test you,' Ivo said. 'If you become embroiled in a fight with Buscarel, you will need more speed and guile than the skills you learned in England.'

'So you think me incompetent with a sword?' Baldwin snapped.

'No. You are good. Just not good enough,' Ivo said.

Sir Jacques chuckled. 'We all had to learn when we came here.'

'If I fought the Genoese, I would die in moments,' Baldwin said sulkily, shoving his sword away. He felt a wave of self-pity. 'I didn't land a single blow on you.'

'If you met with a man as old and feeble as me, perhaps yes,' Jacques chuckled.

'I came here to fight, and at that I am a failure. In my first battle at sea, I was beaten; in the streets you had to save me. I cannot fight anyone. I am pathetic.'

'You have much skill, my friend,' Sir Jacques said kindly. 'But you need to learn how to watch your opponent and anticipate his moves.'

'What, am I to spend my time learning and not fighting?'

Ivo nodded. 'There are no great battles to fight yet. Some time soon, perhaps, we'll have need of more swords. The Sultan Qalawun wants all Christians thrown from this land.'

'You see, he hates us,' Sir Jacques continued, 'and so he should, for we wish nothing less than the denial of all his ambitions: we seek the recovery of Jerusalem for God's chosen people, for the Christians. There will come a day when your arm's strength may lead to the protection of the people of this city. Until then, you must prepare yourself, as the Knights of Saint Lazarus do, and as the Knights of the Temple do: by practising with sword and lance and knife and mace – until you can wield all weapons to their best effect, to the glory of God.'

He stood and rested his hand on Baldwin's shoulder. 'Come! You fought well today. With practice, you will fight still better, and be a great joy to all Christians.'

CHAPTER ELEVEN

It was a few days later that Baldwin met the Templar shipmaster Roger Flor again.

For the last few days, Ivo had been taken up with business. More horses were needed for the Order, and Ivo was the Templars' chief trader in horseflesh. He was known, Baldwin learned, all over the Mediterranean for his fairness, but also for his determination to win a good deal for his clients.

Well, that attitude was fine in business, but Baldwin thought it made him too easy-going. Ivo was happier to negotiate than protect his own interests, but Baldwin was the son of a knight. He had a duty to avenge any slur, and the Genoese had gravely insulted him. Baldwin would have his day.

But not with Ivo's help.

Baldwin took to walking about the city in the early morning before the heat began to hammer at the senses. He liked it best just after daybreak, when he would walk to the cathedral to listen over the hubbub of merchants haggling and children playing to the solemn prayers. The scent of incense lifted his spirits, and in there it was hard to believe the dire warnings from Guillaume de Beaujeu of an army being raised by the Egyptians to overwhelm the city. God would protect His own. He would not see His last city destroyed, giving His Holy Land to the heathen.

Walking from the cathedral one morning, Baldwin stood in the sunshine and snuffed the air. There was a fresh breeze from the sea, and he could imagine the waves chopping at the hulls of the ships in the harbour, the hum of the great cables as the wind plucked at them.

'Master, I am glad to see you once more,' said a familiar voice, breaking into his reverie. 'I hope Ivo the killjoy has not completely destroyed your pleasure in gaming?'

'Master Roger – I am glad to see you,' Baldwin said, grinning. It was easy to smile at such a welcoming face, especially since Roger Flor was only a little older than himself. Baldwin felt a ready affinity for him which he could not feel for Ivo. After all, stern Ivo was old enough to be his father.

'What, no Ivo today?'

Baldwin grinned as Roger made a show of peering high and low in all directions. 'No, he is at the Temple. He prefers to spend his time counting coins there.'

'Ah, an honourable occupation, I doubt me not. Being a Templar, I'm assured there is no nobler way for a man to spend his time,' Roger stated, nodding sagely.

'I would prefer to be busy with my sword,' Baldwin said. 'I came here to fight the enemies of all Christians.'

'You should be a Templar, then. We exist to serve the pilgrims,' Roger said.

Baldwin laughed at that. 'What, *serve*? With the riches owned by your Order? You'd do better to give money to people so they can afford to travel here!'

Roger looked at him, and there was an unwonted seriousness in his voice. 'Don't make that mistake, Master. There are many who deride the Templars, but we need that money. It is essential. If pilgrims are attacked here, they need help here, and were it not for the Poor Fellow Soldiers of Christ and the Temple of Solomon, they would be entirely at the mercy of the Saracens. But come! We will not fall out over such affairs.'

'No, indeed,' Baldwin said, 'but I should like to know, if the reason for the Templar Knights' existence is to protect others, how can they do it from inside a great fortress like that?'

Roger followed his pointing finger and gazed at the tower of the Temple. 'We don't,' he said simply. 'Our service lies in bringing people here by ship, like you, and then protecting them all about here.'

'In the city?'

Roger looked at him. He still wore his customary little smile, but there was a hardness in his eyes Baldwin hadn't seen before. 'If you want to see what we can do, come with me today. I'm riding with a reconnaissance out to the south, into the bay. You may join us, if you wish.'

CHAPTER TWELVE

Their journey had been a great success, and the trader Abu al-Fida was glad as he paid off the leader of the caravan and took his leave.

Abu al-Fida smiled at his son. 'You did well this time, Usmar.'

'I had a marvellous teacher, Father.'

'This is true,' Abu al-Fida said contentedly.

He and his son had hired a pony, and now, with the proceeds of their sales in Damietta laden on the beast's back, they began to walk along the narrow streets to their home. Many Muslims lived here, in the Christian city of Acre, but few had a past like Abu al-Fida's. He had once been a warrior, but for him the days of lust and slaughter were closed away behind a sealed door in his mind. Once in a while he had awoken his darling Aisha with his screams in the night, but she would comfort him through his nightmares, and over time, his dreams had lost their virulence. It was many years now since Antioch's fall, when he had clambered up over the rubble with his sword drawn, to deal death to the inhabitants. It was to escape his past that he had come here to Acre, to forget machines of war, to become a simple merchant. A man of peace.

He shuddered. It was peculiar that he should have begun to have such dreams again.

They were passing the castle now, and soon would be at Montmusart, where they would go along the alley to their little house. There, his wife and daughters would be waiting. It was a good place to live, a good city. Acre was rich, and had made Abu al-Fida comfortable. He had a good reputation.

Passing under the gate of the inner wall that separated Montmusart from the old city, he entered the lane that would take him to their house.

'Usmar – you should buy a gift for your mother,' he said with a frown.

'I shall buy her flowers, Father.'

'Very good. I will meet you at home.' Abu al-Fida watched as his son hurried away. He smiled to himself. His boy, already twenty, was becoming a masterful negotiator in his own right.

He continued, anticipating his welcome, turning over in his mind different ideas for new ventures, and how he might make best use of his son's skills, until he reached the house, and there he stopped.

He must have come to the wrong street, he thought at first. This wasn't his home.

For where his house had stood only a shell remained, a twisted mess of charred and broken timber and rubble.

'What has happened? Where is my wife?' he called, but no one came. Only Usmar, who reached him gripping a brightly coloured rose in a clay pot.

'Father?' he said. 'What has happened?'

Abu al-Fida did not answer. He fell to his knees, his hands scrabbling in the ashes and stone as if searching for his family.

CHAPTER THIRTEEN

His first view of the lands about the city surprised Baldwin. When he had climbed onto the walls near the Lazar Gate in his first week, he had looked out over square, mud-built homes with low roofs on which were tables and cushions laid below stretched awnings for shade. Many slept on their roofs at night when the hot, humid air sucked a man's energy.

Today he saw a different land. Riding from the Patriarch's Tower, they rode through the little homes built close to the wall, and thence out to fields bright with orchards and vegetable gardens, and the ever-present olive groves. The land was ablaze with colour, with flowers and fruits: pomegranates, roses, sweet-lemon and grenadine all grew in profusion, he had heard. Before them, heat-haze made the horizon wobble and dip confusingly.

'It hardly looks like it needs protection,' Baldwin commented.

Theirs was a party of fifteen. A knight in a white tunic led them, but he was an old-school Templar who arrogantly ignored the others. The rest were all like Roger, brown-clad sergeants, with lighter arms. This was only a reconnaissance, not a force in strength.

They followed the coast, past beached ships and on until they reached a road that led away from the sea.

Baldwin was already sweating profusely. He wore a new shirt, but even with the fine muslin, the heat was intolerable, and the fine dust thrown up by the hooves before him made breathing difficult. He had copied the men about him, pulling a scarf over his face and trying to breathe through that, but it was uncomfortable and he felt as if he was lurching along the road to Hell.

They had ridden up a slight rise, and all about here was scrubby vegetation, with an occasional olive grove. They stopped at a village, where the Templar demanded water and bread, and Baldwin was glad to climb down from his saddle. He soon drained the goatskin he had brought with him, and went to the well to refill it.

When he returned, Roger motioned to him, and he sat at Roger's side to share flatbread and olives.

'So, do you like the countryside?' Roger asked.

Baldwin looked around at the dry walls of the village buildings, the pale soil and sparse plants. 'I think it could do with a little Devon rain,' he said.

There was a shout from the edge of the village, where a man had been set to watch the road, and Roger sprang to his feet. The knight was already at his side, and staring out towards the distant hills.

'What is it?' Baldwin asked.

'Looks like people on horseback,' Roger said, and there was a suppressed excitement in his tone that Baldwin could feel in his own breast.

In the distance, travellers had been betrayed by the cloud of yellowish dust that enveloped them. Now, in the midst of the dust, Baldwin saw figures. Horses or camels, he couldn't make out from here, but he felt they were likely camels because their legs were so long. Surely these were Saracens, he thought, and the idea brought a tingle to his blood: he would see his enemy at last.

The knight snapped a command at Roger, who hurried to his horse, calling Baldwin as he went. Baldwin mounted, still chewing his bread, and the two trotted from the village and down a slight incline to the roadway. Side-by-side to avoid dust, they loped along.

'Saracens often ride into our territories,' Roger said. 'Usually they are just travellers, but occasionally we get the odd outrider who is here to study our defences. When we find them, we send them on their way.'

Baldwin nodded. He stared at the men riding towards him, but was already prepared for disappointment. Nothing in the Holy Land was as he had expected.

'What now?'

'We shall talk to them,' Roger said, glancing at Baldwin. 'This isn't a riding out.'

'Yes, I understand. I just wasn't expecting to come all this way and not fight. I want to be useful.'

'Maybe later,' Roger said. 'You're game, Baldwin. You'll be a good friend in a fight, I think.'

Baldwin brooded. 'Scouts for the enemy are to be left to ride home – no matter what information they carry?' He was a knight's son, and pride dictated that enemies should be engaged and vanquished, not sent on their way.

'Oh, there will be time for profit later,' Roger laughed. 'Yes, later we can see what such men have, if we're lucky. I think I'm glad I found you.'

Baldwin wasn't sure what Roger meant, but it was clearly intended in a friendly light, and he was prepared to take any compliment.

As the party drew nearer, Baldwin saw that the heat haze had deceived him. The three newcomers were all on horseback. The horses' legs had seemed longer because of the mirage.

Holding up his hand, Roger walked his horse to them.

Baldwin heard him give the Muslim greeting and studied them as they chatted. The man in the front was a tall, thin fellow with a grey beard that covered half his breast. Behind him were two younger men, both also bearded. The one nearest Roger had narrow, suspicious eyes, and Baldwin thought he looked the sort who would be glad to kill a Christian.

Their mounts were all well-caparisoned, sturdy ponies, designed for stolid journeying rather than for racing, and looked as if they had covered many miles already. As spies' beasts would, Baldwin thought to himself. Deep in his belly, he felt misgivings grow.

Three was an odd number to be wandering, he thought. And it was peculiar that there were two young men with one older man. He would have expected all to be similarly young. But perhaps this leader was an experienced spy, with knowledge of the area hereabouts, and had been sent with two young guards to assess the land, to find the best routes for an army to take to invest Acre.

There was no news of an army from Egypt, but Baldwin had heard that the army which had overrun Tripoli had appeared from nowhere . . . yet it had brought machines of war and tens of thousands of men. Perhaps, in the weeks before that battle, there had been men such as these, who had ridden about the land before the city had realised an army was on the move. Parties like the one of which he himself was a part, could have been surrounded and cut to pieces so that they were unable to return to the city to warn of the approaching disaster.

He threw a look over his shoulder. The Templar stood watching. Baldwin returned his gaze to the three, feeling a heightened alarm. If they were to draw their swords and set about Roger, it would be difficult for Baldwin to protect him. Still, he remained where he was, his hand resting on his saddle's crupper near his sword hilt. If need be, he could draw steel quickly.

Over the shoulder of the old man, a patch of dust caught his eye – a rider, making short work of the roads.

Baldwin's distrust increased. If there was one rider, there could be more. He shouted to Roger, pointing, and set his hand on his sword. In a moment, the two younger men had drawn theirs, too. Roger snapped something at Baldwin, shaking his head, but Baldwin couldn't make out his words as he hefted his sword to charge the group about Roger. His feet were out, preparing to spur his mount on, when he realised that all three and Roger had turned to face the gathering dust-cloud.

There was more than one man approaching, he saw. There were two, and both were cantering with a lazy motion that could eat up the miles with ease.

Roger bowed to the older man, hand on breast, and remained on his horse, staring at the approaching pair as the other three rode on towards Acre and the sea.

'This doesn't look too good,' Roger said.

He could not have been more wrong.

Their ride back was a hurried affair.

When Roger was given the news by the two messengers, his roar of laughter could have been heard in Acre, Baldwin reckoned. Roger had turned and spurred his horse towards the village at full gallop, Baldwin struggling to persuade his own mount to turn and join him.

By the time he reached the village's wall, all the other Templars were already packing and mounting. Roger bared his teeth as Baldwin appeared. Great news, isn't it?' he said heartily.

Baldwin eyed him helplessly. 'What is?'

'The leader of our enemies, man! He's promised peace!'

Baldwin heard no more. The command was given, and in a moment the horses were off at a swift, loping trot, the two messengers riding in their wake.

'Who do you mean?' Baldwin said when they were under way.

'Sultan Qalawun,' Roger said, looking at him with exasperation. He had thought Baldwin would have picked up a little Arabic by now. 'The murdering fiend who overran Tripoli, and wanted to take Acre too. It seems he's sworn peace for ten years, ten months and ten days!'

'You would take the word of a heathen?' Baldwin asked. 'What of his court? Wouldn't they force him to attack?'

'They'd soon be put in their place. Qualawun is a warlord to be feared. If he wants peace, we're safe. His barons and nobles wouldn't dare argue. They bicker and fight amongst themselves more than we Christians do, but not with Qalawun. He doesn't brook any dispute. No, this is good news. With luck we can turn to the old ways soon.'

'I don't understand.'

Roger shot him a sharp look. He liked this tall English fellow, but he was as yet untried. Still, he seemed game enough. 'There are many traders come here from Egypt,' he explained. 'We stop a few, ask them to pay our tolls, and that helps us all.'

'Tolls?' Baldwin had not heard of any tolls on the roads here.

He had thought that the roads, such as they were, were built by slaves.

'That's what I call 'em,' Roger winked. 'The travellers have to pay if they want to continue on their way. And if they refuse, we take their money anyway. It only needs the rumour of a couple of dead men for others to fall into line.'

Baldwin was shocked. It sounded no better than banditry – but Roger was so open about it that such behaviour must be approved. If it was the custom of the country, he was in no position to question it. He was a newcomer, after all. The idea left him uneasy, but he did not want to embarrass himself or lose his new friend.

'I will call you to join me, next time I go,' Roger said, taking Baldwin's silence for tacit agreement, and the rest of the way, he chattered inconsequentially.

Even as they entered the gate to Acre, Baldwin was still uncomfortable. Admittedly these people were Saracen, and therefore not to be accorded the same privileges as Christians, but still, the idea of holding them and demanding ransom made him feel like a felon.

They continued on to the Temple, the two messengers attracting the notice of the crowds as they passed, and many men and women pointed and muttered amongst themselves. At the gate of the Temple, a groom came and took their horses, and the two found themselves alone.

'Master Baldwin, I think this calls for a well-deserved pint of wine each!' Roger said.

CHAPTER FOURTEEN

News had already spread about the arrival of the messengers, and tongues were wagging with speculation about their mission. Roger took Baldwin to a little tavern which had a wide seating space outside, with vines growing over a wooden frame for shade. The two took their seats at benches near a small rickety table.

Baldwin was in the company of a good friend, and his day had been more than a distraction – it had been an education. He felt he was coming to understand the way of this country. After the first two cups of wine, he was certain Roger could teach him more about the Holy Land than Ivo or Jacques. After the third, he was convinced that he was more at home here in Acre than he had ever been in Devon.

'You get on well with Ivo?' Roger asked as he called for another pint of wine.

'He has been kind to me. I was lost when I arrived,' Baldwin said.

'But do you like him?'

'He is a good man.'

'Aye, but depressing, eh? Not the sort of fellow to enjoy a game with dice?'

'He doesn't approve of gambling,' Baldwin said with a snigger.

'What about women?'

'He doesn't have any about the house.'

Roger belched and shook his head. 'He ought to become a Templar. The knights aren't even allowed to kiss their mothers or sisters, in case they get unclean thoughts.'

'What of you?'

Roger pulled a face and his Italian accent grew more pronounced. 'Can you imagine me taking a vow of chastity? I don't think so. No, I am fond of feminine companionship. But I am a shipman: I have not taken the three oaths of poverty, chastity and obedience. They are the vows taken by monks. The knights, they are all monks, you see? Not me. I have agreed to become a lay-brother for a period of five years, and after that, in two years, I will be free again.'

'Why did you do that?'

Roger shrugged. 'When I was eight, I joined a ship. I'm a sailor, but I had no ship. I learned my craft well, and the Templars wanted shipmen. With them I was able to gain access to ships, and be my own master. Perhaps some day I will be rich enough to buy my own ship. I could bring grain to Acre to sell at market, and take away sugar-cane to sell in Lombardy or Tuscany. I'll make my fortune.'

'Tell me, what do you know about Ivo? He is so stern, like a disapproving father.'

Roger stared into his drink. 'He was a strong fighter, I heard. He came here when your King was a Prince – that must be twenty years ago. But when your King returned home, Ivo remained here. He married, had children, and I suppose he was happy.'

'What happened to his wife?'

'Did he not say? She was in Tripoli when the assault came last year. She and their son were there.'

'He was away buying horses?'

'Aye, and when he came back it was too late. The siege had begun and all he could do was wait for news. There was nothing he could have done even if he'd been there, of course. One more sword wouldn't have aided them. But that reflection would not help a man who saw his family slain.'

'How could the people of Tripoli have been so easily taken?'

'They did not think they were in danger. Just like Lattakieh before them, three years ago. Qalawun is a wily old devil. He gives peace treaties, but carefully hoards exclusions. Lattakieh was a principality, so Qalawun declared that it was not a part of the treaty with Tripoli. When Lattakieh was assailed by a great earthquake, and her walls tumbled to the ground, Qalawun took advantage: he rode straight in and the city capitulated. Last year, there was a dispute about who should inherit Tripoli when the Lord Bohemond VII died. Some sent to Qalawun to help them prevent the Genoese from taking the city, and he considered that absolved him from his oath and the treaty.'

'Yes, but the city must have realised it was in danger. Were there no outriders to keep watch for an invasion? Even if there were not, surely some people from villages far away would have seen the army's approach?'

'He sent his army to Syria, but the people of Tripoli didn't understand their danger,' Roger said. He leaned forward on his elbows and explained.

The Templars knew the true target of Qalawun's army, he said. For years the Grand Master had made good use of Templar gold, bribing officials in the Sultan's court, and he alone had advance warning. He sent messengers to warn Tripoli an attack was imminent, but his urgent exhortations went unheeded. They thought he had his own mercantile interests at heart rather than the defence of their city and sneered at his prophetic alarms.

At last, seeing little more could be done, Guillaume de Beaujeu sent his Marshal and many knights to help, but they were too few, too late. The city fell, and all were enslaved or slain in the wholesale slaughter that followed. Only a few lived to tell of the devastation.

'That is why Ivo is hurrying from Grenada to Lombardy and Tuscany seeking horses,' Roger concluded. 'The Order lost three hundred or more in Tripoli, and it is not so easy to replace trained warhorses.' Roger looked at Baldwin, and with a wolfish grin nodded towards three women in the corner of the room. 'Hey, we have need of celebration, yes? We should ask those pretty things to join us.'

Baldwin was nothing loath. It was a long time since he had grappled with a woman, and the middle of these three was a goodly height, just as he liked.

Beckoning to them, Roger leaned back on his seat against the wall, appraising them as the women crossed the floor, giggling to themselves.

To Baldwin, they were almost painfully exotic. Their skin was moderately darker than the olive complexion of the Venetian ladies he had seen while taking ship, and their eyes gleamed in the dim light in the tavern, while their clothing was as skimpy as decency would permit. Baldwin could hear the blood thundering in his ears at the sight of long hair framing slender necks. He could almost feel their soft flesh, and the thought of their kisses was a sweet agony.

They stood before the two men, and one sidled nearer to Baldwin. She touched his cheek with her cool hand, and he looked up into brilliant green eyes.

It may have been the wine, but the sight of her kohl-rimmed eyes was enough for him to lose all desire. He didn't want this woman, he wanted Maria of Lydda, the woman in green.

CHAPTER FIFTEEN

Abu al-Fida learned what had happened from their neighbours.

A fire in the middle watches of the night, and screams from within, but none might enter to save his family. Two men tried, so he was told, and one, a brawny Galician who had the house next door, showed him arms still raw and hairless where he had got burned in his attempt to rescue them.

'I couldn't do it, old friend,' he said.

'What caused it?' Abu al-Fida asked him brokenly.

'Who can tell? A falling lamp? A candle? It only takes a little to set a curtain alight, and when that happens, the whole house will catch fire. We did all we could, my friend.'

All we could. If they had only realised that there was a fire sooner, if they had gone to his poor Aisha and his girls, perhaps they would still be alive now.

But such dreams of what might have been served no purpose. His old life was ended, and he must take stock. He must find a new place to live, think about how to renew his fortunes. Grief was a luxury he could ill afford.

At least he still had Usmar.

Baldwin returned to the yard where Roger was still laughing, one of the other women on his lap. He smacked her smartly on the backside and sent her away with a coin. 'So, you enjoyed your filly? She looked keen.'

Baldwin flushed. 'She was very kind.'

He could not explain that he had not enjoyed the encounter. The girl had been eager enough, but there was something still about the woman with the green eyes that haunted him. The air of mystery that encompassed her only added to her allure, and this little wench was only a cheap imitation of her.

'They were good little tickle-tails, I thought?' Roger said, picking up on Baldwin's reserve.

Baldwin nodded. 'It's not them, it's another woman.'

'Oh, you have an object for your affections? Who is this woman?'

'She is a lady I have seen, a woman in emerald silk.'

'Maria of Lydda?' Roger whistled, and surveyed Baldwin with concern. 'My friend, if you seek to lose your head, there are less painful ways to do it. She can bring you nothing but misery.'

Baldwin gave a weak grin. 'What would you have me do?'

'Forget her and make good use of these ladies?' Roger suggested, turning to point at the women, but they were already gone in search of more lucrative companions. 'Ach! We shall have to hope to meet them another day, eh?'

Baldwin nodded as Roger chuckled to himself. He rose, threw down some coins for their wine, and the two walked from the tavern and out into the light. There, Roger wished

Baldwin godspeed and returned along the street towards the Temple.

It had been too exciting a day for Baldwin to think of going home. Instead, he made his way along the street in the opposite direction. He had a vague thought of going to see the castle, but as he reached the Monastery of San Sabas, realised he had taken too southerly a course. He decided to cut through the Venetian quarter – it would be faster. He continued on, and tried to ignore the enticing odours of fish grilling on a charcoal fire as he passed. After the wine with Roger, his head felt woolly, and he was tempted to go and ask for water from one of the houses near, but the men and women were unwelcoming.

As he was coming from behind the Arsenal, he caught sight of the German Tower ahead of him. Hearing a noise, he turned and saw a woman clad all in emerald. She was standing in a sun-filled alley, and the yellowish rock made her glow with a green fire.

Baldwin could not resist her. This time, she made no move to run from him as he approached. There was something other-worldly about her, as though she would disappear in a moment if he once looked away from her. She attracted his gaze with a magnetism that was impossible to break.

He entered the alleyway and strode towards her, and as he came closer, he saw her smile at him. It was a smile to make his heart melt.

And then the first blow caught him over the ear, and he fell at once into the abyss that opened in front of him.

CHAPTER SIXTEEN

Ivo returned from the Temple to find that Baldwin had left, and for his part he was relieved. The younger man had been grumpy ever since the day they had encountered Buscarel in the street.

During the hottest hours of the day, Ivo routinely took his rest, but today there came a babble from the streets that intruded into his peace, and soon he rose to see what was the matter. Outside was a stream of people hurrying past. He followed, feeling the tension grow in his breast, until he reached the Temple. There the throng was so thick, he could not hope to push through.

'What is it?' he asked the man beside him.

'Messengers from Egypt.'

Ivo looked up at the tower, and the gilded lions seemed to blaze with sudden brilliance. 'An army?' he wondered with quick dread.

'Army? No! That old bastard Qalawun has agreed peace!'

For an instant it felt as though a leaden cloak had been drawn from his shoulders. 'What? Do you really mean it?'

Ivo could hear music, the wailing of a stringed instrument, the blaring of horns, cymbals and drums, as men and women danced with joy. A woman was shamelessly picking up her skirts and dancing with a man over at the next street, while all about her, people clapped and cheered. There was a sickening lurch in his belly at the thought that this was what should have happened in Tripoli. How dare these people survive and celebrate, when his family was dead? It was enough to make a man beat his head in fury.

The city would be making merry all night, but he wanted no part of it. He had never felt so lonely. He wondered for an instant where Baldwin was, but reflected that the boy would be sunk in a tavern, just as Ivo would have been at his age. Let him drink. There would be time for work later. This was a glorious day – for those who had not already lost everything that mattered, everything that made life worth living.

'My friend, you are glad at the news?'

He wiped his eye quickly. 'Jacques, I wish you a good day. God has saved us.'

'So it would seem, old friend. You are torn, aren't you?'

'You always could see through my moods.'

'Where is that lad, Baldwin?'

'Who knows? He has wandered off on his own. He doesn't need me!'

'Ivo, don't be twisted by jealousy. He's a good man, but young. He will show his quality before long. No doubt he's out celebrating, along with everyone else.'

'Yes.' Ivo was pensive. 'I wonder if Qalawun is as pleased as these folks.'

'Peace should gladden any heart,' Jacques said.

'Yes . . .' Ivo agreed, a poisonous thought coming into his head. 'But Qalawun is determined to exterminate Christianity. We both know that.'

'What of it?'

'If he put his enemies off their guard by swearing peace, that would be a good strategem, would it not? He destroyed Tripoli while he was "at peace". It required only a pretext for him to break it: a dispute between Genoese and Venetian interests.'

'True enough.'

'It was rumoured that Venice sent an embassy to Qalawun to ask that he intervene to prevent Genoa becoming too powerful – not that they anticipated that their request would lead to the city being torn down stone by stone!'

'Come, Ivo,' Jacques said gently. 'Do not suffer your bile to rule your head. Qalawun is a man of his word. He can be trusted if he swears peace. More so than a Genoese, anyway,' he amended with a smile. 'Only something dreadful would force him to break his oath.'

When Baldwin woke, his head thundered like a destrier at full gallop, and when he tried to roll over, there was a sharp pain at his wrists and ankles: he was securely bound. Overwhelmed by the need to vomit, he retched, his body convulsing, but there was nothing to bring up but a little bile, and he sagged back, panting.

It was hot here. He was in a small square, with the sun directly overhead. Perhaps it was a garden? There, at the edge of his hearing, was the tinkle and splash of water. Looking about him, he saw a pool of water, and sitting beside it, his Maria with the emerald dress. Her face was still veiled below the eyes, but that only added to her beauty, he thought.

'You must not move. Your head will hurt,' she said. Her French was heavily accented, and he found it captivating. She took a scrap of linen and soaked it in water. Wringing it out, she brought it over to him and rested it on his head. He tried not to wince at the sudden pain, instead staring up into her eyes.

'Maria,' he croaked.

Her eyes widened. 'Not me. That is my mistress.'

'Then who are you?' he demanded.

'I am Lucia. Maid to my Lady Maria of Lydda.'

He stared. She had the olive complexion of a woman of Granada, but her eyes were the cool green of water in a Dartmoor pool. He felt instinctively that he could rest by her all his life and never feel his time was wasted.

'Lucia, you are beautiful.'

She withdrew, alarm in her eyes. 'Do not say that!'

'It's the truth,' he said. He tried to rise to his feet, forgetting his bonds, and winced as pain lanced through his body. His ankles, his arms, his temples, all rebelled at any movement. He groaned and closed his eyes, gritting his teeth.

'I saw you on my first day here,' he said. 'Down the alleyway near the Venetian quarter. Do you remember? You were there, in your finery, and I followed you – called to you, but you ran away.'

She nodded hesitantly. 'Perhaps.'

'And then again in the streets at the market, but that time with your men.'

'That was my Lady, not me.'

He was surprised by that, but now other considerations intruded. 'Why am I tied? What happened? I remember I saw you, and then I was knocked down.'

'I am sorry,' she said, and her voice was tearful. She looked up at a sound, and swiftly retreated.

As she did so, he heard steps, and when he looked, he saw Buscarel the Genoese marching towards him with two henchmen. They went one to either side of him and picked him up by the arms. Buscarel chuckled at the sight.

'So, Englishman. You wanted my ring, I think?' He smiled,

holding up his hand so that Baldwin could see the ring on his forefinger, and then he clenched his fist, and before Baldwin could think to prepare, he slammed it under his ribcage.

The air left his lungs in an explosion of pain, and he collapsed, writhing, trying to breathe.

'I will keep my ring. And now,' Buscarel added with a kick at Baldwin's kidneys, 'now, I would learn what . . . news the two riders had . . . for the Temple. Is it news of an attack on Genoa's interests? You will tell me everything . . . just as soon as I have finished enjoying my . . . self!'

With each pause, he punctuated his speech with a kick until Baldwin felt that his spine must surely break. Then Buscarel's boot caught his head – and everything went black.

CHAPTER SEVENTEEN

Ivo and Jacques were returning homewards when they saw Roger Flor walking along the street. He was waving his arms to make a way for himself among the crowds that thronged the square and streets.

'You will find the roads blocked all the way to the gate-house,' Ivo warned him.

'They won't hold up a Templar,' Roger said. 'You have heard the news?'

'Yes. It's remarkable. I had assumed that Qalawun would overrun us,' Ivo said. He could feel Jacques' eyes on him as he spoke, but he refused to meet the Leper Knight's gaze. It wasn't his fault he distrusted Roger Flor. There was something excessively mercenary about the man.

Roger curled his lip into a smile. 'It is the wrong time to remove the last port where his traders sell their produce, I suppose.'

'Perhaps.'

'Oh by the way, your boy enjoyed his ride with me.'

'Baldwin went riding with *you*?' Ivo asked sharply.

'Do not concern yourself. He didn't have to draw a sword, although he thought he might when we met the messengers. It was we who escorted them back.'

Ivo glared at him. 'Do not think to teach him your ways, Roger. I will not have you hire men from my house to help you rob and kill.'

'Perhaps you should tell him that? He was a willing enough student on the ride, and back here too with wine and women,' Roger said, smiling lazily, but with his hand near the knife on his belt.

'If you pollute him, I will kill you myself!'

'Ivo, you are too old to be making threats to a man like me. Go and find him if you are so concerned about his morals.'

Jacques stepped between them and said pleasantly, 'Where is he now?'

'Last time I saw him, he was heading up the street,' Roger shrugged.

Ivo left without further speech, Jacques hurrying at his side. Roger Flor was a low felon who would murder for a clipped penny. He was not worth talking to. But if Baldwin had walked up this street here, he would be safe; it did not lead to Buscarel's area.

Still, Ivo could not help but glance down into the alleys that led to the Genoese quarter as he strode up the street, a feeling of apprehension niggling at him all the way.

This time, Baldwin was not out in the open. The air was cool on his flesh. He woke to the sensation of a damp cloth being pressed against his brow, and he revelled in the gentle touch of muslin. It was delicious. He moved his fingers, but it was diffi-cult. The bonds tying his wrists and feet were so tight, they might as well have been cut from his own skin.

'We must hear all he knows,' Buscarel was saying.

'In good time. Whatever he has overheard, a single evening will not change matters. If you had not so belaboured him, my dear friend, he would have answered much sooner. I shall report your hotheadedness to your Admiral, if you wish?'

There was steel in that gentle voice. Baldwin relished the note of concern in Buscarel's as he apologised.

'It is unlikely he knows too much,' the gentle voice continued. 'If, as you say, he was with the party returning with the messengers, that does not mean he overheard secret communications, does it?'

Baldwin opened his eyes as the cloth was removed, and found himself looking into the face of a different woman.

She was clad in a similar dress to that of Lucia, and her eyes too were green, but that was where the similarity ended. Lady Maria had higher cheekbones, and while her eyes were green, they were closer set in narrow features. Her lips were less full, and there was a slight twist to the upper lip that gave her a sardonic appearance, as if she saw something amusing that all else had missed. Her emerald clothing was lighter, and more beautifully tailored, and the aura of wealth that surrounded her was emphasised by the gold she wore at wrists and throat.

She wiped at Baldwin's forehead again and threw her cloth away.

Following its trajectory, Baldwin saw that Lucia was in the room. She caught the cloth adroitly, and stood with it in her hands, eyeing her mistress and Buscarel warily.

Baldwin smiled at her. He was lying full length on a carved stone bench, and the door was some distance away. It would be hard to flee this chamber even if his feet were untied. Buscarel had two men with him, and they looked robust, reliable types.

It was not a happy reflection. Behind Buscarel was a brazier, smoking lazily, and Baldwin wondered if this chamber was far below ground, to require the heat.

'So, Master Baldwin. You are here in Acre for your soul, are you not?' Lady Maria asked. 'I wonder what crime you have committed that needs such a desperate penance. Perhaps you will tell us later. But for now, we need to know what it was that the messengers came to tell the Templars.'

Baldwin turned his head to peer at Buscarel. The man stood sullenly in a corner, and Baldwin silently swore to himself that he would avenge his beating.

'Qalawun has agreed a peace treaty,' he said wearily. 'He has confirmed it for over ten years. There is no secret.'

Lady Maria looked up at Buscarel. 'You see? Easy. All I needed to do was ask him. Now, Master pilgrim, what would you say about Genoa? I am sure that there was news of our city, too.'

'Why?' Baldwin asked. He tried to sit up, but it hurt so he lay down again. His back felt as though it had been pounded with leaden mauls, and his arms were painful where his hands were tied. 'That was all I heard.'

'But you must know that there was a dispute between Genoa and Venice. What was said of that?'

Buscarel approached, fists bunching. 'Speak when my Lady asks! What did they say?'

'Lady, could you silence your terrier?' Baldwin said. Before Buscarel could hit him, he continued, 'They said nothing in front of me. Why would they? They were messengers for Guillaume de Beaujeu, and if they had secrets for him, they kept them for him.'

'What do you think of that, Buscarel?' Lady Maria said.

'He's lying! Look at him! He is a dog from the north. You

cannot trust a word from such as he. Let me have him with my sailors for a day. We'll brand him and get all we need.'

'Perhaps that would be best,' Maria said. She put her thumb and forefinger on Baldwin's chin, one at either side, and moved his head this way and that, smiling. 'It would be a pity to spoil his looks, but if there is no alternative, such must be done. So, burn his face to make him unrecognisable, and cut out his tongue when he has finished talking, so he may never speak of things again. Then we could use him. Or sell him to the Moorish slave dealers.'

'Lady!' Baldwin protested. He hoped she was joking, but a look into her compassionless eyes told him that pleading was pointless. She looked on him as she would have looked at a cat, or a rat. Or a slave, he thought with mounting trepidation.

'I will do your bidding,' Buscarel said. 'Genoa must be protected.'

Baldwin was transfixed with horror, his mind filled with images of coals searing his flesh. He did not see how he could free himself, but perhaps if he was carried to a ship, he might get away. Surely that was what they meant when they spoke of torturing him with Buscarel's sailors.

But the smell of burning coals was already in Baldwin's nostrils, and he realised there would be no journey to the sea. He was to be tortured here in this foul chamber. He struggled against his bonds, but nothing helped. In desperation, he threw himself from the bench to the floor. The stone flags struck his brow and knees with a shocking jolt, and he thought he would fall senseless, but then hands grabbed his shoulders and he was hauled to the brazier where the grinning Buscarel stood with a poker.

'It's all perfectly straightforward,' the captain told him. 'I have need of information, so I'll burn and hurt you as I may, and then leave you to Lady Maria's tender mercies. Now, while I heat this iron, think carefully about the question I asked you.'

CHAPTER EIGHTEEN

Jacques pounded on the door with his mailed gauntlet again, and this time an elderly Moorish servant opened it, bowing low in terrified respect as the two men barged past him.

'We want the lad, Baldwin de Furnshill. He was seen brought here, Lady,' Ivo rasped as he strode into the house. He glared about him. 'I will search the house if you do not produce him quickly.'

'You? Search my house?' Lady Maria said coolly. Two of her guards were close behind her, and now Buscarel and another sailor appeared at a doorway.

Jacques smiled. 'I am sure that there is no need for us to argue about him. He is only a young fellow. But I would have him freed, madame.'

'And if not?'

There was a rasp of steel as Sir Jacques drew his sword. 'I will fight for him. And there will be the embarrassment of all your dead men, and the necessary explanations as to why I was here. You do not need such indignities.'

She nodded. 'I have no use for him, in any case. He was struck by a footpad in the street and I had him carried in for his own protection. But if you wish to have him, you may take him,' Lady Maria said with a patrician hauteur. 'He is through there. Please, be careful with him. Don't let him vomit on my floor. He has been knocked on the head.'

Ivo hurried through the door she indicated, and found Baldwin lying on the floor, rosewater being applied to his brow by a maid. 'Baldwin? Are you able to stand?'

Baldwin gave a weak smile. 'Cut my bonds and I may.'

With the thongs sliced from wrists and ankles, he slowly rose, and with Ivo's arm to steady him, Baldwin managed a step or two, not without pain, the sweat standing out on his forehead as he made his agonising progress, through the doorway and out to the hall. There he gave a grateful nod to Jacques.

'I thank you for my life, sir,' Baldwin said. 'You have today saved another pilgrim.'

'My friend, I am taking responsibility for your safety from now,' Jacques said with a cold fury. 'If any man attacks you in this way again, they will answer to me and my Order,' he added, sweeping a look around the assembled men.

'Do be careful in the streets,' Lady Maria called to him. She smiled, her curled lip making it look like a sneer. 'I would not want you injured again.'

'Now I know who are my enemies and my friends,' Baldwin said, 'I shall be careful to avoid the former, and stay close to the latter – until I am ready.'

Ivo helped him through the door and out to the street. 'What happened?'

'They wished to torture me to learn about a message concerning Genoa,' Baldwin said. 'But I know nothing of it.'

There were two Muslims at the street corner, and Sir Jacques took a coin from Ivo to persuade them to help Baldwin.

Baldwin was reluctant to have their aid. All he had heard of these people said that they were murderous and evil, but so far in his time at Acre, most appeared to be cultured and generous. Perhaps, he thought, it was the way of a subject race living cheek by jowl with their rulers, but somehow he doubted it.

Sir Jacques nodded, speaking quietly. 'I know what they wanted to learn. Genoese galleys attacked an Egyptian ship and sacked the port of Tineh.'

'So that's why Qalawun is leaving us for the nonce,' Ivo said. 'He is planning revenge against them.'

'What, he will build a navy to destroy them? I think not, old friend. No, they will have cause to regret their behaviour, I am sure. He will tax their goods extravagantly and make them weep,' Sir Jacques said with a quiet grin.

'How did you know to find me here?' Baldwin asked. His throat was sore, and he felt an overwhelming desire to close his eyes and sleep.

'It was a whim,' Ivo grunted.

In truth it had been, too. It was a mere whim that had taken him to Buscarel's house with Sir Jacques, and when a servant told him that Buscarel was with Lady Maria, Ivo was filled with disquiet. When they reached Maria's street, they spoke to one man who described a fellow much like Baldwin, who had been carried into the Lady's house by two sailors and Buscarel. That had been enough.

Baldwin nodded as Ivo explained, but then he asked, 'Genoa is to suffer? I don't understand.'

'All the mercantile cities have their favourite ports,' Ivo said. 'Genoa had Tripoli. That is why they attacked Tineh and a ship:

to make their point. They are angry that the Sultan has wiped out their trading capital in Outremer.'

'But surely it will hurt all the Christian seafaring nations?' Baldwin asked.

Jacques gave a chuckle. 'It should, but Venice detests Genoa, and has her own centre of operations here in Acre, so it was more a source of amusement to Venice that Genoa's city was destroyed. It won't affect them much, because they will be able to trade direct with the Egyptian merchants, and won't lose profit to the middle-men in Tripoli.'

Baldwin couldn't understand. This was all over his aching head. The talk of mercantile ventures was making his mind swim. He closed his eyes. 'The Lady Maria had contempt for the Templars, too, I felt,' he murmured.

'When she sought to question you,' Ivo said, 'she was thinking of her friends, the Genoese, no doubt. I think she has a close relationship with them, so her feelings are coloured against the Templars.'

'She dislikes the men of the Order?'

Sir Jacques tried to explain. 'It goes deeper than simple dislike, Baldwin. In past disputes, the Templars have tended to ally themselves with the Venetians, while the Hospitallers have been more associated with Genoa. Therein lies the source of many rancorous arguments that have led to the death of Christians.'

'What of Pisa?'

Ivo glanced at him. 'All these three states make money from trade, and from transporting pilgrims and crusaders – and all want to make more money than their competitors. So while they exist, the three cities will fight, and since each has allies, their allies will fight for them and with them. And, of course, there are some who will fight only for themselves. Like Roger Flor.'

'Roger? What of him?'

'He used to go on illegal raids into Moorish lands, to kill and steal from the merchants he found. He preyed on those less able to defend themselves. He will do so again, before long.'

'I was with him today,' Baldwin admitted shamefacedly.

'I know. You're old enough to make your own mistakes – but be careful if you make him your companion. It would not take many of Roger's attacks to upset this fragile peace.'

Ivo sat in his garden drinking strong wine. He had been profoundly shocked by Baldwin's battered and beaten body. It brought back that horrible nightmare of the destruction of Tripoli. He often dreamed of it. Ivo could see the streets in his mind's eye as clearly as if he had been there. He could see *his* street, the flames leaping higher and higher, outlining people who ran from their doors, only to be cut down. He saw his neighbours kneeling on the stones of the road, offering money, jewels – anything for their lives – and then having their throats cut. Then he saw his own wife, Rachel. His son, Peter. Saw the blades stabbing and slashing, the men taking their pleasure with her before killing her too. Poor Rachel.

'I would have been there, if I could,' he said quietly to himself, his voice broken with sorrow.

And afterwards, he also knew how it had looked. Bodies lying at the roadside. Men, women and children, cut to pieces and left with their blood draining, houses looted and ruined, churches despoiled, and nothing left alive. He had been to visit once. The bones were everywhere, but the city he had known was destroyed.

He had dreams in which he rescued them, Rachel and Peter. Waking afterwards was to return to a living nightmare in which they were still dead.

110

'I hope you didn't suffer,' he murmured to himself. It was his abiding prayer, that they had been killed quickly. The siege would have been hard, but at least if they hadn't been tortured, that would be a comfort.

But how would he ever know?

CHAPTER NINETEEN

It had been a nightmare journey for the pilgrims who arrived at the city that November. The seas had been storm-tossed, and some ships had been wrecked, killing passengers and crew alike; fortunately, many had got through, and as the cogs docked in the harbour or beached on the sands outside the city, a thirsty, ill-disciplined rabble was disgorged.

Edgar Bakere was among them.

A tall fellow with a lazy smile, Edgar had been apprenticed to a London baker, but he had never enjoyed the trade. His mind was not attuned to kneading and setting dough to rise, nor to wakening a little after Matins to set the fires in the ovens, ready for a long day of sweating exhaustion. He had long dreamed of leaving England's damp chill, and making his fortune in a land where the sun shone. A place where he would not have to slave, where others would do the menial work for a change.

No, he was not going to be a baker. He was determined upon that. It was why he had invested what little money he had in taking lessons from a Master of Defence, learning how to handle a sword, a stick, or even his fists. while doing this, he had heard of Outremer, the land where men could go and find themselves a patch of land, and where, if they could hold on to it, they could become barons.

It was such a relief to be off the ship and on stable ground again that Edgar could have kissed the sands. He and the other men were only the advance: thousands more were being recruited from Lombardy to London, and before long more transports would reach this shore, full of men eager to protect Acre.

Their ship was a heavy-built transport, and to allow the horses to disembark, the master had beached the vessel. While the passengers copied Edgar and descended the ladders to the shore, shipmen were hacking at the caulking about the door in the hull. There were two other ships beached alongside, and Edgar eyed them without affection. It would, he decided, be many long years before he would willingly submit to sailing again.

Three bodies were being removed from the ship now. He saw the first thrown over the side to dangle from a rope under the arms, gradually being lowered. That was the man who had got into a fight after a gambling dispute. He had been stabbed, and bled to death in front of everyone. No one had gone to his aid. Then there was the body of the young mother, who had simply gone to sleep and not woken up. Even now her child, a boy of perhaps ten years, was wailing as his mother was let down. Why she had sought to come here, Edgar had no idea. Perhaps she was a prostitute, and believed the tales of a land flowing with milk and honey? A whore could make a good living in a town like this, especially with an army arriving. Women of that profession always followed an army.

The third man to be set down on the sandy shore was the kindly-faced old fellow who had befriended Edgar on the first day, and who had slept at Edgar's side, eaten with him, and shared biscuits with him during their passage.

Edgar watched the body being deposited alongside the others, and then rose, looking about him. The city lay a scant half-mile distant, and he hefted his pack, adjusted the knife at his belt, and set off. He didn't think of the man in the sand again. The man whom he had discovered in the middle of the night going through his pack searching for money or gold, and whom he had strangled.

CHAPTER TWENTY

Baldwin saw the first of the Lombards arrive.

Ivo had gone travelling, first to Cyprus and thence to Tuscany. The horse-dealer had been instructed to acquire more beasts for the Temple – be they destriers for the knights, or faster, lighter horses for the Turcopoles and archers. Before leaving, he had specifically instructed Baldwin to stick with someone like Sir Jacques when he went outside, and to avoid any contact with Lady Maria and Buscarel.

Baldwin had no desire to see either. For Lady Maria his infatuation was entirely flown, and he knew he must fully recover before repaying the Genoese shipmaster for his beating.

'Master Baldwin, would you join me for a ride?' Roger asked one morning. He had knocked, and now stood gazing about him with interest while Pietro eyed him with dislike.

'Gladly,' Baldwin said, grunting as he rose from his seat. He was still stiff and sore. 'But I don't have a horse.'

'A horsemaster's house without a horse?' Roger laughed,

but then jerked his head. 'Come, I will arrange for a beast for you. We ride east. Bring your sword.'

Baldwin would not have ridden outside the city without his sword, but on hearing those words, he looked at Roger askance. There was a subtle meaning there, he felt sure, and he sensed the thrill of impending action. He remembered Ivo's injunction not to embarrass him, but looking at Roger Flor, he found it hard to believe the stories of his robbing people. Tolls were one thing, robbery and murder quite different. He had a devil-may-care look about him, but that was the way of Templars.

In any case, he was Baldwin's friend.

There were more men in the streets than usual. Some hundreds of scruffy pilgrims were straggling up from the harbour, and he gazed at them with disapproval. They were – as most travellers were after days on a cramped ship – filthy. Lank, greasy hair framed faces that were pinched from lack of food, while some had been unfortunate enough to befoul themselves.

It only served to make Baldwin realise how disgusting he himself must have been when he disembarked from the *Falcon*. He tried to steer clear of the newcomers as he strode on by with Roger Flor.

A steady rhythmic tread intruded upon his thoughts, and he stood aside to permit four Templar men-at-arms to pass. All clad in their brown uniform habits with the red crosses, they marched in step – a picture of military efficiency that was particularly pleasing among these raggle-taggle Lombards, Baldwin thought, as he trailed behind Roger down the hill towards the Temple.

On the way, he saw a familiar figure with a white cloak and red cross. 'Sir Jacques,' he called. 'God's blessings on you.'

'And on you,' the older man responded. 'You are not approaching the Genoese quarter, I hope?'

Baldwin pulled a face. 'No. We are going for a ride outside the city.'

'That is good,' Sir Jacques said, but there was little humour in his eyes as he surveyed Roger Flor. 'Beware, my friends. These fellows are new to the city, and I do not think they appreciate the land in which they have landed. I fear riots.'

Edgar Bakere walked into Acre by the gate at the Patriarch's Tower. It was a good city, he reckoned.

The arrival of the crusaders, however, was no cause of joy to the citizens. One or two spat on the ground as the Lombards tramped past. Edgar walked about for some while, wondering where he should go, before finding his way to the castle.

At the door lounged three bored sentries. The castle was not so large as the King's White Tower in London, but with the strength of the city's surrounding walls, that was hardly surprising. Defences here would serve only to protect the castle's inhabitants against the city, not from outside attack. If city walls that thick didn't suffice to keep invaders out, the castle could hardly hope to do so.

'I am here to serve in the defence of the city,' Edgar said self-importantly.

'Good for you,' was the unpromising response of a guard. 'Hope you enjoy it.'

'I want to join the garrison.'

'As it happens, just now we don't have any vacancies.'

Edgar frowned. 'Where do I go, then?'

The guard sighed heavily and thrust his thumbs into his belt. He had a pitying look in his eyes as he studied Edgar. 'Anywhere you like, mate, so long as it's not here. Pick an inn, all right? There are plenty all over the city.'

'But I don't have much money,' Edgar said. He wore an apologetic smile, but in his heart a resentful anger was kindling.

'Then get a job,' the guard said. 'Now piss off. We have work to do.'

Edgar walked down the street, past idling servants, merchants with gold gleaming on fingers and about their necks, and then almost bumped into a party of men-at-arms, but not warriors such as he had seen before.

They were Saracens, and wore swords with curved blades. He eyed them with interest, wondering how it could be that representatives of the enemies of the city could have gained entrance. And then he saw to his astonishment that they were making their way to the castle! The guard who had been so insulting to *him*, stood aside and bowed to *them*.

This was incredible. Edgar walked on more slowly as he digested the fact that the people from whom he had expected to defend the city, actually lived inside it.

All over Acre, the inns were filling quickly. Edgar soon learned that to the local people, a fresh influx of pilgrims and crusaders meant only one thing: profit to the men who rented rooms and sold food. The place was hideously expensive, the cost of bread and meats much higher even than in Lombardy, where he had taken ship. The people here were acquisitive to a degree Edgar had never experienced, and he was shocked to see how the innkeepers tried to gull the Lombards – and himself. Prices were inflated, and while many tried to haggle and dicker, they ended up paying with sullen resentment when they realised they had little choice.

He then had a bit of luck. There was an inn in the Genoese quarter with a stable at the back. Just now, the inn was almost full, he learned, but when the innkeeper heard why Edgar was in the city, he immediately professed himself delighted to meet a brave warrior come to protect him and his family.

'You can take some space in my hayloft, if you want,' he said.

By that stage, Edgar would have taken a privy. All he wanted was to sit down and close his eyes for a little.

CHAPTER TWENTY-ONE

Riding out of the massive St Anthony's Gate, Baldwin felt his troubles fall away.

It was two weeks since his beating at the hands of the Genoese, and most of his wounds were healing. As he bent to duck under a low building, his saddle creaking, he could feel the bruises complain, but that was all. Outside in the open air, past the shanty town that had sprung up about Acre's walls, he felt refreshed, and it was with joy in his heart that he trotted at Roger Flor's side.

There were six others with them, all sailors from Roger's *Falcon*.

'We'll head east, and see what we find,' Roger said easily. He looked over at Baldwin, wondering. The Englishman sometimes was so sure of himself, like today, whereas on other occasions he could seem deliberately juvenile. 'You never know what you might see, and it's good to ensure that there are no spies about.'

'Yes, of course,' Baldwin said mildly. For his part, he was keen only to exercise. It was prodigiously hot, but he missed

120

riding. Back at home he would ride every day, no matter what the weather, and he could feel his muscles growing flabby. 'Will we have time for a gallop?'

'Perhaps later,' Roger said with a chuckle, relieved that the lad appeared to understand. There were some men who would be less keen on the idea of a raid against local houses. Maybe Baldwin was a man after his own heart. He might be young, but there was fire in his belly. 'You are a keen horseman?'

'Very. But at home the weather is not so hot. My land is cool.'

'So is mine,' Roger said. 'At least here, when you ride, there is a purpose to it, eh?'

'Yes,' Baldwin laughed.

Roger suddenly lashed his horse into a canter, and the others spurred their beasts to keep up. This, he thought, would be a good day for a chevauchée. He looked over at Bernat and grinned.

Baldwin was filled with the joy of comradeship. There was also a heady sense of freedom to be leaving the city. He was a man born to the country, and in Acre he was always aware of being hemmed in. The seas to south and west, the walls to north and east, left him with the impression of being imprisoned. This ride was a liberation.

They rode on for several miles. To save the horses from overheating, they soon slowed to a trot, and the dust again caused Baldwin to cover his face. Before long, they were riding between two hills, and it was here that Roger slowed to a walk, rising to stand in his stirrups, and peering ahead with a frown.

Baldwin could see nothing at first that could have caused the man to pause, but then he made out a dust cloud some distance away. Not enormous, certainly not caused by an army, but of a moderate size. Perhaps there was a slow-moving caravan.

'Come on!' Roger said. His blood was stirred at the sight of beasts in the sand. They must be carrying something for there to be so many – and whatever it was, it would be worth good besants in Acre. He gleefully anticipated a clash of arms.

At first, Baldwin could make out little. The travellers were far distant, and the heat haze in these parts made any accurate assessment of people or horses utterly impossible.

And then, as they came closer, he saw long-legged creatures. He had seen strange sights before when the land was hot, as though the air itself would reflect the landscape like rippling water. Occasionally a horse would look as though its legs had doubled in length, as he had noticed on that first ride with Roger.

'Ready?' Roger shouted suddenly. Then, with a yell, he swept out his sword, waved it over his head, and spurred his horse into a gallop.

As the others screamed battle cries and pursued him, Baldwin's beast laid his ears back and stretched his neck to join the race. Baldwin had not yet unsheathed his sword, but found himself crouching low over his mount's neck, galloping for the sheer thrill of the wind in his hair, the snap and crackle of his cloak in the wind, the protests of leather and harness. The wind bore tiny grains of sand that stung his eyes and face like flying needles.

The clattering of hooves on the roadway's stones was deafening, but over it he heard the first cry.

A blade whirled towards him, and he ducked, panicking, almost forgetting he bore a weapon. He grabbed at his sword, and had it free even as the Saracen came at him a second time. Baldwin felt a lurching horror in his belly that seemed to rise to his chest, but he forced it aside and concentrated on his opponent. Terror would only slow him.

The Saracen was shorter than Baldwin, his black beard unfrosted, his eyes keen as he sliced again with his curved sword. Baldwin had to lurch back to avoid that horrible blade. He could imagine that if an arm or leg was snared by that, it would slice the limb away like a scythe, and at that hideous thought he lifted his sword into the True Gardant, his fist up and near his brow, the sword's point dropping away from his hand, pointing down and away from him.

The scythe-sword came back at him, the wicked outer curve aiming for his chest, and he dropped the point of his sword to defend himself. The man lifted his hand, and the point of the scimitar flicked upwards, almost eviscerating Baldwin as the point came towards his groin. He chopped down with his sword, knocking it down and away, and instantly lifted his point again, trying to cut the man's thigh or groin, but both targets evaded him, and the two whirled about, their swords flashing in the sun as their horses moved this way and that.

There was a brief cry of pain, and Baldwin and his opponent were distracted enough to glance about them.

Baldwin felt his jaw drop. Three men lay on the ground, their bellies opened, their throats slashed. Hacked limbs littered the sand, while blood stained it black. And the man fighting him gave a sob and lunged.

The attack caught Baldwin by surprise. The blade caught his right flank, and he felt it as a sharp pain, much like the lash of a whip. He didn't realise that he was cut, but thought he had taken a slap from the flat of the blade.

While the man's attention was on his injury, a snarl on his face, Baldwin slammed the guard of his sword into his cheek. He felt the metal crush bone, and the man tumbled from his horse, stunned. He tried to rise, but before he could do so, one of Roger's men turned and kicked him on the jaw, then stabbed him through the throat with a long-bladed dagger.

Baldwin panted, lightheaded after the action, and was aware of a sudden relief. He had fought, and had not embarrassed himself. He had kept calm, and traded blows with the enemy. It was a source of pride – and then he felt a shiver run up his spine and a black reaction set in as he took in the bodies lying all about. None of the sailors was injured, so far as he could tell, but all the Saracens were dead. Their horses were docile enough, apart from one which had taken flight, and even now Roger was almost at it. He was soon trotting back, leading the horse by the reins.

'Who were these?' Baldwin said.

'They're Saracens who assumed the right to use a Christian road,' Roger said with a grin. 'And as a result, we've made good money. These horses can be sold, the arms and armour too. And then, their goods can be taken to market at Acre.'

'What goods did they carry?'

'I don't know,' Roger said.

Baldwin felt a sudden cold certainty: Ivo was right. These men preyed upon Saracens. They had launched their ferocious attack purely to rob an innocent party of travellers.

And he had participated. He too was guilty.

CHAPTER TWENTY-TWO

Baldwin was struck with shame as he looked again at the murdered innocents. They had been carrying spices.

'Look – balm!' Roger said gleefully as he pulled a pot from a sack, opening the lid and holding it out. 'Smell that! The Church will pay well for that – they use it in the censers. This is going to reward us well,' he gloated as he rifled though the other packs.

'So we came here to rob?' Baldwin said.

'We're in Acre to take back the Holy Land. What, would you have us leave the Muslims here unhindered? That won't help our cause, will it? We must harry them as we may. And this way, we increase the money in the coffers at Acre so we can fund more fighters. That cannot be bad.'

Baldwin's misgivings were not soothed by this glib response. Not that Roger appeared concerned whether Baldwin cared or not. His man Bernat was close now, eyeing Baldwin impassively.

'I thought you were as keen to come as I was to invite you,'

Roger said. 'It's a shame if you're not. Still, you will have your share of the booty.'

'I want none of it,' Baldwin said, staring at the man who had been his opponent. The fellow's wounds were already covered with a seething mass of flies.

'No?' Roger said. He glanced at the other men. 'All the more for us, friend Baldwin. This is the manner of our survival in this land. You understand?'

'Oh yes, I understand,' Baldwin said miserably. He was sure that the activities of these men were no worse than those of others. While they gathered up their booty, and a pair dragged the bodies a little away from the road so they might not be discovered too quickly, kicking limbs before them, Baldwin swore at himself for his folly in coming here. He was a knight's son. Chivalry was his whole life, and chivalry did not include murdering like common felons. The shame was overwhelming.

Roger stood, and Baldwin saw that the others had noticed their argument. There was a moment's stillness.

'Look, lad, I don't want to see you unhappy,' Roger said jovially. 'We're all friends here.'

'Ivo is away, but Jacques d'Ivry knows I am with you,' Baldwin told him, fearing some kind of retribution. 'If I don't return, he will want to know why. The blame will attach to you.'

'Baldwin, be calm,' Roger said, still smiling. 'You're safe. But if I learn you've been talking of our little chevauchée, you will die before me. Somewhere in a dark alley, you'll be found, and with a Genoese dagger in your back, I expect.'

'We understand each other, then,' Baldwin said.

Roger nodded. It was a shame, but the fellow was not going to be an ally. Nor could Roger kill him with impunity. Better to keep an eye on him, and if necessary silence him later, in Acre, when it was less likely any blame would attach to him.

Baldwin remounted with the rest of the party. His flank stung, and he looked at it nervously. A raking slash had skimmed his ribs, but it did not hinder his sword arm. Just as well, since one glance at Roger's face told him he must look to his own safety on the ride back.

Baldwin rode back alone, using his injury as an excuse for riding slowly at the rear of the column, from where he could keep an eye on the others, but to his considerable relief, nothing untoward happened. It seemed Roger was content to trust him for now. Yet it was good to see the city once more, and as he rode in under the gate, Baldwin was aware of a sense of relief. He only wished he could lose his feelings of guilt and shame as easily.

After seeing to their horses, Roger Flor found one of his sailors falling into step beside him. It was Bernat.

He spoke quietly. 'That fellow today – Baldwin. I don't know if we can trust him.'

'How do we know whether any man can be trusted?' Roger said. 'The only way is to let him have enough rope to hang himself.'

'He isn't safe, I tell you.'

'He won't let us down. I trust him.'

'He may hang us.'

Roger smiled. 'I said, I trust him. I have spoken to him before, but if you wish, I'll have another word with him and make him realise he must hold his counsel.'

Bernat nodded and said no more. There was no need. They both knew that the young Baldwin was potentially a threat to them.

CHAPTER TWENTY-THREE

It seemed to Edgar Bakere that all the peoples of the world congregated here in one babel of sound.

The sight of Saracen warriors had shaken him, but the more he walked about the city, the more he grew to notice others. It was astonishing to see so many Saracens tolerated. Merchants, traders – they seemed to be everywhere. Almost more than there were Christians, and yet this was supposed to be a Christian city, with Christian beliefs. How Christians could trade with their enemies, and worse, allow them to live in the same city, Edgar did not understand.

Nor did the other crusaders.

He was on his way back to his inn in search of a little food when he saw the first of the fights. A woman, veiled and swathed in black material so voluminously that only her eyes could be seen, was walking with two men to guard her. For a moment Edgar reflected that Saracen women were harder to admire than Christian ones, and for that he was sorry. Edgar had always liked the company of women, and on the journey here he had enjoyed mild erotic fantasies about exotic Saracen girls ... only to learn that they would have to remain pure speculation.

It was not the woman who held his attention, however: it was the jeering, taunting men behind her.

Edgar could see that she was terrified. Her eyes were wildly shooting from one side to another, and her men were as fearful. They didn't know what to do to escape the baying mob. For that's what it was: a mob of unruly Lombard mercenaries who had no idea how to occupy themselves. They had no discipline, and what order there had been was degraded by drink. Edgar could understand their language moderately well after spending days in their company, and now he listened with a careful ear to their insults and taunts.

'Why's she covered up?'

'Come on, girl, give us a kiss!'

'What's the problem, eh? Don't you like real men?'

One man, bolder, or more foolish than the others, pushed his way to the front. One of the guards shot a look at his companion, and then the two tried to block the man's path, but he truculently set his hand to his knife and stared them down, before shoving past them.

The mob enveloped her guards like a wave washing over pebbles.

Edgar frowned. He could leave matters, return to his hayloft and forget this woman and her guards, and yet the behaviour of the man and the rest of the mob showed that the woman would probably be raped, perhaps killed. The death of other men did not bother Edgar unduly – he was unconcerned that the two guards would almost certainly die – but he disliked the idea of the woman being ravished or slain. It offended his sense of chivalry.

As she retreated, Edgar smilingly went to her and stood between her and the man.

'Out of the way, boy,' the man threatened, his hand still on his knife. His French was rough and, for Edgar, hard to understand.

'Your pardon? What was that?'

'Out of my way, fool!'

'You are troubling this lady. I would see her left to go on her way.'

'She's only a Moor.'

'That doesn't give you the right to pester and annoy her. There are taverns throughout the city where even *you* can find a woman. You don't need this.'

'What's she to you?'

Edgar shrugged. 'Nothing. But I dislike seeing a woman harried.'

'You're still in my way.'

Edgar nodded happily. 'I am, yes.'

The Lombard muttered a curse and drew his knife, holding it wide of his body as he crouched. On his breath was the unmistakable reek of cheap wine.

In the London streets in which Edgar had grown, a man soon learned to defend himself against drunk apprentices or clerks. His strength was good, his technical skills honed by the Master of Defence. He eyed the man now, his eyes moving from the Lombard's face to the knife, gauging when the man would make his attack.

There! The point jabbed forward, then withdrew and slashed towards Edgar's belly, but both were feints. They hardly reached close enough to tear his tunic. Edgar didn't move.

'When in a fight, get inside your opponent's reach,' his Master had always instructed, 'but if he has a knife, you must be fast and sure. Or you will be cut.'

Today, Edgar tested his theory.

The knife stabbed forward, the Lombard's arm straight. Edgar darted towards him. His left arm went over the Lombard's right, clamping the man's knife-hand under his armpit, while he wrapped his left arm about the Lombard's gripping his clothing at the shoulder. The Lombard was locked in his grasp, and Edgar punched twice, with stiffened right fingers, quickly, at the man's throat. The man choked and retched, and Edgar span him around, ramming his face into the wall, then, as the man wailed, his nose flooded with blood, Edgar slammed his open hand into the man's elbow, wrenching it sideways.

He screamed and dropped the dagger, clutching his ruined elbow. Edgar turned him around, placed his boot on the man's backside and pushed, hard.

As the Lombard fell amongst his companions, Edgar picked up his dagger. It was a good blade, strong and well made. He tucked it away into his belt and eyed the crowd. 'Anybody else want to try their luck?' he challenged mildly.

As he spoke, the two Saracen guards pushed through the crowd and went to his side, one setting his hand on his sword, but Edgar hoped he wouldn't draw it. If someone pulled out a weapon now, the mob could become nasty. They had the ugly temper of London apprentices on riot, he thought, and he could all too easily imagine them ripping stones from the roadway to hurl at him and the two beside him. That wouldn't be good.

'You a Moor-lover, boy?' someone shouted, and another jeered, 'You want a whore, they're cheaper in the tavern. She'll cost you dear!'

Edgar said nothing, but waited unmoving, alert. Some hotheads were all for attacking him, but already many had begun to drift away in search of wine, or easier prey.

Before long, he was alone with the three, and he wondered

as he looked into the woman's splendid dark eyes, what she looked like. He could not even tell how old she was.

She gave him a long study, from his head to his boots, before murmuring to one of the guards.

'My Lady wishes to express her gratitude. She says you saved her when her own guards were incompetent,' the man said stiffly.

'Tell your Lady I was pleased to be of help,' Edgar said. He tapped his belt. 'I have been rewarded for my efforts with this dagger.'

'What is your name?'

'Me? Edgar – of London,' he said with pride.

'Where do you live?'

Edgar chuckled. 'At an inn. They have a spacious chamber for me, where they store the fodder.'

'My Lady would like to present you with this,' the guard said, taking coins from a purse.

Edgar stared at them, and then smiled, bobbing his head as he took them.

'I am grateful to you,' he said, and as he returned to his inn, he was pleased. Now, he thought, he would buy new clothing to replace these reeking garments. He was on his way to becoming a man of position.

Two days later, more ships arrived with soldiers from Lombardy and Tuscany, and almost immediately the riots started.

CHAPTER TWENTY-FOUR

The first Baldwin knew of the trouble was the shouts. He grabbed his sword, buckling the belt as he went from the house. 'Pietro! Keep the gate locked and barred, and don't let anyone in except me or Sir Jacques!' he shouted as he went.

Hundreds of Muslims and Christians were running from the city into Montmusart, and he was shocked to see the naked terror in their eyes, but then, as he hurried into the city itself, he found the reason for their panic.

It had been a wonderful harvest that year. There was grain aplenty in the markets, and traders had come in from farms all about to sell their wares. Muslims, Christians, Jews – all were to be found in Acre, generally living together without dispute or trouble.

The arrival of the Lombard and Tuscan crusaders would change that forever.

Leaving their ships, full of zeal to hunt down and slay Muslims, the newcomers were appalled to find the enemy walking freely about the city. They were peasants, not politicians, and their understanding of the situation in Acre was flimsy at best. They were disgusted to discover that Muslims were not only tolerated here, but for the most part were treated as equals. To those who had sailed hundreds of miles to protect Acre, it was intolerable to find that the city was already over-run.

Later, Baldwin heard that a man had been set upon in the street for molesting a Christian woman. They didn't realise he was not only Christian, but her husband. His beard confused the crusaders, who thought all bearded men were Muslims and therefore the enemy. They saw a Muslim walking with a woman wearing a cross, and murdered him for his supposed offence.

That first death was only the spark that lighted the fire. Soon fights had broken out all over the city as Lombards and Tuscans ran through the alleys, far down through the Venetian quarter, up through the Pisan and Genoese sectors, and back into the main city. A hothead tried to batter his way into the Temple, but was quickly disabused of his belief that he could enter – and his unconscious body was taken away by his friends.

Many fought with resolute incomprehension. They saw strange clothes, beards and dark skin – and did not think beyond those manifestations of an alien culture. Baldwin wondered whether they could even think. They were the poor, the unedu-cated, the dregs of society – and most of them were drunk. All they knew was that the Pope had sanctioned their journey here to fight Muslims. So they did, wherever they found them.

His flank still smarting, Baldwin entered the old city. There was screaming from the area near the Hospital, and more from the market close to San Sabba, and he smelled burning. Wafts of smoke filled the alleys as he ran.

It was as he made his way through the streets with others summoned by the shouts that he found the first bodies: a man, his face horribly disfigured by a blow, a second victim a short distance away who had been stabbed many times. Their blood was pooled in the gutter, and Baldwin waved away flies with disgust as they tried to settle on his face. It was repellent that they would gorge themselves on the dead and then smother his face. He hurried on, and when he came near to the Genoese quarter he suddenly found himself in the middle of mayhem.

There must have been at least two hundred peasants, ill-armed, and poorly trained. A sergeant was bawling himself hoarse ordering them to stop, but those at the front were filled with bloodlust. There were already six bodies on the ground, three decapitated, and as Baldwin watched, three dragged a man forward, forced him to kneel, and a fourth, laughing with a lunatic joy, hefted a heavy butcher's cleaver, aiming at his neck.

As his weapon reared back to strike, Baldwin reached him.

Afterwards he didn't remember a conscious decision to protect the man kneeling and weeping with incomprehension in the dirt, but the sight so enraged Baldwin that his legs carried him across the square in an instant. He slammed into the executioner, and the man was sent sprawling, the cleaver clattering on the flagstones.

'Release him!' Baldwin bawled with rage, his sword already pointing dangerously at the three gripping their captive. They obeyed at once, seeing the savage anger in his face. They let go of their victim, stepping away carefully, and Baldwin felt a momentary pleasure. He had failed to protect the merchants against Roger Flor, but he would not fail this man.

There was a scrape, and he turned to see the executioner grabbing for his cleaver. Baldwin placed his booted foot on it and held his blade to the man's breast.

'It's mine!' the man said.

'Leave it where it is!' Baldwin rasped.

The crowd muttered angrily, and all might have ended badly, had it not been for a party of Hospitallers who entered the square, swords at the ready, closely followed by twenty Genoese crossbowmen. The mob-lunacy dissipated at the sight of the weapons facing them. The victim had fallen, and was retching drily on all fours in the blood of the other bodies, and Baldwin felt a pang as he glanced at them.

'Why have you done this?' he demanded loudly to the people nearest. 'Isn't it enough that we are in danger already, without killing our friends?'

'They aren't our friends,' the executioner spat. His face twitched, while a hand scrabbled at his lice-infested beard. 'They're Moors – our enemy! If you don't kill them, you are a heathen like them! Blasphemer!'

'Really?' Baldwin sneered. He reached down to the throat of the nearest corpse and pulled away the simple wooden cross he had seen there. 'So now you think Muslims worship Christ as do you or I? You've murdered Christians, you fool!'

He dropped the little necklace back onto the body. A Hospitaller stepped forward and grabbed hold of the executioner to lead him away.

But Baldwin had heard another scream, and he hurried to a nearby alley. As the Hospitallers led away their captive, other men of Acre appeared. There were five behind him now, and seeing that he had their support, he called them to him, and ran into the alley.

Into the Genoese quarter.

It was after prayers, and Abu al-Fida was feeling that tempo-rary ease which always struck him afterwards. Prayers helped him think of his lovely Aisha and his daughters more calmly. It took away the harsh edge of sadness, and replaced it with a softer pain that was at least bearable.

'What is that noise?' Abu al-Fida said as they left the lane and entered a broad roadway.

Usmar's face was white. 'A rabble – they are beating men, Father!'

'Come – here,' Abu al-Fida said, thinking to evade them. He led the way back down the alley, and at the end was going to turn up the next, when they saw more men coming towards them. This time, there were only six or seven – not enough to alarm him.

Usmar murmured, 'Father, shouldn't we go—'

'Come. This is Acre, not some provincial village,' Abu al-Fida said. He continued, and smiled politely at the men walking the other way.

One nodded, and a second grinned, but then there was a shout behind him, and Abu al-Fida turned in surprise to find that another group of men was pointing at him and calling out. As he watched, they started to run towards him.

'Usmar,' he said, 'go!'

'I cannot leave you!'

'You must! Run!'

Usmar set off, and perhaps it was that which made the men act as they did. Usmar was grabbed as he bolted past, and his body slammed to the ground. Then, although Abu al-Fida shouted and tried to get to his son, he saw the flash of a blade.

Strange. Afterwards, all he could recall was that flashing blade, as it rose and fell again, until a red mistiness enveloped him.

A hideous blow caught his neck and he was thrown to the ground, his head an insupportable weight, as though made of lead, and he lay with his cheek against the gravel in the roadway, while he heard the sound of a man choking.

Later, when the men in the white tunics arrived and drove the mob away, he realised the choking had come from his son.

But by then it was too late to help him.

CHAPTER TWENTY-FIVE

Lucia had not expected the crowds. At first their appearance was not alarming, just surprising. It seemed impossible so many people could have poured into the alleys.

When the alarm was heard, Lucia was at the market with her mistress and two men. The sound was like the rushing of a torrent in full spate, and sent terror into Lucia's heart. Lady Maria jerked her head, and they hurried towards the house, but even as they quickened their pace, a man hurtled from an alley, a bloody knife in his hand, his eyes wild. One of Maria's men barged Lucia aside and cut at him. He died quickly, rolling in the dust with his hands at his throat.

Now they were running. Maria was panting, panicked, but Lucia was past worrying about her. This was awful: peasants had risen to kill the wealthy. It was a reversal of normality, as if the Day of Judgement was come. Lucia felt as though her heart must burst with horror when she tripped over a man with an obscene slash in his belly. She fell into his entrails and screamed, trying to wipe her hands clean on her emerald dress, but nothing would get the blood off; it was sticky, foetid, disgusting. Already the others were running ahead of her along an alley that should take them to the house, and Lucia suddenly had a clear premonition that they would enter and bar the door whether she was with them or not. Maria would not risk her property or life to save a slave.

Lucia lurched to her feet, weeping, but even as she sped along, she realised she had not taken the right route and must retrace her steps. It was already too late – too late – and she could not see Maria or the men, and she was all alone, and she could hear men approaching from the street where the house lay, and she couldn't go down there.

Her heart thundering in her breast, she stopped and stared about her wildly. There was an acrid taste in her mouth, as though she was about to be sick, and her heart was racing.

And then she heard, and turned with a whimper to see Baldwin, accompanied by several men.

Baldwin saw her as the mob appeared. One held a bloody knife aloft, while in the front rank, three held skins of wine.

'Sweet Jesus,' one of Baldwin's companions muttered.

The mob saw Lucia, and smiles overspread their faces. One had his hand at his cods, pulling his hosen down, when Baldwin and his men raced to them.

'Back to your ships!' Baldwin bellowed.

They didn't listen. The would-be rapist spat on Baldwin's boot, while the knife-wielder ran at him.

Baldwin stabbed the knife-man in the breast, his left hand grasping the man's knife as he did so, then booted him from his sword; he kicked the spitter in the ballocks, and rammed his pommel into the face of the next. The crowd was forced onwards by the crush behind them, and Baldwin and the men with him had to hack and stab and bludgeon to hold their ground. It was a tight lane, barely wide enough for two horses abreast, and Baldwin lowered a shoulder, shoving the crowd back by using the nearest man as a shield, stabbing with the point of his sword . . . but there was nothing he and his men could do to prevent the mob gradually advancing. They were too many, too reckless.

It was then, just as Baldwin thought they must soon be overwhelmed, that an unearthly shriek came from a nearby alley some yards behind the front of the crowd. Baldwin could see little of what was happening, but suddenly the press was lessened. There was another high-pitched scream, and this time he realised it was a war-cry. A sword hacked at the back of the man in front of him, and Baldwin stabbed from the front, and the man fell. Behind him stood a man in a pale tunic, with longish mousy-coloured hair. The man nodded at Baldwin, a lazy smile on his face, before returning to hacking and stabbing in a wild frenzy.

The newcomer's intervention at the flank was enough to alarm many of the mob. At last, when six men lay dying or dead, the crowd began to pull away.

Baldwin wiped an arm over his brow, staining the linen with sweat and blood, and stared, until he was convinced that the mob was returning to the harbour.

'Are you well, maid?' he panted to Lucia.

She looked up at him.

Her veil had been torn away during her mad rush, and to him she looked like a terrified faun. Her green eyes were still startling, all the more so because her face was flushed, and her wide gaze was fixed upon him with so transparent a look of vulnerability that he felt he could take her up now and never let her go. He would battle the armies of Islam and Christianity alike to protect her.

'I thank you, Master,' he said to the stranger. With a man like this to help him, he would conquer any army. 'My friend, I am glad to meet you. What is your name?'

'Edgar,' the fellow said. He paused, and then, 'You can call me Edgar of London.'

Lucia was in a turmoil as the men walked her up the street and away from her mistress. She submitted, because it was clear she could not go home, not yet. The mob would rape her, maybe kill her. 'What can I do?'

'You must come with us,' Baldwin said. 'When the streets are safe, I will bring you home.'

She nodded. He inspired trust. Confident and tall, he strode ahead. He had a cut on his left arm, three of his companions were also nursing wounds, and the man calling himself Edgar of London followed.

Bodies littered many alleys and corners. At one, a man lay sprawled with a dog lying dead on his body. She saw Baldwin stop and touch the dog's head. She shivered at the unseeing eyes on the dead man. It would be a long time before she could feel safe again in this city.

Unconsciously, she leaned against Baldwin. He was kind-looking for a Frank. Usually they stared at her with unbounded lust in their eyes, but this man did not. He made her feel safe. She was attracted to him.

The other, Edgar, looked dangerous. He scared her. Certainly he was bold, and courageous, but there was something in his eyes that frightened her, a cold unfeelingness like an avenging angel come to earth. During the battle in the street she had caught a glimpse of him, and saw only a terrible glee at killing that chilled her.

It made her realise that there was nowhere safe in the city. Not for her.

To be safe, she must return to Lady Maria as soon as possible.

CHAPTER TWENTY-SIX

Roger Flor and Bernat had instructions to go to the port and check on the Temple's ships. There was concern that the mob could have damaged them.

Nothing loath, Roger took the Templars' tunnel to the harbour. There, the curved arch of the tunnel's roof radiated calm with its coolness. It was difficult, down here, to imagine that only yards above, men and women could have been fighting and killing each other.

As they reached the farther end of the tunnel, and Roger walked past the guards at the door into the daylight, the day's heat was growing more bearable. Earlier, when the mobs first rioted, the heat had been intolerable.

He had with him three Templar sergeants and Bernat. In their brown tunics, they looked less like Templars and more like the peasants who had rioted, he reckoned. There was something about the pure white tunics that sent fear into the bowels of enemies. It was a thought: white and steel – they both petrified. Stand against them, and a Muslim would know he would soon die, because the Templars were known to be the most fanatical fighters in all Christendom.

The ships all looked secure. He ran up the gangplanks to the first three, making sure of their moorings, seeing that nothing had been stolen from below, and then he went to his own ship, the *Falcon*, in which he had previously concealed a number of items. He had caused a step to be built beside the steering oar to give him a better view of the way ahead. It was a perfect hiding-place. A wooden peg concealed a trapdoor. Taking a quick, lookaround he surreptitiously opened it and he drew out the chest hidden within.

He had enjoyed his time in the Temple. It was harsh and restrictive, but no more so than life in a manor would have been. At least no one knew the seas of the Mediterranean better than him. With his position as shipmaster came freedom. Which was why he was able to ride outside the city. But soon his period of service would be ended, and when that happened, he needed to have money saved so he might start out again. Perhaps buy his own ship and take up a new life as a merchant – if he could cope with the boredom. Fighting was in his blood, and he would find it difficult to give up.

He restored his chest to its hiding-place. A Templar was not permitted to possess anything during his period of service. Even a secular knight serving the Order for a fixed term could not own the horses he brought with him. They must be sold to the Order, and when he left the Temple, he would have to repay the Temple half that sum as a gift. But Roger had no intention of giving up any of his hard-earned money.

He couldn't be a knight even if he wanted to. Only sons of knights could become knights within the Order; even then only legitimate sons. Bastards from Brindisi were not permitted the white tunic. He didn't care. The thought of the three vows was not appealing. Instead he would buy a ship and become rich in his own right, trading from port to port, bringing valuable rarities to Genoa and Brindisi, taking pilgrims and crusaders to the Holy Land. That would be a good life, he thought.

Provided Sultan Qalawun left Acre alone.

He put men-at-arms to guard the ships in case of more mob violence, then set off to walk through the city.

'Have you thought any more about that man?' Bernat asked as they walked.

'If Baldwin says nothing, we are safe, and if he does speak, he implicates himself. So he will be silent.'

'In his eyes there was disgust. He may decide to cleanse his soul.'

'More fool him! He'll soon become accustomed to death here.'

Acre had been taken from the Muslims by Richard the Lionheart, and the wholesale slaughter of the people at that time had shocked even Christian chroniclers. The blood of men was set into the very mortar of the buildings here: Outremer was held by force of arms, by strength. The strong vanquished; the weak perished. That was the way of Outremer. Roger knew it. Baldwin would learn to appreciate it too.

'He may accuse us,' Bernat went on.

'If he does, he will be removed.' Roger didn't want complications. 'I told you before, I will speak to him.'

'When?'

Roger looked at him. Ivo was away at the moment, so now was a good time.

'Today.'

Baldwin banged on the door and was relieved to see the peephole slide open to reveal Pietro's suspicious eye.

'Eh? Who's that?' the old man demanded.

'Open the door,' Baldwin snarled, and as he pushed Lucia and Edgar inside, he added, 'and fetch us wine.' He led the way to the garden, where the air was a little cooler, and indicated a bench on which Lucia could sit.

As Edgar took a quick, appreciative look around him, Baldwin asked, 'Have you been in Acre long?'

'A matter of days.'

'Yet you wear flamboyant, local clothing – expensive muslin and silk. And your sword is of the best Damascus steel.'

Edgar said, 'I came here to make my fortune. I had tired of baking bread in London.'

'You were born there?' Baldwin asked, taking a goblet of wine from Pietro.

'No. I come from a small village in Surrey called Clopeham. My father sent me to be apprenticed. He thought if I learned my trade in London I would be more valuable, but he forgot one thing: I had no desire to be a baker.'

'So you left your master and took a ship?'

'Yes. I studied with a Master of Defence, and he told me of the Fall of Tripoli, and how there should be a new Crusade to protect the Holy Land. A priest gave me money for my journey, so here I am. And I like it,' he added, staring at the masonry, the roses, the silken cushions on the benches. 'This is how a man can live in Acre, and how I want to. It's better than a stinking street near the Bishop of Winchester's stews.'

'I wish you fortune,' Baldwin said. 'But the man who lives here has been settled in the East for many years. It's taken him time to earn this.'

'I will work faster,' Edgar said with a patronising air, thinking of the gold he had been paid by the woman in the street. 'All I need is a patron, and I should find one quickly enough.'

'What makes you think that?'

Edgar gave a quiet laugh. 'After today? This city is seething with suspicion, fear and hatred. All the rich will want more guards.'

'You think they'll trust a newcomer?'

'They will trust me rather than a dough-faced Lombard peasant with the swordsman's skills of a seven-year-old.'

'So I saw. You are competent.'

'My Master of Defence taught me well.'

'You learned well,' Baldwin said and Edgar nodded. He was gifted with the ability to be still.

'So . . . how will you find a patron?'

A small cloud passed over Edgar's face. 'I'm determined. I will succeed.'

Lucia said quietly, 'You should speak with Philip Mainboeuf. He is rich, and has need of guards.'

Baldwin looked at her. She sat quietly, hands in her lap, face fixed in despair. 'Maid, are you well?'

'Lady Maria will want to know what has happened to me,' she said miserably.

'We will soon have you home, when it is safe.'

'She will be angry because I failed to stay with her. That makes me deserve punishment, in her eyes. I am a slave, you see. She owns me.'

'A slave? There are none here in Acre.'

'I was captured when I was young, and her family bought me. I have been with her ever since.'

'What of your family?'

'They were with me when I was taken. I think my mother was sold off. My father would have been killed. It is the way.'

'It is a hard way,' Edgar said. 'Still, if you can stay away from her, you will be free, won't you?'

'No,' she said with surprise. 'I am hers.'

'But no Christian can be held slave,' Baldwin said.

'I am not Christian. I am Muslim.'

Baldwin's mouth fell open. 'I . . . I had no idea.'

'She took me many years ago. If I do not hurry, she will have me flogged. Then set me to work in the kitchen, or send me to the farms to work.'

'Well, she locked the door against you, so it is not your responsibility, it is hers, that you are not with her now. For now, Lady, I think you had best remain here with me. I will see to your needs. I can help return you to your mistress too.' He thought, but didn't add, *If you really want me to.*

Because looking at her again now, he thought he had never seen such a beautiful young woman.

CHAPTER TWENTY-SEVEN

Baldwin was not sad to see Edgar leave. There was something unsettling about him, an aura of scarcely restrained violence.

'You are cold, maid?' he asked, seeing Lucia shiver.

'No, I am warm,' she said, but there was fear in her eyes.

'You need not worry. The rioters will soon be calmed and the city will be as safe as before,' he said. She did not appear soothed by his words. 'Why are you troubled? Is it the way your mistress treats you? Is she cruel?'

'No, no. She is a good mistress.'

'Please, maid, if there is anything I can do to help you, command me! I would protect you.'

'What could you do to protect me?'

'Keep you here, safe within my house. I can guard you night and day. If you would have me, I could marry you . . .'

The words were out before he knew it, and he stopped, dumbfounded by his own speech.

Lucia was as silent as he, the two a scant yard apart, but it felt as though the length of the desert lay between them. He wanted to reach for her, but feared he would scare her away, like a terrified mouse. He hesitantly lifted his hands in mute appeal, but she said very quietly, 'I may not marry without my mistress's permission. I am a slave.'

'In a Christian city, if you agree to be baptised, you can marry whom you will,' Baldwin pointed out. 'No Christian may hold another Christian as a slave. Renounce your faith and we can marry. I could speak to the Prelate – he would help, and—'

'I cannot.'

'Why?' Baldwin asked. His heart was pounding, and he felt light-headed as though drunk, her sad beauty was so entrancing.

Before she could respond, there came a knock at the gate and Baldwin cursed as Pietro opened it.

'Master Baldwin, I hope I find you well,' Roger Flor said, and then his eye fell on Lucia. 'Ah, you must be feeling refreshed!'

'This maid was caught in the riots,' Baldwin said stiffly.

'So you brought her here?' Roger peered closer. 'The lady with green eyes?'

Baldwin felt a sickening lurch in his belly as he recalled the whore in the tavern. 'She is Lucia.'

'Where are you from, wench?' Roger asked with a smile.

Baldwin stepped in front of her, and his glower made Roger laugh aloud.

'Well, I may be a Templar shipman, but I know when I'm not wanted! I'll see you soon, Baldwin, eh?'

Baldwin walked with him to the door, where Roger paused. 'She is the woman you were after? I thought you wanted Lady Maria.'

'She is the lady's maid. I hadn't realised.'

'Enjoy yourself. And Baldwin – I know you didn't enjoy

your ride out with us, but keep it under your hood, eh? We don't want news of the caravan getting out into the city. That could embarrass me.'

'I see,' Baldwin said.

'Good, good,' Roger said, and chuckled. 'I like you.'

He patted Baldwin's shoulder and walked off, laughing quietly, and Baldwin closed the door. Roger Flor was another like Edgar. Unsettling, and not only because of his propensity for violence. There was something else in him Baldwin found disconcerting: an appeal.

He felt Lucia's hand on his arm, and smiled down at her. 'Yes?'

'Do you want me to stay here now?'

'Only if you would have me. I would marry you and have you live with me.'

'I cannot. I must go back to my mistress. It is my place.'

'There is nothing I can say that would tempt you to remain with me?' he asked.

Her eyes flashed with something like anger. 'Would *you* surrender your faith to become Muslim?'

'Of course not!'

'But you ask me to convert?'

'I shall walk you back,' he said.

The words almost choked him.

She felt safe with Baldwin walking at her side. There were two men from Ivo's stables with them, both strong and carrying staffs in case of violence, but they saw no sign of rioters. While there was still some shouting from towards the harbour, people were walking the streets again, nervously and not in great numbers, but it was a beginning. They saw Templars and Hospitallers in groups of two or three, often glaring suspiciously at each other, and men in the livery of the King of Jerusalem.

Baldwin was about to knock at Lady Maria's door, when Lucia put her hand on his breast. She was wearing her veil again, and her eyes stared into his seriously. 'No further,' she whispered. 'Please, stay here.'

He nodded reluctantly, but she was glad to see that he stopped. She would have liked to kiss him, but she dared not. Not in the street where anyone could be watching. Instead she smiled, and hoped her eyes would speak of her gratitude. His face held pain. There were no words she could use to soothe him.

She walked away without turning back. If she had, she knew she would be lost. So she walked to the door, rapped sharply on the old timbers – and entered.

Baldwin stood there a moment or two longer, gazing down the lane, hoping that the door would open and she would reappear, perhaps run to him, and throw her arms about him. But no. The door had closed, and she was gone. Unless he bought her, she would remain there forever.

Baldwin came to a decision.

He would have to earn the money to buy her. And perhaps he could persuade her mistress to sell her for a reasonable amount.

It was a sustaining thought as he made his way back up the street, and over towards the wall to Montmusart.

Lucia was grasped by the bottler. He pulled her with him into the room at the rear of the house, overlooking the gardens, where her mistress was sitting with a thin muslin sheath draped about her against the heat of the afternoon. She was sipping from a goblet of wine.

'So, you returned at last?'

'I came as soon as I could. The mob was in the street—'

'Silence!' Maria snapped, and gestured.

The servant shoved, and Lucia was thrown to the ground, moaning with the pain of scraped knees.

'You went with that man Baldwin, did you not? You were seen in the street with him. Have you been whoring?'

'No! No!'

'Stop the snivelling – it doesn't impress me. I think you fell back deliberately when we were hurrying home. Didn't your friend want you when he learned you were a slave? I thought so. You cannot trust these fine, chivalrous men. They take fresh rump when they can, but they are less keen on rotten meat.'

She went to the terrace, picking a rose and sniffing at it. 'You have disappointed me, Lucia. Now answer truthfully: did you mention my business?'

'No. Not at all.'

Maria crossed the floor, her leather slippers making no sound. 'Tell me the truth, child.'

Lucia could feel tears welling. It didn't matter that she was innocent. When Maria looked at her like that, it made her feel guilty.

'I think you told him,' Maria said softly. 'And now you seek to come here to listen to my conversations. Was that the idea? You were to come here and spy for him? What, is he from Venice?'

'No! He is English.'

'English? They are all pirates and felons,' Maria said with contempt. She snapped her fingers. 'Take her to the cellar and question her. I want to know what she told that man, and I want the truth.'

CHAPTER TWENTY-EIGHT

When Ivo disembarked, he was glad of the sudden silence.

Aboard a ship, the constant din of creaking timbers, the whistle and hiss of wind about the ropes, became deafening after a short time. In the past he had enjoyed those sounds, because it reminded him that the ship was like a living creature, a beast that could be soothed and cajoled into better behaviour. But at times the noises became a torment. He had spent long enough with the sea for now, he thought.

He knocked on his door and waited impatiently until he heard the shuffle of his old servant Pietro. At last there was a rattle of the bolt, and the door swung open.

'You took your time! And why only the bolt? Haven't you used the other locks?'

'There's not so much to protect here.'

Ivo scowled. 'As I walked here, I passed three places where there had been fires. Someone mentioned riots.'

'Only little ones, and not here,' his servant said mulishly, and turned to fetch him wine.

Ivo called after him, 'If I could find a servant who was more civil, I'd throw you on to the street!'

'I will find you one. I don't need this complaining every day.'

Ivo fumed while he waited, and took the mazer ungraciously. 'Where's the boy?'

'If you mean Master Baldwin, he's out.'

'Where?'

'Taking his little wench home.'

'What? The moment my back was turned he brought a whore to my house?'

Pietro glowered at his master. 'Eh? He rescued her from the mob, that's all. He's an honourable young fellow.'

As he finished, there came a fresh knock at the door, and when Pietro opened it, Baldwin walked in. Seeing Ivo, he smiled. 'I'm glad to see you back. The rioting today – you should have seen it. I was worried they'd break into the place. It's a relief to have you home. Was your voyage successful?'

'That will be all, Pietro,' Ivo said pointedly. The servant pulled a face, shrugged his shoulders, and slouched away. 'Old fool!' Ivo muttered. Then, 'I hear you had a woman here today?'

'Yes. She was caught in the riots.'

'Couldn't you have taken her to her house? To a church? Why bring her here? I won't have my house used as a . . .'

Baldwin's face paled. 'Don't accuse me of that! I did nothing to her, and I wouldn't, on my mother's life.'

Ivo nodded. 'My apologies,' he said, and clapped him on the back. There was something in Baldwin's face that caught his attention. And then he saw how Baldwin held himself, favouring his flank. 'What is it, boy? What have you done?'

Baldwin wanted to tell Ivo about the ride with Roger Flor,

but he had promised not to speak of it. Still, Ivo might learn from another source, and then he would think Baldwin had been intending to conceal his crimes, not from shame, but from a desire to repeat them. He might think Baldwin a dedicated mercenary. 'It's nothing.'

'Show me.'

Baldwin lifted his arm and his shirt, and Ivo whistled. 'This wasn't today. How did this happen?'

Baldwin bent his head. 'I did not realise he wanted me to join him on a raid,' he began, and told the whole story.

'That bastard! So, he traps you into joining him on the raid, and then ensures you run the risk of punishment for complicity? The shit!'

'It was my error. What should I do?'

'Nothing! He has you by the short hairs! If you accuse him, his men will deny it, in which case your punishment will be the same as theirs would have been, were they to be found guilty. You must remain silent.'

'The guilt tears at my soul.'

'That is the way of guilt,' Ivo said.

'But I cannot bear more guilt!'

'*More* guilt? What do you mean?' Ivo demanded. 'Come, I never asked you what you had done. I think it's time I heard.'

'I am here because I killed a man in England,' Baldwin admitted quietly.

'That was the sin you wished to expiate by coming here?'

Baldwin sighed. He trusted and liked Ivo. He didn't want to spoil their friendship, but he wouldn't keep this secret any longer.

'When my father died, there was never any dispute of the inheritance. My brother is older by several years, and Furnshill is his. I was glad that the manor would go to Reynald.'

157

'What happened?'

'I fell in love. She was beautiful, Ivo. A round, smiling face, with eyes as green as emeralds, a happy, cheerful woman who would warm the heart of any man.'

Ivo listened in silence as Baldwin walked about the room distractedly.

'I wanted to marry her. I offered her my hand, but when my brother heard, he was furious. He had been trying to marry me to a woman from the next manor so that I would have a secure income, and,' he raised a wan face, 'here I was, proposing marriage to a peasant.'

'You truly loved her?'

'Sibilla, yes, I adored her. I refused my brother's proposal, and he swore that I would not marry Sibilla. He threatened to evict her family.'

'So you left?'

'Yes,' Baldwin said, 'but not as you think. You see, I learned that she was pregnant.' He saw Ivo's face darken. 'I had not touched her – it was another man. She didn't truly want me; it was her father, I think, who wished me to take her. There would be cachet in having a bastard son fathered by the brother of the manor's lord.'

'I see. So, your eyes were opened.'

'I saw them lying together, and in my rage, I killed him. Afterwards, I sought sanctuary in the cathedral. I was angry and bitter. I was torn from my brother, my home, my life. I felt I could never be happy with another woman. But in the cathedral church, I heard God speak to me. Outside, a house was being torn down. A vicar told me it had belonged to the Dean, but he paid men to murder a rival, and as penance he was pulling down his house in order to erect a chantry chapel. One churchman murdering another. That reminded me of Thomas á

Becket, and his killers: to atone for their sins, they came here, to the Holy Land, to fight for the cross.'

'So you chose the same path?'

'Yes. After speaking with the vicar I took up the cross.' He looked over at Ivo. 'You look sad. If you don't want me here, I'll understand.'

'No, it is not you – it's me. I'm thinking about my wife Rachel and Peter, my boy, who died in Tripoli. I miss them badly,' Ivo said with a catch in his voice.

Baldwin eyed him. 'I asked you once, what it was about visiting the Holy Sepulchre that made you feel whole again. That was what you said then. Was that your wife? Did you go there to ask God about her?'

'I wouldn't presume to ask Him such a thing, no.' Ivo sighed, and closed his eyes. At his age, he should be resting. After his journeys he was exhausted. But he had a compulsion to explain. 'When I came here with Prince Edward, I was high in his favour. Only a man-at-arms, but he respected me. It was a pleasure to serve him. I adored him.'

'He turned from you?'

'I failed him. He came to regain Jerusalem, but when he reached Outremer, he saw the bickering, the way the Orders would help their allies, the war between the Genoese and Venetians, and he saw he'd never forge an army from so many disparate groups. So he negotiated. And the men who were his enemies grew alarmed, because they could see what many could not: that the Prince was capable of making peace between rivals, and welding them into one army. So they sent a murderer to him.'

'A murderer?'

'An assassin. A mercenary paid to kill his victim and then die. They believe that they will be taken up to Heaven, if they die in that honourable way.' He spat contemptuously. 'Honour-able! To try to murder an unarmed man! This fellow was disguised as a Christian, and used guile to get into the King's tent. He was very convincing, you see. I couldn't help it. I let him inside, and told the Prince there was a message, and when my Prince came, the man drew a knife and stabbed him.' Ivo closed his eyes and let his head fall into his hands. 'It was awful. Blood, everywhere. I cut the assassin down, but his blade was poisoned, and it was only because Princess Eleanor sucked the poison from the wound that Prince Edward lived.'

'Well, that is good,' Baldwin said.

'I am glad that he survived. But the hatred in the Princess's face, in her voice . . . it was enough to chill my blood. I left that night, and never returned. My Prince nearly died because of my stupidity.'

Baldwin saw the tears silently running down his cheeks. He refilled their mazers as Ivo continued.

'After that, I had no occupation, no Lord. I wandered, and one day I heard a sermon, and I heard that those who travelled to Jerusalem could be healed of any earthly offence. I went, I saw the Holy Sepulchre, and I felt renewed. It was that which healed my heart.'

The two sat side-by-side, sipping wine as the sun fell and the evening grew cooler.

'Don't speak to anyone about the raid with Roger Flor,' Ivo said at last. 'I will deal with him.'

'Will you tell the Grand Master?'

'No. I'll tell Flor that I know his secret. Hopefully he won't try anything else like it.' *And if he does*, Ivo added silently, *I will personally see to it that the Order punishes him.*

CHAPTER TWENTY-NINE

Lady Maria was in a towering rage as she stalked back to her chamber. Snatching up a goblet, she was about to hurl it at the wall – but then forced herself to be calm. She carefully set the glass on a table and sat sedately beside it, her hands in her lap.

She was not going to lose her temper. She needed to think.

The stupid wretch! Lucia knew Baldwin was an enemy to Buscarel, and after their capture of him, he would be resentful. A man like that was a danger to them. To Maria. She would have to dispose of Lucia. It was infuriating, after so many years. When Maria had a need for a confidential messenger, Lucia was ideal. Maria had always been able to trust her. But no more. That trust had gone.

Lady Maria sat on warm cushions and fabrics, swirling wine in her goblet. The news about the peace was interesting. Buscarel only cared about Genoa, of course. He had a particularly single-minded focus. Anything that aided Genoa was good, all that hurt her, bad. Lady Maria had a more flexible view of the world.

Her husband had been a clever man, but a tyrant. His death had been a relief. She should not have suffered the indignities he forced upon her. He was a rural knight, when all was said and done, not one to inspire affection, but the match had seemed a good one when he pressed his suit, linking his lands at Lydda with her family's nearer Acre. It was only after their wedding that she felt the rough end of his tongue, the clenched fist.

Since his death she had escaped Lydda to live here in Acre. She was still beautiful, as the number of her lovers attested. There would come a time when she could not attract, but the loss of her beauty did not concern her so much as the loss of her lands. Lydda was a valuable asset, and no one would willingly lose land. It was the natural basis of wealth.

Her lover, Philip Mainboeuf, had assured her that Acre was safe. Well, perhaps so. His single-minded pursuit of money and trade with Egypt led him to believe that Qalawun did not want war, his capture of Tripoli having been forced upon him when the Venetians demanded his help; Genoa had been demanding more rights while trying to force Venice and Pisa from the city – and it was that which had led to Qalawun's attack. Acre, though, Acre must be safe. That was Philip's belief.

Lady Maria was content with his assurances for now. But it was essential that she keep her contacts in Egypt. If Acre were to be captured, she could return to Lydda until the fighting was over – so long as she maintained her friends in Egypt.

Maria knew she trod a fine line. Politics in the Holy Land were always tortuous and dangerous. In the past she had allied herself to Greeks, to Pisans, to Arabs, and now to Genoans too. She promised to use her influence to help them, and in return, she was paid.

Philip Mainboeuf was determined to prevent war. Wars cost money; he preferred peace and increased trade. He knew the Lady Maria had contacts with the highest in the Commune, and he hoped to make use of them.

Little did he know that she also had influence at Qalawun's court. When Tripoli fell, much of her land had been taken. Only by offering to help the Sultan did she retain control. She advised him on the political atmosphere in Acre, in return for which she kept the revenues from her estates. It was a nice arrangement.

She must see Philip and test his knowledge of recent discussions. Then a message must be sent to Qalawun to justify her position as his spy in the city.

Lucia must go. She knew too much of Maria's business with Qalawun. How much had she told Baldwin?

The stupid girl!

Ivo saw Roger Flor in the market the next day.

The citizens were doing the best they could to make the city wholesome once more after the riots. Bloodstained paving stones were scrubbed clean, the smashed remains of pots swept away, broken doors were taken down and replaced, and all over the city there was a feeling that disaster had been narrowly averted.

Roger Flor was standing at a stall with Bernat.

'Good day, Master Flor,' Ivo said. He kept on the left side of Roger Flor, away both from his knife hand and his companion.

'Master Horseman. How are you this fine day?'

'Well enough. But I think I warned you some while ago to keep away from my friend Baldwin, did I not?'

'What one man may threaten, another may decide to ignore,' Roger Flor said airily.

'When a man threatens to take proof to your Grand Master that you are involved in robbing Muslim caravans, I think you will listen.'

Roger Flor took an olive and tasted it experimentally. 'No, too old and sour. I wouldn't buy one such as that,' he said, and then turned to Ivo. 'Old man, you should be careful who listens to you. Some might think you were being threatening, and paunch you to see whether the cause of your bile was in your belly. Don't threaten me.'

'If you involve him in another raid, if he becomes ill, or if he is beaten and slain here in the city, I will hold you responsible, Roger, and I will have you dragged, if need be, to the Grand Master, where you will answer.'

'Me? I don't know what he has told you, but you'll find he was my companion on a ride. Am I accused of something more?'

'He admitted how he gained that wound. Otherwise he'd have kept your secret. And now your raids will cease, or . . .'

Bernat said quietly, 'Or what?'

Ivo grabbed Roger's forearm and swung him around and over his leg, hurling him to the ground. Then he was at Bernat, and although the seaman had already pulled his knife free, he held it low, and too close to his belly. Ivo kept moving forward, his right hand on Bernat's knife hand, pushing with all his strength, his body's momentum turning the blade to point at Bernat's stomach. Then, just as Bernat's eyes widened with shock as the blade point scratched his belly, Ivo let go, and slammed the heel of his hand up under Bernat's chin. It struck with a sound like wet sand hitting two stones; a sudden click as Bernat's teeth met, and the man fell.

Turning, Ivo snatched his own dagger out. Roger Flor was still smiling, but his eyes were filled with grim hatred.

'Keep away from Baldwin, I said,' Ivo told him. 'I won't see you pollute him. If you try to, I will make you wish you had never been born.'

CHAPTER THIRTY

It was Ivo who told him of the arrival of the English.

Their appearance was a shock to Baldwin. Somehow he had not expected to find so many of his countrymen in the city which he had come to think of as his adopted home.

'Best come with me before the deofols attack a Christian because he's wearing black,' Ivo muttered.

They made their way to the harbour and found it in a state of turmoil. Sailors, many with their arms folded in disapproval, watched as English men-at-arms moved about the place. But this was not the arrival of bitter, impoverished peasants with neither leaders nor discipline; this was a small, efficient army. Sergeants marched along the port, bellowing at the lines of men three abreast. All were dressed in tunics with a small cross on the breast to show that they were bound for the Holy Land, but the effect was spoiled by the fact that all were befouled from their long journey. Still, their weapons looked clean and well-cared for, and as an order was given, the polearms all rose, gleaming.

166

Baldwin eyed them jealously. If he could, he would have become a knight. Even to be a squire would have been an improvement. To be a warrior serving a lord meant to have certainty in life. His brother Reynald now enjoyed that. But Baldwin, although he had trained for his knighthood, leaving home at the age of seven so he could live with Sir Hugh de Courtenay and his men, had not yet gained the honour of his spurs. He was still a mere rural man-at-arms, with neither lands nor money to advance him. If he had not quarrelled with Reynald, and killed Sibilla's lover, perhaps he would be a squire by now. Then knighthood would have been achievable.

The men had gathered up their packs, and there was a pause while a horse was brought forward, and a tall, heavy-set man clad in gleaming mail with a distinct coat-of-arms, was helped into the saddle.

Ivo was staring at the man. 'Your eyes are better than mine. What are those arms?'

Baldwin peered. The knight was still a hundred yards distant. Fortunately, a banner was unfurled as a horn blared and the men began to march towards the city.

'It has alternate blue and yellow vertical stripes, but there's a red line angled down it. There are gold marks on the red band, too.'

'Dear God in Heaven,' Ivo muttered. 'A paly of six, silver and argent, with a bend gules and charged with three eagles in gold . . .'

'What?'

'That man. I think it's Otto de Grandison.'

'Who?'

Ivo shot him a look. 'Your King's most loyal servant these last thirty years. He was here with Prince Edward.'

'He looks well for such an old man,' was Baldwin's only comment as the men approached.

Ivo glared at him. 'He's not that old.'

'No, I mean, I . . .'

Ignoring his flustered apology, Ivo stood watching the men approach. As the knight came nearer, he called out: 'Sir Otto! God bring you fortune.'

The knight stopped. He had blue eyes in a square face with lines etched heavily into his leathery cheeks, and seeing Ivo, he frowned suddenly, his gaze wandering all over Ivo, absorbing his dress and features, before a smile appeared.

'Ivo de Pynho? God's teeth, it's good to see you!'

'In God's name, I'm glad to have met you,' Sir Otto said. 'It is good to be briefed before a conference. Is the King here?'

'Not yet. I saw him recently in Cyprus, gathering more men. As you can see, we have strong enough walls, but without the men to protect them, we have nothing.'

'Who controls the city?'

'Amalric, brother to King Henry II, is Castellan. The Commune of the city also wields power: the merchants and barons have their say for the benefit of all.'

'A gathering of merchants and stall-holders?' Sir Otto said disdainfully. He took up a small unleavened loaf and broke it into four. Chewing, he eyed Ivo questioningly.

'Years ago, there was a dispute about who should run the city, when the people rejected the man foisted upon them. Since then, they have decided their own issues. It works.'

'Aye, perhaps,' Sir Otto said, unconvinced.

He was not so tall as Baldwin had thought. His height was not far off Baldwin's, but he had a way of holding himself that made him seem bigger. His hair was shorn in the way of English knights – a military pudding-basin cut. While Ivo had assured him that the knight was fifty-five, Baldwin found it hard to believe. There was a vivacity and power to him that seemed out of place for someone so old and his face, while lined, was not ancient. Even his fair hair had no sign of silver.

They were in quarters near the castle. Otto's hall was a good size, with a pair of good chairs at the lord's table. Trestles were set out with benches for the first mess of soldiers, and now, as Otto sat and washed his hands, drying them on a pristine towel, his servants busied themselves preparing food. Otto and his guests had silver plates and fresh white bread, while the men below had bread trenchers with their meats, and Baldwin watched them jealously in the light lancing in from high above. Dust motes danced in swirls of incense. No one looked at him. They were too busy with their food.

'What do you say, Baldwin?' Ivo asked with asperity.

'S-sorry, Master Ivo?' he stammered.

'Woolgathering, lad?'

'I asked you: what is the quality of the city's men?' Otto said. 'Ivo tells me there's been rioting. What was the cause?' He was leaning forward, his jaws moving rhythmically, as though Baldwin was the only man in the room. It was intensely flattering.

'I think it was the indiscipline, Sir Otto. Lombards and others arrived, most of them peasants.'

'It is the way of the peasant,' Sir Otto agreed. 'No one who has seen the London mob could doubt that. They are like a mountain stream: calm, until roused, and then they become a torrent that can wash away boulders.'

'They must not be permitted to run wild,' Baldwin said. 'There are hotheads among them, and if they get into the open country, they could attack villages or caravans. That could force Qalawun into retaliating.'

Otto glanced at Ivo. 'You agree?'

'Certainly. We must not provoke the Sultan.'

'How many men can he muster? I remember vast numbers when I was last here. Now he has encircled the city, I understand.'

'There are some outposts. The Templars have Castle Pilgrim and Tortosa, we have Beirut, Haifa, Tyre, all small cities with defences that are not so strong as ours. Also, Acre can be replenished from the sea. She is strong, so long as we have the men to defend her walls.'

'Would Qalawun attack, do you think?'

'If he were provoked, as Baldwin says, his response would be overwhelming. I said Acre is strong, but we could not hold her against his full might.'

'Then we must ensure no further insults are given,' Sir Otto said. He waved to a servant, who brought cooked meats and a bowl of salad leaves. 'I am grateful for your advice. Is there anything else I should know about before I see the Constable?'

Ivo pulled a face. 'There is one thing I would say: trust the words of Sir Guillaume de Beaujeu. He is a crafty man, with the resources of the Temple behind him.'

'What, you mean I should borrow from him? I have no love of moneylenders,' Otto said impatiently.

'Money is not his currency: de Beaujeu deals in information. He bribes the most important men in the Sultan's court – their avariciousness is legendary. His knowledge occasionally offends those who depend on God, especially the Patriarch. Not that I blaspheme, but many would say that God helps first those who seek to help themselves.'

'In what way?' Sir Otto asked.

'An example: the Templars warned of Tripoli's plight long before it was recognised.'

'Yes – so?'

'Others thought the Templars were cowardly, and said so to Sir Guillaume's face. Now all can see the truth. What I wish to say is, if Sir Guillaume asserts that the Saracens will do this or that – trust him. He is well-advised.'

Edgar had not found it difficult to locate Philip Mainboeuf's house. A young maid in a tavern near the cathedral found him irresistible; he found her a useful source of information.

Making a mental note to return to her later, Edgar approached the Mainboeuf house, which was close to the main square. A vast-looking building, the golden stone of the area had been carved wonderfully to make pillars and decorative chevrons all over the front. Large windows gaped open to let cool air inside. At the door three men lounged in the heat, and Edgar eyed them critically. They did not look competent guards, he thought. All had leather jerkins, but while one wore a mail shirt, that was all the armour they possessed. They looked like the dregs of a lord's host: underpaid, scruffy and ill-disciplined.

'Friends, is this the house of Philip Mainboeuf? I would like to see him.'

'Does he know you?' The mail-clad sentry was not rude. He looked at Edgar's new tunic and boots with open respect. Edgar was a man with money, the sort who would usually be permitted to speak to his master.

'Perhaps we should ask him,' Edgar said.

He was soon inside a long, rather narrow hall. Drapery hung from poles overhead like banners, moving gently with the breeze. Two clerks were seated at tables, writing urgently, while more clerks and a Saracen steward hurried about, bringing scrolls and records.

There were pictures on the walls. Paintings of Christian scenes, and some few of warfare. As Edgar walked, he studied them with interest. One showed the sack of a city, before which he stopped.

'You like that? It was painted so we should not forget.'

Philip Mainboeuf was a man of perhaps thirty. He had a narrow chin and lively, amused eyes, as if he found all about him immensely delightful.

'What was it?' Edgar asked.

'The end of the Siege of Acre, almost a hundred years ago. It depicts the taking of the town by King Richard, and the slaughter of the innocents in the city. It was always noticeable that when Richard Lionheart took a town, the inhabitants were invariably slain, whilst when Saladin captured cities he invariably showed mercy.'

Edgar nodded politely.

'You wished to see me?' Philip Mainboeuf said, looking him up and down. 'My man said you were a merchant, but I confess I do not know you.'

'I am Edgar of London, and I have the honour to be a known master of defence,' Edgar lied blithely. If he wasn't now, he soon would be, he thought.

'And what would I want with a master of defence?'

Edgar merely smiled in reply.

'Did you see how many men I have on my gate already?'

'Yes – three. You have another two in the yard behind your door, you will say. *I* will say, they none of them would match me.'

'So, my bold friend. You wish to see to my interests?'

'And you will pay me.'

'How can I tell you would be worth my money?'

'Look at my clothes. How many of your guards have been so well rewarded for their service, to you or to friends you know?'

Edgar was pleased to see that Philip Mainboeuf smiled at that. 'You are very certain of your abilities, sir.'

'I have reason to be. I am the best servant you could have.'

'But I am safe already. I have many men to guard me.'

'How many are in here with you now? If I were an assassin, you would be dead.'

'But you are not a Muslim enemy, are you?'

'How would your guards know that? You remember how Prince Edward of England was attacked by a man pretending to be a Christian? Assassins are highly trained. The Old Man of the Mountain makes sure of that. They can hit a fly with a thrown knife, and they are expert with garotte and poison.'

'How do you know all this?'

Edgar smiled. He didn't want to admit that it was tavern gossip. It sounded good.

Mainboeuf studied him closely, considering.

'Very well', he said finally. 'I will take you – for your boldness, if nothing more. And the city does feel more dangerous since the arrival of all these soldiers. I would be happy to have you at my side, I think.'

CHAPTER THIRTY-ONE

Lucia woke in the under-basement – a cold, a stone-walled, stone-flagged chamber with no furniture, only pots and barrels.

The pain was enough to make her weep. When she fell, the bottler had kicked her repeatedly. Even so, that wasn't the worst. She had never endured the sort of punishment meted out to other slaves, because of her favoured position, but that was at an end and she had endured the very limits of a slave's suffering.

Her clothes were a ripped heap over at the wall; she rose to all fours and made her way to them, sobbing with the pain and having to stop, hanging her head, after a yard, tears streaming. She tried to push her mind past the rawness that flared between her legs. The torment would pass. It must.

A swallow, and then she deliberately lifted a hand and placed it before her, shifted her knee, and another few inches were covered.

She should have stayed with Baldwin. What could have happened that would have been worse? She couldn't swear to follow his religion, but he might have forgiven her that. But perhaps he was like all the Franks, and only looked at her for her body. Like the bottler.

Last night he had taken her like a whore from the meanest tavern. He didn't want information – he knew she hadn't lied. No, he took her just to satisfy his lust. She had tried to fight him off, but he only laughed and hit back. She couldn't resist him. He was too strong.

Sobbing at the memory of his sweating, red face over her, she reached for her clothing and pulled on the shreds. She had no idea what the time was, but surely she should be at prayer? She bent forward, and the movement caused her back to flare. She had to give up in despair. Instead she crawled to the wall, and sat with her back to it.

If only she were still in Baldwin's house. He would be kind. He would remember how she had dabbed his face when Buscarel had hit him, and he would take her head in his lap and soothe her, caressing her hair and washing the pain away. And he would look after her forever.

If she were with him.

If he asked her again, she would not hesitate to agree to do anything he asked, provided he only took her away from this place.

'What did you think of him?' Ivo asked Baldwin as they walked towards Montmusart.

'I can see why men would follow him.'

'Yes. He inspired trust even all those years ago,' Ivo said. He paused. They had reached a market, and he peered into the produce. There were fresh olives, and he indicated the pot. The seller nodded and soon Ivo had agreed on a quantity which were spooned into a small basket. He proffered a coin, and the trader recoiled in horror. 'No, no! It is not enough!' and suggested a price double that which Ivo had in his hand.

'No,' Ivo said, and there was a resolute look on his face as he and the seller haggled.

Baldwin studied the goods on offer. There was evidence of the dire situation, with good Damascus knives and swords on sale. Many crusaders would want to buy one to take home as a memento – provided they *did* get home. If they looked upon the land as a source of profit, like Roger Flor, the country could soon erupt in rage and murder.

It was an appalling idea. Surely God would not allow His land to be overrun by heathens? It would speak much of His feelings towards the Christians here if He would see them slain and thrown from it. Baldwin shook his head. God couldn't permit that. Not until the end of the world would He allow the Christians to be thrown from their last toehold on His Holy Land.

There was a man before him, and Baldwin was about to pass around him, when he noticed that the man carried a basket full of clothing: shirt, hosen, tunic – all soiled with dried blood. Baldwin looked at the man, who met Baldwin's look unflinchingly. He was a fellow of perhaps forty or more, from the white-shot beard and hair.

'Your clothes?' Baldwin asked.

Abu al-Fida curled his lip. 'No,' he said, in a surprisingly deep voice, speaking French fluently. 'My son's.'

'I am sorry,' Baldwin said sincerely. 'So much foolishness.'

'It was not foolishness that killed my son,' the man said heavily. 'It was Christians. While there is strife, innocents like my boy will die.'

'Let us pray that the strife ceases,' Baldwin said. 'And no more need die.'

'You think we shall see that in our lifetimes?' the man sneered.

'I shall pray for your son, and for you, my friend,' Baldwin said, feeling ridiculous. The last thing a father would want would be the prayers of those who had killed him.

The man nodded once, pensively. 'I thank you for your words.'

'I fear words are inadequate.'

'You meant them, and for that at least I honour you,' the man said, and walked on, the basket held carefully in his hands like a holy relic.

Baldwin returned to Ivo. He was still shaking his head as the market trader made a fresh offer, and then made as if to walk away. The seller narrowed his eyes, turned his head slightly, and muttered a final offer. Ivo hesitated, and the trader peered closely before a broad grin spread over his face. 'Aha, I have you, you bad bugger!' he cried, pointing an accusatory finger, and Ivo smiled, nodded, and passed him two more coins.

There was a shout from the direction the Muslim man had taken, and Baldwin idly glanced after him, only to see the man stumble and fall. Baldwin pushed through the crush to help him.

The Muslim was on his knees, scrabbling for the clothing, which had pitched from his basket, while two Lombards and another man stood laughing.

The third man was Buscarel.

Baldwin did not hesitate but lunged, grabbing him by the belt and his shoulder, heaving him backwards over his knee, as he had learned in wrestling. Buscarel gave a startled cry, and then he was on the ground, his hand grabbing for his knife. He had the blade half out of the sheath before he realised Baldwin's sword-point was on his throat.

'Leave him!' Baldwin snarled at the Lombards.

Both were young and inexperienced. They eyed Baldwin and his sword with alarm. The Muslim had gathered up his clothing once more, and wearily rose to his feet.

'Sir,' Baldwin said, throwing him a glance, 'I am sorry for these fools. Please, go in peace. I pray Our Lord will watch over you.'

The Muslim gave a sharp nod, and was gone.

'As for you!' Baldwin snarled, staring down at the Genoese.

He remembered the ship – the men with whom he had travelled cut to pieces or pierced by arrows; he remembered the beating he had received in Lady Maria's house, the iron bar in the brazier. It was tempting to kick him – in the groin, in the belly, in the head – to exact revenge for all he had suffered.

And then he recalled the Muslim who had lost his son. Were he to consider that murder a feud, where would it all end? How many Christians would pay for his son's death?

This was the same. If Baldwin killed Buscarel, what purpose would it serve? He would have upset the Genoese, and perhaps they would send men to kill him and Ivo. And then Christians might take up Baldwin's cause . . . it was endless.

'Give me my ring and go,' he said.

Buscarel looked at the faces all around. The two Lombards had fled, and now there were only dark-skinned Muslims staring at Baldwin and him, and none would get involved in a fight between two Franks.

'Take it!' he snarled, pulling it off and hurling it, before rising.

Baldwin saw it hit a man's turban, and darted to where he heard the metallic clatter as it hit the ground.

Buscarel sprang up, and his hand was on his knife again as Baldwin turned, but Ivo's voice came as a rough hiss at his ear.

'You try it, Buscarel, and I'll open you from prick to throat.'

Buscarel moved away, and soon disappeared in the crowd.

'He is a danger,' Baldwin considered.

'Perhaps. But we have wine and olives. Let's get home and break some bread.'

'We've only just eaten!'

'Aye,' Ivo said with a belch. 'But there's nothing can beat good wine, good olives, and fresh bread. When you've been a warrior, you'll learn that.'

CHAPTER THIRTY-TWO

Abu al-Fida left the gate and kept walking. There was nothing for him here, not now. The attack in the street had shown him that. One man had helped him, but what was one man amongst the teeming thousands of the city?

His entire family was dead. His life had ended.

He stared about him as he passed through the tents and shabby houses erected at the outer wall, his feet moving mechanically. Every so often, he peered down, half-surprised that he still carried the basket. It was such a heavy object, and ungainly. But it held his son's clothes.

Some said that the Sultan would avenge the murder of Muslims. The Sultan believed in justice and honour. Perhaps he would listen to Abu al-Fida about Usmar, his son.

His son.

The clothes in the basket were rough with dried blood, and he felt the air leave his lungs at the sight of them again. His breast was empty. All love, all hope were eradicated, for what point was there in either of those things when a man had lost

180

his son? A man lived to raise his son, because that was the greatest duty.

Tottering, he fell to his knees in the sand and dirt of the roadway, the basket tumbling before him. His right palm scraped along a sharp edge of stone, and he stared at the thick, welling blood. So bright and dark, like his son's had been. But he could not weep for his boy. There were no tears in him. Not yet.

Rising, he took his son's clothing and balled it in his fists, gripping it tightly. This city was a place of evil, a city founded on hatred. While the murdering Franks remained, there could be no peace in Islam. It was an affront to Allah that they remained. They should be slain to show that no matter who attempted to steal the Holy Land, they would suffer the same death. Their wailing and screams of agony would rise from Hell to give a caution to the living, so that no more would cross the seas to come here and slay the innocent.

In his hands there was a ball of material, and he gazed at it again, and then the horror returned.

His son Usmar was dead.

He had reached the outskirts of Acre now and he stopped, staring north and south. Where should he go? Where *could* he go?

And then a ruthless determination made itself felt. Once, he had been a warrior. He had seen death in all its forms, and he had decided to give up the path of war, but he still had those former skills. He knew how to make machines that could reduce the walls of Acre to rubble.

He turned and stared at those walls now, his entire being filled with loathing. That was his duty. He must bring the walls down. And there was one place to go to ensure that.

Abu al-Fida set his face to the south-east.

181

Behind him, he heard a pony whicker, and in a moment a merchant with a cart was rumbling at his side.

'*Salaam aleikum*,' the man said, peering at him. 'My friend, are you unwell?'

'They killed him. The Franks killed my son,' he burst out, then clamped his mouth shut to prevent more words escaping. He knew he must keep them inside, imprisoned, so that when he could give witness, he could allow them all to fly free and tell of the guilt of the men who had murdered his son.

So that he could win the justice he needed, the justice his son deserved.

Lucia spent a second uncomfortable night and woke hungry. There was a pot of water, but she had not been given food, and when she rose to her feet, all her muscles ached. Her flank and back were one enormous bruise.

The bottler came again. He took her by the arm and half-dragged her up the stairs to the house itself, and thence to the garden. Lady Maria sat on a stone bench while one maid washed her feet and a second used a reed to dab henna onto her hands in intricate patterns.

She looked at Lucia without feeling. 'You look awful, child.'

'I have done nothing wrong,' Lucia said, and rebelliously held her chin up.

'So you say.' The woman's voice was dispassionate. 'If that is true, so be it. Wipe your eyes. You need not worry about the bottler again. He will remain here.'

'What do you mean?' Lucia said dully.

'I cannot trust you. You will go to one of the farms.'

'No, please,' Lucia said. The farms were out in the plains – hot, harsh places, where overseers whipped and raped their charges. 'Please, let me stay with you, Mistress.'

'With me? Looking like that?' Maria said with a laugh. 'My friends would think I had lost my mind. No, you must go. And if . . .' She took her hand away from the maid with the henna and stood, walking slowly and deliberately to Lucia. 'If you tell a soul about me, and you hurt my reputation, I will have you flayed alive. Or perhaps I should put your eyes and tongue out before you go?'

'Please!'

Maria stared down at her as she fell to her knees, hands up in supplication, but when Lucia looked up, there was only contempt in her face.

'Go!'

'The best way, Sir Otto, is to begin at the west side and cross the walls to the other,' Ivo said.

They were walking to the outer wall, and Baldwin paid scant attention as he peered at his ring, rubbed at it, and rotated it on his finger with his thumb. He had not appreciated how much he had missed it, in truth.

Sir Otto had been sent to help protect Acre, and, 'Whether the Sultan has agreed peace or no, I should investigate the defences in case his attitude changes.'

Ivo led the way through Montmusart to the Lazar Gate and then up the stone steps.

'Here is the tower built by the Order of Saint Lazarus. There is another strong tower over there, by the sea.'

'From here the wall extends back to the old wall, thence to the sea again?' Otto asked, leaning forward and staring along the line of the walls. He spoke crisply, a commander getting the measure of new responsibilities.

'Yes, Sir Otto. The double walls form a line north to south, with a dog-leg halfway.'

'Where are the weakest points?'

Ivo considered. 'I would be less concerned about this section. It is newer, and should be able to take heavy punishment. I would be more worried about where the dog-leg lies. The point of that has a new tower recently rebuilt by King Henry II, and outside there is King Hugh's new barbican. The inner point is held by that tower, named the Accursed Tower – I suppose because before this new wall enclosed Montmusart, it stood all alone. I would feel cursed if I were in that tower, too.'

'I see. Let's walk the walls.'

They descended the inner wall and made their way through the gate to the outer wall, where they climbed another series of steps, and began to make their study of the defences.

On the way, Baldwin saw a tan-coloured cur scavenging about a foetid heap of refuse. It was only as high as his knee, and painfully thin. Spotting a discarded crust by a guard's boot, he bent to pick it up, whistled, and the dog stopped, head tilted. Baldwin threw it the bread before rejoining the others at the wall's top.

'Yes, you are right about this line of wall,' Sir Otto said. 'The base is good and broad and there is space enough for plenty of men to stand here in safety. How many people live in the city?'

'Around forty thousand.'

Sir Otto nodded, his mouth reflecting his unhappy thoughts. 'That is a great many mouths to feed, even with control of the seas. And all those,' he added, waving a hand at the tents and hovels outside the walls, 'their clutter could give succour to the Saracens. We'll have to fire their rubbish.'

'Yes, Sir Otto.'

They had made their way to the corner where the new wall met the old. Here Sir Otto stood for a moment, gazing out over the plains before the city. It was the scene that Baldwin had admired during his first ride out with Roger: lush fields, olive groves, and numerous small houses of mud, much like a peasant's home in Devon.

'They will march right over all that,' Sir Otto said. 'They will want to site engines of war out there. We will need to look over the plain and consider where they will want to place their machines so that we can spoil the ground.'

'Yes,' Ivo said.

Baldwin felt a scratch, and, turning, saw that the little dog was sitting behind him, pawing at his leg. He tried to gently push him away, but the animal stared at Baldwin with hurt in his eyes.

'Of course, the walls need to be prepared,' Sir Otto said, turning and looking back at the bulk of the inner walls. 'We must build hoardings. Any man leaning over the parapets to drop stones on attackers would be the target of all their arrows. It is a shame there is no moat.'

'In this heat, it would be impossible to keep it filled,' Ivo shrugged.

'Quite so.'

'But this is all speculative, isn't it?' Baldwin said, trying to ignore the dog. 'The Saracens have promised to uphold the peace for ten years, after all.'

Ivo gave him a long, considering stare while Sir Otto continued gazing out past the barbican towards the east.

Neither answered.

CHAPTER THIRTY-THREE

Had Baldwin but known it, as he stood near the tower built by King Henry II, far below him, a small party was setting out from the gate.

It consisted of two men, and one woman, dressed in old grey linen. The men were on horseback, but she followed them on foot, a cord bound about her wrists attached to a stirrup. Sometimes it was felt necessary to have slaves bound more securely, but if Lucia tried to escape, she would be at the mercy of the sun and the parched lands.

She had no thought of escape. There was nothing in her mind apart from the pain in her back and between her legs.

All hope was gone. Only misery and despair filled her heart.

Try as he might, Baldwin could not shake off the little cur, who had adopted him after that first gift of bread. Surrendering to fate, he named the mutt Uther, and now Uther followed Baldwin everywhere. The little fellow was so dependent, Baldwin felt he couldn't discard him.

Many sections of wall required repairs before the hoardings could be constructed. The wooden platforms would jut out from the battlements, with trapdoors for rocks or oil to be dropped on enemies beneath. Their weight would put a great strain on the old walls.

In the city itself, already there were a thousand knights and mounted men-at-arms, along with perhaps fifteen hundred infantrymen, and there was a need to find space for them. Arguments and brawls were commonplace. The Templars and Hospitallers had taken to wandering about the city to try to keep the fighting to a minimum, but every so often fists would fly.

In the square outside the castle, Baldwin saw the result of yet another fight. Two men were caught up in a gambling dispute, and one drew his knife. As Baldwin passed, they were holding the guilty man before the castle's two-legged tree: two timbers planted firmly in the ground with a beam across their tops. A rope was thrown over the top-piece, the noose set about his throat, and as Baldwin paused, the man was hauled up, kicking and thrashing, as the rope squeezed the life from him.

At home, a felon would have his suffering eased by his family. They would jump on his body to break his neck, or at least speed his throttling. Here, the Lombard had no family. He could dangle for ten minutes or more before he died. A horrible death.

There were more crusaders at the far side of the square, he saw. For some, this was a grim event, and they stood about with faces drawn as they witnessed their comrade's death. But for others, it was merely a spectacle.

The man's legs jerked violently as he fought for life, and Baldwin could imagine the burning agony as his lungs strug-gled against that rope – and then, as if that were his final peroration to life, his struggling all but ceased. An occasional jerk of his legs, a brief fluttering of the feet, a tremble, and his life was fled.

Baldwin stayed staring, rooted to the ground, struck with a premonition.

Acre would be like that man, were Qalawun to come and attack. Alone, watched by many, and with no hope of aid.

The thought made him shiver.

CHAPTER THIRTY-FOUR

Abu al-Fida was not alone as he entered the great court. He was only one of a long line of men and women who wailed and prostrated themselves. Each crossed the patterned tiles to the space before the Sultan and laid down the blood-stained clothing of murdered relatives. Here a shirt, there a tunic, a robe, a turban – all with their unique blackened patterns of death and horror. In his mind's eye, he saw the smiling face of his son. White teeth gleaming, eyes flashing, so like his mother. Looking about this hall, with Mameluk guards standing silent, the sun making their mail and helmets sparkle, he felt as though Usmar was here with him, giving him support.

It was Abu al-Fida's turn. He walked with slow dignity and stood before the Sultan. Silently, he shook out his son's chemise and robes. The rents in the fabric told their story. He need say nothing. Bending, he set the clothing on the floor. The robes, then the chemise with the terrible cuts and slashes in the fabric, the foul brown stains.

Sultan Qalawun stared down at the clothing arrayed on the tiles, and studied each from his chair, taking them in, one by one.

Abu al-Fida watched him closely. He appeared shocked. Over seventy-five years old, the Sultan was experienced in death, but this scene of wailing parents and siblings had moved him.

'What was the reason for this massacre?' the Sultan demanded in a hushed voice.

'Some said a Muslim had raped a Christian woman, some that there was a fight after drinking in a tavern,' Abu al-Fida said. 'My son was not in a tavern, and he never raped a woman. He and these others were not criminals. They were not guilty, my lord. These deaths were caused by the bloodlust of the Franks. The rioters killed any man with a beard. They even killed their own: there were Christian merchants slain, just as there were Muslims.'

Qalawun stood and spoke in a voice hushed with emotion. 'I have agreed peace with these people, assuming them to be rational. I offered them terms by which they and we could live side-by-side without war, because I am a man of peace. But these Franks have by this despicable act demonstrated their bad faith. I will not tolerate these murderers to continue to live on our sacred land.'

He stared at the mourning people.

'Your dead will be avenged. All of them. I swear this on the holy Koran.'

Afterwards, as the petitioners bowed low, thanking the Sultan, the women still sobbing as they moved to collect the pathetic scaps of cloth, Abu al-Fida alone stood and made no move. Even as the others filed from the court, he remained.

There was a Mameluk behind him. 'You must go.'

'Yes,' Abu al-Fida said. He nodded, and turned to leave, but the Mameluk called him back.

'Your clothes,' he said, pointing.

'They were my son's. I leave them as reminder of why we must punish the people of Acre, for their violence towards the people of Islam.'

The Sultan called to the Mameluk, 'Let him come to me.'

Abu al-Fida made his way to the Sultan's throne, standing with his head downcast.

'Do not be fearful in my presence,' the Sultan said. 'I am Qalawun, friend to all Muslims. I am here now to listen to your petition, not to punish. Tell me, these clothes were those of your son?'

'Yes, Sultan, my son Usmar.'

'Have you lived long in Acre?'

'For five years.'

'You know the city well?'

Abu al-Fida nodded.

'Can you sit with my people and draw with them a map of the city? I need to know the walls, where the strong points are, and the weak, where they keep their stores of food and weapons. Everything you can tell me. Can you do this?'

'Yes. I was once the servant of Baibars and served in his army at Antioch. I understand what is needed.'

'Ah! That was a great battle,' Qalawun said, 'and the Christians still have not returned there.'

'We destroyed them all,' Abu al-Fida said. 'I was with the party at the middle who stormed the walls.'

'It was a brave battle. You were fortunate to be with the first of the men there.'

'Yes, lord.'

In his mind's eye, Abu al-Fida saw that battle again and it almost turned his stomach. His bloody sword hacking at infidels, blood spattering his arms, breast, face; blood in his mouth. At first, he recalled a blood-madness, when all he could see was the sunburned crusaders, eyes flashing with hatred beneath their helmets. A lunatic scramble up rubble and bodies, slipping on a man's arm cut from a body, almost soiling himself as an arrow flew straight at him, and he ducked and it rattled against his helmet, and then he and his friends were on the wall, and dealing death.

It was a truth that hand-to-hand fighting was deadly, but this could not describe the slaughter that began when the Christians fled from the holy rage of the besiegers. It was a massacre such as he had never before seen. Abu al-Fida recalled with shame how he and his comrades screeched their war-cries as they rushed down the inner ramparts and into the fleeing enemies.

And afterwards there were the searches of the houses. In one, he found three children – and when he tried to save them for slavery, other men slew them all. Grandmothers were found in a house, and they too had their lives taken. The city was a stinking charnelhouse. Bodies lay everywhere.

It was that which deterred him from war.

When you have once had a man on his knees before you begging for his life, a woman – perhaps a sister, perhaps a wife – wailing and pulling at her hair with horror and despair as you thrust the sword in, hoping to kill quickly but failing, and witnessed the man scream with the pain, writhing, and not dying – and then seen your companions rape the woman before killing her . . . how could any man of honour who loved beauty and God want to destroy men and women in this manner?

But according to Qalawun, he was 'fortunate' to have been there.

'We shall avenge your son, Abu al-Fida. We will wash the streets with infidel blood.'

Abu al-Fida nodded. He thought again of that man, curling into a ball on the ground before him. At least he had tried to kill quickly and kindly. He had not wished to make the Christian suffer. Others were not so scrupulous.

He had no scruples about Christians dying now. Not even the women and children . . . If it removed the infidels forever from these lands, it was worth it. No man should ever suffer the death of his son, like Abu al-Fida had.

Qalawun called a servant and muttered in his ear. Then he said, 'Abu al-Fida, go with this man and help my secretaries draw up plans of the city. In return, is there anything you would like?'

Abu al-Fida fell to his knees and would have prostrated himself, but the Sultan called on him to stop.

'No, my friend, I would not have you worship me. I am only a man.'

'Then permit me this one thing, my Lord. When you march on Acre, let me join you, and let me once more use my sword in the destruction of our enemies.'

'I can make use of any number of men. I would be glad of your sword.'

Abu al-Fida hesitated. Then, 'I am not only a soldier, Sultan. When Baibars took me to Antioch, it was not for my sword, but for my skill with artillery. I built him catapults.'

'You can build them still?'

'Yes.'

'Then build me a monster, Abu al-Fida. Build me the biggest catapult in the world. We shall call it al-Mansour – *Victorious* – and with it you shall destroy the city that killed your son.'

BOOK THREE

WARRIOR, AUGUST 1290–APRIL 1291

CHAPTER THIRTY-FIVE

The great courtyard before the castle was ideal for open-air discussions for the whole commune. It was a square space, with ornate stonework that reflected the history of the city, and Baldwin joined Ivo near Sir Otto de Grandison's men.

Baldwin had never seen such a congregation before. There were the four Orders, the Templars and Hospitallers eyeing each other distrustfully, the German Order with their black crosses watching sternly, their Grand Master Burchard von Schwanden glowering about him, while the Leper Knights stood slightly apart.

More and more men were pouring into the square, and already the Hospitallers and Templars had grumpily moved closer as they were jostled by newcomers. All the commune's richest and most important representatives were there.

'Look at all these people,' Baldwin marvelled. 'How could the Muslims expect to take the city when there are so many knights of great standing?'

He was overwhelmed: he had never seen so many nobles and lords gathered together. Mail and helmets shone, and the white tunics of the Templars gleamed so brightly it was painful to look at them. Here, Baldwin thought, was the reason for the survival of Acre. No godless army could defeat so many men dedicated to the defence of His Holy Land.

Ivo cast a measuring look about him. His tone was half-weary, half-contemptuous. 'Do you think they will look so marvellous when they are spread thinly over one mile of city walls? I just want to know why we've been summoned.'

Baldwin frowned, but then the city's herald bellowed for silence, and the Constable walked in from a door behind the throne.

Sir Amalric stood before the throne and gazed about him. Baldwin was struck by his expression. There was a savage anger there. When he spoke, his voice reflected the fury within.

'My Lords, Sir Knights, and Gentlemen, I have today received a message from Sultan Qalawun.'

There was a quickening of interest. The men exchanged glances, and Baldwin heard a muttered oath.

'He demands we submit to him all those responsible for the riots and the murder of Muslims in our city. They will be tried in his court and punished.' He gave a frosty smile. 'Who would advise me on this?'

'You cannot send Christians to a heathen court,' Sir Burchard shouted. 'It is unthinkable! None could agree!'

There was a rumble of approval from the German Order and the Hospitallers; the Templars too were nodding. Only Guillaume de Beaujeu maintained a calm demeanour.

Then, from behind Baldwin, a voice demurred. 'Those fools brought it on themselves. What, do you want to incite a war to defend the murdering bastards who put us in this position? I say they should pay the price.'

'These men were brought to Acre by the galleys of Venice.' This was a stout, red-faced shipmaster, who glared towards the merchants as he spoke. 'I would not have it said that men brought here under the protection of Venice could be so easily discarded. They are Christian.'

'No! These men were murderers, and if the price of our safety is their lives, so be it!'

'What of the other Orders?' Constable Amalric asked.

'It is said we may not send Christians,' Sir Guillaume de Beaujeu said slowly. 'But if we do nothing, how will he react? We should placate him if we may.'

'He is a heathen,' Sir Burchard grated. 'We need do nothing. He demands, but his threats are empty. Meaningless.'

'Have you forgotten Tripoli?' the merchant spat.

'He had no treaty with them,' Sir Burchard said dismissively. 'He has agreed a peace with us. He won't break that.'

'So, he is a heathen with a sense of honour,' Sir Guillaume said. 'But he has cause, if we refuse to provide him with the felons who committed these gross acts of violence against his people. These rioters caused the trouble.'

'What do you suggest?' Constable Amalric said.

'For my part, I would empty the prisons of all those convicted for felonies, and send them to him. It would cost us little, and they will die anyway. Let him execute them. We appease him without damage to our ability to protect this city.'

A merchant shouted, 'Are you mad? You think to give up our people to this monster?'

'I think to protect our city!' Sir Guillaume roared. 'What, would you prefer to see Acre fall and your wives and children slaughtered or enslaved? These men are felons in any case!'

'You just seek to protect your Order! Templars make money from the Muslims!' a man shouted.

'It's because he is a coward!' another bellowed.

There was an immediate uproar. Guillaume de Beaujeu was white with fury, and at the accusation of cowardice, he and two Templars behind him had to be restrained by their Marshal, who snapped an order as they began to step forward, gripping his Grand Master's sleeve and whispering urgently.

Sir Guillaume swallowed his wrath. 'I have the fortune to enjoy good relations with some Muslims, yes, and I make use of them. If you had invested in understanding your enemy a little more, perhaps you would not be so poorly advised now, Master Mainboeuf! My friends tell me that Qalawun seeks only a pretext to destroy our city and God's Kingdom here on Earth once and for all. You do his job if you seek to defy him now. He can gather an army in weeks.'

The man whom de Beaujeu had addressed eyed the Grand Master coolly. Baldwin was impressed by his patrician manner, and then saw, over his shoulder, a face he recognised: Edgar. Edgar gave him a faint smile, and Baldwin had the distinct impression that he was being patronised.

Mainboeuf stepped forward and addressed the whole gathering. 'I have my own men in Egypt. They tell me that Qalawun is perfectly well aware of our importance to him. Look at us! He has made us the most powerful city in Christendom! We have ships and we have merchants – and he needs both. Do you think that because he is a heathen he must be a fool? No! Qalawun knows that with us here, he can control the flow of silks and spices. These trades are valuable. Would he willingly destroy the most important market he has? Is it likely? By God's grace, we are in the fortunate position of being able to do His will while also making profit. Qalawun will leave us in peace. Besides, he has more important troubles in other lands on his borders than with us. But, to send a Christian to a heathen's court to be tortured and killed like a slave is not doing God's will. God will protect us from Qalawun and his armies if we stand firm, but if we were to send these poor Crusaders to Qalawun, God would abhore our cowardice.'

'Cowardice?' The Grand Master's hand was on his sword. Through clenched teeth, he said, 'God did not defend Tripoli!'

'That is blasphemy!' was shouted, and Baldwin saw that the Patriarch had risen to his feet, and stood pointing accusingly at the Templar. 'You dare suggest God was responsible? It was the unholy behaviour of the people living in Tripoli that caused their downfall, just as Sodom and Gomorrah collapsed after leaving the true path of God's will!'

'God did not save Tripoli, whatever His reasons,' Sir Guillaume said. 'We must protect Acre ourselves.'

'I say we are strong!' the merchant shouted. 'And if we hold to our faith, we shall remain so! The Sultan has no interest in destroying us.'

'The monopoly serves your interest, not his,' Sir Guillaume pointed out. 'If he wishes, he can crush us without hurting his treasury.'

'It's your treasury you care about,' Mainboeuf sneered. 'Isn't it said that the Temple was founded on money, and the greed of the Knights?'

'That is a lie!' Sir Guillaume bellowed, and in an instant the room degenerated into furious accusations and insults.

Merchants tended to side with the Templar Grand Master, while the Hospitallers and Teutonic Knights agreed with Mainboeuf and the commune. Sir Otto held his counsel, while Ivo shook his head, but Baldwin was concerned. He liked the Grand Master, but to suggest that Christians should be sent to be killed in a Muslim city, no matter what their crimes, was not to be borne.

He was pushed by a man behind him who stepped forward waving a fist in the air, and then another, whose face was puce with bellowing rage, and suddenly there was movement. Sir Guillaume took a pace to one side, while his Marshal and others spread themselves. The Leper Knights moved imperceptibly, but now they too formed a fighting line, for all that their swords were still sheathed. It would take them no time to draw their weapons.

Ivo looked at the Swiss next to him. 'Sir Otto, we cannot afford a fight.'

'No.' Sir Otto held his hands high, and spoke in a calm voice. 'Gentles all, we are Christians discussing possibilities. Come! If we bicker amongst ourselves, the winner will be Qalawun. Do you wish to do his work for him? Be still! Let us talk.'

His words had an immediate effect. Merchants and barons muttered to themselves, but the shouting ended, and men returned to their places.

'This is not possible,' the Constable said when order was restored. 'As a Christian city we cannot send these ruffians, no matter how vile their crimes. They must suffer punishment here in Acre.'

Baldwin nodded his approval. But when he looked at Ivo, he was sure that there was a glistening in his eye, as though Ivo was close to tears.

'In that case,' the Grand Master declared, 'we must prepare the city. Because if Qalawun is not impressed with our refusal, he will send an army to take the city apart: stone by stone.'

CHAPTER THIRTY-SIX

Philip Mainboeuf's house stood overlooking the harbour. From his door, a street ran straight to the water's edge, and from the roof, a man could see all over Acre, from sea to city wall. Edgar liked to walk about the roof. It reminded him why he was here: wealth and comfort. Edgar of London was glad to be living in such a prestigious house.

Today, Philip Mainboeuf hurried back before the end of the discussion, and then rushed upstairs to the roof where his clerks worked under a canopy. Edgar went with him, and peered at the harbour a quarter-mile away. The sea was a fabulous turquoise, and waves glistened as if filled with pearls. From here he could see the cathedral, and heard the tolling to announce the service, a moment or two after the bells within the Temple, and then those of the Hospital. Each of the Orders had their own bells, which pealed in a discordant cacophony, but Edgar didn't care. To him, their sound was just one attraction of this exotic new life.

There were many – especially the women. He was enthralled

by their dark skin and their lustrous brown eyes gazing at him from over their veils.

There was no comparison between this and his past life. Here, people had luxuries he had never dreamed of, from sweet sugars to silks. When he thought back to London and the filthy, dark alleys and streets, the grey Thames, it was as though he was harking back to a nightmare in comparison with this sumptuous grandeur. Heaven must be like this.

There was a loud knocking at the door below, and Edgar strode to the front of the house to peer down into the street. There, he saw a woman in green with three guards. Soon she was up on the roof with Philip and Edgar.

He had seen her before, of course. This was Lady Maria. Edgar saw her eyes go to him as Philip stood, and Edgar held her gaze with a smile on his face. She was a forward woman. The sort who would be a challenge. Not that he could hope to bed her – she had her sights set far over Edgar's head.

'You can leave us,' Mainboeuf said to his clerks, and they gathered up their tablets, inks and reeds, and made their way to the stairs.

Edgar made no move to follow them. His attention was still fixed upon Lady Maria.

'Edgar, you can leave us too,' Mainboeuf said.

'While there are these strangers with you?' Edgar said, indicating the three men who had come to the roof with Lady Maria.

'I am safe with Lady Maria. You can leave us.'

Edgar paused before obeying. There was no reason for him to remain, because after all, if the three men wanted to attack his master, they would simply kill him first. He walked to the stairs at the side of the building, and as he was about to descend, he saw Lady Maria go to Mainboeuf's side, and he heard their voices clearly on the warm, humid air.

'You must send to Cairo. We cannot afford to leave him in any doubt.'

'He will seek profit. This is a negotiation.'

'Then we must ensure he wins it.'

Baldwin found Ivo sitting in a nearby tavern, muttering to himself, a quart of wine before him.

'I was here with my Prince, and I would've laid down my life happily for him and the Kingdom of Jerusalem, but this? It shows how low the Kingdom has sunk. Putting God's land in peril to support drunks and murderers! In Christ's name, don't they realise what they're doing?'

'We shall be all right,' Baldwin said, and he truly believed it. The debate had been harsh at times, and the men had been determined to push forward their views with force, but the right decisions had been reached.

'Baldwin, if you live to be an old man, you will never forget the coming weeks,' Ivo said sourly. 'And when the end comes, my friend, remember your words.'

'I will.' Baldwin smiled, and was relieved to see that Ivo returned it, albeit weakly.

'What is that cur doing with you still?' the older man asked, glancing down.

'Uther is a good companion. He doesn't snap as much as some,' Baldwin grinned.

'Companion!' Ivo sneered, shaking his head. He noticed Otto de Grandison marching off with his men, and the sight made him narrow his eyes.

'Qalawun won't want to attack us,' Baldwin said. 'You heard what that merchant said.'

'Do *you* think Guillaume de Beaujeu is a coward?' Ivo demanded.

'Of course not!'

'So, although the merchant could say something that stupid, you trust his judgement on other matters? On which matters is he more likely to be accurate, would you think?'

He wandered away, and for the first time Baldwin was struck by his age. It made him feel sad. Poor Ivo was upset and anxious, and it was hardly surprising. War was a young man's sport. An older man would find it a great deal harder to survive a battle.

'So, Master Baldwin. And are you well?'

He turned to see Sir Jacques. 'Yes, but Ivo is disturbed.'

'So he should be,' Sir Jacques said mildly.

'You think we are in danger?'

'I put my trust in God, but I will sharpen my sword.'

The next day, Baldwin saw Edgar again near the market.

'Master Edgar, I hope I see you well?'

'God has seen fit to reward me,' Edgar said.

'So I see,' Baldwin noted. He had never before seen a man so richly attired who was not a merchant.

'This is Philip Mainboeuf, my master,' Edgar said.

Baldwin bowed to him. 'I was impressed by your speech, Master.'

'Yes, well, there were some points that had to be aired. One must ensure that right prevails,' Mainboeuf said.

'It is reassuring to learn that Qalawun values trade with us so highly,' Baldwin said.

'When you have spent a little time in this land, you will learn that the Muslim enjoys profit every bit as much as a Christian,' Mainboeuf said condescendingly. He did not like to discuss such matters with those he felt to be inferior, and so he walked away to chat to two other merchants.

'Is your woman well?' Edgar asked.

'Lucia? I have not seen her,' Baldwin said. 'Not since the day of the riot.'

'No? It is strange that she has made no contact. You did save her life,' Edgar said. He was standing negligently, his arms folded as he eyed his master. 'You yourself have made no effort to see her?'

'It would be difficult. There is a man near her who seeks to do me harm.'

'But of course. So, you wish to remain safe, and thus you avoid her.'

Baldwin scowled. It sounded as if Edgar was teasing. 'What of it?'

'Nothing. But if I was enamoured of a little strummel like her, I don't think I'd let a man who sought to prevent me, succeed. She had a keen eye for you.'

'You think so?' Baldwin said. The words sent a tingle through him, and he thought of her calm, green eyes.

'I know so. She only had eyes for you. I'd go and tumble her while you can,' Edgar said off-handedly as he moved away to follow his master.

Baldwin frowned again at Edgar's words, but as the fellow wandered away, he was filled with gratitude. 'She only had eyes for me?' he murmured, looking down at the dog. A smile broke out over his features as he began to walk homewards.

But unaccountably, soon he found his feet had taken him towards the Genoese quarter, and Lady Maria's house.

CHAPTER THIRTY-SEVEN

Lady Maria reclined on a couch covered in silken cushions. A fresh pomegranate lay opened on a silver dish before her, and she speared a seed with a pin as she eyed Baldwin. She was a most disconcerting lady. Her eyes were coldly calculating, but now, with her veil removed, Baldwin could see how finely her face was moulded. Her lips closed about the pomegranate seed.

'Why do you come here?' she demanded. 'To insult me? I can have six men in here at the click of my fingers.'

'I insult no one, lady.'

She saw Uther. 'What is that cur doing in here?'

'He is my dog.'

'You collect any waifs and strays?' She laughed quietly, but made no move to call her men. Besides, there were already three men and five women servants moving about the garden. She was not without a chaperone. 'You think you can come here and question me?'

He had knocked on the door to ask about Lucia, but as soon as the door opened, the porter indicated that he should enter, and led him out here to the small garden courtyard. It was silent, apart from trickling water and the wind in the little trees. Almonds and lemons, he saw. It was a peaceful enclosure, but he felt endangered from the moment he entered. He remembered his last visit.

'You are a strange man,' she said. 'You have been held here and beaten, yet you return to ask me about her. Why, do you think you are safer now than before?'

'I do not. But I would speak with Lucia. Where is she?'

'Did you think to court her?' She smiled at that. 'How sweet! How endearing! A slave wooed by a reckless crusader! That would make a wonderful tale: many would be touched by it. So, you are not interested in money and property, then? You do not care about her being a nothing, a simple chattel.'

'I care nothing for that. But I do love her, madame. I would be honoured to take her hand.'

'Then we would have to discuss her value, would we not? How highly do you value her, I wonder? Would you offer anything for her? That ring, for instance? Yes, I heard how you recovered it from Buscarel. Or your sword? Would you give away your sword to buy her freedom? No, I thought not. You set no great value upon her, do you?'

'I esteem her highly,' Baldwin said stiffly. 'But I do not think a man or woman's life to be worth pennies.'

'Nor do I, Master,' she said tartly. She adroitly stabbed another pomegranate seed and popped it into her mouth, eyeing him narrowly. 'I think a slave is worth much more than mere pennies.'

Baldwin felt miserable. She would inflate the price to a ridiculous amount. 'I would pay anything you consider suitable.'

'All I need do is name my price?' She laughed. 'You are so young, so noble, so ignorant! You think it polite to ask a woman what she would have, in the hope that she might be generous to you? This is the East, Master. Here men are used to negotiating. So am I.'

'I agree. But I would not insult a lady. It would go against my concept of chivalry.'

'Chivalry? Yet you are no knight, nor even a squire. What exactly are you, I wonder?'

'My father was a knight, and so is my brother.'

'So that is why you are here. Another sad English knight who suffers under the yoke of primogeniture. Your brother inherited your father's estates, and you were forced to make your own way in the world. *That* is why you came here.'

'Yes,' Baldwin said, seeing Sibilla's face, but without pain. He suddenly realised that his desire for Lucia had overwhelmed his affection even for Sibilla. He could recall her face, but it was Lucia's which intruded upon his thoughts. It was a matter of dishonour that he had killed Sibilla's lover. Suddenly he felt a depth of shame at that murder, an overwhelming appreciation of a crime he would never be able to escape.

Maria shook her head patronisingly. 'You are the biggest fool I've ever met. A woman can be bought for so little out here: a brief liaison, a hurried encounter in an alley or a room, but no: you seek an affair of the heart. Very chivalrous.'

'You sneer.'

'What do you expect? You think you can marry her kind? You think you may take her up and ride to some glorious future in which you and she live in peace forever?'

She suddenly swept her legs from the couch to the floor and stood. Shorter than he by at least a head, yet she exuded power, and as she stepped towards him, it was hard not to step away. He felt much as he would on encountering a snake: she had the same lissom grace – but it was more than that. There was a sensual tension in her that was alarming. He had never been seduced by an older woman. His experiences included younger maids from the stews in Exeter and the taverns here in Acre, and immature fumblings with willing peasant girls at Fursdon. This was entirely different. Maria was offering herself to him, and he did not know how to respond. He dare not offend her.

'My lady . . .' he began.

'You prefer her to me? You would take my slave and make her your woman? And what then? What would happen to you both? Would you live contentedly, or would you find that each day your friends would look down upon her a little more, until it was difficult to leave your home, since you had married a mere slave-girl. One who had been purchased. And so you would sit in your cold home, with her, and never mingle with your lords and important comrades. Until the day when you realised that you hated her.'

She had approached so close now that her breath was upon his face as she spoke. Her head was tilted up so that she could look at him, and he imagined he could feel the warmth of her body. It sent heat to his heart, to his belly, his loins.

'And when you realised that, Master Baldwin, what then? Your life would be over. You would be stuck in your hovel with your slave, and you would be forced to the whores at the inns. Or do you think you would remain here? I assure you, here we do not believe in nobles who have married their maids or slaves. Perhaps a great lord could do so without being punished socially, but for most, the men must marry good wives. If they want their little strumpets, they can have them, but only as a diversion, to toy with, without broadcasting the fact. If you tried to marry her here, you would become a source of amusement. A joke.'

'Then what would you have me do?' he asked.

She smiled up at him, and cocked an eyebrow. 'Am I so repellent?' she asked. 'I am better than a slave girl.'

It was too much. He recoiled, thinking of the moment when he had woken and discovered her with Buscarel in the room with him, the feel of the bruising and pain, the sight of the brazier.

There was pain in her face at his rejection. A great spasm passed through her, making her quiver like an aspen in a gale – and then, a veil seemed to draw over her eyes, and she stepped away. The moment was over, and she returned to her couch. She bent and took up another pomegranate seed, and for a moment he thought she was going to offer it to him, but she didn't. She placed it into her mouth, and sucked it.

'You will never have her. She is my slave, and now I see what she is worth to you, I will keep her.'

'Please, let me see her. May I just speak to her?'

'No. She is not here. I have sent her far from the city, and I doubt if you could find her. But if you do, if you try to take her: hear me! I will have her put to death!'

CHAPTER THIRTY-EIGHT

Abu al-Fida stood at the junction of the roadway and studied the immense catapult. The great sling that would release the massive rocks and pots of Greek fire was the largest Abu al-Fida had built, a great deal larger than the machines used against Antioch.

Huge beams from the forests north of Venice had been cut, laboriously brought down from the mountains and floated along the great rivers, until they arrived at the city built on water. They had been sailed across the Mediterranean, then loaded onto wagons and brought here, to Kerak, where, under his supervision and with the ready help of hundreds of craftsmen, the beams had been cut and shaped. Adzes of many types had squared the sections of timber, and a ropemaker and his men had taken the bundles of hemp and created from them a wonderfully strong series of ropes. Already it was completed.

Abu al-Fida knew that there was only one last proof of his workmanship. He clenched his fist and punched. The chief gynour nodded, and waved the others away. When they were safely removed, he looked about him one last time, and then pulled the pin from the restraining rope. There was a slithering of leather, and as the huge counterweight dropped, the long arm rose, dragging the sling after it, the rock caught within its embrace. It swept along its trough, then up, until the sling released it and the stone flew up and forward.

He had selected as his missile one of the largest rocks he could find, and the task of shaping it to be more nearly round had taken much time, but he knew that just as a stone flung from a sling should be rounded and smooth, so should the missiles from this great machine. And now he felt a sense of pride to see how the great lump of rock hurtled onwards.

It rose as smoothly as a heron leaving the water, climbing ever higher, until it reached the zenith of its trajectory some two hundred yards from the machine, before crashing down to fall three hundred yards away.

'Load it again,' Abu al-Fida said quietly.

The men reached for the windlass, and as soon as the counterweight was still, they began the laborious task of hauling the arm down again. In a matter of minutes, the arm was locked, the steel pin holding it down. Masons rolled the second of the great stones to the channel, and the sling was looped over it.

He punched his fist again, and the arm swept up. The stone flew high and straight, and fell with an audible crack only twenty or thirty paces from the first.

Abu al-Fida smiled. It was the first time he had done so since the death of his son, but now he could see the result of his efforts, he was content. This machine would break the walls of Acre as easily as a man crushing an egg.

CHAPTER THIRTY-NINE

For Baldwin, it was a relief to feel a horse beneath him, the comforting weight of a sword at his belt, the hot air flowing past his face. He felt whole again, a man again. For the last weeks he had been little more than a labourer, like a peasant on his brother's estate.

He had worked with the masons at the base of the Lazar Tower, helped construct new ramps and walkways, and once dangled over the walls with terror in his heart, helping to hang the hoardings. And all the while, Lucia was never far from his mind. Often, while on the walkways, he would stop and stare out eastwards, wondering where she might be.

It was the dearth of information which tormented him. He worked to empty his mind, but his mind refused to be distracted from endless speculation: where she might be, what she might be doing, how harsh her life was now that she had been exiled.

When the Templar Marshal Sir Geoffrey de Vendac had appeared yesterday and asked Baldwin if he would like to join today's reconnaissance, the young man had leaped at the chance.

'But leave your dog behind; he would never survive in the desert,' the Marshal said, looking down at Uther with distaste.

Baldwin had taken his advice and left Uther with Ivo.

He glanced now at the knights of the troop. While he had always considered knighthood to be the pinnacle of human achievement, some of the knights he had met had not impressed him half so much as Ivo. The latter was not a member of the chivalry, yet he had depths of integrity and honour to which many knights could only aspire.

In the same way, Baldwin now realised that women were not merely chivalric ideals, nor decorative adornments for knights: they could be dangerous, too. Women like Lady Maria were powerful and intelligent. Baldwin feared her more than Buscarel.

Thinking of Lady Maria and Lucia, Baldwin felt a curious emptiness in his throat. He had experienced shame and despair when he realised that Sibilla did not love him, and that was what had impelled him to kill her lover, leave his country, and travel all this way: embarrassment at having been made a fool. But he hadn't expected to find a woman here like Lucia, who could erase his misery with a smile.

And now she was taken from him.

'You are thoughtful?' It was the Marshal. He had slowed, and now rode at Baldwin's side.

'Where do we ride?' Baldwin asked, instead of answering.

'We ride south and east for a day, and then we shall ride north. We are looking for signs of warlike preparations.'

'In the desert?'

Sir Geoffrey grinned – which totally transformed his features.

Up to that moment, Baldwin had only ever seen him look intro-
spective and austere. With a smile on his face, he was more like
a kindly old uncle. 'No! But I have spent long enough in the
Temple worrying over ledgers, and you have spent too long
slaving in the heat. I thought a few days away from the city
would be good for all of us.'

Baldwin smiled. He doubted that the ride was for his benefit,
but as he studied the Templars around him, he thought they
already looked less worn down.

They were a mixed group, consisting of five knights in
white, each with a squire in a black tunic with the red cross,
riding a spare destrier or charger, and each with a sergeant,
who was responsible for the sumpter packhorse. Baldwin had
heard how these men would fight in the same manner as
squires at home. As the knights crashed into the enemy, their
squires would be behind them in a second wave, bringing the
destrier as a remount, and fighting while the knights reformed,
ready to charge again. The Turcopolier would rally the
sergeants and the lightly armoured turcopoles, and they would
ride in support, or charge together as a fresh rank and shatter
any resistance.

'You are impressed?' the Marshal asked.

'With the troop? Your Templars are an awesome sight. I only
hope I might see them fight.'

'I think that is all too likely. What do you think of the
defences?'

'At Acre? Strong,' Baldwin said. 'I have never seen so
magnificent a city.'

'Let us hope that we may keep it.'

'With so many knights, and such a committed population, I
don't see how we can fail.'

'I am glad of your faith, my friend,' Sir Geoffrey said.

'God will permit us to hold it, or force us to relinquish it, at His will.'

Baldwin nodded. 'God alone can bring success.'

'But men can occasionally guarantee failure,' the Marshal added wryly.

CHAPTER FORTY

They rode across the dusty plains south of the city, following roads that had lain there for centuries, whipped by the wind until they were hidden under drifting sand. Each year experienced travellers exposed them with their great caravans, creating ruts in a seemingly endless expanse of sand.

At the end of the first day, the Templars busied themselves. The Marshal selected a location near a pool of water and the men waited for the command to dismount, and only then did they begin to unload their equipment. Sir Geoffrey's pavilion was placed at the centre, and while Baldwin struggled to remove his saddle, squires and knights silently made the camp. Tents were pitched, fires lit, and men saw to the horses. Baldwin was impressed to see that the men who groomed the horses and saw to their needs tended to be the knights themselves.

'The Marshal asks that you join him, Master Baldwin.'

The air was already cooling as the sun sank below the horizon, and Baldwin followed the young squire through the maze of guy-ropes and huddled figures to the Marshal's tent, where he was given a goblet of wine and waved to a seat.

For all the deference shown to the Marshal by both knights and squires, Baldwin was struck by the fact that the man's equipment was precisely the same as that of the other knights. Even his food was taken from the same cookpots. There was no favouritism.

'You look surprised, Master Baldwin,' Sir Geoffrey said when Baldwin glanced about him.

'I am unused to the ways of your Order,' he said. 'I had expected more display of wealth.'

'We take the threefold oaths, of chastity, poverty and obedience, as Saint Benedict demanded,' the Marshal said mildly. 'You see, our purpose is to serve God in the best manner possible for a knight, as both warrior and monk. So, we are careful to be frugal, while also maintaining our strength. But we take our oaths seriously, naturally.'

Baldwin nodded. 'Why do men join the Order?'

'I can answer that easily. For the same reason we interest you.'

'Me?' Baldwin said and gave an uneasy chuckle. 'I don't think I would be good Templar material.'

The Marshal peered at him over the rim of his goblet. 'That itself makes you better qualified than most,' he observed, and Baldwin suddenly realised he was being sounded out to join the Order. He began to feel very nervous.

'You were born to a knight?' the Marshal pressed on.

'Yes.' Baldwin cleared his threat. 'But that does not mean—'

'And to that knight's wife? You were not born out of wedlock?'

'Well, yes – I mean, no. They were married, I mean.'

'And you were trained as a knight?'

'I was taught how to handle weapons of all sorts, yes.'

'With whom?'

'Sir Hugh de Courtenay at Tiverton. I went to him from an early age.'

'But because your elder brother survived, he took the manor and the title?'

'Yes.'

'That is why so many of us joined the Brotherhood of the Temple. Like you, Master Baldwin, we were second brothers. Others, of course, were knights who inherited, and donated their worldly wealth to the Order, but most were like you. Religious, men of commitment to God. And we *all* joined the Order because we sought to serve Him as best we may. Just as a monk would serve in a scriptorium because of his skill in writing beautiful script, so I joined the Order because my skills lay in fighting and killing heathens. But I am no better than any of my brother monks in the Order. I am one of them. So my food comes from the communal pot, and my allocation of meat and wine is the same as that for any other Brother Templar.'

'It is a harsh responsibility, surely?' Baldwin said.

'It *is* a responsibility,' Sir Geoffrey agreed. He sipped wine and gazed through the tent-flap. Tonight his eyes held an inner calmness which Baldwin had only ever seen before in the faces of priests. 'If you consider your duty to God, it is also an honour. To be accorded the responsibility to protect His pilgrims and His lands, *is* a marvellous privilege, after all.'

'Was it a difficult choice?'

'To come to the Order? No more than it would be for you. One reaches an age when secular pursuits no longer hold their former fascination. When one has chosen to eschew those natural pleasures, and instead select a life of duty, it can, in fact, come as a great relief. We were all brought up in the worship of God, so to make our oaths involved only a minor alteration in our lives. It is not as if we were forced to take up the sword and the cross.'

'No,' Baldwin said. 'Any Christian should be proud to join the Order.'

'Most are,' the Marshal said.

Baldwin heard the tone of enquiry in his voice and replied honestly: 'I am not yet ready to shun the world.'

'It is not really a matter of shunning the world. We do not hide from the world, we embrace it – but forego transitory pleasures that mean little. To spend a life in contemplation and prayer, firm in the knowledge that what you do each and every day will help God and the poor souls here on earth – *that* is glorious, my friend.'

'I hope to marry some day.'

'I am glad for you. You are a strong, good-hearted man.'

'You know that from two brief conversations?'

The Marshal smiled. 'I have spoken of you with Ivo, and respect his judgement.'

'What has he said of me?' Baldwin asked, torn between amusement that Ivo had little better to speak of than him, and annoyance that he should be discussed behind his back.

'That you are a fine young man, but have much to learn.'

'That is true.'

The Marshal leaned forward. 'Why are you here, my friend? Ivo tells me that you came here to escape something. Is it a matter for which you need feel shame?'

Baldwin looked out over the camp. The tent-flaps caught and rattled in the wind, and he could feel Sir Geoffrey's eyes on him.

'I killed a man over a woman I wished to marry. And when I

heard of the disaster that overcame Tripoli, it seemed the most natural thing to come here and serve. But I had no idea of the situation.'

'Our position is perilous,' Sir Geoffrey said, so quietly that Baldwin was not at first sure he had heard him aright. 'It would take but a single blow from the Muslim army to destroy our city. And without Acre, there is nothing. No Kingdom, no Patriarch, no hope. It would mean the end of our Crusading endeavour.'

Baldwin smiled. 'Marshal, I know little, but I do know that Acre is a strong city. I have never seen any to match its defences. With God on our side, we would prevail against any foe. And the Sultan has given us peace, has he not. We are safe for ten years, as he swore.'

'I believed that once, but we have suffered much and lost much in the last years,' the Marshal said. He sighed. 'So you think that Sir Otto and the Orders are wasting our efforts in strengthening the city? You think *you* waste your time?'

'I believe strengthening the defences will not harm us,' Baldwin shrugged. 'But the timbers will be ancient by the time they see a siege, I think.'

'I hope you are right.' The Marshal stared out over the encampment. 'I was there in Tripoli, Baldwin. I went to help protect her, and I failed, along with my companions. We were as much use as a single dog against a pack of wolves. We could sound the alarm, but the numbers were overwhelming.'

'It must have been terrible.'

'You can have no idea. Until you have seen friends crushed to a smear of blood and bone, or seen men smothered in oil and pitch, burning like candles and screaming – you never heard such screams! I hear them in my dreams . . .'

He glanced at Baldwin, and brightened, not without an

effort. 'But while there are fit, honourable young men like you to serve with us, we can protect our lands and peoples.'

'I shall do everything I can to help.'

'Consider joining us, then,' the Marshal said briskly. His eyes were fixed keenly upon Baldwin once more. 'We lost many of our men in Tripoli. Your quality is already noted. You would be welcomed into the Order.'

'I am no knight.'

'We have need of all men-at-arms. Watch us, while we are on our little journey. See if you enjoy the camaraderie of our Order, and if you find you could work with us, then join us. You need not sign for your life's course, if you do not wish to, but if you would consent to taking on a black mantle for a time – during the defence of Acre, for example – you would be serving God.'

Baldwin nodded, aware of the honour being paid him. Not many were invited to enter the ranks of the Templars. Shortly thereafter, he bade the Marshal goodnight and walked from the pavilion to his sleeping space. Lying under the sheet the draper had provided, he stared up at the stars. The Marshal's offer was very tempting. He did believe most strongly that the Templars were a good, dutiful and principled force, but he did not believe this was the best way for him to serve God.

Would he do so, were it not for Lucia? he asked himself. Perhaps he should forget her. Let her pass from his mind and aim at a more honourable ambition than merely marrying a woman and raising a family. As he closed his eyes, he saw her face again. *No.* While she lived, he would join neither the Templars nor any other Order. He would marry her, and make her the focus of his life's efforts.

* * *

Lucia halted and straightened slowly in the field as the overseer shouted at them to stop. She took up the mattock, and followed the shuffling line of exhausted men and women back towards the farm buildings a half-mile away.

Her mind was empty. To allow thoughts to intrude was to permit pain to return. Her hands were blistered, the base of her right thumb bleeding, and there were sore patches on both palms. If she were to look at them, she would notice the black, broken and ruined nails, too. Once she had enjoyed the attentions of the best manicurist in Acre. No longer.

They were at the outer gates. These were locked at night, but why, she did not know. If a slave were to attempt to escape, they would have many miles of dry, waterless lands to cross. There was no escape. Only death.

Many sobbed themselves to sleep. Lucia listened with the detachment of a slaughterman listening to fasting cattle. They meant nothing to her, they were only companions in this torment. She squatted on the floor beside her bowl of pottage and flat bread, eating with a slow precision to stretch out the experience. If she closed her mind, she could imagine the rich tang of lemon and orange, the subtle savoury tone of olive, the sweet odour of lamb roasting on charcoal. She could almost imagine herself back in the garden in Acre.

In those days, she had delighted in life. The softness of silk under her fingers, the cool, swept paving slabs of the yellow stones underfoot, the constant scent of jasmine and spices.

It was enough to make her weep. They were gone, all a mirage. Her life in Acre was ended, and so too was her hope. She would remain here until death claimed her.

CHAPTER FORTY-ONE

Although his decision had been made, Baldwin watched the Templars with interest that second day, awed by their organisation and efficiency.

They rose and ate together in contemplative silence while one brother read from the Gospels. The camp, he learned, was always set out in the same manner, with the Marshal's pavilion at the centre, with a portable altar set up in a tent alongside, where the Brothers all met for their services.

When it was time to strike camp, the Templars waited in silence until the order was given, and then all was taken up and carefully stowed away. At another command, they packed their paraphernalia onto their horses, and at last, on the final bellow, the men all mounted and prepared to ride.

It was an impressive sight, to see so many men ready and prepared to be commanded before performing the least task. Impressive and at the same time alarming, for Baldwin knew many knights – 'ruthless individualists' described them well – and to see these men submitting to a commander was a big shock.

At evening on the second day, he finished his meal and lay back. The effect of sun and sand on his face had made his flesh feel like old leather, and he was bone-weary. He soon drifted into an utterly dreamless sleep.

His eyes snapped open at the first shout.

A dark mass was rolling towards the Templar camp. There was a strange thrumming noise, as of drums, in the distance, a bellowed command, and then, before he had thrown off his sheet and blanket to snatch at his sword, he saw three knights were already at the outer edge of the camp, their great shields firmly planted in the ground, swords at their hips, their lances held low, butted into the sand. Sergeants joined them, the Marshal among them, while turcopoles took position at their flanks, and squires rushed forward with more lances, gripping them like their masters, the points low, menacing the breasts of any horses foolish enough to come close.

A shriek, and a whistle, a thwack as an arrow cracked into a shield . . . and as Baldwin scurried towards the line of Templars he saw that the ghostly rolling blackness was a troop of cavalry cantering straight at them. He had his sword in his hand now, and threw the scabbard away, gripping the hilt with both hands.

This time, although he felt sick, he was aware of less fear than he had experienced on the ship.

There was a cacophony of noise as the first enemy mounts broke in upon the line of shields. Arrows zipped all about, and he felt one skim over the front of his breast, miraculously not breaking his skin. He had no mail.

There was a screamed command from the right, and he saw a pair of Templars rammed backwards. The foe's horse, whick-ering high like a banshee, flailed at them with vicious hooves, blood spurting from a ragged wound where a lance had pierced his breast, and then Baldwin had to concentrate on his own post. A roar, a shout, and another horse was almost through, and Baldwin sprang forward, all thoughts of fear or anger passed. Now there was only the urgent need to support the front line, and he grabbed a shield that had fallen, his sword at the ready. The shield was a ponderous weight that felt as though it must drag him down, but he resolutely thrust the bottom edge into the sand and held his shoulder to it, peering over the rim.

Another horse was charging him. It was tempting, so tempting to drop the shield and run, but if he did that, he would present that spear-thrower with a broad back at which to aim, and he had no wish to die spitted on a Moorish lance. He grimly held his position as the leaf-shaped point hurtled towards him, and at the last moment ducked well below the shield's protection.

The concussion as the brute crashed into his shield was tremendous. It felt as though his arm was shattered. There was a roaring in his ears as he felt the great mass of horse and rider roll him back, and then he was on the ground, beneath the shield, and the horse had gone over him. His face was full of sand. It was in his ears and mouth and nose. He could scarcely open his eyes, but he must, if he were to avoid the lance. Pushing the shield aside, he scrambled to his feet, and felt the sand trickle down beneath his chemise as he gripped his sword firmly once more.

The horse had passed him, but now turned and the rider spurred to aim at him.

Baldwin had no time to plan. He slipped his arm from the shield and waited. As the lance was almost on him, he hefted the shield up, blocking the weapon before it struck him, and felt the point pierce the wood. He threw the shield down immediately, and it took the lancepoint with it, its great weight bearing the lance to the ground, and making the shaft shoot upwards. There was a cry of pain from the Muslim rider, and then Baldwin's sword span around, and the edge caught the rider behind the knee. A spray of blood hissed over Baldwin's face, and then he saw another horse speeding towards him and turned to face it, sword up, before recognising the Templar's symbol.

The knight glanced at Baldwin, but then his lance was down and he speared the Muslim almost without effort, so it seemed, and as he passed, the Templar flicked his wrist and the Muslim was thrown to the ground behind him, writhing.

Baldwin whipped round. A second Muslim was riding towards him, and even as Baldwin crouched, staring about him in an urgent search for another shield, the rider's horse gave a loud whinny, stretched its neck and fell sprawling, its hind-quarters caught in the guy-ropes of a tent. The rider was thrown, and landed on his head with an audible crack. He didn't move again. Another man lay sobbing near the wreckage of a tent, his horse's leg entangled in guy-ropes, and as Baldwin watched, a sergeant despatched the rider.

Baldwin's first man lay moaning and choking still.

He had a narrow face, and a thin, black beard. From the look of him, he could not have been more than two years older than Baldwin himself. He looked up at Baldwin with agonised incomprehension, a hand pressed to his belly below his ribcage, and Baldwin could see he was dying. The blood seeped from his wound thickly, and there was a foul odour. His intestines were punctured too.

The man's eyes were pleading, and Baldwin ended his misery with a quick downward thrust of his sword.

He saw the life leave the body as it slowly slumped, the man's eyes on Baldwin's face, until it was nothing more than a sack of bones and muscle. The dark eyes seemed to fade, some-how, and then go dull, like a dead fish's.

For some reason, Baldwin muttered a prayer for the man's soul. It seemed the right thing to do, but as soon as he finished, he wanted to weep. He had never prayed for Sibilla's man, he realised.

He knelt, set his sword before him, and rested his brow on the cross as he begged forgiveness for that murder, and prayed for the man's soul.

And afterwards, for the first time since killing him all those miles away, Baldwin felt as though God had heard his prayers.

Perhaps he was forgiven.

CHAPTER FORTY-TWO

Baldwin and the Templars returned to Acre on the fourth day. After the excitement of that night attack it had been an uneventful reconnaissance. There had been no signs of Muslim forces, only the occasional caravan slowly lumbering along the ancient roadways.

As they came nearer to the city, Baldwin found the Marshal at his side once more.

'You acquitted yourself with honour in that fierce little fight,' Sir Geoffrey told him.

'I am glad you think so.'

'There are many who would not have bestirred themselves so swiftly, nor thrown themselves into the fray with such eagerness. Your training is a tribute to your old master.'

'I only sought to protect myself.'

'You did better than most,' the Marshal said. 'You would be a credit to the Order.'

Baldwin shook his head. 'I am deeply conscious of the honour you do me, but—'

MICHAEL JECKS

'You still have hopes of a wife and marriage.'

'Yes.'

'That is good. But you could do much for your fellow Christians if you joined us.'

Baldwin was thoughtful for a moment. 'I love a woman who said she cannot marry me because she is a slave. And she would not give up her religion to be free.'

'So you question the primacy of your God?'

'No. I question everything,' Baldwin said. 'I believe in God and Christ – but if another man believes in another God, is that reason to kill him?'

'No. But we must yet fight for the true God, and try to defend His city, His Kingdom, here on earth. It is our duty.'

'I see that,' Baldwin said, 'but I need time. I want to find her . . .'

'You fought well,' the Marshal repeated. 'You would be welcomed, even if you take a month or a year to decide. Christian fighters always beat Muslims, with God's grace.'

'You say that, but we were fortunate that the riders were hampered when they rode in among the guy-ropes. Many of their horses became tangled.'

'God was on our side,' Sir Geoffrey said confidently.

'Yes,' Baldwin agreed. But in his heart he was doubtful. That phrase would come to haunt him.

They trotted in under the great gate of the city, and thence along the main thoroughfare towards the castle.

'You are released now, Master Baldwin,' the Marshal said as they came to the castle's gate. 'Go and tell Ivo about the fight. He will be interested.'

'Godspeed,' Baldwin said. He walked his horse back along the lanes, under the old wall and into Montmusart. Ivo, he

232

found in the little yard after he had given the beast to the groom.

'You managed to survive your first riding out, I see?' Ivo grunted.

'And you tried to have me recruited by the Templars,' Baldwin said, distracted by the attentions of little Uther, who pranced and leaped with joy on seeing his master return.

'I did,' Ivo said. 'It would do you no harm to have a little of their patience and discipline.'

'I didn't need it,' Baldwin said proudly, 'when we had a fight.'

'Fight?'

'Our camp was attacked by Muslims,' Baldwin said offhandedly. 'I don't think we need fear them so much, Ivo. There was a strong force, and while some broke through the shields, they were not able to go far. We killed them all.'

'It was a large force?' Ivo asked. He was intent, listening with great care. 'How many men were there?'

'At least five and twenty, I suppose,' Baldwin said. 'Perhaps more, but that was all we saw and killed.'

It was gratifying to see how his news was received. Clearly Ivo was exercised by the news that Baldwin had fought, and in his manner, Baldwin hoped that he portrayed the calm demeanour of an experienced warrior. It was good to be able to surprise the old man.

'By Saint Peter's pain, that's bad,' Ivo said.

'Eh?' Baldwin was snapped from his smugness.

'If they're bringing raiding parties that size, they must be scouting the lands, don't you see?'

'We saw no sign of any others.'

'Perhaps not – but the deserts are wide. If a party that big is raiding, there are more.'

'What if there are?'

Ivo stared at him. 'Are you still so dull-witted? We could be facing an army of sixty, eighty, even a hundred thousand, if Qalawun decides to unleash his full might upon us! How would we survive that?'

'This city has walls that would grace London.'

'Krak des Chevaliers had stronger ones, with a mighty fortress on top of a great hill. Qalawun mined beneath and destroyed them. There are no walls strong enough to withstand his reckless hatred if he sets his mind to destroying them!'

'He has not declared war on us, has he?' Baldwin asked.

'Not yet. But who can say what will arrive tomorrow morning?'

'You worry too much,' Baldwin said soothingly. 'Think how many knights there are here: Templars, Germans and Hospitallers, and how many others from all over the world. Even he would find this a hard city to take while we have men such as Otto de Grandison.'

'Hard? Yes. He may have to spend a whole month here,' Ivo said harshly.

CHAPTER FORTY-THREE

While the first meeting had been held against a chorus of anxious demands, this second was more restrained. Everybody had heard that a party of Muslims had attacked the Templars. Baldwin saw Guillaume de Beaujeu look about him when the Constable asked him to speak. The Templar's expression was fierce, especially when it lighted upon Philip Mainboeuf. Baldwin was glad it didn't land upon him.

The Grand Master began quietly. 'I have been accused of cowardice in this chamber. That, and worse: being prepared to endanger Christian lives for profit, as though I care more for money than their souls. I state here it is *not* my desire to enrich myself or my Order. I have only one ambition, and that is to see Jerusalem return to our faith. Christians must reconquer the Holy City, and to do that, we must hold tight to Acre!'

There was a murmur of approval at this. A murmur that was only stilled when the Grand Master held up his hand.

'Qalawun is calling on his vassals in Egypt and Syria. In Palestine his men are building siege engines to attack our walls.

A vast host is gathering. We cannot hope to prevail, unless we plan. We need more men, and should send all useless mouths away. Can we demand of Venice, Pisa and Genoa that they remove all those who cannot fight? Send them to Cyprus, to safety. Returning ships can bring more men and food.'

'How many more men? For how long?' Philip Mainboeuf demanded, and now he stepped forward to address those present, saying patronisingly, 'Citizens of Acre, we are aware that the good Templar is devoted to the city. We know that he is an enthusiastic proponent of all forms of warfare against the heathen Muslims, but come! Let us be rational! Qalawun is a sensible man, no less than any of us here. He would not seek to destroy the key trading city that brings him so much in gold each year. Look at us – panicking over attack, when we are the only city that should be safe! If we overreact and respond in a warlike manner, then yes, we can guarantee that Qalawun will attack. But I have a note here,' and he held aloft a scroll, 'that proves all concerns to be mistaken. Citizens, noble Grand Master, please, let us not be precipitate. Let us discuss, consider, and behave accordingly.'

'What does your note suggest?' Constable Amalric asked.

'That the armies he raises, and the machines of war he builds are for the east and north of Africa. Our city is safe.'

There was a hubbub at that. Baldwin looked over at the Grand Master, and saw his pinched expression. Perhaps the Grand Master had misjudged the meeting. Or perhaps he had hoped to incite war?

'*I* have had messages too,' Guillaume declared. He took a step forward, commanding the whole assembly. 'I say this: there have been orders sent to his men in Egypt and Syria. In Egypt the muster continues unabated, while he has ordered his commander of the Syrian army, Rukn ad-Din Toqsu, to move

to Palestine where there is timber, so that they might construct
siege machines. Where are the cities in Africa that he would
wish to attack? Is there a single city with a great encircling
wall, such as we have here? I know of none. His strategy is
concealed from us deliberately. He has created a misty decep-
tion, a fog about his plans, in order to confuse us. When he
feels it safe, he will launch his attack, in a great torrent of fire,
rock and men, that will overwhelm even our great city, just as
he did with poor Tripoli. This man is insatiable. Qalawun will
not rest until all Christians in the Holy Land are slain. He has
no interest in trade. It matters not to him whether the trade is
allowed to flow through Christian Acre or through Muslim
Damascus. Why should he care that our city can trade with
Venice or Genoa? It means nothing to him.'

'He needs our trade,' Mainboeuf said loftily, with a super-
cilious glance at the people all around. 'He knows we make
him lots of money.'

'You think that,' de Beaujeu said flatly. 'You are wrong. He
knows he can make more money by having trade fully controlled by his own people. That means having Muslims at the coast.
Not Christians to make their own profit.'

'I think that here we can discern the inherent panic of an
Order which sees its own destiny written,' Mainboeuf sneered.
'The Templars are always honourable. They try to support
friends and allies. Venice has been a good ally to the Temple,
has it not?'

'What of it?' de Beaujeu demanded.

'We all know that the Venetians have in the past profited
from selling timber to the Egyptians. Their buildings are
dependent upon Venetian wood, as is their manufacture of siege
engines, as you so astutely point out. And when we look at the
present situation, do we not see only a Templar's desire to help

his allies? We know Qalawun is determined to punish those in Africa who have offended him by refusing to accept peace with him, and he is to build siege machines. The Templars would prefer to have the machines built at their profit or the profit of their friends, so they have persuaded the commune to pay their allies for all this timber here: we buy wood and use it prodigiously, constructing hoardings. It is normal, certainly, for them to support their Venetian friends, but I am surprised that the Templars should have fallen for such a ruse. For I am certain that the good Grand Master is not dishonest. He has been convinced in this tale, I have no doubt, by his friends in Venice. They put this—'

The rest of his words were drowned by roars of disapproval from Venetians and Templars alike.

A body of sailors and merchants from Venice tried to force their way towards Mainboeuf, while Pisans and Genoese jeered and bit their thumbs at them. The Templar Grand Master stood glowering. Behind him, his knights were holding themselves back only with great restraint, and Baldwin saw more than one of them shuffling forward as if to prepare to attack.

'Enough!' Amalric bellowed at last, standing and holding his hands aloft. 'This ridiculous noise will cease! Be still! Master Mainboeuf, I hope you have some evidence for the wild allegations you have made.'

'"Wild allegations"? What is wild about them? We know that the Venetians supply timber to Egypt. That is a fact known for decades. They have been censured for such sales by the Pope. We also know that the Temple and Venice have been allied for many years. This, too, is fact. So what have I invented for this meeting?'

'I have nothing to say to a fool who suggests I would lie, nor that I would succumb to the blandishments of others to deceive this company,' Sir Guillaume growled. 'I state again: the city is in grave peril. Our enemies gather their full strength to assault us. We shall succumb unless we can hurry the pace of our efforts.'

'We have already succeeded in making our city as near impregnable as it is possible to conceive,' Mainboeuf said flatly. 'There is no need to worry about this latest rumour. Our enemies are occupied elsewhere.'

Baldwin thought the look Guillaume de Beaujeu threw at Mainboeuf must surely scorch him, but the merchant smiled as though he were careless of any insult he might have given.

Only later did Baldwin begin to wonder about Mainboeuf's supreme confidence.

Out in the field, Lucia continued with her labours, digging a trench for new irrigation, her pick rising in unison with those of the other slaves. She felt like the soil she was tilling. Invaded. Violated.

Some nights ago it had begun. A vicious, one-eyed Kurd with the body of a wrestler had been taking his pleasure with another slave woman, thanks to the connivance of a guard, but now he had selected Lucia.

She fought him, that first night. His fist felt as though it must break her skull when he punched her, and after that she daren't resist, but lay quiescent while he rutted on her like a hog. And then, when he was done, he laughed as he left her. *He laughed.* And so it continued, every night. After the long day's work, she would wait for the sound of his approach, brace herself for the torture of his rapes.

At first she had tried to turn her mind away from him, to think of other things, while he forced her on all fours and grasped her hips, but it was impossible.

No means of defence occurred to her. Every day she sought a tool, but the rocks were feeble sandstone, and not heavy. Her pick wouldn't serve, since the tools were taken from them each evening. For her to attack the Kurd, she would have to do something that would hurt him badly, but which didn't require a long weapon or steel.

And then she saw the little bush with scraggy branches.

That night, Lucia heard the guard approach, the lumbering steps of the Kurd with him. She had not been touched by the guards. The Kurd was the only man who had taken her. It was strange, to know that she was to be attacked again while the other women lay on the floor all about, listening. Perhaps some would even be jealous. Any attention was better, maybe, than this life of steady, crushing work.

They would get his attention in time. The guards needed the women served so that more slaves could be born, just as the farmer needed his cows served by his bulls. Slave-children could fetch good prices.

The door's bolts were tugged back, but this time she wasn't worried. She wanted him in now, to get this over and done with. Lying on her back, she waited. The door opened, and there was a moment's hush as the guard and the Kurd peered in, a solitary candle throwing a faint glimmer over the room.

He could be smelled two yards away. She detested that smell. It had been on her, about her, within her, for days now. A repugnant stench, like that of death.

'Ready for me, little sparrow?' he asked in his grating voice.

She felt his hands on her breasts, her hips, then down between her thighs, and she parted her legs willingly, which made him chuckle. Reaching out her left hand, she put it about his neck, pulling him closer to her face. Even in the darkness, she could sense his smile of conquest.

'Want me now, sparrow? I'll reward you, then,' he said breath-lessly.

That was when she took her short, sharpened little twig, and stabbed his good eye, shoving it in as far as she could, ramming it with the heel of her hand, feeling his juices running down her wrist, relishing his sudden high screams and the spasms in his body in that long moment before his fist hit her face and she knew no more.

CHAPTER FORTY-FOUR

When the messenger arrived the following morning, Baldwin and Ivo responded immediately.

'Marshal, how may we help you?' Ivo asked as they were brought into the large chamber of the Temple. Two men sat at a big table, both hooded, wearing the white habits of the Order.

'It was not he who asked for you, it was I,' Guillaume de Beaujeu answered, standing. Slowly, the Marshal followed suit. Baldwin thought Sir Geoffrey looked as if he had aged a great deal in the last hours. His face was haggard.

Pulling down the hood of his habit, the Grand Master eyed Baldwin. 'I have heard good reports of you, Master Baldwin.'

'I hope I've justified them.'

'You heard the comments of that primping foumart, Mainboeuf. What do you think of his words?'

'Me?' Baldwin responded with surprise. 'Grand Master, I do not think I am in any position to comment.'

'You are old enough to judge a man. Would you judge him as honourable or not?'

Baldwin opened his mouth to prevaricate, but catching sight of a quick frown on Ivo's face, he considered the Grand Master's question. This was not, apparently, a time for false modesty.

'I do not know the man. From what I have seen, he is keen to give the benefit of any doubt to the Muslim leader. I find that strange, for he must know that the Mameluks have destroyed the other Christian cities. He seems convinced that the Muslims will allow this city alone to remain.'

'Do you have any impression of his honesty?'

'I would not cast a slur upon him or his integrity. He made arguments that sounded rational. Beyond that, I could not say.'

'Well, I suspect him,' Guillaume de Beaujeu said. He bent his head, deep in thought, and paced the room.

Ivo looked from him to the Marshal. 'What is the matter, Grand Master? You have more news to alarm you?'

'Other than the news of the greatest army Qalawun has yet mustered against us?' the Grand Master asked bitterly. 'Yes, I suspect that there is a traitor amongst us. It greatly concerns me that we may fail to defend our city, and if that is so, we will fail to save the Kingdom!'

'Do you think that Mainboeuf *wants* the Kingdom to fall?' Ivo asked. He could not believe that any Christian could wish for such a terrible thing.

'I don't know what to think. It is possible that he has been deceived. But he is no fool. I know Mainboeuf of old.'

'For my part, I don't think him a traitor, if that is what you fear,' Ivo said. 'Philip Mainboeuf is a fair enough merchant. He is a true Christian, and would not willingly see Acre fall.'

'Is there anyone else who can speak for him?' the Marshal

asked. He wiped a hand over his face. 'We must know whether he has been deceived, or . . .'

'Or whether you have,' Ivo finished for him.

'Yes,' the Grand Marshal agreed.

'How can you tell what is passing in a man's heart?' Baldwin wondered.

'One way is to send an embassy to Cairo to speak with the Sultan,' Guillaume de Beaujeu said heavily. 'We need to learn whether our news is true or not.'

'If he says he intends nothing of the sort – what then?' Baldwin asked.

'We will be no worse off,' Sir Geoffrey said. 'But I doubt he would say so. If he sees we are keen to learn the truth, he will not be slow to try to profit from us. He will demand money to leave Acre free, I would expect.'

'I will go to him, if you want,' Baldwin said.

'*You*?' There was a smile hovering on the Grand Master's lips. 'Tell me, how much of the Muslim tongue can you speak? How would you tell what was in his mind?'

'I am not an expert in the language, but I could watch and listen,' Baldwin said. 'I can understand men's faces, and I would be able to tell much from how they look and speak.'

'I think not,' the Grand Master said.

'Who will go?' Ivo asked.

'I have two messengers. I will send a small guard with them.'

'Templars would be killed as soon as they arrived.'

'Yes – I intend sending secular members of our Order.'

'Then let Baldwin join them. He can do little harm, and his extra eyes and ears may just help,' Ivo said.

The Grand Master glanced at the Marshal. Neither spoke for

a moment, and then Sir Geoffrey gave a faint nod. Guillaume de Beaujeu turned back to Baldwin.

'So be it. You will ride with my men to Cairo, and there you will listen carefully and watch, to see if there is any clue you can pick up that tells us what the Sultan plans. Be careful and beware! There are many dangers in Muslim cities for men who are friends of the Temple.'

That night, Lucia's back was still sore from the beating, but she had no broken bones. She had not cried, she had not wept or sobbed. That satisfaction she refused them.

A week ago, she would have welcomed death. The toil during the day was bad; the fumbling rapes at night worse, but now she could at least hold her head high again. She only regretted not having pushed the stick further into the Kurd's good eye until it found his brain. With luck he would develop gangrene and die.

She had expected death. Even as she thrust the stick into the Kurd's eye, she welcomed the thought. For a slave to harm another was punishable by death. But the *overseer* made it clear that she would not escape her torment so easily. Her life itself was to be her punishment.

She rolled over, the pain in her back agonising as the weeping scabs pulled where the whips had lashed. The overseer had used every ounce of malice in him. No matter that it was he who had brought the Kurd to her each night. She was a slave, she had no rights.

Her hand on her belly, she prayed not to bear a child. There was no sign of it – only a deep soreness that seemed to start at her brain and ran through her body to her groin. He had hurt her so much, than Kurd; more in the mind that between her legs. It made her want to vomit, remembering his hand grabbing her, wrenching her knees wide, smiling down at her.

She had no regrets about blinding him. It had felt good. Never again would she sit back and endure. Even if it meant death, she would gladly accept it as the price of her freedom.

CHAPTER FORTY-FIVE

They had arrived by ship at the coast near Damietta, a voyage of some two hundred miles, and Baldwin was fascinated to see the land as the galley deposited him, along with Roger Flor and three others, at the mouth of a wide river.

Their route took them down to Damietta, thence to Mansourah, and onward to Cairo, a journey of another four days.

The huge city stood on the side of the river. Gold glittered from its domed buildings, and the minarets gleamed white. All about the city was a vast series of canals and smaller waterways. Baldwin had heard how the river broke its banks each year, and he guessed these channels were dug in order to take flood waters, but it was a passing thought as he took in the citadel on its own prominence behind the city.

'Grand sight, eh?' Roger Flor said as they trotted towards a gateway with tall towers either side.

Baldwin nodded. Roger Flor's presence on the journey had been a worrying development, but the other man had gone out of his way to be pleasant. Neither had mentioned the riding out, and Baldwin found his company refreshing although he heeded Ivo's warning to beware and watch Flor during the journey. Ivo had been more worried about Flor than Baldwin thought necessary, but it was worth being on his guard.

Roger Flor shook his head. 'It would put Acre to shame, this. By Saint Peter, it would put even Jerusalem to shame!' He smiled at Baldwin, but then caught sight of the young man's expression. 'What is it?'

'Look!'

They had come around a small hill, and beyond it Baldwin had caught sight of a vast gathering of men. The land rose behind them, so the full immensity of the camp was plain. Black and white pavilions stood dotted all over, with gaily fluttering flags, but it was the sheer number of men that shocked Baldwin. It was as if a giant had kicked over the top of an ant heap, and exposed these teeming black-clad figures

'Sweet Christ's cods!' Roger swore with shock. 'How can they feed and maintain such an army?'

The rest of their party were, like Baldwin and Roger, staring with wild speculation. It was a relief to ride nearer the city and lose the view behind other hills.

Cairo was a maze of small alleys on either side of one broad road that cut through the middle, paved and clean. Shops lined the streets, and above were living quarters; their owners stood and discussed their trades, all falling silent as Baldwin and his party rode past. Baldwin wondered for some while what it was that caused the people such concern. 'You would think that they have never seen horses before,' he muttered from the side of his mouth. 'The army outside the walls had horse-lines, I am sure.'

'No, horses they have aplenty,' Roger chuckled. 'It's you they're interested in. They won't have seen too many Franks here in the city. Not since King Louis was captured.'

'That was more than twenty years ago, wasn't it?'

'Nearer forty. An entire Crusading army destroyed by the French King,' Roger said, and spat into the street. '*And* he destroyed the Templars who were with him. All for no gain.'

They were riding through the city and then they were out the other side and heading towards the main castle – but before they were halfway there, their guide took them over to a large lake, and here Baldwin and the others could at last drop wearily from their horses and take in their surroundings.

'What a city!' Baldwin said. 'It is vast!'

'Beats Genoa – or even Paris,' Roger agreed.

'Cairo is the leading city in the whole of the Mameluk lands,' a voice said, and Baldwin saw a tall, turbaned man walking towards him. '*Salaam aleikum.*'

Baldwin responded politely, studying him. He was chubby, and carried a curved sword at his side, but for all that he was heavily bearded, and had a face as dark as any Saracen, he was plainly not a natural Muslim. He smiled and grasped Baldwin's hand before waving the party to a pavilion by the side of the lake. 'Come, you will need to refresh yourselves. I have water and juices to slake your thirst, and there are many fruits. Please, come and rest.'

Baldwin sat on thick cushions in the pavilion. It was held aloft on four tall shafts like spears, and cords anchored the roof to pegs. There was a soothing snap and rustle overhead, and it was good to feel the air soughing past. He opened his neck to it, allowing the breeze to cool his skin. After the ride in the hot sun, the soft wind from the lake waters was giving rise to a sense of well-being. He could happily have closed his eyes – but were he to do so, he knew he would be unable to stop his snores. Even so, it was difficult to keep his eyelids open, and he had to smother many a yawn. Food was brought, delicate cakes and pastries. He ate and drank with relish, gratefully accepting juice from another servant.

Refreshed, he took in his surroundings. There were many of the strange palm trees he had come to recognise, and plenty of bushes. Roses bloomed in profusion, and other flowers. This garden belonged to their wealthy host. He was about five years older than Baldwin, who thought he looked rather dissolute. Perhaps he had spent too much time here with the Saracens.

'How long have you lived here?' he asked when there was a moment's pause in the conversation.

'I have lived here all my life,' the man said. 'My father is the Emir al-Fakhri. I am his son, Omar.'

Baldwin was thrown into embarrassment. 'My apologies. I assumed you were Christian.'

'No, but my mother was, and I have lived amongst Christians. You hold less terror for me, than for my countrymen.'

'How is that?'

'I have dealings with your masters, the Templars,' Omar said easily.

Baldwin nodded, but immediately felt less secure. He disliked the thought that he was surrounded by Saracens, in a Saracen land, being fed by Saracen hands. Never before had he felt so entirely vulnerable.

Roger Flor saw his face and laughed, reaching for dates. 'My young friend is anxious.'

'Why? He is our guest,' Omar said, bemused.

'He doesn't realise that you earn much of your money from trading with the Templars,' Roger said.

Baldwin bridled at being ridiculed. He listened as the two discussed the present situation, and Omar expressed sadness that matters had reached such a pass.

'He will not draw back from the brink, I think. Qalawun has a pretext for war in all the dead Muslims. Why did your people have to kill them? It was ridiculously stupid.'

'They were drunk,' Roger said with certainty. 'Peasants and wine. A bad mix.' He spat out a date stone.

'Such rashness. It is a miracle the Crusaders have held their lands all this time,' Omar said.

'So, will we meet the Sultan?' Roger asked.

'Perhaps, or perhaps one of his officials. I do not know. He will expect good compensation to save Acre.'

'So his armies will march on the city?'

'Of course. Men have been killed. That, to the Sultan, means you have broken your treaty of peace, so he must come to enforce his peace over the land.'

'What would he accept to prevent it? Money?'

'Perhaps.' The man considered, leaning back on his elbow and gazing over the water. 'But if you would know my mind, I would say that if he does demand money, it will be only a short-lived peace. He is determined to take Acre and all within it.'

CHAPTER FORTY-SIX

Baldwin and the others were led to a huge house that seemed more of a palace than a home. There, quarters were made available. To his surprise, Baldwin was not to share a bed with his companions. Each had their own mattress. Baldwin's bed had clean linen sheets smelling of roses, and when he tumbled between them, sleep took him swiftly.

He slept well, and for the first time in ages, he dreamed of Lucia. He was desperately searching for her in a crowd of veiled women who were similarly clad in emerald. He rushed from one to another, seeking her eyes amongst a multitude of brown, blue, hazel ones. But they were never hers. Never the ones he sought. Then, as he came to the last woman, he saw it *was* her, and ran to her, pleading for her to marry him . . . but even as he drew near, Maria appeared behind her, and he saw the knife's blade draw slowly across Lucia's throat. She collapsed, the gush of blood turning her beautiful gown to black, and Baldwin could do nothing but clench his fists. Even his wail of despair was somehow stifled. He could do nothing, say nothing, to save her. Then Maria's face changed, until it became that of Emir al-Fakhri's son. He smiled as he stared at Baldwin over Lucia's body, and Baldwin saw more bodies lining the streets. All the women he had seen were dead.

A hand on his arm shook him from his dreams, and he grabbed for his sword, until the world returned, and he recognised a servant. The man bowed low, and Baldwin realised it was daytime. For a while he could not move, as his heart returned to its usual rhythm. He only hoped no one had been disturbed by his dreams. He would be a laughing stock.

Baldwin did not like being so far from those whom he trusted: the grim but homely Ivo, the stern, resolute Otto de Grandison, the Templars . . . He felt like an exile.

He rose, washed his face in water that held rose petals to give a delicious scent, and dressed himself. His clothes had been washed, and now the tunic that had been filthy after more than a week of travelling, smelled fresh and looked almost new, apart from the many marks of fading.

On a paved terrace outside, he found Roger Flor, who was glancing at the rich decorations and gilded figures with the eye of a man who could assess the value of goods from thirty paces. Servants brought meats and watered wine, bowing low, as though Baldwin and Roger were royalty.

'Where are the others?' Baldwin asked.

'Already gone. We weren't necessary. With luck they'll speak with Qalawun, and we can soon return to Acre. Have you seen the quality of this workmanship?' he asked, lifting a goblet of glass. 'The best the Venetians could produce, this is.'

'Venetian?'

'Aye. They don't make much, but what they do make is very good. Look at this! Fine, light and robust.'

'What of it?' Baldwin asked.

'I was thinking: the Venetians make good profits from trading with Egypt. How hard will they fight to protect Acre if it's against the will of Qalawun?'

'They have the best location in Acre,' Baldwin pointed out. 'They would be mad to compromise their position for a little profit. They need Acre as much as anyone.'

'I hope they remember that.'

Baldwin left him, following the path they had taken the previous day to the water's edge, staring out over the smooth, still lake, and he was there when Omar appeared with an older man.

'Good day, my friend,' Omar said. 'This is my father, the Emir al-Fakhri.'

The Emir was shorter than Baldwin, and above his black, glistening beard, his face was sorely pocked. His belly asserted his wealth, and his eyes were surrounded with laughter lines – but today those eyes were not merry. He looked troubled.

'Please, you will walk with us,' Omar said, a hand indicating a path that led about the lake. Columns rose on either side, as if it had once been a building. 'My father speaks your language only poorly, so he has asked me to come and translate for him.'

'Of course,' Baldwin said. 'How may I serve him?'

'Your envoys are with Qalawun now,' Omar said, watching his father's mouth. 'They are in the chamber with Qalawun's men even as we speak. He will demand money.'

'I suppose it will be a vast sum,' Baldwin said.

'A vast sum, yes. But worthwhile, if the Franks wish to remain. However, it is high in his mind to remove the Christians from Acre. You must let the Grand Master de Beaujeu know this: if the city pays this money, it will buy a little time. In a year, perhaps two, Qalawun will see Acre demolished.'

'What of the value of the city as a trading centre? Without the Venetians and Genoese, how will he sell goods to the Christians?'

The older man stared at Baldwin with amusement before speaking to his son.

'My father says, "Why would he care?" You have to understand that to a Muslim, the sight of your people is an abomination. They do not belong here. We have a duty to protect our holy places, and those of your religion do not honour them.'

'But it must be good to have so many ships bringing money to buy your goods?'

'If Acre is destroyed, we shall have more ships come to Cairo, or to one of Qalawun's other cities. But the merchants who earn the money will be Muslim, and our people shall wax strong and wealthy, while yours will wane. Do you think Muslims may not negotiate for themselves? We are perfectly competent to buy and sell without your intervention.'

His voice had grown angry. Baldwin placated him. 'I meant no insult to you or your peoples, Omar. It was my only desire to learn.'

'And now you have. Be assured that before four years are passed, your city of Acre will be destroyed. Qalawun will take it apart stone from stone, just as he did Tripoli. And then the churches will be consecrated in the True Faith, and all vestiges of Christian rule will be eradicated. Only then will the Nation of Islam rise again.'

'Why does your father tell me all this?' Baldwin asked.

'Because your Templar master pays us well and because there is nothing you may do to prevent the inevitable. So while we speak, it will not benefit you. We do not betray our peoples or Islam. We tell you what must be.'

'Should we pay the ransom?' Baldwin asked, staring at the Emir.

'My father says, "It is up to you. Pay the sum demanded, and see the Sultan's armies destroy Acre in a year or two; or do not pay and see the city laid waste in weeks".'

'Is there nothing we might do to protect ourselves?' Baldwin asked, feeling a cold certainty that the Muslim's words were spoken from conviction.

'Nothing. Acre will cease to exist, and all those within her walls may expect the same pity as those who lived at Tripoli.'

CHAPTER FORTY-SEVEN

It was eleven days later that Guillaume de Beaujeu marched into the broad space before the castle with the Marshal and five knights at his back. His white tunic was spotless, and gleamed in the sunlight as he pulled off his helmet, loosening the thongs that bound his mail hood. He pushed it back, and stood, left hand on his sword, the right gripping his helmet as he surveyed the men ranged about.

It had fallen to him, perhaps, to be the last Templar Grand Master to address the Commune of Acre. That was a sobering thought.

He had no misapprehensions as to the severity of their situation. All the Christians of this city, forty thousand souls or more, were dependent upon his ability to convince these men of the danger they faced. The reports of the envoy he had sent to Cairo had been uncompromising, as had the impression of the young man, Baldwin. He was a strong-willed fellow. Knew the value of a clear report.

Their news was appalling, but it only supported Guillaume's

own convictions. There was no man so stupid as one who could not read the signs when they lay all about him – and yet there were men here in this room who were fooling themselves into believing black was white.

Constable Amalric appeared, and Guillaume took a deep breath. 'My Lord,' he said, 'I have news from Cairo.'

'Please share it with the Commune,' the Constable instructed him.

'At our last meeting, I warned you that the threat posed by Qalawun was real,' Guillaume stated, addressing them all. 'He has already constructed the largest siege artillery ever seen, and his army is enormous. There is talk of over one hundred thousand men. It is not a force designed to wage war. It is an army brought together to eradicate the last Christian outpost in the Holy Land.'

Philip Mainboeuf had been sitting on a stool but now he stood and held his hands aloft. 'My friends! Men of the Commune of Acre! How many *more* times must we listen to the same old song? My ears are tired with hearing the same allegations at each meeting. Where is this army? Is it here? Is it marching to us now? No! Are their siege engines before our walls? No! Do we have news of Qalawun leaving his capital city? No! Yet every few weeks the Templars seek to petrify us with vague threats and rumours. In God's name, how much longer must we put up with this nonsense?'

De Beaujeu could see that the majority sided with the merchant. Very well. He waited for the tumult to die down, but now he did not speak in the mild, gently persuasive manner he was accustomed to use before the Commune, he used the tone he employed when speaking to subordinates. A cold, resolute voice that brooked no argument.

'My Lords, Squires, Gentles, listen to me carefully. An army is assembled against us. It will leave very shortly. There are siege engines enough to destroy our city and forever dispel any hopes of winning back Jerusalem. We risk not only our own lives, but the souls of all Christians if we fail here: for if we do, God must turn His face from us. We have a holy duty to protect that which we hold.'

'Against a will o' the wisp!' Mainboeuf laughed.

De Beaujeu did not look at him. 'Not only have I been warned of this, I have been warned too that there is a spy in our city who seeks to convince us that the danger is not severe. I am told that this spy has been given much gold to persuade you, the Commune, that you are safe.'

'You accuse me of taking Muslim gold?' Mainboeuf roared.

Before he could cross the floor, three Templars stepped before their Grand Master, and stood, hands on hilts. The Hospitallers were irresolute, while merchants bellowed and shouted, fists waving in the air.

Constable Amalric stood and boomed in a voice that reflected his anger, 'Be still! Grand Master de Beaujeu, I hope you have evidence to support this allegation?'

'The evidence of my eyes and ears in this assembly is all I need, Constable,' the Grand Master said. 'There is one man who is determined to undermine the defence of the city at every opportunity. He is there.'

Philip Mainboeuf snarled in response, 'Look at him! A Templar, secure in his arrogance and pride! He tells us to prepare for war, and why? So his Venetian friends can make money bringing crusaders here – and we know what that achieved, don't we? The very danger he warns us of was caused by the last influx of Lombards. How many more does he think we need bring to our city to guarantee its utter collapse?'

The Grand Master motioned to the Marshal, who snapped an

order, and the three Templars moved aside. Guillaume de Beaujeu stopped before the irate merchant.

'I do not spend money foolishly in the hope of gaining information. I spend carefully and wisely to ensure that I have the best intelligence I can acquire. If you are uninformed, your opponent is not. He will make sure that he knows as much as it is possible to learn about you. About your forces, your defences, your food stocks, your water – everything. And that is exactly what I try to learn about Qalawun. I pay a lot for the best results. And I have sent people to Qalawun directly to gain information about his forces.'

'And you say that we have a spy?' the Constable said.

'We have. Someone who is greedy and debased enough to sell his city for gold.'

'What should we do?'

'Master Mainboeuf should be held so he may not earn more from Qalawun,' Guillaume said. He stared at Philip Mainboeuf for a long moment, before turning and facing the Commune once more. 'I have sent an embassy to Qalawun. He agrees to peace and the renewal of the treaty for as many Venetian Sequins as there are men and women living here in Acre.'

If the noise before had been loud, now it was a roaring torrent of sound that threatened to deafen even the strongest. Guillaume de Beaujeu held up his hands. 'Listen! Listen to me!'

'You say this deofol will bring an army to engulf us, and then you tell us to pay him? What stupidity is this!' Mainboeuf bellowed.

'We can hold him off for a little – if we pay,' de Beaujeu explained, but no one wanted to hear.

'You tell us to pay our enemy? First you state that he is on his way to kill us all, and then you tell us to bribe him! This is Templar logic, is it? I tell you, you wouldn't last long in my world!' Mainboeuf jeered. 'If you were to run a business in this way, you would soon have no trade and no money!'

'This is cowardice!' someone else shouted. 'The Templars want to surrender. If Qalawun *is* coming, then surely it's better to hold on to our money to pay to protect ourselves!'

'There's a traitor here all right, and it isn't a merchant!' another roared from the back of the room. 'The Temple wants to give our money to heathens? This is an insult to our intelligence!'

Guillaume de Beaujeu felt his rage rise to encompass his whole soul. He drew himself up to his full height and stormed from the court, his men behind him, and out in the road, he turned towards the Temple, shoving his helmet onto his head as he went.

The fools! Their brains were in their arses! They had no more hope of protecting themselves against Qalawun than a sparrow against a hawk.

But already, as he marched past the Genoese quarter, past the cathedral, and down St Anne's Lane to the great gate of the Temple, he was thinking strategically. He must write to the Holy Father in Avignon, apprising him of their dire situation, and asking for men and money to defend the last Crusader city, and then there should be plans laid for emptying the city of all but essential people.

Reaching his chamber, he pulled off his helmet and set it aside. Then he began to remove his tunic. His squire was already at his side, and helped with the coat of plates, the mail, the thick padded habergeon, and all the while Guillaume de Beaujeu was thinking, assessing, analysing, considering.

'Leave me!' he said when his armour was off, and he could shrug himself into his white habit.

The squire left the chamber with a graceful bow, and the Grand Master was alone. He walked to his chair and sat, staring into the middle distance, meditating – until it came to him.

No matter what he plotted and schemed, there was little he could do against the army Qalawun had gathered. Without God's help, the city must fall.

And suddenly Guillaume de Beaujeu was aware of a heat at his eyes, and mistiness in his vision.

CHAPTER FORTY-EIGHT

The next weeks were for Baldwin and Ivo a time of unparallelled effort. There was not a single part of the walls which was not resurveyed, and every week brought more timbers for the defence of the city. Some were to go to the construction of engines of war, while others were stored. During a siege they would be brought out to shore up buildings, or strengthen mines.

No matter that some continued to deny that the Sultan would attack; there were enough now who believed Guillaume de Beaujeu's contention.

Ivo had been made a vintenary, responsible for a group of twenty men recruited from pilgrims, crusaders and city men. His first decision was to install Baldwin as his sergeant. Baldwin had already decided that if he was to die, it would be with his countrymen, so he was glad to hear they would take a section with the English under Otto de Grandison. Ivo came and watched Baldwin with a grudging approval as his sergeant took men aside and gave them lessons in fighting with spears or swords.

'Ye'll have your work cut out teaching that lot to fight,' he said that evening.

'They'll fight better when there's an army outside the city walls,' Baldwin said.

'Perhaps.'

'You know it's true.'

'They'll fight, all right, because they'll have little option when Qalawun appears over that horizon. When men see him, some will fall to wailing and weeping, some will be beshitten, and a few will stand and defy them. It's the way of a siege.'

Baldwin remembered those words as he walked along the new hoardings atop the wall. He had taken to traversing his section, from the Lazar Gate all along to the Accused Tower, staring through the hot air towards the horizon. He came here most mornings now.

Today, he saw a speck in the distance trailing a cloud of dust. Clearly it was a horse, and moving quickly. Baldwin peered through the haze, wondering who it might be. As the rider approached, he saw it was a Turcopole, who waved and shouted as he rode, and Baldwin stared into the distance, fearing that at any moment the great army would appear. But there was nothing: no sparkle of weapons, no cavalry, no sand rising from hundreds of thousands of feet.

He was still on the wall, when he heard the first great cheer from the gate, mingled with screams and sobbing.

Hurrying down the steps to the gate, almost tripping over Uther, he saw guards being kissed and hugged by women. The Turcopole had all but fallen from his mount, and stood, red-faced, his back to a shaded wall, facing the sky, panting, while his horse puffed and blew nearby, head drooping.

'What is it?' Baldwin demanded.

A woman took his face in her hands and planted a kiss on either cheek.

'He's dead! Qalawun's dead! We're all safe! Our city's safe!'

And Baldwin felt as though his stomach had fallen to his boots with the shock.

When he was called to Lady Maria's house, Buscarel was intrigued. A maid led the way to the paved garden. 'My Lady,' he said with a bow.

'Master Buscarel, I should be glad of your assistance,' she said. She lounged on a comfortable couch in the shade. 'As you know, I am a friend of Genoa.'

'Yes.'

'Venice is not, however. Nor are the friends of Venice. One such is this Baldwin de Furnshill, Ivo Pynho's friend. I would pay you to kill him.'

He rubbed a thumb against his beard. 'Why?'

'Ivo wishes to foment war with Cairo. It serves his purpose, and that of Venice. We must stop that. Kill his friend, and he will have other things to consider.'

'Very well.'

She watched him leave with a feeling of contempt for all men. They were so transparent. This Genoan, Buscarel, he was as dull-witted as the rest. Typical of the breed, he would fight for his purse, but as soon as he was back in port, any money he had taken would be frittered away on whores and drink. It was the way of sailing men.

Taking a mazer of wine, she sipped contentedly.

That was why it was so easy to pull the wool over their eyes. Over those of the Sultan too, who thought he was gaining so much from her reports, while in truth she was learning more about him than he did about the city. Over those of men like

Mainboeuf, also. Oh, he had a pleasing thigh, and a nice tarse, but she was not bedding him for fun. He was the most prominent merchant here, and he could tell her about the defences of the city and what matters were discussed in the Commune before anyone else knew.

He was the source of her value to the Sultan. And for that reason, her farms were safe. She would give away the secrets of the Pope at Rome to protect her lands.

The evening was warm and sultry, with wind blowing in from the sea as Baldwin walked back from the cathedral.

All had wanted to participate in the service of thanks which the Patriarch of Jerusalem had held. The bells had been ringing all afternoon, making a cacophony that was at first exhilarating, but now tedious. Not that Baldwin cared. Like others, he was euphoric. And, to be honest, slightly drunk after all the wine he had quaffed.

Otto de Grandison and Ivo were chatting, walking in front of him. Suddenly a man bolted from a doorway. He almost lurched into the three, burped, apologised, and smiled crookedly, saying, 'God has saved us! God be praised!'

'God be praised,' the tall Swiss agreed, and the drunken man walked away unsteadily up the road.

'For Qalawun to die so suddenly, it must be a miracle,' Baldwin said.

'Or a poison given to him by an enthusiastic politician,' Ivo said sourly. 'They have different ways of ensuring their succession. Does anyone know who will be taking his position as Sultan?'

'No. I doubt me it matters,' Grandison said comfortably. 'Whoever it may be, he will spend his time consolidating his position, not worrying about war.'

'But a man with a vast army must occupy it,' Ivo pointed out.

'This is true,' Grandison replied. 'But he will be concentrating on putting down plots about his succession, and the army will be useful for that. All I know is that the worst threat to the Holy Land is dead. And that means I will be taking my men back to England soon. It will be good to get away from this infernal heat.'

'I do not know what I shall do,' Baldwin said, only half-realising he spoke aloud. It was a curious thought. For the last months, his mind had been completely focused on the defence of the city. Without that spur, there was nothing to keep him here – only the memory of Lucia. He passed a couple fornicating against a wall, and thought perhaps he should go to the whores and dispel his natural passion. But he remembered the unsatisfactory coupling all those months ago when he had first arrived, and pushed the thought from his mind.

'Well, what do you *want* to do?' Ivo asked.

'I don't know,' Baldwin said. 'I cannot return home.'

'Remain here, then.'

'What, and join the Templars?' Baldwin laughed.

'You could join a worse organisation.'

'I am not ready to become a monk.'

Grandison looked at him. 'You could become a merchant in your own right.'

'I know nothing about trade,' he protested.

'Then permit Ivo to teach you,' Grandison said.

'I would be glad if you remained,' Ivo said.

Baldwin felt a welling that blocked his throat. 'I . . . I am grateful.'

'Good. That is settled, then,' Ivo said.

They were passing a large mound of broken lathes and spars burning merrily, while people danced about it, hands linked.

Men with bells buckled to their knees were dancing too, and behind them people were drinking and eating. A man with a huge tabor drummed enthusiastically, piping at the same time, and a hurdy-gurdy was taking up the rhythm. Women sang and laughed, and Baldwin saw children scuttling about and playing. It was a scene of joy. All were happy.

'Everybody is celebrating. All the stores saved for the siege are being devoured,' he said.

'And the wine, too,' Ivo said.

'There will be more than a few children conceived tonight,' Grandison sighed. 'My men will leave many a young maid with an expensive present.'

Ivo glanced at Baldwin. 'Is there any news of her?'

'No.'

Grandison looked at him. 'You have lost a woman?'

'Yes. A maid. But her mistress sent her away.'

'If it was a servant, you need only consider where your mistress owns houses.'

'Lady Maria owns many,' Baldwin said.

'Then you will need to visit many, won't you?' Grandison said. 'Faint heart never won fair maid, boy.'

Baldwin resented his bluff confidence. It was tempting to snap back at him, but then he found himself considering the Swiss's words. He was right, after all. And if he were to search, he might find his Lucia. 'I will do so,' he said.

'We can sleep better tonight, anyway,' Grandison said.

'Yes,' Baldwin agreed.

'I hope so,' Ivo nodded.

'There is surely reason for a little more confidence than a vague "hope",' Grandison said. 'God has saved us.'

'For the nonce, yes. But I just wonder what will happen to that army.'

'Ivo, you could make Bacchus miserable!'

'Not as miserable as a hundred thousand warriors marching against us.'

The people thronging the streets made it hard for Buscarel to follow Baldwin. As soon as he saw the young man in the crowds, he gripped his dagger's hilt under his cloak and pushed forward. The drunks would shield him from view, and he could reach Baldwin, stab him, and be away before anyone was any the wiser. It was the perfect place for an assassination.

But there were too many celebrating for him to be able to get close without trampling all in his path in an unseemly manner. It was one thing to push men and women from his path, another to cause such a disturbance that Baldwin must hear and seek the cause.

He followed, hoping to find the right moment.

In the last weeks he had been moving regularly amongst the men of Genoa. The mood was not good. All feared the loss of business if the Sultan arrived, and the Genoese had enough spies of their own to know the Templar warnings were valid. Many spoke of leaving.

Buscarel trailed after the young man all the way into Montmusart, and thence to Ivo's house. He stood in the alley-way near the entrance to the house for some little while, watching and thinking. Acre was the only place he knew. It was the home he loved. He had his wife here, his son. The thought of fleeing to some other city was depressing.

It was a relief to know that the threat was receding.

CHAPTER FORTY-NINE

Baldwin lay on his bed and stared at the ceiling, his mind full of thoughts of Lucia.

It was the scenes all over the city tonight that had provoked this. Happy, cheerful faces had loomed in the flickering torch-light, people dancing, singing, kissing, laughing – the whole of Acre making merry. Baldwin alone was miserable.

The pleasure-seekers should realise that although their enemy was dead, his army was still in Cairo, he thought. Yet how *could* they realise, for they had not seen that vast army.

Uther jumped onto his lap, making Baldwin start violently. He growled, 'Clumsy brute,' as the dog lay down, his chin on Baldwin's belly, staring up at him. 'You wouldn't be as foolish, would you?' Baldwin muttered, scratching him behind the ears.

He was being irrational. It was jealousy: he wanted Lucia back. Here in the city it seemed everyone had a partner, and he wanted his. The idea that she was somewhere far away, toiling under the harsh sun, made him shudder. Her delicate skin was not made for such torment. 'His woman' – it was ironic that he thought of her in that light. She was hardly known to him. He had met her and spoken to her briefly, and she had spurned his advances. As she had said, she was not of the same faith, and unless she were to change, she could not marry him. It was unthinkable that he might change from the True Faith, after all. So it was impossible for them to marry, and he suspected she would not tolerate being a concubine.

Yet the man Omar had said that his father, a Muslim, had married a Christian wife. Perhaps there were ways around the strictures of their religions without compromising?

This was ludicrous, anyway. He had no idea where she was, where she was living, or how. He would have to search all the farms and manors owned by Lady Maria, if he were to find her.

A shriek of delight came to his ears from the roadway outside, followed by a burst of giggling. Baldwin gritted his teeth.

How many different manors did Lady Maria own? Not that many. He had heard that she possessed lands near Lydda. Perhaps he should visit them and search until he found Lucia. Better that, than lose her forever. What sort of a suitor would he be, were he to desert her to a life of slavery?

He would take Otto de Grandison's advice and find her. At least now, with the threat of war receding, he could search.

Under Abu al-Fida's careful direction, the great engine was taken apart.

Moving a massive machine like al-Mansour was a major undertaking. All parts had been marked by the carpenters under Abu al-Fida's piercing gaze, so it could be brought together with speed and rebuilt. The base was constructed from timbers pegged together; there was the support structure for the counterweight and arm, and ironwork for hinges and counterweights. There were many parts which could fail individually and cause the whole machine to break down. Even the simple loop which hooked over the arm, to slide free as the arm rose to release the stone, was prone to wear. If that happened, the engine was no more use than firewood.

But Abu al-Fida would not have it cease its bombardment because of a failure of planning. There were spares for all components: multiple slings, coils of rope, vats of grease for the bearings and to keep the slings supple. In a series of chests were kept spare pegs, two for each hole, and all the paraphernalia of the machine was stowed in a logical sequence so a man could place his hands on the relevant item at a moment's notice. In all, al-Mansour and the items necessary for its continued running, were stored in more than a hundred wagons, which formed a column half a league long.

And all for nothing. Because the Sultan was dead.

Abu al-Fida walked from the wagon park, and up to the castle, struggling to control his emotions.

This castle had been built by Christians, and the fiend Raynald de Châtillon had won it when he married his wife. The hero of Islam, Salah ad-Din, had captured it, and in recent years Baibars had enhanced it.

It was as dark in history as Acre. Both were steeped in the blood of innocents. All because of the Franks. They took a place and perverted it, with their intolerable greed and brutality. Acre, like Tripoli, should be torn down.

Over the entrance to his new tower in the north-west corner, Baibars had masons carve two lions facing each other. Abu al-Fida paused and looked up at them now, wondering, as he had so often, what drove men like Baibars and Qalawun. He did not know. But while their ambitions matched his own, he was content to do all he might to support them. He wanted to see the last Christians thrown from these lands, to see that befouled city, Acre, pulled apart so that the blood of the innocents could be avenged.

Qalawun had sworn – but now, now what would happen? The Sultan's son, al-Ashraf Khalil, had taken power, but he was a weak man, from what Abu al-Fida had heard, and had been mistrusted by many, including his dead father.

Abu al-Fida climbed the stairs and stood on the tower's roof, staring out over the hills to the north, his fists clenched. Why was his beloved Usmar taken from him, when men like al-Ashraf Khalil survived?

Poor Usmar. Poor Aisha. All his family gone in a matter of days.

Abu al-Fida struggled to hold back a sob. He could not believe that he had come so far, achieved so much, only to see this great war machine lie disassembled and idle. It was built for a purpose. Without that, Abu al-Fida's life was meaningless. His sole reason for existence was the destruction of Acre. Without the Sultan, without the army, there could be no release for him. He had lived in Acre, he had lived amongst the Franks as well as in cities which were resolutely Muslim. If possible, he would prefer not to see further slaughter: in the final days of Antioch he had seen enough to last a lifetime. After the appalling aftermath of that siege he had run away to discover a life which did not involve death. He had become a merchant, trading goods between the cities.

His life had been good. Alas, that his wife had died with their daughters in that fire. Alas, that Usmar had died. All dead, and the city was responsible. He could never forgive that. There was no hatred in him now, only a driving passion. He must see that city of devils destroyed. It was unthinkable that it should remain. It was an insult to God.

God wanted him to destroy that city – he was sure of it. To do His will, Abu al-Fida would bring such a shower of horror upon Acre that all would regret Usmar's passing.

He only prayed that the son of the Sultan would grant him his ambition.

CHAPTER FIFTY

Baldwin was glad of an opportunity to join the Templar forces riding south.

'This is only a reconnaissance. We ride to ensure that there are no elements of the Sultan's grand army on their way to us,' the Marshal said as they tightened cinch-straps and checked their armour. 'There have been rumours of spies over recent weeks. Our task is to see whether there are Muslim forces spying out the land.'

Roger Flor glanced at Baldwin. Roger was wearing the brown tunic of a Templar sergeant, the red cross a blaze of brightness on his breast. His beard had been trimmed and he grinned as he caught Baldwin's eye. They had not spoken since their return from Cairo.

'Not like our last riding out,' he murmured. 'I'm glad you kept that quiet.'

'It was not my place to denounce you,' Baldwin said. He had no desire to recall that shameful action – he would be happier to forget it.

'Godspeed, my friend,' Baldwin heard, and turned to find Sir Jacques smiling at him.

'You are joining us?' he asked.

'I was glad to ask to accompany the party.' Sir Jacques peered ahead through the open city gates at the landscape outside. 'It is time for us all to prepare for war.'

'You think so too?'

'I have no doubt. The son will want to keep his army busy, and demonstrate his determination to follow his father. He will want to end what Qalawun began.' Sir Jacques glanced shrewdly at Baldwin. 'I heard from Ivo that you seek a woman?'

'Yes. She was once the maid to Lady Maria.'

'Then I wish you joy in your search. There is a manor of Lady Maria's down to the south and east, which is on our way. Perhaps she will be there.'

Baldwin nodded. He would be glad to find Lucia there. Even if she was, of course, he was unsure what he might achieve. Her mistress had refused to sell her or give her her freedom, and if she remained intransigent, there would be little Baldwin could do to force her. Still, if nothing else it was good to leave the city for a while, and make a journey in the more mild temperatures of the winter.

The order to mount was given, and Baldwin and the others rose into their saddles, and were soon trotting under the broad gatehouse of the city and into the open lands beyond. Much had changed since Otto de Grandison's arrival. The shanties were gone and their occupants evicted. Where lean-to shacks had rested against the walls, now there was only cleared sand, while above, along the line of walls, and atop the towers, the new hoardings concealed the sentries on the walls. The place had the appearance of an armed camp, as indeed it was.

Some distance from the city, the first of the farmed lands stood, green and verdant and full of promise. Baldwin hoped that the harvest would be good. He was at heart a rural fellow, and it grieved him to think that good crops could be wasted by war.

They rode for a day and a half, heading first east and south, and then sweeping back towards the coast again. On their way, Baldwin told Sir Jacques about Lucia, and how he feared for her because she was a slave.

'Well, it makes your task easier.'

'What, that she is a slave?'

'Of course!' he smiled. 'She is a Muslim, you say. Well, that means she must be nearby. She will not be in Muslim-controlled lands, but close to Acre. Otherwise she would have been released. Muslims would not permit a Muslim to be enslaved any more than a Christian would allow that to happen to a Christian.'

'I see.'

'Slavery has created unique problems for us,' Sir Jacques said musingly. 'Baibars once settled a peace on the Christians, suggesting a free exchange of all prisoners of their wars – but of course the Templars and Hospitallers could not agree.'

'No?'

'For them to maintain their castles and lands, the Orders had need of craftsmen: masons, leather workers, smiths. So after every raid, they would learn the skills of their prisoners, and those who could be used were kept as slaves for life. It was the only way to maintain the Orders. They couldn't rely on enough workers arriving from Britanny or Guyenne.'

'I am sorry to hear that. I would never hold any man as a slave.'

'The Templars paid for it. Have you heard of Safed?' Sir

Jacques asked as they rode eastwards that first morning. 'It was a Templar castle.'

'No, I don't think so.'

'It was after the breakdown of the peace, some forty years ago, that Baibars tried to destroy Safed. He attacked it time and again, but could not break the resolve of the occupants. So he took another tack. He made those inside understand that the Turcopoles would be welcomed, if they left. The Templars held them in a rigid discipline, but even beating them could not stop many from climbing over the walls in the dead of night. Without them, there were only two hundred Templars left inside. Not enough to man the walls. And so they were forced to accept terms. The Sultan offered them safe passage from the castle if they would only open the gates. So, reluctantly, the commander finally did so.'

'And that earns them a place of pride?' Baldwin questioned.

'Yes, because as soon as his men took control of the castle, this same Baibars had the Templars gathered together. He made them a new offer. Those who submitted – you know that "Islam" means "submission"? – would live. All those who refused would be executed the following morning. The Sultan left them the night to consider, and next morning, he had the men lined up. The commander ordered his men not to forget their oaths and their faith, and for that the Sultan had him flayed alive before his men. Imagine: all those knights standing and watching while their leader had the skin peeled from his body in front of them. And then they were asked, one by one, whether they would accept the Muslim faith. It is said that as each refused, he was beheaded. And yet not one agreed to the terms. All remained firm in their faith. That is the sort of man a Templar is. Resolute, you see. Guillaume de Beaujeu is one of the mould of Safed. It is in his blood to do all he can to protect the people here, and if necessary, he will die trying.'

'I hope he will not need to,' Baldwin said.

A little later, Baldwin found Roger at his side. 'So, you like his story of death and glory at Safed?' Roger asked.

'I would prefer to think they had retained the Turcopoles in the castle and had not lost it and their lives,' Baldwin told him.

'Aye,' Roger said ruminatively, studying the men in front of them. 'But they'd think they'd won a glorious victory by dying as martyrs.'

'I think winning is better than a glorious death and losing the battle,' Baldwin said.

'Me too,' Roger said. The sand was rising from the hooves in front, and he snorted, hawking and spitting, then adding, 'Stiff-backed hairy-arses, the lot of them. But good men to have on your side in a fight.'

Baldwin smiled, confused. 'But you are one too.'

'Nay, only for a short time. Soon I'll be free again, and I'll buy my own ship and make a fortune bringing pilgrims here – *if* there is a "here" to bring them to.'

CHAPTER FIFTY-ONE

At the city's gate, Baldwin felt his failure overwhelm him. With the Templars he had visited two farms of Lady Maria's, but there was no sign of Lucia in either. All the long ride back, he had kept his face covered. Partly against the sand, but in truth more to hide his dejection.

'Good day, my friend,' he heard, and Sir Jacques trotted up to join him as he walked his horse back to the stable at Ivo's. 'If you do not object to the observation, you appear less than content after our ride.'

'I am desperate to find Lucia,' Baldwin admitted. 'But how can I? Lady Maria has hidden her away.'

'That is the counsel of despair,' Jacques said. 'Continue to join reconnaissance parties, and you will find her. I have faith that you will. You must have it too.'

Baldwin nodded without conviction. It seemed ridiculous that he should hold such a heaviness in his heart. 'I would see her again. I am sick for love of her. Without her I feel like a flower missing the sunlight. I am nothing.'

Sir Jacques smiled sympathetically. 'I understand.'

'You cannot – you are a monk!'

'Even monks were once men,' Sir Jacques said mildly. 'I loved deeply before I joined my Order. I was an enthusiastic hunter and gatherer of feminine hearts, if you can believe that.'

'What made you join your Order, then?'

Sir Jacques sighed, and Baldwin saw for the first time that behind his smile there was a great sadness. 'I loved one woman with more devotion than I had been able to summon before,' he said. 'She was beautiful to me, a generous, warm woman, with the natural grace of her people.'

'She was Muslim?'

'No, a Christian, but of the Jewish race. Her name was Sarah, and I adored her. If I had been able to marry her, I would have.'

'What happened?'

'She fell prey to leprosy. It is not uncommon. I would have married her and tended to her, but it was not to be. When she became leprous, I lost her. She was declared dead, and left me to join the Order as a nun. She was based here, in Acre. And when I heard she had done so, I chose my own path.'

'I am sorry.'

'I had thought that we would become wealthy. I saw myself as a baron to rival any in Guyenne, while she would be a glorious wife and mother to a brood of children who would be our constant pride. A man begins life with so many plans and hopes, does he not?'

Baldwin felt his throat constrict at the tone of sad acceptance in the knight's voice. 'You do not forget her?'

'How can a man forget the only woman he truly loved? I knew many before her, but not a single one since. I could not gain pleasure from any after her. So, I went to the Grand Master and asked if I could join. And after I had been questioned as to my commitment, I was permitted to take the threefold vows and entered the Hospital.'

'Have you regretted your choice?'

'What a curious question, Master Baldwin. Why should I regret my vocation? I am a calmer, better man for my position. And one day, when I die, I will die here, in the Holy Land, not far from my Sarah.'

'She is still here?'

'She died many years ago. Her body is buried in the Convent of the Nuns of Saint Lazarus in the old city.'

'I do not know how I shall ever see my Lucia again. Perhaps I shall have the same fate as you.'

'Master Baldwin, do not be disheartened. You are young, and so is she. There is always hope, until death. And then we go to a better place than this. So all is good. Still, I wonder . . .'

Baldwin glanced at him, but the knight was peering into the middle distance with a speculative frown and would not speak of his thoughts. The most he would say was, 'I have some friends. I will speak with them.'

The day was hot, and the sun bore down upon them like a blast from a forge as Lucia stood in the field with the heavy shovel, digging up the sodden soil where it had blocked the irrigation trenches and banking up the field. She had never been so close to wet soil before in her life. Just now, the thought of lying down in the cool earth was very appealing.

Her back was healed now, but not her mind. She had been raped by that foul Kurd, time after time, and she would never forget how it made her feel inside, as though her womb had been shrivelled.

She thrust the wooden shovel into the soil. It had a metal

blade fixed to the edge. Perhaps she could use it to escape? But that was foolish. There was nowhere to escape *to*.

The work was mind-numbingly dull. Her hands were sore where they had been chafed by the wooden shaft, there were blisters on her palms, and the soles of her feet where they had been soaked with the water, and now her back was beginning to complain. Not the scars from the whipping, but the muscles deep at either side of her spine, above her waist. They ached and complained, and she closed her eyes as she stabbed once more at the ground.

A few yards away was another slave, legs wide, bending from the hips, as she picked at the weeds that infested this patch. God forbid that Lady Maria might see a single stray plant here in her garden when she deigned to visit.

When she did, Lucia hoped she might have a stick ready for her too.

Baldwin was sitting with Ivo, when the knock came at the door. He was relieved to hear Jacques d'Ivry's voice. It seemed to calm Ivo, too, as though he had been expecting someone else.

'Masters, it is a good morning, and I think a wonderful opportunity for a ride,' the Leper Knight declared, pulling his gloves from his hands as he entered. He gladly accepted a beaker of watered wine, and peered at Ivo and Baldwin over the rim with eyes that danced with happiness.

'What are you talking about?' Ivo demanded. He set his wax tablet on the floor and scowled up at his friend.

'The sun is up, and I consider it possible that a short ride to north and east may provide our young companion with a profoundly desirable encounter.'

'You mean you've found her?' Baldwin said, standing quickly and gaping. 'My Lucia?'

'I may have, yes. A slave-trader told me he took a woman to Lady Maria's manor towards Tiberias. I would not be surprised if we were to find your woman there.'

'My friend! I don't know what to say!'

'Then it may be best to say nothing until we know that she actually is there, Master Baldwin,' Sir Jacques said, recoiling from Baldwin's enthusiasm.

'Aye, yes,' Baldwin agreed, trying to control his grin of delight.

'How sure are you?' Ivo asked.

'The man said that there was only one woman and it was shortly after the riots. I trust our friend has not seen the woman since then? Then it is possible, if not probable.'

'That road is not safe.'

'No, Master Ivo. But if the young woman is there, it would be a kind act to rescue her.'

Baldwin's face fell. 'How can I do that? If she is being held, I have no right to take her. Even if I wanted to, it would be hard with one against a number of men.'

'Perhaps you would not be alone,' Jacques said with a smile that Baldwin could only think of as sly.

He had never seen such an expression on his friend's face. 'W-would you come with me?' he stammered.

'There is need of a patrol to the north,' Jacques told him. 'The Templars and Knights of Saint Lazarus will be leaving later. We should be glad of your company, Master Baldwin.'

CHAPTER FIFTY-TWO

A short time after Jacques had left, Baldwin was ready to go out on patrol with him. He had pulled on a mail shirt and tunic, and with his sword belted over the top, he looked almost like a squire in his own right.

Ivo was about to clout the lad over the shoulder in an unaccustomed display of affection, when he heard the sound of men at the door again. The moment Ivo clapped eyes on the messenger, he felt his elation subside.

'Who is this?' Baldwin asked.

'A messenger from Cairo,' Ivo said. He beckoned the man to him, and took the proffered message.

'What is it?' Baldwin wanted to know next.

'I must visit the Marshal,' Ivo said heavily. 'Ride fast and safe, and return quickly, lad.'

Ivo then took up his sword and made his way to the Temple, where he was soon brought before the Marshal. Geoffrey de Vendac was looking pale, Ivo thought.

Squat pillars supported the ceiling, and candles flickered and smoked from sconces set into pillars and walls of the Temple. The Marshal waved Ivo into his chamber, and when Ivo was seated, he motioned to his servants to leave them.

'I am glad you could come, old friend,' he said, and cleared his throat. 'We have heard more from Cairo.'

'I guessed as much.'

'There has been an attempt upon the life of the new Sultan. As you know, all too often a man's blood is dissipated in his children. Our misfortune is that our foe has left another capable leader behind.'

'His son?'

'Al-Malik al-Ashraf Salah al-Din Khalil ibn Qalawun,' the Marshal agreed, rolling the lengthy name over his tongue like a man suspecting a poison in his wine. 'Yes. When Qalawun was dying, he called al-Ashraf Khalil to him and made him swear to continue the war against us. This the man agreed. During the time he took to have his father buried, we hoped we might get another chance for negotiations.'

'What happened?'

'An Emir called Turuntai attempted to hasten the process of succession. He organised a plot to remove al-Ashraf Khalil, but the Sultan came to hear of it. Turuntai is dead, and the Sultan more firmly installed on his throne than before. He has already issued commands to the army.'

'They won't attack yet,' Ivo said. 'It's winter. They'll not advance until spring.'

'That's right. Our spies tell us that there are sixty thousand horse and a hundred and forty thousand men-at-arms. Two hundred thousand, all told.'

'That means nothing unless there are machines and miners.'

'He has them. Thousands of miners, and over a hundred engines.'

'Over a hundred?' Ivo asked, shocked.

'Some of the largest catapults ever created, Ivo.'

'How many men are there here in the city?' Ivo asked, calculating.

'There are perhaps forty thousand souls all told. Of them, fewer than a thousand are knights, and perhaps there are sixteen thousand men-at-arms. The rest . . .' He let his words hang in the air for a moment, then continued: 'There is no need for horses now. When the army of al-Ashraf Khalil descends upon us, they would serve only as food for the people of the city.'

'I understand.'

'However, you can help the Temple and the city with other work.'

'How? Tell me how I can assist you?'

To Ivo's consternation, the Marshal let his face fall into his hands and could not speak for some moments. Ivo stood, unsure what to do or say. He shuffled, looked about the room. Sir Geoffrey had always been so strong and purposeful. To see him reduced to this was deeply disconcerting.

'Master Ivo, I am sorry,' the Marshal said. He took his hands away and stiffened his back. 'My apologies. I must soon go to the chapel, so I shall be brief. I know your wife and child were in Tripoli.'

'I tried to return to them,' Ivo said steadfastly.

'I know. I was there, as you are aware. I was persuaded to leave on a ship before the end, and my comrades remained to do all they could. It was little enough. All died. Master Ivo, I saw that city in all her glory, and I saw the devastation of the Mameluk attacks. The rocks thundering into walls. Men and women crushed – babies, too. I have never seen such appalling sights. Those who survived the fury of the missiles were slaugh- tered by the Muslims running through the streets. Master Ivo, I would not have that happen again.'

'I see.'

'I wish you to plan for all those who are not committed to fighting for the city, to be taken away. The Genoese and Venetians should be able to evacuate the women and children to Cyprus. They will be safe there. And with them gone, my friend, we shall all be able to fight more bravely, knowing that whatever we do, we do not risk the lives of the poor and weak. We fight for God and God's land.'

Ivo nodded. He was still thinking of Tripoli.

Buscarel could see the Temple towers from his door.

While he despised the Templars, being more comfortable with the Hospitallers as a Genoese, he appreciated the sight of their great building with its immense towers. He had always held a fierce love for this city. It was where he had installed his woman, and two sons too. His love for Acre was as strong as his hatred for Venice and her allies, but today, walking through his door, he felt only relief to be back at his home.

The door gave onto a short passageway that led to the square enclosed garden within. It was not enormous, but was fitting for a merchant seaman of his importance and wealth. He was lately returned from a short journey seeking fruits, and hoped to surprise his woman.

She stood, flustered and surprised as he entered. 'I thought I should visit my wife,' he said affectionately.

'You will need food! Wine! Please, let me . . .'

'Cecilia, sit, wait with me.'

She made as though to go to the kitchen, but his calm beckoning persuaded her, and she walked to him, her face downcast. 'Was it a successful voyage?'

'Master Mainboeuf will be content. Where are my sons?'

She smiled. Cecilia had the olive complexion of a south-ern woman, and although she was almost thirty years old, her looks had not faded. When she smiled, her eyes danced with joy.

'They are with their nurse at the house of the merchant of Pera.'

'Manuel? Good. It would be pleasant to have some time alone with my wife,' he said.

He walked with her to their bedchamber, and they kissed, then made love. When they were done, he remained naked on the bed, drinking wine as he gazed out of his window towards the sea and the great port, over the roofs of the Venetian houses and palaces.

Venice! he thought. The thieves of the Adriatic! Their piracy was notorious throughout the Mediterranean, especially with their alliance with the Templars. Look at Acre! The city could be the jewel of the East, if the Genoese had their way; unfortu-nately, the Genoese quarter had no access to the sea, without passing through the Venetian quarter. The harbour was all theirs, and they had their lands and privileges guaranteed by the Templars. No one could fight both.

He was no hypocrite. It was true that Genoa had profited from her investment in Tripoli. If that city had survived, Genoa's wealth would have been guaranteed, for the merchants there were keen to deal with Genoa, almost to the exclusion of all others. That was why Tripoli had fallen. All knew it. Someone had travelled to Qalawun to demand that he intercede on behalf of those poor men from other cities who could not trade in the way they had in their past. Because Genoa was become the monopolistic trader with Tripoli.

Yes, all knew what had happened. Venice had sent an

embassy to Qalawun in Cairo, and he had responded with over-whelming force. Poor Tripoli. Poor Genoa.

'What is it, my love?' Cecilia said, walking back into the room. She bore a tray with more wine and a flat bread.

'I was thinking of those murderous bastards!'

She was still for a moment. When he allowed his anger to show, it always scared her, and her fear was a spur to his anger. There was no need for her to be scared of him, unless she actively sought to enrage him. He would not hurt her, and the alarm in her face was demeaning to both.

He swallowed his annoyance, and tried to force a less bitter expression into his eyes. 'Come. I am not angry with you. I was thinking of them – that was what enraged me.'

'I am fortunate to have such a good husband,' she asserted, and sat on the couch beside him.

'They have cost us much,' he said.

She nodded, pouring him wine.

It was because of Venice that Genoa was fighting for survival. The Venetians possessed the bulk of all trade from the East because they controlled the sole remaining city. In future, everyone must go to Venice for silks, for spices and sugar, for all the luxuries that cost men in Saxony or Paris so much. All the items which allowed a shipman to make good on his invest-ments would be denied to Genoa.

His people must defend their trade. Except no one was willing to do so. They sat in their houses and drank wine and dreamed of the days before the loss of Tripoli, or proposed stupid plots to retake their city, or to remove the Venetians from Acre.

'You are troubled?' Cecilia asked.

'It is nothing for you to worry about,' he said reassuringly. He closed his eyes so that she would not see the anxiety in his face.

Acre was the last stronghold on the coast. While she lived, Genoa would be impoverished. But Acre was his home. And while he hated the thought of serving the interests of Venice, he would defend this city to the last.

CHAPTER FIFTY-THREE

It was a tense ride for Baldwin. He was glad to be out, but still more glad that there were so many men about him. There were two other Leper Knights with Sir Jacques, as well as their squires and sergeants. The remainder of the thirty were Templars.

Their way took them over the plains, and thence between some low, yellow hills.

'All this land once was ours,' Sir Jacques said, looking about him. He was wearing his full armour, and the nose-guard looked incongruous, being slightly bent at the bottom. It pressed upon Sir Jacques' nose, pushing it in and to the right. Baldwin was tempted to ask why he didn't have it bent back. 'The Kingdom stretched all the way from Antioch in the north, down to Gaza,' he went on. 'The Templars and other Orders built strong defences along the border to protect Jerusalem and the other cities, but over time we have lost all.'

'How?'

'You mean, how did men's folly permit such a disaster? Or how could God have allowed heathens to take His land?' Jacques asked lightly.

'Both, surely.'

'I think not. God gives us the strength to do His will, but that does not mean He commands us in all we do. He likes to test us with new trials, and this is just one more.'

'But how can it be a trial when we know He cannot allow us to lose?' Baldwin said.

Jacques looked at him. 'And you are certain of that? Perhaps the trial is to see whether we have the resolution to see this through. But if we fail, perhaps it will be for another brotherhood of Christians to return to wrest the land from the heathen, and thereby bring about His divine wishes.'

'He cannot allow heathens to take it, surely?'

'Why not? If we are not strong enough, someone must have it.'

'If God were to allow the Kingdom of Jerusalem to fail, surely that must mean the end of the world.'

Jacques smiled at the solemn young man. 'And would that be so terrible? He has already given Jerusalem to the Muslims. What would it mean to give up Acre as well? Not so very much in comparison. I do not think He has been very impressed with His people in recent years. If He were, would He truly have allowed the slaughter at Tripoli?'

Baldwin closed his mouth and stared ahead. Speaking was painful, for every word meant swallowing sand kicked up by the horses ahead. Still, the thought that God might permit His lands to be invaded was ridiculous; He must help Christians throw back the godless.

'Look there! I think that is the Lady's farm.'

Baldwin followed Sir Jacques' pointing finger, and saw some drab buildings in the distance. 'There?'

'It is a small farm for her slaves, I think,' Jacques said.

Lucia was bent at her work when she heard the approaching thunder of hooves. Dimly, she could make out the white tunics, grubby with sand and dust, of the Templars. They were a large force, and dressed for battle. The knights wore mail, with helmets on their heads and swords at their sides. The overseer cracked his whip, and the slaves bent to their work once more. Lucia watched as two knights rode forward at an easy canter, reining in at his side, and began to speak. And then she saw him. The strange Frank called Baldwin.

It almost made her drop her spade. She tottered and, as the overseer shouted at her, she ducked below his lash. Too late, for the leather end caught her across the shoulders, and she cried out with the pain. A second blow struck her torso, and the end whipped about and caught the side of her breast.

The pain was unimaginable. She wept as she struggled to return to her work, feeling the slickness of fresh blood running down her spine.

Baldwin saw the overseer lift his hand, and felt his face grow black with rage. He spurred his mount onwards, thrusting himself and his horse between the slave-driver and Lucia.

The overseer glanced up at Baldwin with a frown of incomprehension. This was one of his slaves, and he was right to maintain control. It was his duty and his job. He edged around Baldwin's horse.

'Keep back, churl!' Baldwin snarled. He looked down at Lucia and his heart was almost broken to see her. She was nearly unrecognisable. The lady in green he had fallen in love with was now a broken woman in soiled, torn linen.

'My Lady,' he said, 'I offered you my hand once. I offer it again.'

The overseer darted around, to stand before Lucia, smiling wolfishly, daring her to speak.

Baldwin forced his horse on, and it barged into the slave-driver. 'You try to hurt her again,' Baldwin said, 'and I'll kill you!'

She stood, leaning on the haft of her spade wearily. 'Sir, I cannot. As I told you, I am Muslim. I cannot betray my faith.'

Even as she spoke, the overseer darted round Baldwin's horse and the whip cracked.

Baldwin didn't hesitate. His sword flashed, and he thrust it into the man's throat. There was a sudden gout of blood, and the man fell back, both hands clutching at his neck as if trying to stem the flow.

'No!' Lucia cried as he collapsed on the ground.

'I will allow no man to hurt you again,' Baldwin said. He was looking about him at the other slave-masters. One had already cast aside his whip and was fleeing, back to the farm. Another stood gaping, but made no threatening gestures.

'Lady Maria will hear of this! She will have me killed!' Lucia wailed.

'I offered you my hand,' Baldwin repeated steadfastly. 'Come, Lucia, ride with me. It's many leagues to Acre, and I do not think you can walk it.'

Ivo sat in his garden as the sun sank, sipping wine and thinking about the Marshal's words. Sir Geoffrey had been deeply moved. Perhaps he felt guilt for escaping when he had. Just as Ivo felt the guilt of being absent when his wife and son needed him most.

He drank. Wine dulled the pain.

The knock at the door made him start. Pietro was in his little chamber near the gate, and he rose, complaining loudly as usual, and went to the door. And then, to Ivo's surprise, Baldwin walked in, carrying a young woman in his arms.

'I am sorry if this causes trouble,' he said, standing in the doorway. 'But I couldn't leave her to suffer. Not like this.'

Ivo nodded, and stood aside to let the young man pass. But somehow, as he watched Baldwin walk through his little garden, the image was strangely familiar. And then he understood: in his dreams he had seen himself, just like Baldwin, carrying his wife and child, bearing them to safety from the flames of Tripoli.

At least Baldwin had been able to save his woman, he thought, and his eyes fogged with tears.

CHAPTER FIFTY-FOUR

Baldwin woke late that morning, and arched his back as he stretched. In the past months he had slept on the roof, but with the recent rains he had taken Ivo's advice and now slept in this comfortable chamber.

He would never have thought to live in such luxury. Soft linens made his bed, and even though others said it was chill at night, for him, used to the miserable damp and cold of a Devon winter, it was balmy and delightful.

Rising, he pulled a tunic over his nakedness, and made his way to the chamber where Ivo had installed Lucia. Her room was empty, and for a moment his heart fell, as though finding her again had been nothing more than a dream. Surely she had not left in the night to return to Lady Maria? But then he saw that her bed had been slept in, and there were blood spots on the sheet where her scabs had wept overnight.

The memory of the overseer taking his whip to her made Baldwin grit his teeth. Hearing a sound, he walked through into the garden and his rage disappeared at the sight of her sitting on a bench near the front door.

'I like these moments,' he said.

'I am sorry?' she asked, starting to her feet.

He waved her back down. 'Before the full heat of the sun. I like this time, when the breeze is cool, and the air is still gentle. It is the best time of the day.'

'Yes,' she said.

He sat beside her. She was painfully beautiful, he thought, as she averted her gaze. She wore a simple shift of linen, and while she had tried to bind her hair decorously behind her head, the lack of hood or veil made her anxious, made her feel wanton and shameful.

'You are troubled,' he said quietly.

'What should I do? I am a runaway slave! If she catches me . . .'

'You are safe here,' he said reassuringly.

'My Lady Maria may not see the affair in so clear a light.'

'It doesn't matter. You're free, and here, and that is all I care about.'

She closed her eyes, but the tears forced their way past. She would like to believe him, but she could still see the Kurd leaning over her. She was not meant for happiness. 'You don't understand. She is powerful – here, and elsewhere in the land. If she decides to have me killed, I will die. If she decides to see you dead, you will die.'

'I am not so easy to kill.'

'Please! You saved my life. But now, if I remain, your life will be endangered.'

'Let it be. I shall defend us both,' Baldwin said. 'This house is guarded, and Ivo and I are both trained in the use of weapons. Even if someone wanted to attack us, they would think twice because we are friends to the Templars.'

She nodded, miserable.

He was persuaded to promote his offer of marriage. 'If you wished to be safe and demonstrate that you cannot be a slave, you could—'

'No. I will not renounce my faith. I am a Muslim. I believe in Islam. I cannot change my beliefs for a temporary convenience.'

He wanted to persuade her, to show her that the only True Faith was his own – that of following Christ – but he didn't know how.

'I would marry you if I could,' he said at last.

'I know. And I am grateful.'

He smiled and moved to kiss her. Her horrified expression startled him. 'Why? What is it?'

'Do not do that, I beg!' she said, but her voice was full of suppressed rage rather than offended pride. She could not escape the picture in her mind of the Kurd, the feel of his hands on her, the rasping, sour breath.

Baldwin was hurt. Her reaction convinced him that she did not love him as he loved her, and he stood at once and walked away. She was the same as Sibilla, he thought bitterly. He had thrown away everything for her in England – home, prospects, everything – and come here to fight in the Holy Land, and now God mocked him by causing him to fall in love with another woman who did not want him.

God did not mean him to be happy with a woman. Instead, he would remain here and fight for the Holy Land as he had originally planned, and if he lived, he would find a small, quiet space far from all women, and forget about them.

He kicked at a rock and sent it flying. He would never love again.

CHAPTER FIFTY-FIVE

Grand Master de Beaujeu took off his habit and donned his mail and tunic. He would not walk through the streets without protection and weapons. His squires bustled about, pulling on his mail hosen, his thick felted undershirt, then the coat of mail. He had a tight-fitting, padded cap under his coif, and over all went his Templar mantle. In preference to the usual pot helmet, he chose a cap with nose-protection.

When he was dressed and armed, he walked from his chamber and met Geoffrey de Vendac and four knights in the yard.

'So, Grand Master, we try again,' the Marshal said.

'If we can't get the decision we need, I will leave the city and the Commune within to their fate,' Guillaume de Beaujeu growled. 'I will not tolerate the jeers of ignorant commoners again.'

'If it is your wish, Grand Master.'

'In God's name, I would rather surrender myself than see a single drop of blood fall from these miserable citizens, no matter how ungrateful they are!'

300

He strode through the Temple's gate and up St Anne's Street to the castle. People in the roadway paused to watch as the Templars marched past, but at least this time there were no cat-calls, as there had been before. Such insults were hard to endure for men born to pride. But many citizens thought them greedy, lazy men who sheltered in their Temple without a care for the rest of the city. Some said that if the Templars could, they would flee the city before the army of al-Ashraf Khalil arrived. Anyone who thought sensibly about it would remember that the Templars had a tunnel connecting their fortress to the docks. They had no need to conceal their movements: they could go whenever they wanted.

But Templars existed to defend pilgrims to Jerusalem and the Holy Land. They would not lightly throw away their God-given duty.

Guillaume de Beaujeu did not look to left or to right when he reached the castle, but continued on inside, his men behind him like the outline of an arrowhead.

The Commune was gathered, and as he took his position, he glanced at Mainboeuf. The man rejected the notion of Acre's peril. Was it because he was a fool and could not see the danger? Perhaps so. He was a merchant, after all, a man who would commit usury to advance himself. The Templar held such beings in contempt.

'I have come again to demand that the city prepares for siege,' he began.

The jeers erupted almost instantly. One voice cut through the rest and Sir Guillaume heard the words clearly over the hubbub.

'He's still determined to see us waste our time and money. He demanded that we send Christians to die in Cairo – then that we should pay for our lives. What happened? Nothing!'

'The son of Qalawun has gathered the greatest army ever seen in Outremer. It is reckoned to be two hundred and fifty thousand strong,' Guillaume said without responding to the noise. 'He has been building siege machines for months and has more than a hundred of them, all different sizes, to attack our walls. He has more miners than we have men inside our city. We should send away all those who cannot fight. We have ships – let our weaker citizens be withdrawn to safety, leaving only the strong and healthy.'

'Sir Guillaume,' Otto de Grandison said with his accented French, 'I am sure that you argue from conviction, but many will wonder why your warnings have not come to pass. You spoke of these threats last year.'

'As you know, Sir Otto, no army would have marched through the winter. It would be a guarantee of failure to attempt it. The army has been camped outside Cairo while the machines were prepared. Soon they will march. This is our last chance! We have weeks, no more, in which to prepare.'

'The city is as prepared as we need,' Philip Mainboeuf stated. He lifted his hands to the heavens as if in despair. 'We have the most powerful defences of any city in the whole of Outremer.'

'The strongest fortress will fail if miners dig beneath walls and towers,' Sir Guillaume said.

'*If* you are correct and he comes here.'

'He has stated so,' Sir Guillaume snarled. His temper was fraying at repeating the same arguments. It was demeaning for a man used to issuing commands.

'We know that there was an attempt on his life,' Philip Mainboeuf went on. 'Of course he said the things that those in his court wished to hear. It's hardly surprising! If the Devil makes work for idle hands, He is even more adept with idle generals! I say again, as I said at the last meeting, the Muslims are good

men of business. In the name of God, surely we should capital-
ise on our strengths? We all want trade, Christians and Muslims
alike. So let's discuss trade.'

'The army will march to us soon,' Sir Guillaume said. He
felt an overwhelming despair. His powers of persuasion were
inadequate, and he knew he was failing. 'At least evacuate the
women and those too old to fight.'

'What, lose the solace of our wives and children?' Mainboeuf said. 'And, worse, leave them unprotected in a dangerous
land? I would never do that to my family. However, I do have a
suggestion to make. Constable? May I speak of another option?'

Constable Amalric nodded.

'I believe we are in no danger. The Grand Master thinks we
are. I propose that we send another embassy to Cairo. Hopefully it will calm the Grand Master's fears if we can gain
assurances of al-Khalil's good intentions.'

'Whom would you send?' Constable Amalric asked.

'A Templar, an Hospitaller, a layman who is competent in
Arabic, and a clerk or two.'

'Can you speak Arabic?' Sir Guillaume asked.

'Yes, and I would be happy to volunteer.'

And so it was decided. Sir Guillaume nodded. 'I will supply
a knight, if my friend from the Hospital will do the same.'

Later, as he left the meeting, Sir Guillaume felt a grim satisfaction. If Mainboeuf was proved wrong, at least he would not
have to argue with him any more.

Baldwin left the meeting believing that the Templar was right.
His own journey to Cairo had convinced him that the army of
Sultan al-Ashraf was a very real threat, and he viewed the prospect of a siege with less enthusiasm than once he had. The city
was strong, true, but there was an inexorable quality to that

army. If all those men reached the walls of Acre, they must succeed in taking the city.

He was useless here. What was the point of a man like him, who was not a squire, let alone a knight, when battle threatened? He was just another useless mouth who would deplete the stocks of food and drink when the city could scarce afford it. Better that he should leave.

It was not only the city, of course. It was the atmosphere at Ivo's house. Lucia was quiet and submissive, and Baldwin felt like grasping her and shaking her. He didn't understand, and she would not tell him what was wrong. Their religions were a bar to their marriage, but there was more to her reluctance than that. There was fear in her eyes whenever he approached her. She shivered like a cowering hound. The only creature to whom she displayed affection was Uther. It was painful to see the woman he adored every day, knowing he inspired only loathing.

'Master Baldwin, I would be grateful for a word,' Sir Otto called as people moved out of the ward.

'Of course,' Baldwin said, pushing thoughts of Lucia from his mind.

'You have been here longer than my men. I know that you are sergeant to Ivo, but one of my vintenaries has fallen prey to an unfortunate malady, and has died. I would appreciate your aid.'

'How so?'

'I would ask you to take his place.'

Baldwin felt his face break into a smile. 'Me, Sir Otto? I would be honoured!'

'Then it is decided. You will fight alongside Ivo, I trust, on the wall?' Sir Otto looked around. 'What is that noise?'

There was a sudden clamour from the gate, and when

Baldwin glanced towards it, he saw the flash of swords, and heard a scream, but then he was running, with Sir Otto following closely. All he could see was a tightly-packed group of Templars with their swords held ready over their heads.

CHAPTER FIFTY-SIX

Edgar of London had not anticipated trouble as he left the castle.

He swaggered, confident that his master was one of the most powerful men in the city. With his pacifist approach, blocking those who sought war, Philip Mainboeuf had elevated himself to the very pinnacle of the social elite in Acre, and as his standing rose so, by association, did Edgar's.

It had been a good decision to come here, he thought smugly. He had money, the best clothes he had ever owned, and his choice of women in the city – many of whom were grateful for a distraction from fears about their future. Life was good.

His mood was suddenly punctured when he saw the men pushing and jostling all about the Templars and his master; an alarm began to scream in his head.

Edgar darted forward, trying to get to Mainboeuf and pull him from the crush, but even as he did so, there was a sudden shout as the Templars drew their weapons.

Edgar's sword was already out when he reached his master. The air was full of bellowing, and a woman gave a scream at the sight of blades. Edgar didn't care – he ducked as a Venetian shipman nearby aimed a cudgel at his head, and as Edgar dropped, he stabbed upwards with his sword. He felt it sink into the man's breast, and the sailor toppled with a look of intense surprise on his face, which gave Edgar a brief flare of satisfaction before something crashed against his head, and he felt himself tumble onto the rough gravel of the roadway – and could only watch numbly as boots moved all about him. Just ahead of him, he saw the shipman he had stabbed. The man's mouth was moving, but no words were coming. At least, Edgar heard none. He remained staring, but then, too exhausted to continue, he closed his eyes.

Baldwin arrived as the crowd began to turn nasty, and it was a relief to hear Otto de Grandison bawling orders, barging his way through the men encircling the Templars, three Englishmen with him shoving people aside.

'Move away! I won't have the mob attacking unarmed men!' de Grandison roared, ignoring the fact that the Templars were standing in a group with steel glinting in the sun. None had dared approach them. Nobody had any doubts of their ability to protect themselves.

Baldwin was standing with the remaining Venetian. 'What was this about?' he demanded.

Sir Guillaume spoke through clenched teeth. 'The mob jostled us. Someone made jokes about Templar cowardice and whether we would find anyone who dared travel to Cairo.'

'I'll wager you won't go!' a man shouted.

Baldwin felt the crowd's evil mood. One man was dead, and Edgar lay unmoving before him. He didn't want any more injuries. In an instant, Baldwin grabbed the man who had spoken by the neck of his tunic, his sword resting against the fellow's throat. He had never seen a man's eyes open so wide before.

'Is there anybody else who wants to make a comment?' he snarled rhetorically. He shook his prisoner. 'Now, since you are unconvinced about the Grand Master's willingness to fight, would you offer him a challenge to single combat?'

He was wrong. Eyes *could* open wider, apparently.

'Me? I'm no knight!' the man squeaked.

'You were brave enough when you had the mob at your back!'

'He has armour and all!'

'It was your choice to insult him. If you don't apologise, I will take you to the castle's yard now, and you can fight Grand Master de Beaujeu.'

'I agree! I submit! I apologise!' the man blurted.

The tension had already dissipated. Instead of angry mutterings, Baldwin heard chuckles at the fellow's predicament. Someone imitated his high, anxious tones.

Baldwin thrust the man forward, then booted him in the backside, directing him into the crowd.

'Disperse, the lot of you. Go on – clear off!'

'Master Baldwin, I am grateful to you,' Sir Guillaume said as the people moved away, and he and his men felt safe enough to put up their swords. 'What is happening to the world, when a mob will take it upon themselves to attack Templars?'

Baldwin nodded. But there had been two groups in the crowd. Now the remaining Venetian was rising from the side of his dead comrade, scowling at Mainboeuf. Baldwin jabbed his sword out before he could move towards the merchant. 'Why did you attack him?' he demanded, his sword almost touching the man's throat. The man's face was familiar, but he couldn't think how he knew him.

'He sent the Genoese after my ship! You were there – you were on my ship when his men attacked us and killed half my crew! I had to sail to Venice to make good the damage he caused my ship, and only returned two days ago.'

'That was not Master Mainboeuf, it was a man called Buscarel,' Baldwin said. 'I know him.'

'Buscarel was the shipmaster, but this piece of shit *told* Buscarel to attack my ship. You ask him! See how his eyes shift? He knows it's true!'

'If he did, that was out to sea,' Sir Otto said. 'Whatever happened out there has no force on land. You have broken the law in trying to kill him here. Murder on the streets is not permitted.' He motioned to the three men-at-arms who were with him, and two moved towards the Venetian, kicking his knife away and grabbing him by the arms.

'What of justice for me?' the Venetian declared wildly. 'That man tried to ruin me, he had many of my crew killed, and now what?'

Sir Otto shrugged and jerked his head. 'Take him to the gaol and meet me back here,' he said. 'So, vintenary, I am impressed with your turn of speed.'

Baldwin was only half-listening as he studied the figure on the ground. 'I know this man,' he said.

Philip Mainboeuf peered down too, saying, 'He is Edgar of London, my Master of Defence. I was expecting to take him with me to Cairo. What will I do now? It is extremely disappointing.'

'It would have been worse if he had not saved your life,' Sir Otto pointed out. 'He is your man. You will need to have him taken to your home to be nursed.'

'How will I protect myself on the way?' Mainboeuf snapped grumpily. 'The man's a fool, he doesn't deserve to be nursed.'

Baldwin stared in disbelief. 'This fellow was injured saving your life!'

'And by failing to guard himself, the fool's left me without protection. Ach!' The merchant looked about him and seeing a scruffy urchin nearby, commanded him to go and fetch two strong men from the house, and a cart or some other means of transporting the body. 'And be quick if you want payment for your effort,' he called as the boy scuttled away.

Baldwin watched Mainboeuf walk away. 'What will happen to the Venetian?' he asked Sir Otto.

Sir Otto considered. 'I trust he will pay a fine for breaking the peace, and then be released. That is what I would do. We cannot afford to lose a single man from the city.'

'So you do not think that Master Mainboeuf will succeed?'

'With the embassy to the Sultan? In God's name, no! The embassy is doomed. The preparations are too advanced, from the information which the good Grand Master has gleaned. They will never have an opportunity to fight like this again – not with so many warriors, if the reports are true.'

'So what do we do now?'

'Practise with our weapons, Master Baldwin, see to the defences, gather food, and put our trust in God.'

Abu al-Fida rose from his devotions and walked out into the sun. Kerak had been a good staging-post. Now, he was happy to know that his time here was at an end. Orders had been received, and his machine was to go to Acre.

His clerk and servants were outside, all packed and ready, and he took the reins of his horse and mounted. It was a beautiful day, dry and hot, but with the edge of heat taken away by the remaining cool of winter. A time of year he had always enjoyed, before the unendurable heat started again in the late spring.

The small mare was frisky, and he patted her neck as he looked back over the immense wagon train stretching past Kerak and into the distance, and then trotted to the head of the column and waved his arm in the signal to advance.

Behind him he heard commands bellowed along the line. There was a creaking and squeaking of leather harnesses as oxen strained, and the jingle of chains and mail, and the complaining lowing of cattle and whickering of horses as the first wagons began to lumber forward. More cracks of whips, and shrieked urgings from drivers, while the camels and oxen slowly moved off.

Abu al-Fida stopped at the outskirts of the city's territory and watched on his mare while the train rolled slowly past, raising clouds of sand and dust. He had an emptiness in his soul. His son should have been here to see this – but then if he had, Abu al-Fida knew he would not have left his comfortable life as a merchant, would not have been forced from his home by those murderous Frank crusaders, would not have travelled to Cairo to demand justice from the Sultan, and would not have been sent to build al-Mansour. He would not have been created Emir and placed in charge of a force to bear his weapon to Acre.

His son would have been proud to see his father in this position. Usmar had always been devoted to Islam, and ridding the land of the rapacious Franks had always been close to his heart. It grieved him that Acre sucked in the best merchandise, and that the markets there had always paid the best, but such was the case. That was why Abu al-Fida had lived in Acre. And because of that, his family had died.

An inevitable chain of consequences had brought Abu al-Fida to this place, to this position, and would inevitably lead to the destruction of the city.

The wagon train was slow. Oxen moved more ponderously than horses, but their strength was vital. No other creature could haul such loads. As it was, it would be a laborious undertaking to have the machine transported to Acre. In this wet, early springtime, it would take a month to travel as far as another caravan could go in a week. But that meant nothing. For Abu al-Fida, all that mattered was that he should reach that city and set up his machine. Al-Mansour would be one amongst many, but her immense power would do more damage than all the other hundred mangonels and catapults together.

All he need do was get the machine to Acre. And perhaps then, he could lay the ghost of poor Usmar to rest at last.

CHAPTER FIFTY-SEVEN

Edgar slept badly.

When he woke, he remembered waking in the middle of the night and being sick, and as he recalled it so he smelled the vomit all about him.

He rose blearily, and almost fell trying to cross his floor. It was like being drunk. He grabbed for the wall, standing and panting, and his legs felt like jelly. A fresh wave of nausea washed over and through him, and he closed his eyes, feeling that strange spinning sensation again.

There was a chair near the window, where his sword and belt had been set to rest, and he lurched across the room to it, clumsily knocking his sword to the floor.

The door was flung open, and a house servant entered, wrinkling his nose at the smell.

'Water!' Edgar managed. 'Poison . . .'

'You're not poisoned, just hit on the head. You're lucky. The master would've left you there to die in the street. As it was, we had to bring you here. You'll have fun cleaning this little lot up,' he added, staring at the vomit-soaked sheets.

Edgar closed his mouth, his head loose on his shoulders. 'What?'

A vague recollection came to him of the street outside the castle. There were two men, and one tried to club him . . . the Templars . . . then he recalled the man slumping with Edgar's sword in his belly, his eyes dulling – and then someone else had hammered Edgar. He desperately wanted to sleep, but something told him it would not be safe. 'Fetch me water,' he said imperiously. 'Now.'

'Don't order me about, you English turd. Fetch it yourself. As soon as you're well, you're leaving. Master said he didn't want to see you again, so you're to go. Now you be nice to me, or you'll be out all the sooner. And that means after you've cleaned up after yourself.'

'*Fetch me water*,' Edgar repeated, and at last the servant nodded and left him.

Edgar studied the chamber and saw he had been sick all over the sheets and himself. He was disgusted: he had never spewed that much, even when he was deeply sunk in ale or wine. In fact, he reckoned he was fortunate not to have drowned in his own vomit. He rubbed at his breast. The acid was still in his mouth, but no less painful was the pounding at his head.

The servant returned carrying a plain earthenware beaker which he set on the floor near Edgar, who took it up and drank cautiously. In London he had seen an apprentice after a fight, who had drunk too swiftly, and then brought it up as speedily. Edgar had no wish to be sick again. Every muscle on his torso felt strained; merely breathing was painful.

'You say I must go?' he asked hoarsely.

'Master said so.'

'Where is he? I must speak with him.'

'He's not here. He left for Cairo. Have you forgotten already?' the man sneered.

Edgar made a show of setting the beaker on the floor, then his head lolled.

The servant eyed him warily, but after a few moments, with Edgar's breath snoring, he reached towards the purse on the sick man's belt.

Edgar's hand whipped out, fast as a snake's, and he pulled the servant towards him. 'Try that again, and you'll lose your hand,' he whispered.

Baldwin had not slept well after the attempt upon the Templars. The sight of men drawing swords in the street had been disturbing, when all in Acre should have been pulling together. Perhaps the mob was right. Maybe Mainboeuf *would* negotiate a fresh peace treaty. It would be interesting to see the response from Cairo.

The city of Acre had been on tenterhooks since Baldwin's arrival last year, and to think that the situation was as dangerous as ever was disquieting. The populace was a seething cauldron of fear and alarm; if there were no firm response from Cairo, men could no longer continue to pretend that there was nothing to fear. In many ways, it would be better to have a resolute declaration of war and the intention to destroy Acre, as the Grand Master believed, than to have another period of unreliable peace.

Mainboeuf would be well on his way to Cairo now. Baldwin hoped he would hurry back.

At that moment, he saw a white tunic and recognised Jacques d'Ivry.

'I hope God holds you in His blessing,' Jacques said, a kindly smile softening his face.

'Sir Jacques, I am glad to see you,' Baldwin said. 'I was thinking of the embassy to Cairo, and any distraction would be of great service.'

'Yes, I understand how you must feel,' Jacques said. He looked towards the south, as though his eyes could pierce the walls of the houses and city, and see beyond them, all the way to the great city so far away. 'But there are many things still to be done in the city.'

Baldwin groaned aloud. 'What more? I've moved rocks and rubble; I have learned the mason's arts; I have constructed two catapults and helped repair two more. My arms ache, my back is almost broken, and now I have to take on *more* duties?'

'You will find as you grow older, that it is good to be occupied,' Jacques chuckled. 'There is nothing better, in fact. That is why Templars and members of my Order are commanded to work. When a man is idle, his mind and hands may turn to less productive efforts. So if ever we are bored, with nothing to do, we are instructed to carve tent-pegs.'

'You think I should resort to that?' Baldwin asked indignantly.

'I think you perhaps could find more suitable occupation,' Sir Jacques grinned.

They had crossed beneath the inner wall from Montmusart into the old city, and now the two turned towards the castle. Ahead they saw a lurching man.

'I know him,' Baldwin said. 'He is guard to Master Mainboeuf. Master Edgar?' he called. 'I hope I see you well?'

It was obvious that Edgar was far from well. His face was pale, and he moved with a slower gait than before.

'Master Edgar?' Sir Jacques prompted.

Edgar looked as though he did not recognise either of them. He stared at Baldwin with a confused frown, head set to one side. And then he began to sway.

'Let us take him with us,' Jacques said, and the two put their arms beneath his armpits and helped him towards the Mainboeuf house. 'We shall see him home. He should remain there until he is well.'

'He was hit on the head yesterday,' Baldwin said.

'So I should imagine. It has left him disordered. He should rest.'

'Why aren't you at home, man? You shouldn't be out and about,' Baldwin said.

'Thrown out,' Edgar mumbled.

They had reached the Mainboeuf house, and Sir Jacques rapped sharply on the door. There was a grumbled comment from the doorkeeper's lodge, and then a face appeared at a grating. 'Yes?'

Baldwin listened to the conversation while he held Edgar against the wall to stop him falling. It was clear that the doorman would not allow the injured man back inside. 'It's what the master told us when he left.'

'What shall we do with him?' Sir Jacques wondered as the door to the grating slammed shut once more.

'Help me take him to Ivo's house,' Baldwin said. 'At least there I can have him looked after by Lucia.'

'How is Lucia?'

Baldwin was reluctant to answer, but it was hard to ignore the Leper Knight. Rudeness to him was unthinkable.

'She is well enough,' he mumbled.

Sir Jacques cast an eye over him. 'She has been a slave for many years, my friend. Do not be downcast if she takes time to realise she is free. Rather, look on it as your duty to win her

317

over. If you give her the comfort and affection she craves, you will succeed.'

'She is devoted to her faith. She won't consider marriage,' Baldwin said.

Sir Jacques looked at him sadly. 'You would marry her?'

'Yes.'

'I have known many Muslims, my friend. Some were good, some were bad, just like we Christians. But few were so dishonourable as to change their faith to ours.'

'Dishon—! But to change from a false religion to accept the True Faith, that would be an act of . . .'

'Bad faith. You remember, I told you of the Templars at Safed?'

'The castle where they accepted death?'

'Yes. They refused to cast aside their religion just because Baibars threatened them with death. Why should you expect an honourable Muslim to do otherwise? Do you think Lucia would be any less strong in her faith?'

'I can have no hope she might change?'

'You must pray to God, to ask that He too speaks with her. Ask the Blessed Virgin to enter her, and show her the path of truth and honesty. With time, perhaps, you will win her over to Christ by demonstrations of humility and integrity. All I say is, you cannot expect her to give up her past life, and the faith that supported her through her slavery, in a day or even a month.'

'I suppose so,' Baldwin agreed without enthusiasm.

'But for now, what we need to do is bring this man to a bed. Here is your house, I think?'

Baldwin knocked and called for Pietro, and soon they had Edgar lying on a couch in a chamber at the rear of the house. 'Pietro, can you wash him and clean his clothes?' Baldwin said with his nose wrinkled. 'He smells like he's been living in a sty for weeks.'

CHAPTER FIFTY-EIGHT

In the Genoese quarter Buscarel was worried about the possible siege. His wife Cecilia kept to the house as much as possible, fretful about their fate.

It was the same matter that exercised the Council.

In every city where Genoa had a trading presence, an admiral would congregate a small council of traders of standing to discuss how best to achieve greater prominence for Genoa's interests. Today they met over a meal seated about a table in Admiral Zaccaria's house.

'Gentlemen!' Admiral Zaccaria said, when the Council members were all present. He was a short man with a body like old oak, brown and hard, and as he lifted his glass to them in a silent toast, the gold on his fingers and about his neck glinted. 'We are living in difficult times. We all know the situation: war approaches. What should we do?'

'There is only one course open to us,' Grimaldi said. At three and thirty, he was nearer Buscarel's age than the Admiral's, although his belly was larger, and he had taken to the customs of the East more than any of the other Genoese of the quarter. 'If the city is attacked, we have no place here. We should emulate the Venetians and take to our ships.'

'No, I do not agree.' Buscarel stood and leaned on the table, meeting the eyes of each in turn. 'If we depart, we leave the city to others, and we cannot share in any triumph.'

'Triumph?' Grimaldi laughed, but with incredulity plastered on his face. He cast a hand about the others present. 'How many of us anticipate a triumph if there is outright war with al-Ashraf?'

'He has no navy,' Buscarel said immediately. 'If our ships bring supplies, the Muslims must fail. The worst enemy of any army is stagnation and disease. If they remain outside our walls in a protracted siege, they will grow indolent, and then disease must strike, just as all previous armies have learned. They will go, and once they have gone, Acre will be stronger than ever before. Just think of the glory in our status then.'

Buscarel had known Grimaldi would be the hardest man to persuade. He was all for an easy life, while Buscarel was happy to take risks if it meant greater profits.

'Acre would be the jewel of the East – *our* East!' he went on. 'For Venice is known for her cowardice in the face of the Muslims. Look at their actions in Tripoli two years ago. They took all they could, and fled. It was the sight of their ships leaving the harbour that persuaded Qalawun he could storm the city. They will do the same here – they have no belly for a fight. When they leave, we shall be here to bring supplies and maintain the city. And then we shall reap the rewards, too.'

'Rewards? Our likely rewards will be death by a Muslim sword,' Grimaldi scoffed. 'No, I say that when the army comes

– and it will, my friends, it will – then we should be prepared to depart. There is no profit in being slaughtered.'

'There is no profit in running away, either,' Buscarel said. He curled his lip, staring full at the Admiral. If Zaccaria was with him, all the others would follow, with or without Grimaldi. And Zaccaria would not want to take the coward's way out. 'We are Genoese. We know that to get rich, we need to take risks. Would our children feel pride in their fathers and their city, were they to learn that we had fled?'

'This is not a question of pride, Buscarel. This is simple business,' Grimaldi said. 'We are here to make money, nothing else. If the Muslims destroy the city, our reason for being here has gone.'

'What do *you* say?' Buscarel asked of the other men at the table.

Zaccaria sucked at his teeth, then took a long draught of wine. 'This is a matter of money. If we stay, do we make more money, or less? I suspect we would make less.'

'But think of the future. If there is no Acre, what will we lose in the traffic of pilgrims and crusaders across the Mediterranean? The losses would be enormous.' Buscarel was startled that Zaccaria could go against him in this. Surely the Admiral could see that the world would view a flight of Genoese ships as a matter of betrayal. 'We would be looked upon as traitors to the Christian faith, were we to run before heathens. If our action cost us Acre, how would others view us?'

'How would they view us if we remained to be slaughtered, like the poor city-folk of Tripoli?' Grimaldi said heavily. 'For me, there is no choice. To remain would be folly. I say we conclude as much business as possible, and when the time comes, as it must, we return home.'

'This *is* my home!' Buscarel declared.

His vehemence surprised even himself. Others looked on this city as a trading post, he knew – just one of a number of little colonies strung about the seas for the benefit of Genoa. But to him it was much more. He had founded his family here, perhaps even begun a dynasty to rival the Luchettos and Zaccarias. But the Council were taking away his dreams.

'Can you not see that your home is to be brought down over your head?' Grimaldi demanded. 'Don't be a fool!'

'I would rather die here than run and live as a coward,' Buscarel said. He looked at the faces about the table. They were all decided. Not one looked up and met his gaze.

'So be it,' he said.

Pietro hurried by with an anxious expression on his face, and Lucia was intrigued, despite her inner desperation. He had been carrying a basket, and his face looked as though he wished he were not.

She had been working on her clothing, trying to mend a long rent in the skirts with needle and thread, but no matter what she tried, the material was so worn and frayed, the thread slipped through the fabric. She needed a new tunic, if she was to appear in public without embarrassment.

Again, Pietro scurried past like a rabbit with the hound behind, and she was tempted to laugh aloud at his earnest, fretful demeanour. 'What is it?' she called, but he was gone.

With a sigh, she set the needle by the ball of thread, and went to see what was troubling him so. Pietro had been a surly old man since the moment he had set eyes on her, but she wasn't afraid of him. Sullen looks couldn't scare her, when she was used to whips. She saw him slip into a chamber that had been used for storage. This intrigued her, and she followed without trying to conceal her interest.

The chamber was set into the southern wall of the house, parallel with the old city wall, and was sparsely furnished. There was a palliasse on the floor now, and as she craned her neck round the doorframe, she saw a naked man lying on it while Pietro washed him with water. A pot of scented oil stood nearby, the odour fighting valiantly, if unsuccessfully, against the stench of vomit.

She recognised Edgar from the day of the riot. 'What is *he* doing here?' she asked.

'Eh? Oh, it's you. Master Baldwin brought him here,' Pietro said. 'You remember him?'

'Yes – but what has happened to him?'

Pietro told her the little that he had gathered from Baldwin and Sir Jacques, and she crouched at Edgar's side. 'He has a fever,' she said, resting a hand on his forehead.

'Aye. I could have told you that,' Pietro said, as though infuriated with her for stating the obvious while he was doing all he could to help the man.

'You have enough to do. Let me see to him,' she said.

'I can do it,' he protested, but without his usual stubbornness. He reached to the bucket, dipping the cloth in the water.

She placed her hand on his. 'I have nothing else to do,' she said quietly. She made no move, but sat back on her haunches, staring at him, her hand still on his. 'Please.'

He glanced up and caught the full impact of her sad eyes. 'Oh, very well,' he declared. He passed her the damp scrap of linen with which he had been mopping Edgar's brow, and levered himself upright with an effort. 'Call me if you need anything. Poor devil has been badly knocked about. Someone's tried to break his head, I think.'

She nodded, reaching forward and wetting the material again, wringing it out and placing it gently on Edgar's forehead. He moaned quietly as she did so, and she felt her heart move to think that the man who had helped to save her that day might be in danger of his life.

'You are safe here,' she promised in a whisper. 'Be strong.'

CHAPTER FIFTY-NINE

It was a week since Philip Mainboeuf had set off with Brother Bartholomew and a Hospitaller, along with their servants and a clerk.

Baldwin hoped their mission would succeed, but the more he thought about it, the less sanguine he became. Fortunately, he had enough to occupy him with the twenty men of his command. It was a daunting prospect when he was first thrust in the midst of them. Ivo had gone with him on the first day, either to see to it that Baldwin was safe as he was introduced, or to give himself a laugh; Baldwin was not sure which.

There was a heavy-set, bullish man with a shock of black hair, who went by the name of Hob Atte Mull, and two skinnier, shorter men, with fairer features and paler hair, who were brothers called Thomas and Anselm. A very short, suspicious-looking fellow called Nicholas Hunfrey was the last of the competent fellows. The rest looked confused about every aspect of their duties. They had been gathered together from dribs and drabs of pilgrims and shipmen about the city, and few appeared even to have held a sword before.

'They look like outlaws,' Ivo grunted on seeing them, and Baldwin concurred.

'I only hope that they are a little more reliable.'

'Well, Master Vintenary, that's up to you to ensure, isn't it?' Ivo said with an evil grin.

Hob Atte Mull stood, hawked and spat, studying Baldwin closely and without apparent satisfaction. 'So, Vintenary, what battles have you fought in? Have you always been in the thick of it with the foot soldiers, or cowering away on a horse?'

'I've been in battles at sea and on land,' Baldwin said haughtily.

'Oh aye. Which? Did they merit a name?'

Ignoring him, Baldwin addressed them all.

'Have you seen to your weapons yet?' he asked.

He saw the men glance at each other. There was no joy in their looks. The one called Nicholas Hunfrey pulled a grimace and shook his head, saying nothing, but staring down at the ground. The others began to make a show of chatting amongst themselves.

It was infuriating. A leader needed to lead and show that he was in charge, but just now he could think of nothing else to do, short of demanding that the men pick up their weapons to show him they were clean.

Ivo snorted and walked to his side, looking at each man in turn. 'I think you'll need to ask Sir Otto whether any of them has fought before. Not one of them has any skill with a sword, I'd reckon.'

Hob glanced at him with amusement in his sneering face.

'They won't practise, anyway,' Ivo went on calmly. 'They don't want to show themselves up in front of you.' He pulled his own sword free. 'Very well. I haven't had a test of swords-manship in days. Are you ready?'

Baldwin nodded, drawing his own sword, wondering why Ivo had lied. It was scarcely a day since his last trial with their Saracen teacher.

Ivo drew his sword up into the two-handed guard so favoured by recent visitors to Acre, while Baldwin held his own sword in the outside guard, his right fist gripping the hilt at waist height, the point crossing before his body, tip raised slightly.

There was a flash as Ivo's sword descended. Baldwin blocked his blade and twisted his own blade, but couldn't snatch Ivo's away. Ivo's came back again, and Baldwin knocked it down and away, before launching his own swift assault. Ivo managed to slip away, giving ground, and Baldwin moved forward to harry him, the two swords flashing in the sunlight.

It was curious. Baldwin was pressing moderately hard, and while Ivo would normally defend himself vigorously and then lash out with some startling surprise attacks, today he didn't. Perhaps he was tired, Baldwin thought. He kept his eyes fixed on Ivo's, waiting to see if his master would try to alarm him soon, but there was nothing obvious at first. Not until he saw Ivo's eyes quickly narrow. Then Baldwin was sure he was about to launch a new approach.

Ivo moved his feet, and then, as Baldwin stabbed at empty space, he was whirling, spinning, ready to sweep his sword round at Baldwin's head. But Baldwin knew that move already. It was the first Jacques had shown him, and he blocked it swiftly, returning his own blade to Ivo's, and with a competent flick of his wrist, sent Ivo's away to safety, while Baldwin's rested on Ivo's breast.

'I missed my mark,' Ivo groused. 'That was too easy for you.'

327

Baldwin smiled. But he saw that the vintaine were eyeing him with an increased respect. It was only later, when Ivo walked away and Baldwin caught a glimpse of his grin, swiftly concealed, that he understood.

'You crafty old sodomite!'

Baldwin left his men after a day's hard training, and made his way homewards along the alley that led to the postern near the castle. It was a useful short cut, although it was a narrow, twisting way. Still, Baldwin was confident that his own ferocity was adequate to deter thieves and cutpurses. The day had gone well. The men were beginning to work as a team, rather than a disparate bunch of felons, and Baldwin was just congratulating himself on the way that they were learning their trade, when an arm slipped about his neck and a dagger touched the skin under his ear.

'I have no money,' he said.

'I know that.'

Baldwin felt his face harden at the voice. 'You want my ring again?'

'No.'

Suddenly the knife was away from his throat, and he was pushed away. He turned.

'Remember, Master. I could have killed you.'

'Well? Why didn't you?'

Buscarel was silent a while. In truth he found it hard to answer. 'We need all the men we have. I am Genoese, but this is my city. My family lives here. I wouldn't see the city weakened.'

'So?'

'Lady Maria told me to kill you. I could have done so just then. But I won't kill you, nor take your ring.'

'Good.'

'Why did she want you dead?'

'I have her maid. I suppose she is angry.'

'No. I think it is more than that. Her lands are all she has. If the Sultan takes all this,' Buscarel said, waving a hand, 'she will lose everything. So she seeks to remain a friend of the Sultan.'

'How so?'

'It's said the Templars have a spy in the Sultan's court. Wouldn't he have the same?'

Baldwin gave a dry chuckle. 'That, I think, was Philip Mainboeuf. He was the spy.'

'Really? Then he is safe.'

'Yes,' Baldwin said. And those words would come back to him later.

CHAPTER SIXTY

Edgar woke again that evening. He felt muzzy, distressed to find himself in a strange room, lying on an old palliasse that seemed to have more broken straws sticking into his back than a stook. He would give much for a good English palliasse.

Then his eyes snapped wide as he recalled his last interview with Philip Mainboeuf's household. He had been thrown out like a beggar. If he saw that steward in a dark alley, he'd take a stick to the man's head. God's blood, but the fellow evicted him when he had been injured in the service of their master. When Mainboeuf got back . . .

That was the point, he recalled. There was no telling when, or whether, Mainboeuf would return. It was a dangerous journey, especially now, with the rumours of war apparently justified. Edgar groaned. The thought of having to start again from scratch appalled him. For the last months he had worked hard, ensuring that his master was safe, and reaping the rewards. He had enjoyed expensive clothes, decent food and other luxuries he had only dreamed of before. He wanted them again.

He sat up and gasped, pain lancing through his skull. A hand to his head, he slowly sank back to the palliasse, and moaned.

A light step, and then a soft rustling of material at his side, and when he opened his eyes, he found himself staring up at Lucia's face.

'How are you?' she asked.

'I feel considerably better at this moment,' he croaked. 'I know you – you are the woman we rescued from the mob.'

'Yes. Your head was broken.'

'Someone didn't like me,' Edgar agreed. 'I think it was the way I stabbed his friend.'

'You killed him?'

Edgar shrugged. 'He was attacking my master. I had to stop him. His companion did this to me.'

'You must rest.'

'I should be going,' Edgar said, but without conviction. The thought of rising made the nausea return. He felt sick at the mere thought of walking.

'You can go nowhere today. It is late, and if you try to walk the streets, you will be prey to any cut-purse. You must sleep here tonight.'

'If you are sure,' he said with a relieved grunt. He let his head gently down on the pillow, feeling her cool hands on his head. 'That is good.'

'Sleep, Master. Sleep.'

She heard his meandering thoughts and dreams, and guessed much of his story. It was sad, she thought. He was another like her. Used while the whim took his master, and then, as soon as a fault was perceived, discarded. He too was little better than a slave.

*   *   *

Baldwin was exhausted. There had been a delivery of fresh timber, and he and his men had been ordered to go and unload the great baulks of wood and move them nearer to the walls. In the absence of a great Muslim army appearing at the top of the plain before the city, there was a distinct lack of enthusiasm among his vintaine.

'Come on, haul!' Baldwin bellowed. He eyed his dog with jealousy. Uther lay panting in the shade of an awning while he and the vintaine worked and sweated.

Hob and Anselm pulled with Baldwin on ropes near the head of the horse, while others pushed from the back of the cart as they manhandled the timbers up the hill towards the castle. It was hard, hot work in the rising humidity.

'Be grateful it's not full summer yet,' Baldwin snarled when Thomas complained that the day was too hot, but he knew how they felt. It was impossible to get any citizens to help. People were living in a limbo, in which they could persuade themselves that the Muslim army would not come. Many of them believed that the embassy would be able to talk the new Sultan into agreeing to an extended peace. Where was the profit in destroying Acre, after all?

Baldwin, who could still recall that ant-hill of men outside Cairo, was unconvinced. So many men needed an occupation. He did, too. Perhaps he could become a merchant, as Sir Otto had suggested, but so often it seemed that everything he undertook came to naught. He wanted to marry Lucia, but could not; he had come all this way to help recover Jerusalem, but there was no bid to recover the Holy Land.

Baldwin had these bitter thoughts as he strained and hauled. They finally manoeuvred the cart and the sweating, panicky horse, to the top of the hill, and there they all stopped, a block under the tyres of the cart, while the horse bent to a drinking trough, and men sank to the roadway, panting and groaning to themselves.

'What's the point of a city on a hill like this?' Thomas muttered.

'Swyve me if I know,' Anselm said, wiping his brow with a scrap of shirt. He looked about him. 'Who picked it?'

'The man who didn't want to see the city washed away every time the tide came in,' Hob commented drily. 'Perhaps he was born able to use the brain in his head, unlike you lot.'

Baldwin gave them a little longer, but when all were recovered, he had them on their feet and continuing up the roadway.

At the gatehouse, they offloaded the cart, complaining non-stop, while he walked to a tavern in the shadow of the walls. There he bought two gallons of thin ale. He sent two of the men to collect the ale in jugs, and the team drank deeply, before returning the jugs to be refilled. When all twenty had slaked their thirst, he had them continue, and soon the timbers were stacked moderately neatly, without blocking the street. Then they must go back to the harbour for more. Baldwin could understand their gripes. This kind of work was more suitable for labouring peasants, rather than free men, but there were not the men available to do such work. And besides, Baldwin was all too aware of Sir Jacques' injunction to keep the men busy. It was better that they were occupied than that they sat about drinking without purpose.

He was about to follow the men, when he heard a shout from on top of the tower. Looking up, he saw a watchmen pointing urgently towards the south. Baldwin glanced at his men. Hob was watching him with a cynical look in his eye.

'Hob, get the men back to the harbour', he said. 'You begin on the next load. I'll join you shortly.'

'Oh. Right. *Shortly*,' Hob said, and spat into the road.

Baldwin felt his hackles rise at what sounded like simple insubordination. He was about to shout at the man, but before he could draw breath, Hob had turned to the rest of the men. 'So? What you lot gawping at? Think those logs are gonna get up here without help? Maybe they'll roll themselves up the hill, eh? Now get your miserable, swyving arses back down there, and fetch the next lot.'

And the men moved off, apparently content now someone had cursed them. He heard Hob damning their souls, eyes and arses as they moved off down the hill again, but by then Baldwin was already halfway up the first set of stairs to the wall. He hurried to the tower's door and climbed inside, past the machinery of a catapult, and into the hoarding. Uther followed him. The timbers were slick from the rains of the previous night, and his leather soles almost slid away, but then he caught hold of the wall, and stared out in the direction the guard had indicated.

There, in the haze, perhaps a mile along the bay, he made out a black dot. With fear stabbing at his heart, he peered behind it, then studied the lands to the east and south, searching for the line of black, for the inevitable fluttering of banners and pennons on the horizon – for dust in the air, anything indicating an army. Seeing nothing, he felt a sudden loss of tension that showed how anxious he had been.

'What is that?' he asked the guard.

'Single rider, I think, sir. Can't tell more at this distance.'

Baldwin nodded, looking about the plain. The shanty town was gone, and in its place there had been efforts to dig a trench to make assault more difficult, but the work had not proceeded efficiently. Too few thought there was a serious threat. That was down to Philip Mainboeuf and the contempt he had publicly shown for the promoters, as he saw them, of war.

334

The man on horse back was moving sluggishly, and Baldwin frowned. 'I will go and see if he needs help,' he said. 'That rider looks exhausted. He may have run out of water.'

He took his time descending the stairs, not wanting to slip, with Uther pelting down ahead. He would ask for gravel to be spread on the wood later, he decided, so that in battle the men could stand securely.

At the bottom he spoke to the porter at the gate, and found a stable where he was able to borrow a sturdy rounsey. On that, he rode out to the south with a fresh waterskin, cantering gently, Uther panting to keep up.

The man was a dark stick on the edge of the horizon when he started out, but soon he was able to discern a horse and man, and then the fact that the man had a turban wound about his head. In the midst of the turban a shining steel spike sparkled, almost blinding Baldwin.

'Friend, are you well?'

'I have travelled far.' His voice was hoarse.

Baldwin peered. 'Do you need water? I brought you some to ease your last mile.'

'I am thankful for that,' the man said. His lips were broken and scabbed from dehydration, and his eyes were so narrowed that it was apparently difficult for him to open them more than a small amount.

He was oddly familiar, and Baldwin found himself running through the various Muslims he had met, trying to jerk his memory. Nothing struck him, and he was forced to ask at last, 'I know your face, I think. Do you remember me?'

The man tipped a little water into his hand and wiped it over his face, then more over the back of his neck. 'In Cairo last year, when you were meeting with my master, the Emir al-Fakhri.'

'Of course,' Baldwin said with a smile. 'I hope your master is well? You have come from Cairo on your own? It is a weary long way for a man alone.'

'My master bade me come, and not to rest,' the man said. 'I have news for Acre.'

'It is not secret?'

'No. The embassy sent to speak with the Sultan al-Ashraf has not succeeded.'

'Not succeeded? You mean that they didn't reach Cairo?' Baldwin said. Sometimes the Bedouin would attack people, he knew, but rarely a Templar or Hospitaller. That was curious, certainly, and he was about to ask more, when the man gave a hacking cough and continued.

'No, the men reached Cairo, but the Sultan refused to see them and had them thrown into his cells.'

Baldwin felt the news as a punch in the belly. Then his shoulders sagged. He had wanted a clear and unequivocal response to the embassy, he recalled.

'So it is war, then,' he breathed.

CHAPTER SIXTY-ONE

Baldwin stood with Sir Otto as the Commune met to hear the message.

It was a quiet and attentive meeting. The representatives were gathered in a semi-circle about the Constable. Baldwin noticed that in particular. In the past there had been two groupings: on the one side the merchants and tradespeople who wanted to avoid antagonising the Muslims, and on the other the Orders. Now there appeared to be a feeling of unity in the Commune that Baldwin had not seen before.

The messenger from al-Fakhri stood anxiously before the Constable, who glowered from his throne. 'Speak.'

Al-Fakhri's servant turned to the crowd, and spoke clearly in slightly accented French.

'My master, the Emir al-Fakhri, bids you welcome. He prays that the Franks of Acre are thriving and sends his good wishes to all his friends in the city.'

'Get on with it,' the Constable snarled.

'Your messengers arrived on the Thursday before last. My

master saw them with his own eyes: one Templar, one Hospitaller, and their servants and assistants. They were arrested as soon as they entered the city, and all were refused permission to meet with the Sultan. They were taken directly to the gaol.'

'But they were emissaries travelling under promise of safe conduct!' the Grand Master of the German Order protested.

The messenger shrugged. His manner indicated that if the Sultan did not extend safe conduct, there was little security for them.

The Constable leaned back in his seat. There was a moment's absolute stillness in the chamber. High overhead, a flag flapped and cracked in the wind from the sea, and Baldwin was startled by its loudness. Birds wheeled and soared, their cries oddly plaintive, as if they were announcing the disaster to come. Baldwin reckoned all in the square felt the same wretched discouragement.

'Is there more?' the Constable asked quietly.

'My master bids you prepare your defences. The Sultan swore to bring his army here on his father's deathbed, and it was his generals who advised him to wait until after the winter rains. The rains are finished. The army marches.'

'Do you have any idea of numbers?' Guillaume de Beaujeu demanded.

'I was told sixty thousand cavalry, and one hundred and sixty thousand men-at-arms on foot.'

The Constable's jaw fell open. 'You mean the total of marching men and cavalry was one hundred and sixty thousand, surely?'

'No. The total is two hundred and twenty thousand warriors. There are more, but they are miners and masons to attack the walls.'

There was an appalled silence as the men absorbed this. Only Baldwin and Guillaume de Beaujeu were unsurprised.

'Sweet Mother of God,' a man murmured. It summed up the feeling of the men in the chamber.

'How soon will they arrive?' the Grand Master asked, bringing them back to the present dilemma. 'How long do we have?'

'They will be here in the first week of April, I think. There are many obstacles since the rains. They have more than a hundred siege engines, and the wagons for them take time to cross rivers.'

Guillaume de Beaujeu bowed to the messenger. 'I am grateful for your news. It shows what needs be done.'

The messenger looked warily at the Commune members before him, then at the Constable, who gave a motion with his hand. The messenger then bowed low, wished them all peace, and left, his eyes going from side to side as though he feared to be attacked on his way out. One man did reach for his dagger, but another put a hand on his and shook his head. There was a sense of futility, of despair beyond comprehension.

Baldwin found himself staring at the spot where the messenger had stood. In his breast he was aware of a relaxation of tension, oddly. At last the dreadful waiting was to end.

A merchant Baldwin recognised as a friend of Mainboeuf's, spoke wonderingly. 'This must surely be a mistake? The Sultan would not unnecessarily take a peace envoy, would he? Perhaps we should send a message asking the Sultan to release our friends and explain again the reason for their embassy? Maybe it was the presence of two warlike ambassadors that gave the Sultan the wrong impression? We know he detests the Orders.'

Guillaume de Beaujeu turned slowly to stare at him, and when he spoke his contempt was acid.

'Do you mean he thought we had sent an army of two knights to take his city? Are you blind to the facts? Our position is clear: we cannot negotiate. We had two options: flight – or fight to defend our city. But there is now no choice. All Christians have a sacred duty to remain here. We in the Temple know our duty.'

'The Hospital will remain with the Temple,' the Grand Master declared. 'This is the destiny of our Orders, to fight and die if need be in the service of God and the Kingdom of Jerusalem.'

'The Knights of Saint Lazarus too will fight.'

There was a moment's pause, and then the Grand Master of the German Order, Burchard von Schwanden, grunted his own assent. Baldwin thought he looked distraught, whereas the other Grand Masters were steadfast in their commitment.

The Constable nodded and looked over the remaining members of the Commune. 'The city will soon be at war. From this moment, all supplies of food must be subject to the demands of the city's defence. I wrote last year to ask for more help from our friends, and with luck we shall gain some support from there. What of the Orders? Can we hope for help?'

Guillaume de Beaujeu spoke first. 'I have hope that I can call on more knights.'

The Hospitaller nodded to de Beaujeu. 'I will order my knights to send all who may be spared.'

The only unhappy Grand Master was von Schwanden. 'My men are already involved in the Crusades in Lithuania and Poland. I do not know if I can have men here in time.'

'So, we have a thousand knights and sergeants on horse-back,' the Constable said. 'Against the Sultan's army.'

'Sir, the most important thing now is to send away all those who are no use to the defence of the city,' Jacques d'Ivry said.

Baldwin noticed that Sir Jacques appeared to feel no concern for himself, as always. His faith was so strong, it preserved him from fear.

The Constable considered. 'It will take time to arrange such a plan. We have so many thousands to evacuate.'

'We have planned for this already,' Ivo put in. 'We can begin to remove those people as early as next week.'

'Very well, I agree. Gentlemen, my Lords, we all have much to do. Any questions should be addressed to my clerk.' The Constable stood. 'Good luck, and may God go with us all.'

Turning, he made his way to a curtained doorway. Baldwin watched, and was shocked to see him stumble, clinging to the doorpost like a frail old man.

CHAPTER SIXTY-TWO

When the Genoese ships slipped their moorings and rowed into the bay, there forming up into their fleet, Buscarel was at the harbour watching, gloom filling his soul. He could have gone with them. Perhaps he should have, but the thought of deserting his city was too hard. His heart was in his throat as the first of the ships moved slowly past the Tower of Flies and out to sea, and he felt dizzy, like a man who has spent too much time in the sun. But when the third ship had gone out, suddenly all that disappeared, to be replaced by a bitter rage.

'Damn them,' he swore.

This was his home. He wouldn't run from it.

The ships unfurled their great sails, and he felt a lurch in his gut to see how the pennants fluttered. From over the sea, he heard the creaking of the cordage, the straining cracks of the timbers, as the wind caught the canvas. The sun. It was odd to think that this could be the last time he ever saw his country's fleet – because it would not return. That had been made plain.

Zaccaria had invited him to the Admiral's house. 'We cannot

get back in time to rescue people if things go badly,' he had warned him.

'There are women and children to be taken away,' Buscarel said. 'You could carry some to Cyprus.'

'We are clearing our warehouses,' Zaccaria told him. 'We both know that when the Muslims arrive, they will destroy the city.'

'Not if there are enough men here to defend her. If the women and children could be evacuated, so that only fighting men remained, we could protect Acre,' Buscarel declared.

'No. You cannot hope to do that.' Zaccaria shook his head. 'So we have to empty all our goods from here. The investment in buildings is a sore loss, but we can do nothing about them. Besides, it is good that this city was Venice's jewel. The loss will hurt her more than us.'

'This is a Christian city, Admiral. Could you not bring back men? Even a few thousand would help, and if you—'

'*No*. I will return to Genoa and tell our people what I believe: that Acre is lost. There is no point sending ships or men here to die,' Zaccaria said flatly. 'If you have any sense, my friend, you will come with us.'

'While there is hope, I must remain,' Buscarel argued. 'One question: will you take my woman and sons with you? I would be happier to know that they were safe.'

'They must go to Cyprus with the other women and children. There will be scarcely enough room on my ship for my goods.'

'Please, Admiral. All I ask is a little space. They will take less room than I would.'

'Yes, but they cannot work their passage like you would. Perhaps if you had not lost a second ship to the Templars last year, there would be more space aboard, but as it is, with one ship fewer in my fleet, it is going to be a tight fit.'

'Then I will remain here with them.'

'Then you will die. And die a fool, at that.'

'Perhaps. But I won't die a coward!'

Zaccaria looked at him bleakly. 'Be careful how you speak to me, Buscarel.'

'Or what? You will leave me here to die?' Buscarel laughed scornfully.

Today, he walked along the harbour, then out along the breakwater to the Tower of Flies where he climbed the steps to the very top, staring out to sea.

'They've all gone, have they?' one of the garrison of sentries asked, watching the Genoese ships with him.

'Yes.'

'Are they coming back?'

'No. They sail away to protect their money,' Buscarel said.

'Well, we're better off without them, then,' the sentry said with a shrug.

Buscarel stared at him, dumbfounded. And then he began to feel his despondency fall away. 'Yes,' he agreed. 'Yes, I suppose we are.'

The plans for the evacuation of the majority of women and children were already well advanced, when Baldwin met Ivo for lunch.

The two had been working their men on the walls near the Tower of St Nicholas, and now they sat and rested their backs against the wall in the shade of the new hoarding roof while they chewed bread and drank thin ale.

'This ale's going off already,' Ivo said with a wince.

'Well, it gives you an excuse to drink it all the faster,' Baldwin chuckled.

Ivo gave him a dirty look, but Baldwin was in a good mood. He had the trust of his men, and for all that their situation was alarming, he was determined not to show concern. When the fellows needed to be jollied along, it was Ivo who invariably sprang into action, making them laugh, and forget adversity.

Baldwin and his men spent that day strengthening the catapult-bases on top of the towers. In the last few days they had constructed larger ones behind the city's walls, too, up near the Lazar Gate and the Gate of Maupas, where the defences had been insufficient beforehand. The timber from Venice had been put to good use. With the catapults being built now, the city could retaliate with determination against any attack.

Later, when Baldwin returned to the house, Pietro let him in wearing an expression of great irritation. 'Worse and worse,' he snapped.

'Eh?' Baldwin asked, but then Pietro was gone, and Baldwin walked through to the garden.

The weather was improving now, and the table and chairs had been taken from the house and put back into the garden. Here, the sound of the birds singing in the little fruit trees was a source of delight always to Ivo, and he liked to sit with his eyes closed, listening.

Today, however, he sat with his eyes wide open, a mazer of wine in his hand. When Baldwin walked in, the young man could see the bleak expression in his eyes.

Lucia was there, and she brought him a mazer of wine, bowing her head. He wished she could stop behaving like a slave, treating him like a master who had power of life and death over her, but there seemed nothing he could do or say that would change her manner to him.

'Thank you,' he said, taking the cup and drinking deeply. It was hot working on the towers, and his throat was parched. Then: 'Ivo, what's the matter?'

The older man walked to the table and sat down next to a large bowl of olives. A dish of seafood was soon brought in by Pietro. 'Likely won't have decent food much longer,' the servant grumbled to himself as he set out the food, and left again.

Baldwin sat, and motioned to Lucia to join them. She shook her head quickly, and went out to the kitchen to help Pietro.

'What is it?' he asked Ivo again, his eyes on Lucia as she left.

'Would you believe, the Grand Master of the German Order has resigned.'

Baldwin stared at him. 'Burchard von Schwanden? Why?'

'He thinks himself incompetent for the task ahead. It will serve to demoralise many of the men here in the city, just as we prepare to defend her.'

'Who will take his place?'

'Conrad von Feuchtwangen.'

'Do you know him?'

'No, I've never had any dealings with him,' Ivo said. He stared about him, looking depressed. 'I have done all I can to maintain the spirits of the men here, to try to keep them keen and ready for the fight, but the idea that the Grand Master of a religious Order could resign his position will affect everyone.'

Baldwin was struck by Ivo's sombre mood. If even he could become downcast, Baldwin felt that there was little hope for anyone.

CHAPTER SIXTY-THREE

Next morning, Baldwin was reluctant to tell his team of men the news. He didn't want to see their faces as they absorbed it.

They had been sent to work on a new catapult being constructed near the castle. Hob was a gifted mechanic, Baldwin was learning, and his abilities improved with every machine they built. This was the largest he had so far attempted.

'Why so large?' Baldwin asked as Hob stood eyeing the timbers lying on the ground ready for piecing together.

'It's said that the enemy have some of the biggest machines ever seen,' Hob replied. 'They can move theirs forward or back to change the range. All we can do is make one that will reach them, no matter how far they may be.'

Baldwin was content with that, but later, when he walked along the walls, thinking of the battle to come, he found himself looking over the plain. He was there, near the Maupas Gate, when he met Sir Otto with another man in German Order tunic, the black cross on his breast.

'Sir Otto,' Baldwin said, bowing his head.

'This is the new Grand Master of the Germans,' Sir Otto said. His manner was irritable as he asked, 'What are you looking for? The enemy has not arrived yet.'

'I was wondering how best to aim the machines, sir,' Baldwin replied, not understanding Sir Otto's mood. 'I thought if we could guess where the Muslims would place their camp, where their men would pitch their tents, we would have a better idea where to point the catapults.'

'You need not worry about them,' the German said. He stood and peered over the walls. 'When they arrive, they will place their tents and horse-lines far beyond our reach. Only those devices intended to attack the city will be at a range to be hit.'

'Can we try to estimate where they would place them?' Baldwin wondered.

'I have some men who are experienced in siege warfare,' Otto said. 'What of you, Grand Master?'

'I will ask.'

Baldwin bowed, and then, emboldened by their apparent acceptance of him, 'Sir Conrad, I hope God protects you in your new post.'

'News spreads quickly when a city is in peril,' Conrad von Feuchtwangen said. He gave Baldwin a serious stare. 'Hopefully, we shall prevail against our enemies, be they ever so numerous.'

'God be praised!' Otto said fervently. 'Baldwin, I will have two men sent to you at Ivo's house. Wait for them there. Perhaps they can advise on the best locations to aim for.'

'I will.'

'Have you looked at the towers?' Otto asked.

'Only the catapult platforms. I have been concentrating on building the machines, sir.'

'We have been walking the city walls together, and all the towers have their kitchens and cellars ready. The water cisterns have filled over the winter, God be praised! So now we are ready for an attack.'

Baldwin nodded. Each tower was effectively a self-contained fortress. If an assault succeeded and men gained the walls, the towers at each side of the breach would bar their doors and rally men ready to return to the walls and throw their enemies to their deaths, but if even that failed, the towers could hold on until the city could send a force to rescue them.

'What is the mood of the men?' Otto asked.

'Keen to fight, sir,' Baldwin said. 'If they don't see a Muslim soon, they'll start fighting amongst themselves!'

'Keep them calm. They'll see their enemy soon enough. And then this Swiss will show how men can fight and keep their honour,' he muttered, half to himself.

Conrad von Feuchtwangen shot him a cool look. 'I have no doubt that the Swiss and the German Order will fight bravely, my friend.'

'With knights such as you fighting for the city, it is difficult to see how we may not win a glorious reputation,' Sir Otto said.

Later, resting on a bench, his eyes closed, feeling the ache of overworked muscles, Baldwin mentioned that exchange to Ivo. 'I didn't understand what they meant.'

'Only that both are ashamed.'

'Why both?'

'Because of Burchard von Schwanden. He was the leader of the German Order, so his cowardice in leaving now means that they are embarrassed by association. His resignation has reflected badly on the honour of his whole Order.'

'I can see that. What of Sir Otto?'

'Did you not know he is Swiss? So was Sir Burchard. So Sir Otto feels he too has something to prove with his fighting in the coming days, to show that he is no coward.'

'I see,' Baldwin breathed.

'The impressive truth is,' Ivo said, 'that while the Genoese pigs have fled across the sea, and while one Grand Master facing the most ferocious battle of his life has resigned and followed the Genoese, the majority of the men of the city are still here, determined to fight. And more men arrive each day to supplement their numbers. The Venetians and Pisans have not deserted us. True, they are carting off their best valuables, but they still remain here to protect Acre and the people. I find that reassuring. Perhaps God will give us the means to keep this city.'

'Lucia, please, come and sit with us,' Baldwin said.

It was later in the afternoon and she had been dozing on her bed. Hearing his voice, she sprang up, startled, and followed him into the garden where she found Sir Jacques and Ivo.

'We were talking about your old household. When you were there, you were happy, were you not?' Jacques said. 'Until you were sent away?'

'Yes.'

'But you were sent away because your mistress was displeased with you?'

'Yes. She thought I might have spoken about her to Baldwin.'

'And did you?'

'No!'

'So you have been punished while you were loyal to her?'

'Yes.'

Edgar appeared, wearing a fresh tunic which Ivo had bought for him. 'Gentles, I cannot sleep. I have been asleep for a year and a day already, or so it feels. May I join you?'

'Please,' Jacques said, motioning to a bench. 'We were talking to this maid about her mistress.'

'Ah, I know a little about her, too,' Edgar said. 'My last master knew her well, didn't he, Lucia?'

She looked at him, but said nothing. She couldn't. While she breathed, she was the slave of Maria, and speaking out against her was a crime that would lead to her being beaten or whipped again, if Maria learned of it. She found it hard enough merely being here with all these men. It felt wrong. But then she saw the expression on Edgar's face, and Baldwin's, and felt more secure. They wouldn't see her hurt. Nor would Ivo or Sir Jacques. They were kindly-looking men.

'What do you mean?' Baldwin asked.

'She would visit Master Philip Mainboeuf in his house. They would send away all the other servants, and only have one to serve them – the old bottler whom I still must "thank" for being evicted in so hasty a manner,' Edgar said.

'Mainboeuf was having an affair with her?' Ivo said, and gave a chuckle. 'Randy git! Good luck to him. She'll not see him for a while, though, I'd guess. He'll be otherwise engaged in Cairo for some little time.'

'She is known for her appetites,' Jacques said. 'She is young and beautiful. It is hardly surprising.'

Baldwin shrugged. This was the way of people in Eastern lands, he was coming to learn.

Edgar looked at Lucia. 'Is it difficult to hear us speak of her, maid?'

'No,' she answered honestly. 'She has hurt me so much, I do not think I could be more injured by her.'

'Why did she send you away?' Baldwin asked. 'Had you offended her in some way?'

'I cannot speak. She ordered me not to.'

Ivo grunted. 'She is not your mistress. If there was something you wanted to confide, you can.'

Lucia bit her lip, and thought again. 'It was only this one thing,' she said. She spoke reluctantly, but in her mind, she felt that as a slave living in Ivo's house, she must now answer to him as master. 'She would visit men. She had me wear her clothing so that her subterfuge would not be noticed. She would have me walk about the city with guards, as though I were her, and she would slip out later to visit her men.'

Baldwin suddenly had a flash of inspiration. 'You mean that first time I saw you? In the road, close to the Genoese quarter?'

'Yes. She had sent me to a house to deliver a message, but the man tried to take me when he found me there. And then you followed me, and I thought you would as well, so I ran from you. You looked scary. Almost drunk.'

'Does that mean she was seeing Mainboeuf?' Baldwin wondered.

Lucia hung her head. 'She was very fond of Philip Mainboeuf, I think. She wanted to see him most often. She will be sad that he is lost to her.'

'She should not be *too* despairing on his behalf,' Ivo snapped. 'The man was selling us to the Muslims. Al-Fakhri told you that.'

Edgar demurred at this. 'No. My master was many things, but he was not a traitor. He saw how the city could prosper, and followed that route, but he would not willingly sell his city.'

'So you think,' Baldwin said.

'Aye. I knew him well.'

'Then who *would* be the traitor to the city?'

'The Lady Maria, perhaps?' Baldwin said. 'That is what Buscarel told me a little while ago.'

'You've had dealings with him?' Ivo growled.

'He and I have an accord,' Baldwin said. He was struck with a mental picture of Lady Maria. Her cold, unfeeling eyes as she threatened him with torture, or the time she told him he would never find Lucia. 'She has a heart of stone.'

'She seeks to protect her lands,' Lucia mumbled, head hanging. It was her last betrayal. Now Lady Maria would never forgive her.

'Perhaps,' Baldwin said, thinking how lovely Lucia was, especially when she looked so lost and vulnerable.

That night, he did not sleep for a long time, thinking of her. But the following morning, the first desperate farmers from the environs of the city began to arrive, and he had other things to concern him.

BOOK FOUR

BESIEGED, APRIL-MAY 1291

CHAPTER SIXTY-FOUR

Baldwin was on the wall when they arrived.

The city had been prepared by the sudden inrush of terrified farmers. There was no need to send patrols to check for the direction from which the attack would come. They had all the intelligence they needed from the refugees.

'Here they come,' said Edgar, standing bareheaded beside Baldwin. He said his head was too painful still to wear a helmet, but Baldwin had a suspicion that it was more his vanity that prevented him. Baldwin saw him glancing at women wherever they went. Still, whatever the reason, at least he had insisted on coming here and standing at the wall with the other men.

'Where?' Baldwin asked.

Edgar pointed languidly at the horizon. And suddenly Baldwin saw through the heat haze to a black line, and a thin mist of dust over it. The young man-at-arms was glad to have a friend at his side, because this was a sight like no other he had ever seen. A seething mass of men and horses and machines, all crawling along from the south like a massive black centipede, seemingly flat against the ground. Like a centipede it curved about hillocks and depressions in the ground as if seeking the best route. It was so like a vast, malevolent creature, it was hard to believe it was composed of thousands upon thousands of men.

'So here they are,' the man beside him murmured, and then was quiet, as though embarrassed to have broken the silence, as if his words could bring the rage of the Muslims down upon them all. No one else spoke. They watched the approach with a kind of resignation. This was the beginning of their battle. The final battle for Outremer, God's Holy Land, the Kingdom of Jerusalem.

Drums began to toll.

Over the expanse of beach and flat sands, Baldwin could hear them. And with them came the distant cacophony of cries and shouts, of rattles and squeaks, clattering pots and pans; the inevitable row of an army on the march.

There was a sudden drift of dust, and a hundred horsemen broke away, to canter towards the city.

'Patrol of horsemen,' Edgar said.

They rode across the ground towards the right, where the sea met the Patriarch's Tower, and there the force stopped, eyeing the walls, trotting up and around them from a distance of five hundred yards or more, well out of bowshot.

Baldwin watched as the horsemen trotted all the way up to the westernmost tip, and then made their way back again, stopping opposite the Tower of the Legate. There, they halted to take their rest, while the rest of the men and horses continued their approach at that slow, inexorable pace. They were near enough now that their battle flags could be clearly seen. The sparkle from the steel tips of their helmets was blinding, as was the glitter and gleam of mail and brightly polished steel lance-points. Wagons lumbered along behind bullocks, and as Baldwin watched, men rode hither and thither on horses, apparently directing a wagon to this point, another to that. Clusters of wagons collected at each site.

It was a sight to drive a dagger of helpless terror into the heart of the strongest, Baldwin reckoned.

Emir al-Fida took the route allocated, riding slowly behind the Sultan's messenger, past the wagons and men as the camp was gradually formed. All the way he kept his eyes on the walls of that infernal city.

The man stopped and indicated where they might set up the machine, and the Emir remained on his horse while the wagons were brought up to his firing-point, still staring at the walls. The men within had been busy, he saw. The walls had new hoardings that increased their height and guaranteed the protection of the men within. The outer wall, he estimated, was about thirty-three feet high, while those of the inner were some fifty. Men on the inner wall could loose arrows over the heads of those at the outer, increasing the deadly impact of their defenders' firepower. Yet his stones would easily pass over both, hoardings and all.

His servants scurried, and by the time he had checked the position for the catapult and studied his section of the wall with care, his tent was erected. He walked to it with a feeling of grim pride. Since the riots, all he had felt was misery at the memory of his poor Usmar's death. While trudging the weary miles to Cairo, while going with the men to Kerak, and during the journey to reach the city again, he had been filled with melancholy and despair. Now he had arrived, all he could think of was exacting revenge for his son's murder. All those in the city would suffer for what they had done to Usmar.

'God willing,' he murmured to himself as he sat and his servant brought him a cooled cup of water. It was perfect, and he sipped it as he sat, watching his men pulling the constituent parts of al-Mansour from the wagons and fitting them together in the order he had prescribed.

He was torn between pride and misery.

There was little for Baldwin and his vintaine to do. There were no enemy machines or soldiers within reach, and the garrison was left to wander the taverns and alehouses, soothing their fears with strong wines. It was difficult to imagine how they could drink so much and yet not become drunk, but Baldwin saw many men consuming vast quantities and still speaking as clearly and precisely as a priest at the Mass. Not that he had seen that many entirely sober priests, as he told himself. Not here. Not recently.

The men under his command looked mostly to Hob for their instructions still. It didn't offend Baldwin, if for no other reason than that he was younger than most of them. On this first day, the men had been told that they could remain down at their lodgings. Meanwhile Baldwin and Hob went to look at the enemy's preparations with Ivo.

They made for the angle of the wall, from where they would be able to see the Muslims more closely.

'What are they doing?' Hob asked a man on the wall.

The man glanced at Hob briefly. 'Oh, hello. Didn't recognise you at first. You had a wash or something?'

'Yeah. In a pig's arse,' Hob said conversationally. 'So, what're they up to?'

The man, who was another of Sir Otto de Grandison's English warriors, Baldwin learned, was thin, with quick, alert eyes. He nodded with his chin towards the barbican.

'That's where Sir Otto's most worried about. He reckons the angle of the wall makes it the most vulnerable section. If the enemy break the point there, they can enter the city without hindrance – and they know it. They're setting up their machines to do just that. They'll have had men watching us here for years, and merchants who'll have given them intelligence, too. They know all our weaknesses.'

'How are the men deployed?' Ivo asked, looking around along the walls.

'Far left, Lepers and Templars take the section nearest the sea; then it's the Hospitallers. King Hugh has the Tower of the Countess de Blois, and the Tower of King Henry, up to here. After us, it's the French, then the German Order and the Commune, with Venetians and Pisans towards the sea at the south-east.'

Baldwin nodded. The Orders all had their own towers, which they had themselves erected and maintained, and had an interest in protecting their own. The first call to arms would have each running for their own posts. And because of the number of men-at-arms under the command of Sir Otto de Grandison and Jean de Grailly, who commanded the French, it made sense for them to fill the gap here, to the right of the King's men.

He looked over the men. The mix of colours and symbols on their tunics was warming to the eye. Over to the far west at the Tower of St Lazarus he could see the Beaucéant fluttering, the rallying point for the Templars, with the two squares: black above, white below. There was the Hospital's flag nearer at their tower, with the white cross on the bright red background, while the Hospitallers' black tunics stood in stark contrast to the white of the Templars beyond. It was easy to see who guarded which section.

At the middle, where the King of Jerusalem's brother held the point, Baldwin saw the bright blue of the knights of his guard. Their golden crosses shone in the sunshine. The sight of them made Baldwin feel grimy in his filthy clothes.

He then studied the enemy, watching the catapults being constructed.

'Are they really out of bowshot?' he wondered to Ivo.

'They're careful to keep themselves safe,' was his response. Ivo pointed to the wooden frames being nailed together. They resembled wooden shields with arrow-slits cut through. One was completed already. It had wheels, and was easily large enough to conceal four or five men. 'When they get within range, they'll use those mantelets. They're shields to protect bowmen and others. When they want to get closer they will roll them forward on their wheels, while their men hide behind. When they begin to move, that's when the catapults will be brought up, and the battle will start.'

'Look over there,' Baldwin said, pointing. Near the sea, opposite the Legate's Tower, a massive pavilion of red linen was being erected. Men moved about, tightening guys and setting out carpets. 'It's huge.'

The tall Englishman glanced at it disinterestedly. 'That? It's the *Dihliz*, the Sultan's tent. Too big to be anyone else's.'

Baldwin stared. 'The man who's caused all this, he's in there?' He seemed so close, it was infuriating. If only a small party of knights could ride to him, kill him, and end this siege before it began! But they couldn't. The distance was four or five hundred yards, and the knights would be cut down well before they could reach the tent. It was a shame. Still, he wondered if knights might be able to ride out at a different point. It was a thought.

CHAPTER SIXTY-FIVE

The noise went on all night. Baldwin lay in his bed, arms behind his head, listening to the hammering, shouting and thundering, until he felt as if his mind would explode. He could imagine hundreds in the streets would be drinking to excess, singing, dancing, fornicating – anything to eradicate that horrible row. But he could not do any of that. If he were to go drinking, it would be to raise a toast to Lucia; if singing, he would sing of her; if dancing, he would be thinking of her body near his; and the idea of sex with another woman was unappealing. If he could not have Lucia, he would remain celibate.

At last, in the middle watch of the night, he gave up. He pulled on his chemise and a leather jack, bound his sword-belt about his waist, and made his way into the night, waking Pietro so that the grumbling old man could relock the door after him. Baldwin left Uther behind. The dog would only trip men. It was too dangerous.

It was dark on the walls. Torches were lighted at the towers, but for the most part the men had no need of them. Their attention was focused on the fires outside the city. Baldwin could not count them. From shore to shore, all was a blaze of light: a dramatic sight. He leaned on the wall and stared out in despair. No city in the world could withstand an assault from so mighty an army.

'Master Baldwin, could you not sleep?'

Baldwin found that Sir Otto de Grandison had walked up behind him. 'You couldn't sleep either?'

'Not with their infernal din,' the tall Swiss said. He was clad in a tunic and hosen, a cloak over his shoulders. 'I think it will begin in the morning.' He was peering over the parapets with an eye trained in gauging distance. 'See that great device over there? That is to be brought a little closer, but I fear it is such a monster, it will never be within the range of our own catapults. A shame. A rock landing on that would give the city cause for cheer, eh?'

'There are dozens of them,' Baldwin commented, seeing machines at every point. 'Where did they get them from?'

'Those machines they call "The Black Oxen", I am told. I think there could be eighty – perhaps more. It is those two I dislike the most. That one over there, aiming at the Templars, and this one at the point of the wall.'

Throughout the Muslim army, Baldwin could see the moving men. 'Do none of them sleep?'

'They will sleep in the morning, if need be. When their machines are prepared, they will leave the firing to the gynours. Until the walls are reduced, there is no point in attack.'

'I see.'

'You are feeling the belly wobble, eh? The heart is a little affrighted? Do not be alarmed. When you have seen as many sieges as I have, the sight of another host of men preparing to attack just stiffens the thews and sinews, gives you a sense of being alive!' Sir Otto said with a grin.

Baldwin tried to return it, but his eyes slid back towards the lines of Muslim warriors. They looked terrifying in the flickering light of the fires, like demons preparing pits for fresh souls.

Baldwin woke shivering, wrapped in a cloak, sitting on the steps with his back to the St Nicholas Gate, under the little drawbridge that led to the door from the wall. He looked up blearily, rubbing the sleep from his eyes, gazing about him as he yawned prodigiously and stretched. He remembered sitting here sometime towards dawn, when the sight of the men in the distance had grown more familiar than terrifying. He was not sure he would be so sanguine when their missiles started flying towards him, however.

Smelling fresh bread, he saw a boy with a basket passing rations to the guards. Baldwin took a loaf when it was offered, and mounted the stairs again, pulling it apart and eating.

The lines had changed, he saw. Where before there had been a mass of moving men, now flags and pennons fluttered along the lines, with the massive frames of the trebuchets looming behind them. Wooden towers were rising, and other devices to aid the scaling of the walls. But there was a strange quiet: no shouts, no rattling of swords against shields, no drumbeats. Just that malevolent silence, with the grim lines of horses and men staring over the broad plains before the city.

Baldwin chewed his bread, looking out at the immense force. There was no sign of movement. Perhaps this was all a ruse to increase the tension of the besieged. If so, it was working. Along from him, two sentries stood sweating under their helmets; one had a nervous tic under his eye that he kept hitting with a crooked finger, as though knocking away a fly. The other did not blink. He just stood staring, as though disbelieving the proof of his own eyes.

A company of riders rode along before the lines, and Baldwin wondered who they might be. He thought, for a moment, that they were riding to the front of the lines and would soon give the call to charge, and the whole dread host would begin to move forward. In his mind's eye he could see them, an implacable black tide that would come forward and roll over the walls, smothering everything and everyone in their path.

The riders continued at a canter to the sea at the far side, before turning round and riding back towards the middle, opposite the barbican. There, the soldiers of the Muslim horde parted to create a pathway, and the riders galloped down it, to take their station at the rear of the men.

A drum thundered. All of a sudden there was a great roar, and the entire army crouched to the ground.

'They pray,' the blue-eyed sentry said. 'They think their poxy god will help them.'

The other hawked and spat. 'They reckon He will help them if they give Him the numbers. I'll tell you this: they've done well on that measure.'

'Swyve 'em. Let 'em come here,' the first said, patting his sword-hilt. He wore a heavy-bladed falchion in a black scabbard. 'My blade has one edge for the one God, and I'll see them in Hell before this city falls.'

'You'll get your moment of glory soon enough,' the older man responded, but with a touch of sadness in his voice.

Baldwin watched the enemy's religious devotions with a sense of urgency shackled in time. He wanted to go and find his men, but his legs were rooted to the spot. It was like being in a dream, in which time passed with extreme slowness.

The chanting rose and fell, and Baldwin suddenly felt his breast tingling. He bolted the last of his bread. A boy came past with a bucket of water, and Baldwin took a ladleful, drinking it quickly, then splashing a little over his face, giving it a rub, and when he looked out again, the drums were beating once more.

Then there came a single, enormous thud that Baldwin felt like a blow throughout his body. A bellowed order, and the men started to move, first over on the left, then the right, and finally the middle, a mass of men driven by hatred and fury. And a moment later, the drumming started again.

The beat seemed to echo in Baldwin's head and chest and belly, a sullen pounding like the beat of death. And he heard another sound over the drumbeats: a squeaking and rattling, as of chains being tightened. Baldwin could see that the machines had already begun to move forward. There were the mantelets, just as he had heard, and the great catapults rolled behind them, mangonels with their lower, wide shapes squat and ugly, the tall trebuchets wobbling a little as the gynours pushed and shoved and heaved their massive equipment.

'When will they be in range?' Baldwin wondered aloud.

'The archers will know,' Hob said. He had appeared as if from nowhere, and now he stood scowling at the approaching men.

'Will they come to the walls themselves?' Baldwin wondered aloud.

'Nay, Master,' the older guard chuckled without humour. 'They won't want their men cut down before they've killed as many of us as they may. They'll keep back as far as they can.'

Baldwin nodded, watching the advance of the machines. The sight was daunting: immense catapults and mangonels surrounded by the tiny figures of the gynours. Overnight, timbers had been hammered vertically into the ground, and now men hauled on ropes that were attached to pulleys on these piles, and the machines were pulled slowly forward, while over the cool morning air could be heard the cries urging the men on. It was like listening to shipmen as they drew up heavy canvas sails.

There was a shout, a loud double crash on a drum, and the plain fell silent.

The sudden absence of noise was like the moments sitting on a horse before a charge. The anticipation was gut-wrenching. Baldwin would remember it later as a series of memories, each distinct, but each fitting into a fast-encroaching terror.

First he was aware of the flapping and crackling of the flags all about. There was no sound from the men of the garrison, not even a rattle of mail or creak of the ropes over the catapults, and their silence was itself intimidating. Baldwin had a feeling that he was a solitary man, that he alone stood before that immense horde. It was a shocking idea.

But then he saw the enemy with a fresh acuity.

About the massive catapults, Muslim soldiers hurried. Some hauling on the ropes that would drag down the huge arms against their counterweights, while others brought the ox-carts filled with rocks specially shaped for flight.

Baldwin began to pray.

CHAPTER SIXTY-SIX

It was a morning to praise God, Abu al-Fida thought. He stared at the city looming before him, the sun rising over her double walls as though pointing out his enemy.

The creaking of the machine was always alarming before the first shot. Even now, after months of construction and preparation, he was anxious as the new timbers settled. Each arm would last for many hundreds of shots, with luck, but some failed and shattered with an ear-splitting crack, either when being dragged down like this, or when they were being fired. He had seen both – and each shot, each preparation for a shot, brought the same anticipation of disaster. There was to be no disaster today, however. He nodded to the master of the gynours, who gave the bellow for the arm to be hauled down. There was a windlass, and the men were already sweating as they chanted, heaving on the ropes.

Al-Mansour was a simple design, but built on a vast scale. The arm was a long baulk of timber, with a steel hinge one quarter from the base, about which the arm could move easily.

He had ensured that plenty of grease had been applied to that steel pin. At the bottom was a basket filled with rocks, lead and sand, and when resting, the arm stood vertical with this basket underneath. But as they pulled the arm down, the basket rose, that ponderous weight acting on the arm, and when released, the arm was snapped up to vertical and beyond. The sling fixed to the top of the arm had one end loose that hooked over a projecting steel bolt. When it flicked up, that came free, and the rock held in the sling was unleashed to fly through the air towards the target. A simple, but a massively effective weapon.

Gradually the great arm was dragged down against the weight of the bucket. Ropes and timbers creaked and complained, while men rolled the first of the rocks from the wagon and used levers to position it on the wooden track under the arm. A loop of rope dangled from beneath the sling. As the arm reached its lowest position, the master himself pressed this through a metal ring on the bed of the machine and put a steel pin through the loop to hold it in place. A long cord was fastened to this pin, and the master held on to this as he watched the men ready the sling.

Another command and all the men fell back, eyes on the arm, moving well away in case of accidents. Abu al-Fida himself stepped away from behind. Rocks had sometimes flown from their slings to hurtle backwards, destroying all in their paths. Slings could break, fixings tear loose, steel might shatter or shear, and the effect on a human body was devastating.

Abu al-Fida lifted his arm and stared over to the east, along the line of the army. There, he could see the nearest officer on his horse.

He waited.

*　　*　　*

Baldwin felt the tension in the air as he gazed across at the line of machines. The men had been moving about them, but were now standing aside. Baldwin could only imagine the expectation on their part. For him, this was torture. He needed to go to a latrine, but he dared not turn his back on those missiles. The thought of their sudden deadly impact was terrible. Rather that, he thought, than a protracted death from a gangrenous knife wound or arrow – but surely if a man had no body, he could not be raised from the dead? Would a crushing death mean no journey to Heaven?

It was a hideous thought, and it was that which kept him here, peering out over the first wall at the enemy.

He wanted to see his doom flying towards him, not be hit in the back like a coward.

Abu al-Fida heard the bellow, saw the officer's arm drop, and let his own fall.

His firer pulled the cord, and the arm was loosed. All the energy in the machine was unleashed in a rattling slither of stone and leather. A shudder, a lurch, and the sling was moving, the rock surging up the track, and then it was in the air. The arm swept up, accelerating, the rock whirling, and then the arm was up and over the vertical, and the sling released.

Abu al-Fida felt the freedom in his own heart as the rock rose, suddenly as light, apparently, as a pebble, and from here he could follow its trajectory. It continued up, and up, and then seemed to pause in mid-air, and only then did he become aware of the other rocks, a hundred at least, which also hurtled on towards the city. It was a moment fixed in time. He could see the rocks for what seemed like an age, and then they were falling, a rain of death on the people of Acre.

*   *   *

Baldwin heard someone shout something incomprehensible. They could all see the rocks now, a wave of them, passing effortlessly through the air with the majestic grace of buzzards on the wind. It was almost beautiful.

Then they began to crash to the ground.

It was as if the very land was rejecting the Christians. Baldwin felt the shock through his legs, the wall shivering as a rock slammed into it near the Patriarch's Tower. Another moaned past a hundred yards distant, and there was a flat, crunching sound as it fell on the road outside the castle. A third hit a tavern, and in the blink of an eye, it was gone, just a mass of mud wall, broken timbers and ragged cloth where an awning had been only moment before.

Baldwin felt his mouth open. A cloud of dust was thrown up beyond the wall in Montmusart where another had landed, and he wondered briefly where it was. Surely not at Ivo's house, he hoped. The thought that Pietro or Edgar had been crushed was appalling. He dared not think of Lucia being killed.

Already, when he turned to look, the arms were being dragged down once more. He saw the rocks being rolled, men with levers laboriously shoving them on, until they were fixed in place. Other men set the slings about the rocks, and as soon as they were ready, the rocks were launched.

Nearest him, the missiles were not flying with precision. The second threw up a great gout of sand as it landed thirty or more yards outside the walls, and there was a wave of derisive laughter from around Baldwin. A second landed at the foot of the walls, causing more merriment. The third took off the top of the outer wall's hoarding below Baldwin, and the laughter stopped abruptly as men saw the bloody smear where four men had stood. It was as if a cockroach had been crushed under a boot. All that remained was an indistinct mark where before, four living creatures had stood.

A shivering percussion now. The stones on which Baldwin stood were trembling as though fearing collapse as more rocks thundered into the walls. The catapults which had been set too far away were moved closer so that they might execute their own devastation on the city, and now screams and shouts could be heard all over as more and more men were injured.

And then there was a groaning reverberation, and Baldwin looked up to see that the tower above him had loosed their first stone. It rose into the sky, urged on by a cheer from the men all around, and they watched as it dropped, only to hurtle into the sand fifty yards from the enemy.

'They have the machines for this,' Baldwin's neighbour muttered.

'So do we,' Baldwin said. 'It's just a matter of time, before they come closer and we can hit them as hard.'

The older man stayed staring out at the machines.

'We'll need to,' he said.

CHAPTER SIXTY-SEVEN

After a day of bombardment, Baldwin found that his fear of the artillery weapons had reduced to a manageable anxiety. Despite the constant reverberations, it soon became clear that the weapons themselves were entirely random. The mood of the men of Acre was already changing: the haphazard nature of the enemy's weapons had made them less intimidating. Instead of inspiring terror, the catapults had become a focus for hatred – symbols of the enemy's cowardice, hurling rocks from the safety of their lines at the women and children of the city. It left the men determined to exercise an unrelenting ferocity when they closed with their foe at last.

Baldwin found that his fear increased greatly at night. When, in the darkness, that low thrumming sound came, he was convinced that the rocks were heading directly towards him. When he did hear the reports as they crashed into buildings, it was still some moments before he could bestir himself, the terrror was so intense.

He was with Hob and the men when the new panic began.

They had endured a day of the rocks, and were having a pot of wine and some bread with cheese in a tavern when Baldwin heard a new sound – a whistling, screaming sound – and he stared up at the awning overhead in alarm. They had all been lounging on the floor, but now he rose and hurried to the open window, eyes fixed skywards, still chewing.

'What was that?' he demanded. Even as he spoke, there was a sudden whoosh, and a burst of black smoke told of a fresh disaster. 'Some new machine they have worked on?'

Hob was at his side, and he shook his head, muttering to himself.

'What is it, Hob?'

'Greek fire. They'll use it to burn us to death, if they may.'

Baldwin frowned at him. 'Greek fire? What's that?'

'They throw it in big clay pots, like the rocks, and when the pots land, the clay shatters and the fire is released over everything in its path.'

It sounded to Baldwin like a new work of the Devil, but later that same day he saw the missiles in the sky. Enormous pots, they were, with a trail of grey smoke flying from them. One burst in mid-air, and a gout of flame was vomited at the city, scorching the wall, but missing its target. Another, later in the day, detonated as the catapult arm was released. Baldwin saw it distinctly, the arm springing up, while a flash of fire was sprayed over the machine and the men standing about it. There was a thick, roiling black smoke that rose heavenwards, and strange figures could be seen, cavorting and whirling in the midst of the flames. It was only when one ran out, burning like a torch, that Baldwin realised it was a man. Men from the next catapult raced over to him, smothering him, trying to put out the flames, but it could have served no useful purpose.

Baldwin felt the horror of that man's death, but he was alone. The men on the wall cheered at the sight. To Baldwin, their satisfaction was misplaced. Such a death could only motivate the Muslims to greater efforts. Still, it meant there were some fewer enemies, and one less artillery piece to stand against them.

After their period of duty on the walls, Baldwin told the men to stand down, and made his way to the house.

The roads were almost unrecognisable from the previous week. Clean roadways had thick heaps of rubble sprawled over them. The wagons and carts, which had always been so prominent in this trading city, were no more. Instead, there were only scowling, anxious men, hurrying from one place to another on foot.

Baldwin strode swiftly, glancing around at the damage to the buildings as he went. The castle's south-west tower had taken a hit, and the top of the tower had been wrenched asunder. Now a pile of stones lay beneath. Next to it, there had been a little house. The falling rocks had pulverised it and the family which had lived inside, and now only a few spars and shattered tiles showed where six people had lived.

'This is a battle between God and the Devil,' Hob grunted.

Baldwin agreed.

Today the assaults from the catapults had been varied by the arrival of pioneers. Groups of Muslims dressed all in black had hurried forward.

'To the walls! To the walls!'

Baldwin heard the shouts from the men on the towers, and ran forward with Hob and the vintaine. They made their way to the outer wall, and clambered up the stairs to the hoardings, puffing and blowing when they reached the top, staring around.

'Get your men forward, quickly,' a guard roared, clapping them on the back as they swarmed up the battlements and into the roofed hoardings.

It was strange in here. The crash of rocks was lessened, this far from the city itself. They were shielded by the inner walls from the rumble and crash. Instead there was the suffocating smell of fresh timber. It was hot, for the wood absorbed the sun's heat and made the interior as fiery as an oven. Instantly Baldwin felt the sweat squeezing out under his thick padded jack and shirt of mail. A pair of sentries with their faces blackened and grimy stood at a trap in the hoarding's floor, shouting for rocks and other missiles. About each gap in the boards were other men, and as Baldwin stared, he saw the reason why.

Beneath them were Muslims. Already bowmen were aiming at other pioneers scurrying forward, protected by shields of wet calfskin. The enemy were bringing planks of timber, darting up to place them against the walls, some placing theirs carefully, others hurling them like spears in the hope that they might fall as required. Some, sheltering behind mantelets, were digging furiously a few yards away. Baldwin saw one fall, an arrow piercing his head through his helmet.

'What are they doing?' he said, confused.

'Undermining the walls,' Hob said, swearing under his breath. Cupping a hand about his mouth, he bawled back, 'More rocks! And oil! They'll make a trench from there, which they can cover,' he added. 'Then they'll have access to our wall, and can dig underneath.'

A chain of men was bringing the rocks now, one at a time, and Hob passed them through the battlements to the two sentries waiting. He continued, 'They'll go down, deep as they can, shoring up the walls with timbers as they go, and when they're ready, they'll soak the timbers in oil and burn the lot. The walls'll be left standing on nothing, and they'll collapse. And then we'll have a breach, and they'll flood in.'

Baldwin was passing rocks from Hob to the sentries as he panted, and the two sentries stood, holding the massy weights in their hands, legs braced either side of the hole, until they saw a man approaching the base and released them. Once, Baldwin was peering down and saw their stone hit a man. It fell straight, and he gave a strange keening sound as it crashed into his shoulder, tearing off his arm and ripping a huge gash in his flank. He fell, and Baldwin watched with horrified fascination how the man's blood pulsed in the gaping wound.

That was their work for the day. As the Muslims dug and tried to erect roofs of timber, Baldwin and his vintaine brought up rock after rock and sent them tumbling onto the unhappy wretches beneath. And then the order came for them to leave the hoardings.

Nothing loath, Baldwin clambered over the battlements again, and inside, on the stone walkway of the wall, he found two men holding a great cauldron. As he watched, they slowly tilted it towards the nearest loophole, and began to pour a thick, black oil through. Peering down, he saw the viscous liquid splashing and soaking the mass of timbers where the pioneers had been. There were cries now, and the men digging seemed to hesitate. An arrow caught one man who peered incautiously around his mantelet, and then the sentries were given a lighted torch, and dropped it through the nearest hole.

A gust like the breath of the Devil rose. A thick, roiling smoke engulfed the whole of their section of wall, and Baldwin recoiled, coughing and choking, but even over the sensation of suffocation, he could hear the inhuman screams of the men beneath, and in his mind's eye he saw them burning to death in their little chamber, beneath the flimsy protection of their planks of wood, as the ignited oil ran through and smothered them.

Mercifully, their screams did not last long. As each flaming figure emerged from the trench and pit, they were shot by the archers who stood laughing at the arrowslits.

CHAPTER SIXTY-EIGHT

Hurrying homewards later, Baldwin felt a horror that would not fade. In his mind he still saw the men in the burning oil. It was satisfying to see that the attack had been foiled – but at what cost! He had an instinctive compassion for the men who had been turned into human torches. It was monstrous.

He passed a small chapel in which a guard from the bastion had been celebrating Mass – for the men were forced now to stagger their religious devotions – when Baldwin saw a man he recognised. It was one of the guards from the Tower of King Henry II. He had shared a cup of water with Baldwin earlier in the day, and Baldwin nodded to him as he went by. The man grinned and waved. That was the image that remained in Baldwin's memory as he turned, because at that moment he saw Buscarel.

The Genoese was standing, hunting through a satchel, oblivious to Baldwin.

Baldwin was debating whether to speak to him or not when it happened.

There was a hissing groan in the air, and Baldwin felt a concussion that started in his feet and slammed upwards, with the heat of a furnace scorching his face and hands. Instinctively he shielded his face with a crooked elbow, ducking his head, but as he did so, a splash of acid seemed to burn his temple and his wrist, and he gave a cry, so he thought, as he felt himself thrown aside like a rag-doll, falling on his shoulder.

A missile filled with Greek fire had struck the chapel, and all the men gathered within were enveloped in flames. Mouths open in silent screams, they lurched from side to side, waving their arms in agony. Two toppled from the flames and crawled over the still-hot stones, and Baldwin saw a man dash from a house with a cloak in his hands, throw it over one of the men, and beat out the flames, while from within the cloak, a high keening could be heard.

Baldwin climbed to his feet filled with shock. The burning men had already fallen, some thrashing in agony, while others, mercifully, were already still. Baldwin reached the other who had run from the flames, and found himself staring at a mask. The man's eyes were wide, his eyelids burned away. His entire head was red, raw and blackened like a hog's roasted over a fire, and Baldwin was transfixed. There was nothing he could do to ease the fellow's pain, nothing he could do to help him. The man would die, and that in extreme pain.

Buscarel barged into Baldwin, stared at the wounded man for an instant, and then cut off his head with a practised sweep of his sword.

The body sank to its knees and slowly toppled to one side while Baldwin remained frozen in place. There was a stench of oil and turpentine, combined with the smell of roasted pork.

Buscarel was already gone when Baldwin could drag himself back to the present. The road was full of men and women gazing about them with horror and incomprehension at the smouldering victims, and the man with the cloak had unwrapped the remains of the fellow he had tried to help, and now knelt beside him, weeping silently.

That was the picture Baldwin retained as he reached the house. The man kneeling there, staring at the blackened features of his friend whose face had been burned away.

Pietro saw his expression as Baldwin walked in, and said nothing, only went and fetched a cup of strong wine.

'Master, drink this. You need it.'

Baldwin took it, falling back onto the bench, staring at Pietro's face without recognition. 'His face,' he murmured. 'It was burned away. And I could do nothing.'

'Drink, Master Baldwin,' Pietro said gently. 'It'll help.'

Baldwin sipped, and the first taste made him want to puke, but he drained it. Pietro replenished his cup, and then walked away.

'You are distressed.'

Lucia had come to him, her hands clasped decorously before her. She was dressed in a shift of clean white linen. On her head was a coif of similar material, and she had tucked her hair away beneath the cap.

'You look lovely,' Baldwin sighed, and gestured about him. 'Please, take a seat.'

She looked at him for a moment, a long, considering stare, and then went to his side and seated herself on his right, perhaps six inches from him. Close enough that he could almost feel her warmth, far enough for the distance to be a gulf.

'Pietro said there was something wrong.'

He did not look at her. 'There was a burning missile. So many men killed . . . burned alive.' He felt the shudder start at the small of his back, and then he spilled wine as it shot through him.

She placed a hand on his shoulder. 'I am sorry.'

'The man Buscarel, he was there,' Baldwin said. 'He made no attempt to harm me, but he tried to rescue a man who was burning. His flesh was afire, all over, and he was screaming, screaming . . .' Baldwin stopped to take in a breath. 'It was awful. And I could do nothing to help him.'

'Your arm,' she said. She drew back his sleeve, and he saw for the first time the red blistering. 'You were badly burned!'

'It's nothing.' He felt as tired as death.

Lucia called for Pietro, and with his help, she made a salve from some butter and honey, and wrapped it about the wound with a bandage. After Pietro had left them, she poured Baldwin more wine. 'Rest.'

'How can I rest?' he said.

She looked at him, and then helped him to his feet and took him to her chamber. The wounds on her back were healed, but the wounds in her memory remained.

In her chamber, she helped him to take off his mail and clothes. He sat on her palliasse, and she stared at his body. The wound in his flank was healed to a ribbon of scar tissue, but there were other injuries, small cuts from swords during fighting practices with Ivo, scratches on his hands from handling so many rocks and stones, and fresh abrasions from being thrown about today. He was a mass of more or less minor bruises, gashes and abrasions.

'Wait there,' she said, and fetched a bowl with water. She found a rose in the garden and took the petals from two flowers, crushing them into the water and mixing them, before finding a clean strip of gauze and carrying them back to her room. In the garden as she passed through it, she saw Ivo sitting on the bench. He stared at her with an unreadable expression. He made no comment as she carried on.

She found Baldwin already asleep. She took the cloth, wrung it out, and wiped his face clean. It didn't wake him. She gently used the cloth to wipe away the dirt and grime from him, softly murmuring a song she recalled from her childhood, a lullaby her mother had sung to her. Once, his entire body stiffened, and he cried out, but she soothed him, a hand on his brow, the other on his breast, and his hand suddenly reached up and gripped hers, holding it there, close to his heart.

His hand had the grip of desperation. As a slave, she should remain with him if he wanted her – but tonight she was scared. The flying rocks, the sudden eruptions of flame, made her feel as vulnerable as him.

'I will stay here,' she whispered. 'I will stay at your side.'

And she lay beside him on the bed, rested her head on his shoulder, and both slept.

It was dawn when Baldwin woke. He stirred and yawned, stretching. He felt the pain in his wrist where it had been burned, and glanced at it with a sudden memory of a man burning like a torch, his head cut loose in an instant. And then, he realised that there was a warm body lying beside him.

She said nothing, only watched him as he rose from the bed and began to walk to the door.

Then: 'You are leaving again?' she said.

It was her tone that stopped him. She sounded abandoned, like a recently orphaned child. He turned to smile at her, but found he could not.

'We will die here,' she said. 'Won't we?'

His smile faded. 'I think so.'

She could see his sadness. He was lonely and despairing, she thought. His whole demeanour that of a man who was set to fail in all he had embarked upon. And in that moment, she felt a strange conviction that of the two, she was the stronger. He was no more her slave-master than Sultan al-Ashraf. He was only a man.

'Please,' she said. 'Come back here.'

CHAPTER SIXTY-NINE

Baldwin walked the walls that morning with a feeling of elation. His arm was still sore, but he could not lose the grin from his face. He wanted to tell Ivo and the others how happy he was. Lucia had been so gentle, sweet and loving, and he felt sure that he would be able to persuade her to marry him. That was what he wanted with all his heart: to make her his wife.

He stood at the hoarding where he had stood the day before. Already carpenters had been all over this section, replacing the broken roof where a rock had smashed it to tinder, repairing the supports from bits and pieces of timber lying all about. There was nothing the Muslims could do that would break the resolve of the inhabitants of Acre, he thought. They might throw all their missiles, but men would take heart no matter what.

At the first hissing passage of a fire-pot, he felt his heart quail, but then he stiffened his resolve with a memory of Lucia's naked body on the bed when he left the chamber. Her smile, her beautiful face as he kissed her, all woke in his breast a fierce determination to be as brave as she would expect him to be. He still felt the fear, but somehow Lucia's love lighted in him a shield against any returning terrors. He managed to put to one side the memory of the man's face from last night, just before Buscarel's sword took his head off.

Baldwin was still on the walls when the first assault began with the simultaneous flight of a whole mass of rocks from the catapults. He was stationed once more on the outer wall, ready to repel a repeat of the pioneers' attack, when the rocks crashed into the hoarding.

There was no warning. The men were peering through any arrow slits available, when Baldwin saw the catapult arms all rising with that lazy motion, like a small forest of pines in a gale, he thought. He saw their missiles discharge, but as they reached their zenith, he lost sight of them under the overhang of the roof. There were tense moments as all the sentries waited, braced for the shock, and then there was a rippling thunder as the massive stones pounded the walls. Some, striking further away, made the feet of the men in the hoarding tremble, and then there was a scream, suddenly cut short, and a shudder that made the hoarding creak alarmingly. Daylight entered, blinding them.

Baldwin felt it like a leaping horse. That was how he would later describe it: like being on a charger as it leaped over a hedge – the sudden, belly-swooping moment of flight, followed by the shock of the landing and the rippling of the hoofbeats. Except he was not on a horse.

The missile struck the hoarding at the point of the roof, and crunched through it to the parapet hidden behind. Three men had been there, and Baldwin saw their bodies left as a jelly of blood and bones at the wall. The roof collapsed, and then the floor too disappeared, torn away by the weight of that immense rock. A man at Baldwin's side moaned and wept, a two-foot splinter of wood embedded in his chest. Another was staring open-mouthed at the stump of his left arm, his face white, while Hob was standing precariously at the edge of the hole, shrieking in incoherent rage his defiance at the army on the plain – miraculously, like Baldwin, completely uninjured.

Baldwin bellowed for his men, and soon the bodies and wounded were removed, while planks were brought to replace those lost. Soon he had a rough deck nailed in place, and a low wall to protect them from arrows. At least the rock's progress had improved their view of the battlefield, he told himself.

It was a mass attack from the right that he noticed first of all. Glancing there, he saw an entire line of Muslims rushing forward. Many bore long ladders, and there were three of the tall, protected scaling towers too, pushed by scores more.

Blaring trumpets from the city countered the booming thunder of the Muslim drums, and then there was a loud pealing of bells. Soon a rush of men answered the summons along the streets, and there was a constant bellow of orders. Archers stood preparing, while Baldwin was pushed to the back of the wide walls.

'Hob! We need archers over here!' he bawled, gesticulating with his arms. Hob saw the danger, and brought a number of Sir Otto's men with him. They stood stringing their bows, staring intently down at the battle scene. Then, with wicker quivers filled with arrows set before them, they took one each and nocked it.

'What do you reckon?' one said.

'Out of bowshot for us.'

'Yeah.'

Baldwin leaned forward. 'You must be able to hit them! They're only a few yards away!'

'Still too far for accuracy, vintenary. We're better off not loosing our arrows. If we wait here, we'll soon have targets enough.'

'What?'

The archer glanced at him with exasperation, then jerked his chin towards the men before them. 'Look!'

Baldwin saw that the middle of the army was moving, too. They rolled forward, and as they came, the front ranks paused, and he realised that they were all archers. In the sky, their arrows rose like a cloud of filthy carrion crows, darkening the ground beneath; they hung there a moment, and then began to fly down towards the men on the walls.

''Ware! Arrows!' Baldwin said entirely unnecessarily, and ducked.

There was a clattering, a rattle of arrows hitting steel or rock, and shrieks as men were hit. Baldwin looked about him in astonishment to see that he and all those nearest were uninjured, and he bellowed defiance at the enemy just as the second wave of arrows arrived. The archer to his right coughed almost apologetically, as an arrow plunged into his shoulder beside his neck. He stiffened, and tumbled from the wall.

Baldwin stared at the man's dead body some thirty feet below. His eyes were empty, as though his soul had flown in that instant.

More arrows were falling now, and Baldwin regretted the lack of a roof over his head. It left him feeling as exposed as a tethered chicken before a fox.

There was a shout, and more men ran to the walls bearing shields to protect the archers. One of them was a youth of perhaps fourteen, Baldwin saw. He ran up, carrying a large kite-shaped shield, and as soon as he reached the top of the wall where the roof had been burst away, he was struck in the leg by an arrow and fell, screaming shrilly, on the dead archer inside. His neck was broken when he landed.

But the other men were there with their shields held aloft now, and the archers could maintain their fire from beneath that protection. Not that it was enough. There were so many Muslims that the arrows made no discernible difference.

Baldwin moved aside to leave more space to the archers, and as he did so, he saw parties of men running at the walls, protected by a wagon-frame covered with wet hides. They stopped some distance from the walls, and more men hurried up with mantelets. These were thrust forward, and soon the men behind were neatly concealed.

'What are they doing?' Baldwin demanded.

The older English warrior was with him again. 'Miners,' he said. 'That's a *chat* – a cat. They'll drive a shaft forwards from there to tunnel under our wall and the towers. Just like yesterday, but this time, more effective. It's how they took Krak des Chevaliers.'

'They are experienced at sieges,' Baldwin noted.

'Oh, yes. You could say that.'

CHAPTER SEVENTY

On the third day, Baldwin was called away from the walls with his men.

Sir Otto de Grandison was in the Tower of St Nicholas, where the catapult worked constantly. When Baldwin and Hob reached the top of the tower, they saw a rock fall with a crunch into the middle of the shields protecting the entrance to the mine shaft, and Baldwin felt a surge of delight to see the devastation wreaked upon the miners and their bowmen. Two of the wheeled shields had been crushed entirely, and parts of them, and the men who had sheltered behind, were strewn about the sand. Not far from that lay the shards of wood from the first demolished cat. It had taken a direct hit from a lump of masonry hurled by the same catapult, and now the timbers of the walls stood up like the ribs of a massive beast.

'A good shot! Good shot!' Sir Otto was roaring, slamming his fist on the parapet before him. He ducked as an arrow whistled past his ear, and turned to Baldwin with a savage grin. 'There's a few more there who won't see their wives again!'

'Sir? You wanted me?' Baldwin said.

'You built that catapult in the Montmusart area, didn't you?'

'Two of them, my Lord.'

'I need another one.'

'Sir. You give us the wood, and we can build it.'

'This is a special one,' he chuckled. Pointing over the line of the walls, he said, 'You see that catapult they have up there? The huge one?'

Baldwin peered around the machine that took up so much of the tower's roof. Past the timbers, he could see the great bulk of the catapult in the distance, outlined against the sea. 'Yes.'

'I need that destroyed.'

'I don't think any machine we built would be able to hit it,' Baldwin said doubtfully. 'The largest we have is behind the Gate of Maupas, and that one falls short by some distance.'

Hob agreed. 'We have to have them built far back enough from our walls so that our missiles clear the inner wall. The enemy can throw everything they want at us, and it doesn't matter whether it hits the inner or outer walls, or flies over and lands inside – it's all the same to them. It's different for us.'

'I can get a catapult much closer,' Sir Otto said, 'to half that distance – so a small catapult will do. Can you build me one?'

Baldwin looked at Hob and shrugged. 'Give us the materials, we'll build it,' he said.

'The timbers are at the harbour. There is a man down there who will take you to the shipman – he will help you. With fortune, our idea will work.

'We need something, God knows,' he added sombrely.

Baldwin and Hob gathered the vintaine and left the walls. In the open roadway behind the gates, they found a young boy of perhaps nine. He was short and fair, and had an eager expression on his round face. Once he might have been the son of a wealthy man, but now he was grubby and dishevelled, like all the others in the city. This lad's hosen were torn, the fabric of his chemise frayed.

'Follow me, sirs,' he piped up.

'Do I know you?' Baldwin asked as they hurried after him.

A whistle and howl made them all duck as a rock soughed through the air overhead. It touched the roof of a house and an explosion of debris flew into the air, white like a cloud of swansdown, while the rock ploughed on into a building beyond. There was a crumpling of masonry, and a wall collapsed in an explosion of sound.

The boy stood, glancing about attentively. He reminded Baldwin of a small hunting dog, shaking itself after a brief immersion in an unexpected pool, and looking for his quarry once more.

'I am the son of Peter of Gibelet. But he has died,' the boy said. 'I am called James.'

'I am sorry your father is dead,' Baldwin said. 'I knew him. He was a good man.'

'He was old,' James said. A tear formed in his eye, but he snatched at it, ashamed to weep for his father when he should be fighting.

'It is good to mourn.'

'I won't. I want to kill the men who killed him,' James stated firmly, and carried on.

At the harbour, Baldwin stopped at the sight of the ships docking. There was a constant stream of galleys and smaller vessels, all of them bringing food and arms to the beleaguered inhabitants of the city. A few women and children were taken on board as he watched, the richer folk, or more anxious, paying for their passage to Cyprus. Many had already been

393

taken away under the evacuation plans implemented by the Templars.

And then he saw the man waiting for them. It was Buscarel with a small party of men standing by a cog moored near the *Falcon*.

'Master Baldwin,' he said. 'I am glad it's you.'

'I saw you that night – when the tavern was hit,' Baldwin said.

'I know,' Buscarel said. 'It was a hideous attack.'

'Sir Otto de Grandison sent me. I am here to build a catapult.'

'And I am here to give you your platform,' Buscarel said.

Hob and Baldwin exchanged a glance. Baldwin said, 'What do you mean, "platform"?'

'This,' Buscarel said, pointing at the ship, 'is where it will be positioned.'

Baldwin shared a look of bewilderment with Hob. 'On a ship?' he managed at last.

'Christ's ballocks!' Hob muttered, staring at the cog with disbelief.

'Aye. That way we can get close and attack the big bastard catapult they have opposite the Templars.'

Baldwin eyed him and then the ship once again. 'Can we make it fit?'

CHAPTER SEVENTY-ONE

The ship was fitted with a castle fore and aft, and it was on the forecastle that Baldwin was told they must erect the machine.

Buscarel busied himself with his shipmen shifting ballast into the ship while Baldwin and Hob bellowed at the men on the top. First Baldwin had thought to reject Buscarel's suggestions out of hand, but when he considered other methods of achieving the same result, it was clear that Buscarel was better advised than he. The catapult could not be sited in the middle of the vessel, for the arm would snag on mast and rigging, and he was assured that if it were set at the back of the ship, she would not be manoeuvrable. So instead he decided to carry on as Buscarel had proposed.

By the end of that day, they had a firm platform on which to set the machine. Working through the night by the light of torches and oil lamps, they had the structure built and ready on the quayside, and by the end of the second day, the catapult was completed and in place. There was a moment of panic when rocks were brought aboard in Buscarel's absence, and a pile was built up on the port side of the ship. She was not yet ready for them, and began to heel over dramatically, until there came a warning bellow from Roger Flor, who was standing in his own ship a short distance away, laughing at their antics, and the vintaine ran about the boat at his command, rolling the rocks from one place to another and lashing them down securely.

On the morning of the third day, the ship was ready, and Baldwin and Hob stood on the harbour-front as she was pushed from the quayside and began to make her way out to sea, towed by an enthusiastic crew on a small galley.

'How do you think she'll do?' Baldwin asked.

Hob looked up at him and drew the corners of his mouth down. Nodding in the direction of al-Mansour, he grunted, 'If they manage to lob a rock at that bugger over there, I'll be surprised, let alone hit it. Whoever heard of a catapult on a ship?'

Baldwin nodded. They made their way back to the walls and climbed the steps again.

After their third attempt at storming the walls, the Muslims were resorting to hurling every conceivable missile they could at the walls and the towers, concentrating on the point of the wall where the barbican protruded. Many rocks were landing in the city, but Baldwin reckoned these were simple overshots. The main targets were the defences, he thought, as a cloud of flame burst from the outer wall in front of him. Black, reeking smoke roiled up from the bright yellow and orange flames, and he winced at the blast of heat as it rolled past him.

'They must have brought every rock from here to Cairo,' he muttered.

'Aye, they brought enough,' Hob agreed.

On the towers above them on either side, the smaller catapults were working hard, flinging masonry. Pieces of shattered Muslim missiles gave them plenty of ammunition, along with the rubble from damaged buildings. The thunder of collapsing buildings could be heard every hour. But now a cheer went up from the besieged. The little cog had braved the rough seas, rocking and bucking, but when the men on the walls saw her catapult send the first rock inland, they roared like spectators at a cockfight. Even from here they could see the sudden shock in the Muslim ranks. The first missile missed al-Mansour, but flew straight into the flank of the men before the machine, and rolled over and over amongst them, crushing and killing several. A second flew harmlessly beyond the army, hitting only a wagon and shivering it to splinters, but the third and sixth seemed to reach close to the machine.

In a desperate bid to remove this threat, the Muslims brought up a large mangonel and set it near the catapult, firing heavy steel bolts at the ship. The missiles missed, however, the arrows stabbing harmlessly into the sea. It was a fluke, but a sudden shot from the ship punched into the sand near the mangonel, and one arm was snapped off, rendering the machine useless. But still the great beam-arm of al-Mansour kept rising and throwing rocks at the city, and no matter what the men of Acre attempted, nothing could reach that dread device.

'We have to get it,' Baldwin said, resting his chin on his forearm as another rock flew past al-Mansour. He recalled his thoughts about killing the Sultan in his tent that first day. 'We should attack it.'

Sir Otto was passing him as he spoke. 'You aren't the only man to have that thought,' he said.

Baldwin nodded, turning back to the sea, and was in time to see the ship breast a wave. 'He's very close to shore,' he said.

Sir Otto stopped and there was a moment's silence as the men on the walls stared out to sea. 'He has to be, to hurt them. He must be as close as possible. It is fortunate Buscarel is a good shipman.'

The ship returned, and as it crept in towards the harbour, Buscarel relinquished his steering oar, along with command of the ship, with relief. His armpit, where he had gripped the oar for so long that day, had been rubbed raw by the timber. Blisters had raised and burst, and now blood soaked his chemise. His eyes were salted and tired from all the spray.

'Make her fast,' he shouted, and the sergeant at the forecastle nodded and had two men set about the cables fore and aft, while Buscarel rubbed his eyes.

They had at least done some damage while sailing up and down the coast, but their catapult was not strong enough to reach into the main camp of the Muslims. They were forced to run up and down as near to the rocky shoreline as possible, hurling their missiles as quickly as possible.

Leaving the ship, he saw Baldwin walking down to meet him, his scruffy dog behind him. There were two men along with him, but Baldwin stopped them at the ramp to the harbour, and walked on alone.

'Master Shipman,' Baldwin called. 'You did well today.'

'Aye, well, we must all do what we may,' Buscarel said, his eye falling to the ring on Baldwin's finger.

Baldwin clenched his teeth and closed his fist. He stared at Buscarel challengingly.

'No. Once I wanted that ring,' Buscarel said, 'but not now. I would be happy if I could only have my woman and children sent to Cyprus.'

'Really?' Baldwin found the assertion hard to believe.

'I am Genoese. I wanted to fight Venice for control of the seas. When I saw a ship that was owned by Venice, it was natural that I should try to take her. If our roles had been reversed, the Venetians would have taken mine and slain me. It is only on land that Venice and Genoa live in peace.'

'But you are here, although your countrymen have fled.'

'I was proud to be Genoese – but now? Now, I think I am a man of Acre. I have made this city my own. I would not leave her to be invaded and destroyed. She is the city where my sons were born, and where my woman and I have our home. To flee and hide would be shameful. So, I will stay, and perhaps I will die, but I will do all I can for her while I live.'

Baldwin looked at him with surprise. 'You would renounce your own homeland?'

'I would give up everything to keep this city safe,' Buscarel said. He stared at the line of buildings. There were flames lighting the skies to the north and east. 'Look at her! Acre burns, and for what? My family is here, but what will happen to them, to us? The city must hold.'

'If she does, you will become a valued member of the Commune,' Baldwin said.

'Me? I doubt it. I am not noble, and I wasn't born here. No, they'll express thanks for my efforts and forget me. It's the way of things.'

Baldwin nodded. They both knew that when there was no longer a need to defend the city, the merchants and barons would take control again, and those who had risked their lives would be discarded. 'Your fame will not fade so easily,' Baldwin said. 'The man who could lob his missiles into the Muslim camp will be remembered for many years to come.'

'Perhaps. But then someone will mention that I was a pirate, and all my efforts before that will be overrun. But no matter. I am happy with my place. So long as there is wine to drink, and my woman is safe.'

'Aye,' Baldwin. His face hardened. 'Did you know what Lady Maria did to her maid?'

'Which?'

'Lucia. She is with me now. Lady Maria had her beaten, and then delivered her to a slave farm. I found her there and brought her back.'

'I wish you luck. For me, all I know is I am weary to the bones. I need to rest before I set sail again.'

'You'll continue tomorrow?'

'Yes. If I can provide a harrying fire against them, at least I will feel I am achieving something.'

'Tell me – when you assaulted our ship and took my ring, what would you have done with us?'

'Sold you as slaves. Lady Maria had contacts with dealers in Cairo, and I would have made a lot of money from you and some of the other pilgrims.'

'What of Mainboeuf?'

'He was her willing assistant. A wily merchant, with contacts all over. That was why Lady Maria used him, I think. She wanted to maintain good relations with the Muslims.'

'Why?'

'Because her lands are hard to defend. Lydda is a valuable town, and if the Muslims wanted, they could take it and all within it. Lady Maria did all she could to protect it and herself.'

'Would she have sold Acre?'

'No. She is a Christian.'

'So are many who would sell their city and friends for a purse filled with gold,' Baldwin said.

'Here?'

'It is rumoured that in Safed the Templars were betrayed by a single man who became Muslim,' Baldwin said. 'I did think that Mainboeuf could have done that. But then, why would he have been taken and thrown into gaol? It cannot have been him.'

'Surely no one would have betrayed us?' Buscarel said, but in his mind's eye he saw Lady Maria's green eyes, and he wondered.

'Good luck on the seas tomorrow. And God be with you.' Baldwin hesitated. Then, 'I will pray for you.'

Buscarel stared at him, and then patted Baldwin's dog. 'I never thought to make a friend of you.'

'I think we have both seen much that has changed us in the last days,' Baldwin said.

CHAPTER SEVENTY-TWO

That night, Baldwin did not return to the house. He was desperate to go to Lucia, and to hold her, to lie with her, as though in her bed he would be safe from the rocks flying through the air, but even as he made to return from the harbour, he heard the cries of men pleading for help.

'What's that?'

Hob jerked a thumb. 'Look at the fires.'

Swearing under his breath, Baldwin hurried up the roads to the city centre, Uther at his heels. The scene that met his eyes was one of horror. Fires had broken out through the whole of the eastern section near the Patriarch's Tower: there were eight great conflagrations near the church itself. Gathering himself, he bellowed for Hob to join him.

Hob was soon with him, and began to issue commands. In moments a boy had been sent to find Anselm and Thomas and the rest of the vintaine, while Hob and Baldwin sent another to find buckets. There seemed to be none about the area – all had been taken to the walls, where the fires had been burning already. Baldwin spotted the young James of Gibelet again and told him to run to the Templars and beg for any spare men they had, and all the buckets they could provide.

The Patriarch, a rather short, plump man with a white robe and cap, was standing before his cathedral, praying with his eyes squeezed tight shut. Two of his clerks were behind him, in the same attitude of prayer. Baldwin spoke to one, asking him to join them in helping put out the flames.

'Leave us, man! We are praying to save the cathedral,' he snapped.

'God might consider helping you more if *you* helped put out the fires around your church!' Baldwin snarled back.

'Sir, we have buckets,' Hob announced, and Baldwin was relieved to see a small force of Templars hurrying up.

One of them was Roger Flor, who gazed about him quizzically. 'Not looking good, is it?'

'It'll be better when you've helped put out the worst of it,' Baldwin said.

'Aye,' Roger said. Bernat was with him and the two strode over to join their companions in their brown tunics. Soon a chain of men was organised, and buckets were being manhandled up to the nearest fires, and while Baldwin felt the flesh on his face scorching in the heat, at least he saw that the advance of the flames was being halted.

Uther was running about and yelping with excitement, or perhaps fear, and Baldwin saw a man aim a kick at him. He didn't like to see a dog harmed, but for now he left the fellow alone. Uther retired, with a slinking hurt pride, which may have saved his life.

Moments after he had gone, there was a loud rumble, and Baldwin had to lunge away, taking Hob with him, as a wall collapsed, the stones glowing dully from their heat. Some fell into a pool of water, and instantly a cloud of steam rose. Then suddenly there was an explosion, and bits and pieces of stone shot all about. A man gave a thin scream, and clapped his hand to his face when a shard of red-hot stone lodged in his cheek. Others had to hold him down as he threshed about, and cut the stone out with a knife. Baldwin saw the next buildings begin to smoulder, and to his relief Hob gave orders for the men to hurry with the water again.

And so the work continued all through the night. At times Baldwin thought that they were getting the better of their enemy, and at last the flames were beginning to die down, but even as he had the thought, another wave of clay pots filled with Greek fire hurtled over the walls towards them.

One smashed on the ground before Baldwin, and he felt the liquid hit his tunic, but by some miracle, the contents did not ignite. Three or four others landed in the road or on buildings, and Baldwin and Hob were hard put to have the men stop the fires from taking hold again. It was not easy. The flames seemed impervious to water, and while the men threw bucket after bucket at them, still the flames continued to burn. Then, while the men were running about trying to douse one fire, a further pot crashed to earth near the cathedral, and instantly one of the two clerks was immersed in a column of flame. His figure could be seen encased within the fire, still bent and praying, and then slowly tumbled to the ground.

Baldwin swore under his breath. He grasped the Patriarch and his remaining clerk, pulling them from their contemplations, and shoving them away. 'If you won't help, you can at least get out of our way,' he shouted.

The Patriarch nodded, staring at his dead clerk. 'I don't understand,' he said with a pained voice.

'Who does?' Baldwin snarled.

*　　*　　*

Baldwin and Hob worked until the sun lit the horizon. In the orange glow of so many fires, it was hard to appreciate that this new light was not merely a hellish reflection, but soon Baldwin realised he could see Hob's face.

Every crease was black, filled with soot from a hundred houses, from the remnants of clothing and wood. His eyes gleamed, the whites reddened with soreness, and his lashes were darker, like a woman's lined with kohl. But most of all it was the weariness that Baldwin saw, and knew that he was every bit as exhausted.

They had fought the fires all night, but even now, the sun brought no respite. The thunder and crash of the missiles shattering and scattering their flames far and wide was just as prevalent as it had been in the middle of the night.

'Hob, go and get some rest. I'll see you on the wall,' Baldwin said.

'Aye,' Hob said, and called hoarsely to the rest of their men. Soon they were shuffling away, and Baldwin called to Uther, who was cowering under a cart.

'Come, little fellow,' Baldwin said. He took a moment to crouch and stroke his dog.

The road here had lost many houses. Remains of their masonry stood up like blackened teeth against the glowing sky.

'Sweet Jesus,' Baldwin murmured, remembering his first glimpse of the city from the ship. Back then, it had been a city of gold, he had thought. Now it was possessed by a demonic glow. Gradually he became aware of a strange stillness. There were still one or two crashes as rocks hit the city, but many of the machines seemed to have fallen silent.

He stood, carrying Uther, made his way to the walls and climbed the stairs. At this point, a large section of hoarding had been crushed and burned away, and there was little timber to replace it. It did at least mean Baldwin could see much of the plain.

All about him there was still the rumble of missiles. Before him on the plain, tens of thousands of warriors stood with their banners fluttering in the light morning's breeze. And then, the last of the catapults fell silent. There came a loud cheering from the field, and as Baldwin watched, he saw the appearance of a warrior on a horse.

'The Sultan,' a man next to him said.

He was followed by at least three hundred men on horseback, all wearing armour that gleamed in the early light. As Baldwin watched, the Sultan lifted his arm, and then let it fall, and in an instant, all the catapults fired together.

In the corner of the nearer tower, men were huddled down in the lee of the walls, watching a cock-fight. It astonished Baldwin that men would want to see more death, but at least the cocks meant there would be food later. A sentry, peering over the wall, ducked back and hissed at the men to expect a missile, before throwing down his own coin to bet on the winner.

The Muslims had adjusted their range, and now the machines were aiming solely at the walls, the majority beneath the Tower of King Henry. A vast weight of clay pots filled with Greek fire were aimed at that narrow section. Clouds of flame gushed, billowing black clouds smothered the area, and the noise was appalling. Over it all, Baldwin heard the iron clanging of the huge bolts fired by mangonels, their hideous heads burying themselves in the rock. He detested them.

'What now?' he said.

The man at his side was the same blue-eyed Englishman with the heavy falchion. 'Now? They'll concentrate all their efforts on the walls, and leave the damage inside the city to the two bigger ones over there.'

Baldwin looked to where he pointed, and saw al-Mansour rising over the field like a hideous gallows. He could almost imagine a man being hanged from that vast sling. It made the gorge rise in his throat. But then he saw something else from the corner of his eye. There, out at sea, was Buscarel's cog, and even as he watched, the cog's catapult swung up, and another rock was sent tumbling through the air.

'They will not hit it, you know,' Jacques said.

Baldwin turned with surprise. 'My friend, what are you doing here? You should be at the Lazar Tower.'

'I was aware of my post, yes,' Jacques said with a very slight tone of impatience. 'I have been sent to speak with Sir Otto. Sir Guillaume thinks that the ship will not succeed.'

'Why? Buscarel is doing a good job, flinging his rocks. It's only a matter of time before he has destroyed that damned machine.'

'Damned it may be, my friend, but do not be confused. We will die before it, at this rate. There is need for us to take the initiative.'

One of Sir Otto's men saw Sir Jacques, and hurried to take him over to the English Commander. Baldwin waited, watching them discussing something, both close to each other, glancing through gaps in the hoardings. Then there was a nod of agreement between the two, and they clasped their forearms in a display of trust.

'Wait for me tonight, Baldwin, at Ivo's house. You will come with us,' Sir Jacques said, with that quiet smile on his face.

'Where do we go?'

'We ride to that damned machine, my friend. We shall go there and burn it and send it to Hell, where it belongs!'

CHAPTER SEVENTY-THREE

By mid-morning, Buscarel was pleased with the way that the catapult was working. They had thrown fifteen of the great lumps of masonry, and although the Muslims had tried to fire their darts in retaliation, it had availed them nothing. With the cog bobbing and dancing near the coast, it was impossible for them to hit her. She wove a frenetic course along the coastline here, where the water was good and deep, and then tacked to return the other way, the men frantically working the great machine all the while.

It was good to be on the water again, he thought as he looked up at the sails and saw how she was falling away. This would be the last shot from this tack, he thought, and called to the sergeant in charge of the catapult to get a move on.

The sergeant roared at his men to withdraw, then pulled the pin. The long arm swept up, the sling caught the lump of broken stone, and with a scraping rasp, the missile was hoiked along its channel and up into the air. The sling released perfectly, and the stone flew straight and true.

His heart seem to stop. From here, Buscarel could see the stone moving swiftly away from him, up into the air, and then seem to hang, like a hawk stooping, only to plummet. And all the time, the rock was moving perfectly in line with the hideous bulk of al-Mansour.

'Sweet Jesus!' he prayed. 'Let it hit!'

There was a gout of sand, a spray of bodies, and al-Mansour was gone!

Buscarel bellowed with joy, his fist in the air, but even as he punched at the sky, he saw it was an illusion. The rock had hit men between him and that horrible device, but had missed it. Al-Mansour still functioned. As he watched, he saw the arm rise lazily, and fling a rock at the city wall.

Swearing to himself, Buscarel was hit with a dejection so intense, he could have thrown the oar from his sore armpit and gone to find his skin of wine. This was a fool's errand. How they could hope to hit a machine like that at such a distance, especially from a moving platform like a ship. It was stupid at best, insane at worst. A waste of time and precious materials.

'We go about!' he roared at the men, but the noise of the creaking and whining timbers of the cog took his voice away.

Suddenly, a wave hit the hull and the vessel began a long, slow roll. No great problem – a cog like this round-bellied old sow was capable of weathering much worse seas than this. But then, when he looked at the deck, he realised his error, and the new danger.

'Lash the ammunition securely!' he roared again, and this time one of men heard him. Seeing his frantic wave, the ship-man glanced about him, and Buscarel could see the dawning horror on his face as the rocks began to move.

'All of you! To the rocks! Tie them down!' Buscarel shouted in despair.

The rocks which he had so carefully piled on his deck had been fired from the one side as he beat up the coast and sailing back, from the other. But now, the weight of rock was unbalanced. There was too much on the port side of the ship, and as the wave caught her, the rocks on the starboard deck began to move. The slow sea made her roll sluggishly, and he could see the strain on the lashings over the rocks as the ship edged further and further over, until he was hanging onto the oar in a desperate panic.

Up on the castle, the sergeant was hanging on to a rope, cursing and berating his men while they tried to rope down the rocks, but it was too late. With a sharp report, the first lashing snapped, and a snake of tense cordage flew back. Buscarel heard the scream as it whipped past a shipman, cutting through his body, and flinging him aside. Then the rumble of the shifting load could be felt through the deck. Buscarel gritted his teeth in horror as the entire load moved, and the cracking of the parting ropes sounded like the reports of thunder. The moving rock seemed quiet in comparison, a hollow grating as tons shifted with a terrible inevitability to port. And with every inch they moved, the ship's ability to return to true was reduced, until suddenly she was too far over, and the rocks began to accelerate.

A pair of shipmen stood in the path of the avalanche. One scrambled, agile as a monkey, onto the top of the firmly lashed rocks at the port side, but the second was too slow. As he tried to follow his mate, a rock tumbled over and over, crushing his leg. His wail of agony made his companion stop, and Buscarel saw him gaze back with terror, then continue, leaving his companion behind. The trapped man glanced over his shoulder, and Buscarel saw the madness in his face as the next rocks engulfed him. His shrieks were soon silenced.

Buscarel tried to save the cog, hauling on the rudder to bring her around, thinking perhaps he could turn her port side to the sea, and that way have her forced upright . . . but a final wave thundered into her hull, throwing her over with a squeal of tortured wood. As he leaped from the deck, hit the water and sank in, the cool brine stinging his nose and throat, he heard a distant sound and realised it was a cheer of glee from his enemy.

He had failed.

Back at Ivo's house that evening, Baldwin ate an early supper. It was good to come home. He was so weary, it was hard to keep his eyes open, and the thought of heading straight for his bed was very appealing. At least in Ivo's house there was peace. It was far enough away from the walls to be safe from most of the catapults, although it was impossible to shut out the noise of stones hitting the walls and other buildings. A constant rumble and thud came even here: the threnody of war.

Ivo was at the gate with Pietro. 'How are you?' he asked, looking at the young man with sympathy.

'Tired,' Baldwin said.

When he saw Lucia, sitting on the bench in the garden, he was struck by a sudden embarrassment. He had no idea whether she had welcomed his advances on the night of the burning chapel. What if the poor girl had been too scared to refuse him, with the fear of a slave for her master? Perhaps she had thought he would rape her if she tried to refuse his advances? That was a horrible thought.

Edgar was at the table. 'I was over with the men at the English Tower today,' he said. 'The attacks on the Barbican and the Tower of King Henry are having an impact. It worries me, the way that the walls are shaking.'

'They must hold,' Ivo growled. 'If that point falls, the enemy will have immediate access to the city.'

'Perhaps. But even a baker can see when stones begin to shift in the masonry. A man beside me today was killed by a shard of rock. A missile struck the wall, and a great jagged piece of the parapet snapped off and flew through the air. It cut off both his legs.' Edgar wore a pensive frown.

'There were many on the outer wall today who died,' Ivo said. He sounded weary, and rubbed a hand over his eyes as he spoke. 'Too many.'

Pietro brought some skewered meats from the charcoal brazier. 'God's blood, many inside the city died as well,' he said harshly. 'We need God's protection, or the city will fall.'

'There are plenty of knights here,' Baldwin said. 'You shouldn't fear.'

'Eh? There are not enough men-at-arms. We need archers and axemen to defeat this foe,' Pietro said. He didn't meet Baldwin's look, but stared aggressively at the floor. 'I must go to the walls as well. I can do no good here, but I can wield a bow and arrows.'

'Who will guard the house from looting?' Ivo demanded.

'If the Muslims get in, there will be no house to protect,' Pietro said flatly.

Baldwin shot a look at Lucia. She had been listening, but her eyes were downcast. Feeling his guilt return, he too averted his eyes.

After they had finished their meal, Edgar and Pietro declared their interest in leaving the house for a while and seeing the damage outside. They left soon afterwards.

'What's the matter with you?' Ivo demanded, peering at Baldwin.

'Nothing. But I have been asked to ride out tonight.'

'Ride out?' Ivo echoed. 'What – outside the city?'

'I am to ride with the Templars and try to destroy that damned catapult,' Baldwin told him.

'It would have been better, had that blasted fool on the cog hit the thing,' Ivo muttered.

Baldwin shrugged. 'Sir Otto is determined to remove it,' he said.

'When do you go?'

'Sir Jacques will come for me.'

'Good,' Ivo said, and drained his wine. 'At least he can keep an eye on you, eh?'

As Baldwin rose and left them, Ivo saw Lucia looking after him.

'You should go to him, maid. He may die tonight,' Ivo said, then looked up as a loud rumble came to them: another building struck and collapsing. 'We all may.'

Edgar was already up. 'I will see if I can help,' he said.

Ivo nodded. 'You go. I'll wait here. I need to rest.'

Lucia watched while Ivo poured himself another cup of wine.

'I know you, Lucia. And I know that boy quite well. He's a good man. He needs your comfort.'

'He did not look at me.'

'Did he need to? He isn't used to the sight of men dying. He's not a knight. Treat him with kindness.'

'I do,' she said quietly.

There was another rumble nearby, and then a yelping from outside the gate. Lucia felt a quick alarm. 'That's Uther,' she said, and hurried to the door.

The dog must have followed Pietro and Edgar when they opened the door, and a pair of street urchins had seen him. As

Lucia opened the door, she saw them throw pebbles. Uther was whimpering at the edge of the road, while the boys laughed.

'Stop!' Lucia shouted, running out into the road, but the boys only jeered and threw the last of their stones. They bolted when they saw Baldwin appear in the doorway.

Lucia ran to the dog, and when she looked up, she saw the twisted anguish in Baldwin's face. He reached down tenderly and gathered up the dog, who whined again.

'You poor fellow, Uther,' Baldwin said, and there was a catch in his throat.

He turned and carried the dog back through the door. Lucia followed in his wake, pulling the door closed behind her. Baldwin laid the dog down on an old scrap of cloth he found, and studied him.

Uther had been badly beaten. His fur was matted with blood, an ear had been slashed, and now he lay panting like a hart held at bay. Baldwin touched his head with his hand, and the dog opened an eye and stared up at him for a moment. His tail beat twice on the ground, and then he closed his eyes again and lay, his breathing fast and unnatural.

'Be strong, little fellow,' Baldwin murmured.

Lucia saw the tears in his eyes and heard the thickening in his voice. She stroked Baldwin's arm. 'I will look after him.'

'Thank you,' Baldwin said, and would have said more, but there was a loud knock at the door. He ran to fetch his sword, took his leave of Ivo, and stood beside her.

'Be strong, Uther,' he said again.

'Be careful,' Lucia said. 'Please, my lord.'

He glanced at her with surprise, and then bent to her and kissed her softly. 'I will. Take care of him for me, Lucia, please.' And then he was gone.

Lucia knelt beside the dog and rubbed her hand over his hot pelt. 'You have to live,' she told him. 'He needs you more than me. If you die, that will be an ill omen for him. Don't leave him!'

CHAPTER SEVENTY-FOUR

Baldwin strode through the streets until he reached the Hospital of the Knights of St Lazarus. It was a large space – a fortunate fact, since there was a great force of men and horses gathering. It was roughly triangular, with the church dedicated to St Lazarus on the left, and the great gateway of the inner wall dead ahead. The tower of St Lazarus, which had been funded by the Order, was the other side of the gateway, and not visible from here. All the outer towers were built to be overlooked by those of the inner walls, so that defenders would always have the advantage.

The Templars stood patiently by their horses. They were the largest force here, and Sir Guillaume de Beaujeu was mounted on a massive black destrier who pranced and stepped with barely controlled excitement. This was no sweet-natured horse, but a trained man-killer that would kick, bite and stamp on any man in his path.

'Quick, Baldwin – you can ride with a lance, can you not?' Sir Jacques demanded.

'Yes, of course I can!'

'Good, then wait,' he said, and beckoned a sergeant from his Order. The man carried a mail shirt that was several inches too big for Baldwin, but Sir Jacques insisted that Baldwin wear it over his padded jack. There was a pair of whalebone-reinforced gauntlets, too, and a helmet of steel, but Baldwin found this last to be too large for his head and loose, so the sergeant had to run to fetch a thicker padded coif for him to wear beneath it.

'You will ride with the men behind the second rank, the squires and sergeants, Baldwin,' Sir Jacques said as Baldwin drew the helmet on. It restricted his vision, and he found his breath disconcertingly loud.

'I am glad. But of all the men in Sir Otto's army, why me?'

'Well, my friend, I thought you could do with the ride. And there could be benefits for a man who has ridden in a holy war. We shall see!' Jacques said with a quiet smile. 'But for now, please do me the favour of not getting yourself injured or killed, eh? Ivo would never forgive me. Keep your head low, aim for the heart, and keep your seat.'

'Yes.'

'You know how cavalry strikes. The heavy knights in the first wave will try to hit as one wall, knocking all opposition aside. The second wall will be the sergeants on the remounts for the knights, and finally the third wave is yours. These successive shocks are what should drive the force through the defence.'

Baldwin nodded.

'You will ride behind my sergeant here. Do you keep with him and mark his position, so that when we all pass through the Muslim positions, we shall be together and capable of support-ing each other. If you lose us, look for the Lazarus banner, and if you cannot see that, go to the Templar banner.'

There came a hissed command, at which the Templars mounted their horses.

'God be with us!' Sir Jacques said with a grin and trotted to his position.

At their head, Baldwin saw the Marshal, Geoffrey de Vendac, and beside him the tall figure of Sir Otto de Grandison, who looked about him carefully, eyeing the men all around, before lifting his heavy war-helm up and onto his head. A man passed him his lance, and Sir Otto raised it to the Templar Marshal in salute. The Templars set off, eleven knights all told, with another four English and three Leper Knights. And behind them, another three hundred men, mounted like Baldwin on heavy horses and armed with lances and a variety of other weapons.

And before them, Baldwin told himself, were two hundred thousand or more. He shrugged the thought away. His position was behind Sir Jacques. That was all he need worry about.

Glancing around, he was surprised to see a number of men bearing clay bottles with stoppers; they dangled from their saddles by thongs. They must be some form of weapon, but Baldwin was unsure what. His wrist was sore where it was burned, and he rubbed it against his chin, filled with expectation.

The movement of the horse beneath him was so familiar, it felt as if it was only hours since his last ride. This was what he had trained for since his seventh birthday: battle on horseback. He had practised for it so many times, and yet this was different. This time, it was for real. But the light and the strange atmosphere made everything feel like a dream. He leaned back against the cantle, then to either side, making sure the cinch strap was tight, and shrugged his mail over his back. It caught some hairs at the base of his neck and yanked them out. The lance he had been given felt solid enough. There was no looseness or rattling when he shook it. He felt for his sword, making sure it was firmly held. His mount blew, lifting his head and nodding, before shaking his head. All the brutes were the same – they were eager, like race-horses at the start.

He had a little knot of tension high in his belly – not fear, but anticipation. Baldwin was keen to be out and galloping, as was his horse. He patted the fellow's neck – a good, hard slap to remind him that he had a rider and that his will today was subservient to Baldwin's.

The Lazar sergeant beside him stared ahead, not looking to either side. At first Baldwin thought him afraid, but it was not that, it was merely a stare of concentration. Like the others he must keep his eye on his own knight, so that the line would remain solid as they came to blows. Looking up, Baldwin saw that the moon was almost full. Its light would illuminate the field and make their ride all the easier. But with luck, their attempt would be a surprise to the Muslims. If it were, their mission might just succeed.

There was a squeak of iron complaining, and the first gate was opened. The way between the walls was visible, the barred gates of the outer wall clear before them. An order was issued quietly, and Baldwin gripped his lance more closely as he saw three guards begin to slide the massive bars across to rest in their slot in the wall itself.

Jacques peered over his shoulder and grinned, and Baldwin returned it, and then the gates opened and they were off.

There was a hush as the men rode into the space before the wall. Baldwin saw them funnel into the darkness of the tower's gate, and then he too was beneath the vaulted ceiling of the gate-house, and through, past the portcullis and gates, and his horse's hooves thudded, muffled by the soft sand as they trotted gently onwards.

Sir Otto was looking carefully from side to side, assessing the total men with his force as he went. Gradually the Templars took up station behind their Marshal, he taking the point of their formation, while the knights were each followed by their own waves of squires on heavy horses, then their sergeants on lighter mounts.

Baldwin saw Sir Otto's great destrier rear up, flailing his hooves in eagerness for the fight, and the knight held his lance aloft. All the men were in the plain now, and Baldwin watched the Marshal moving off, Sir Otto with him, and the standard-bearer of the Templars holding position between the two, the Beaucéant banner flapping as they trotted forward.

No cavalry could hold formation for long at the gallop. It was crucial that the front ranks should hit in one solid mass, punching through their enemies, and to achieve that, the charge must be launched as late as possible, so that all reached their gallop together moments before they struck the enemy.

Soft, warm air touched his face. An occasional splash of cool sand flung at him, leaving a crusty residue on his lips. A grain in his eye, making him blink and quickly rub at it. A picture of Lucia's face. Baldwin found his mind wandering as he rode, random thoughts springing into his mind. Sibilla's lover. The Cathedral Church at Exeter, the priest, the house being demolished and the sudden thought that he should come to the Holy Land. All so long ago now.

All this ran through his mind, and then he realised that they were already increasing their speed, and forced his mind to concentrate. They were cantering gently, covering the space between the walls and the army quickly. And then he heard the command from Sir Otto to charge, and immediately the bellow of rage, such as might issue from a charging bull, and Sir Otto leaned forward slightly, his lance point dropping, and there was an echoing roar from the Templars. All their weapons were lowered, and Baldwin felt his blood singing in his veins as they pounded onwards, and there, just ahead, he heard a shriek of terror, and a man sprang up from the ground, only to be trampled by the Templar horses. A mess of flesh and torn clothing. Two sergeants galloped past the line of knights, one desperately trying to rein in his mount, but their horses were paying no heed. All were thundering forward, to ruin and death. Suddenly Baldwin's mind was clear again.

Ahead was the Muslim army. Lights from torches and fires illuminated their path as the three hundred men pounded on. A squeal told of a man impaled on a lance, and Baldwin saw his body sprawled in the sand a moment later, but then he was concentrating on the path ahead. There was the great arm of the catapult, and he saw that Sir Jacques was heading straight for it. The Templars were fanning out slightly, giving themselves more space, and now there was a rippling crash as the front ranks slammed into the paltry defence and through it.

Their arrival was a ghastly shock to the Muslims. The Templars poured through and over their sentries like a tide washing away the sand.

It was then that everything went wrong.

A horse gave a screech of terror and reared, falling into a latrine. Others, swerving to avoid it, rode past a tent, too close, and their legs became entangled with guy-ropes. One fell, crushing his knight, but already their moment was passed. More and more Muslim warriors appeared, wielding vicious axes on long shafts, spears, even a war-hammer or two, and the men were soon engaged on all sides.

Baldwin hurled his lance at one man and drew his sword, clapping spurs to his brute and riding on to the front of the battle. There was a hedge of bladed weapons glinting wickedly in the moonlight, and shouts and roars as the horses moved forward, only to be pushed back. A mount reared in agony, a lance jutting from his breast, and fell amongst their enemies, and Baldwin saw the rider, a sergeant, disappear under a flurry of swords and axes. There was plenty of space between the men, and he urged his horse on, spurring straight at three men who were running towards the Marshal. One had a spear, and was about to thrust it into the Marshal's face when Baldwin crashed into him. The man fell under Baldwin's horse, and he used his sword against the other two.

The Marshal glanced at him briefly and nodded. It was good to see his act had been acknowledged.

A shout, and he saw another group of Muslims nearer the catapult. They set themselves with lances and spears butted into the ground, small, round shields before them. Baldwin rode towards them with Sir Otto and two English knights, but they could not break through the bristling points. Baldwin would have ridden past them, but there was no passage, and he swore under his breath. More Muslims were advancing, warily, from their left, and Sir Otto waved on the rest of the sergeants.

'Use them!' he bawled. 'Hurry!'

Two of the men nodded, and took up the pots they carried at their saddles. They hurled them into the men crouched before them, and a third man, who had ridden to a fire, came up with a lighted torch, and flung it after the pots. Instantly there was a loud shooshing sound, and a thick, yellow flame rose from the midst of the spear-men. The rest were thrown into confusion, and Sir Otto rode into the thick of them, plying a mace with a spiked head. Everywhere he went, the Muslims fell, and even when his sergeant was killed, stabbed by a spear under his chin, Sir Otto carried on.

Baldwin rode to his side, taking the place of his sergeant, and hacked with his sword. Inside his mail coat, Baldwin was sweating profusely. His mouth was dry and he craved a drink. A fresh flash and wash of heat heralded the detonation of more Greek fire, but when Baldwin snatched a glance, he saw that only their enemies were being burned. The catapult stood high overhead still, mocking them, and Baldwin suddenly felt rage at the thing. He spurred and whipped his beast, trying to force a path forward, but the press about him was too strong. He felt a blow at his side, and looked down to see a Muslim with anxious eyes staring at him. Baldwin thrust into his face, and saw the man fall, but even as he did so, he felt a hot lash at his leg. When he glanced down, he saw he'd been cut. It was bleeding, but not profusely. He slashed with his sword, backhanded, at the man who had stabbed him, and aimed another cut at a man with a bill, but had to duck under the fearful weapon's blade, and then a man with a lance tried to paunch him at the same time.

'Sweet Jesu,' he muttered. A weapon flew past his face, almost taking his eye out, and he dodged again.

They had lost their momentum. Those with the fire-bombs were held back, and the knights were involved in furious hand-to-hand combats near their standard. Their position was precarious. He heard a rallying cry, and managed to jerk his mount's head away from the group trying to encircle him, cantering back to the banner. Behind them all, he saw that Muslims were beginning to rush to take up positions.

Sir Otto was now wielding a hand-and-a-half sword with the ease of a child with a stick. He brought it down on the head of a man with an axe, and the man's head was cloven in two. The knight looked over at Baldwin, who shouted, pointing: 'We're trapped!'

'Not yet!' Sir Otto bawled, and then bellowed at the men to retreat to the gate.

Sir Jacques appeared at Baldwin's side. There was a thick smear of blood on his cheek, and his mouth was raw where a weapon had smashed into his teeth.

Baldwin rode at his side as the remaining men, perhaps only two thirds of the number which had left the gate ten minutes before, galloped at the men trying to entrap them. The Muslims were scattered like grain broadcast over a field, and the Christians continued until they reached the gates. And as soon as they were back inside, the gates were slammed, the bars sent across to block out the enemy.

The night's assault was over. Baldwin wearily sat in his saddle and gazed about him at those who had survived the carnage as they rode back into the broad area before the Hospital of St Lazarus again. There were so few, compared with the glorious force that had gathered here only a matter of a few tens of minutes before. The only emotion he could feel was despair at the thought of all those good men who had died. He should have seen it coming, after the failure of the Muslim attack on the Templar camp. They too had become tangled in guy-ropes. But he had not thought.

So many had died. And all in vain.

CHAPTER SEVENTY-FIVE

There was an enormous shudder, and Buscarel came to, in time to receive a shower of grit in his eyes. Coughing, he rolled over, blinking and wiping at his eyes.

'Wait, you fool. You want to shove sand tighter into your eyes?'

'Where am I?'

'In the undercroft of the Temple. You're damned lucky, too.'

He at last managed to open his eyes and gaze about him. The chamber was an old storage room, with squat, solid pillars holding up the massive vaults of the ceiling. Sconces held candles which burned with sickly yellow flames, and there were some torches further away, set into brackets in the walls. Along the floor, palliasses were set out, and on all of them, men were lying. Some appeared to be asleep, but for the most part, the men were awake, listening to the thuds of the rocks hitting the ground overhead.

'Are they hitting the Temple?'

'What, with their rocks? No, these are all landing a long way away,' the man said.

Buscarel glanced at him. He was a short, grizzled fellow with the arms of an archer – immensely strong shoulders and biceps. 'Why are you here?'

'I managed to get a splinter of rock on my head,' the man said. 'It took off my helmet, and I was bleeding so much, they thought I wouldn't last long. Then someone noticed I was breathing. You were the same.'

'You said I was lucky – why? How did I get here? I remember the ship sinking, and the sea washing me away . . .'

'A fisherman found you and brought you in. He thought you were too far gone but the brothers reckon you'll be all right.'

Buscarel remembered. The water, lapping over his nose and mouth, the saltiness on his tongue, the desperate thirst, while he clung to the ship's oar. Every so often he would see the battlefield and glimpse the rocks flying, the darkening of the sky as arrows were loosed at the walls of Acre. And then there would be a wave under him again, and it would pass on to the shore, while he was concealed from that world of pain and anguish.

He had thought of letting go. Of sinking, to drown slowly. Men said it was not so painful. But others talked of the monsters beneath the waves, the little fishes that would feast on a man's flesh, the crabs that would pick at his eyes, the jelly-like creatures, the slugs, all eating his body . . . and he knew he couldn't submit. To do that would be to give away his entire body, and what would he then have on the day God called to the dead to rise again? So he had gripped that piece of timber, and refused to let go, while the shore slipped away, further and further, and the currents pulled him out to sea.

A man clad in brown robes moved along the palliasses, a bucket in one hand, a ladle in the other. He stopped, providing drink to those who needed it, and Buscarel realised he was parched. He swallowed, and called. The monk saw him and nodded, but continued his progress. One man did not move. The monk sighed, placed the bucket on the ground, the ladle inside it, and pulled the man from the palliasse, leaving him on the stone flags, then carried on.

There was a smell about the room, Buscarel noticed now. A fusty odour of old damp stone and mortar, overlaid with a thick, cloying stench. It was the smell of death.

Lucia was in the garden still when Pietro opened the door, and she rose with a start on seeing Sir Jacques helping Baldwin inside, an arm about his shoulders.

Sir Jacques still managed to smile with his ruined mouth as he released his patient and passed him to Pietro. 'Take care of Master Baldwin,' he mumbled. 'He will need that wound seen to.'

'What has the fellow done to himself?' Pietro demanded, standing back and peering down.

He was pushed aside as Lucia reached him. 'Oh, oh!' She fell to her knees and pulled at his hosen, staring at his injured leg with her mouth curled in horror. 'Quick, to his bed, and then fetch me a cloth and hot water!'

'Eh? I suppose I don't have enough to do already?' Pietro muttered truculently, but did as he was bid, while Lucia turned to Sir Jacques.

'Nay, child, not me,' he protested quickly. 'I am not permitted to be touched by a woman.'

'You think you will lose yourself in passion for me?' she said curtly.

He took a step away, a grin twisting his bloodied features. 'Baldwin has, has he not? Go to him, child. He needs you more than I, and I have men who can see to my face. Go on! Go!'

She frowned quickly, but then turned and went back to Baldwin.

His leg was a mess. The cut had gone deep. It was fortunate that the bleeding seemed only slow, but he must surely rest it, she thought.

'It was a dismal failure,' Baldwin panted. 'I should have warned them. I saw the Muslims fail in the same way when they attacked us in the desert.'

She placed a hand on his breast, and the gentle rumble of his voice made her hand tingle. 'I prayed for you, and you returned, so I am happy.'

'A hundred didn't. They'll remain out there. And what will become of us, I don't know.'

'Do not worry. You need to rest your leg, let it heal.'

'No, Lucia, I can't. I have to get back to the walls tomorrow. I have men to command,' he fretted.

'You must have a physician look at your leg,' she insisted. Pietro had entered, for once silently, and placed a bowl of hot water at her side. She took a ball of muslin and soaked it, before beginning to wipe at the blood about his wound. The lips opened wide and she could see the blood moving thickly within, while the white flesh pulling away made it look strangely obscene. She dabbed and cleaned the gash as best she might, then called for Pietro.

'Yes? Can't a man get any rest?' he grumbled as he reached the door.

'I need some egg-white. Give the yolk to Uther, and bring me the white.'

'And then, I suppose get used to watching over the man all day long,' she heard him grumbling as he turned and walked back to his kitchen. Soon she had the egg, and could smear it all over the wound.

'There! That is the best I can do for you,' she said, wrapping his leg in a fresh piece of muslin. 'You must rest now.'

'I don't want to rest. How is Uther?'

'I think he will live. He will be better if I bring him in here. The two invalids may soothe each other,' she added with a twinkle in her eye.

'It will be some time before I can sleep with you again,' Baldwin said sadly.

'If that is all you can think of, you are already mending.'

'Please, lie here with me.'

Fifteen minutes later, Pietro passed the chamber and saw the two lying together. Lucia was asleep, her head on Baldwin's breast, and Pietro saw that Baldwin's hand was clutching hers. It was enough to waken a pang of jealousy, but he refused to give in to that. He continued past them, recalling his own woman. Long dead now, of course. Along with his family.

'Pietro! Get over here!'

He sighed, fitted the accustomed scowl to his face, and shuffled reluctantly to the man who had saved him then, and who was still the only man for whom he would willingly die. 'Sir?'

'Sir Jacques needs wine. Quickly, man.'

Pietro was soon back with a jug, and he set it down beside the two men, passing them cups before he bent, grunting, to serve them both.

Sir Jacques found it difficult to talk. His mouth was terribly battered and bruised, and Pietro could hardly take his eyes from the injury.

'It was a man's gauntlet,' Sir Jacques said, seeing Pietro's look. 'A Brother Templar was lancing a Muslim, and his arm flew up and hit me. Hardly the kind of honourable injury I'd expected,' he added wryly.

'Master Baldwin, he said a third of the men were lost?' Pietro said.

'I think so. The knights returned, but of the sergeants and squires, I fear we lost many. It was a bad game. Very bad,' Sir Jacques said.

'What of Master Baldwin?' Ivo asked.

'He was as bold as a youth could be. He rode himself up with the rest of the force, and made his way to the front, and he saved the Marshal of the Temple, I think, when Sir Geoffrey was sorely pressed. He was a credit.'

'I am glad,' Ivo said. He stared up the garden to where Baldwin's chamber lay.

'But even with him, we'll find it difficult to survive,' Pietro finished for him.

'You still here? If I need advice from a servant, I'll ask for it,' Ivo muttered, but without heat.

'He is right,' Sir Jacques said. He took an olive from the dish between them and carefully placed it in the right side of his mouth, away from his wound. 'If we receive no more help, we will fail. There is food and water aplenty, and we have no lack of weapons, but we need more men. We cannot afford to lose almost a hundred in an evening.'

'I know,' Ivo said. 'We shall have to hope that more men arrive.'

'We must pray for our dead companions,' Sir Jacques said.

'Yes,' Ivo replied gruffly. 'Of course we must.'

*　　*　　*

Ivo walked with Pietro to the wall the next day. Baldwin wanted to join them, but Ivo threatened to have him restrained if he did not agree to remain with Lucia.

'What, do you think that the city can afford to lose any more men?' he demanded. 'You have a duty to heal yourself. The city won't fall this morning just because you have stayed back, boy!' Ivo had taken a good look at his injury already that morning, and was sure that it was not a life-threatening one.

'Come, Pietro,' he said as he and his servant climbed the stone stairs to the inner walls.

Pietro's face was hard as he took in the scene. Where the hoardings had stood only a week ago, now there were only shattered remains. The incessant bombardment had done its job in reducing them to firewood, and from the walls all could see the full sweep of the army facing them, and the machines working constantly. Even as Pietro took it all in, there was a thundering detonation behind them, and he span round, startled. It was only Ivo's hasty grab for his sleeve that prevented him from toppling over the edge. 'Careful!'

'Yes, Master,' Pietro said, staring at the orange flames and coils of thick black smoke that rose from the rubble.

There was a warning shout, and men dropped to their knees or cowered as a quartet of stones and pots of Greek fire slammed into the walls. Three hit the outer wall, but the fourth lazily swooped down towards them on the inner wall. Ivo thought for an instant it would breast the battlements, but at the last moment it dropped, and they all felt the stones beneath them shudder with the impact.

'Christ Jesus! These whoresons are getting serious!' Pietro managed after a moment.

'Aye, that they are,' Ivo said.

'Master Ivo, this is not a war we can win, is it?' Pietro said.

Ivo stared out across the plain. In his heart he was certain that this city must fail, like Tripoli, like Lattakieh, like all the cities which the Christian crusaders had taken over the years. There was no survival against such numbers.

'God will save us,' a man said from the wall nearby.

Pietro was staring at Ivo, almost like Uther staring at Baldwin, a pathetic look of hope in his eyes.

Ivo forced a smile to his face. 'Of course He will,' he said. 'You seriously think God would allow us to lose His lands?'

CHAPTER SEVENTY-SIX

When Lucia would finally allow him to rise, Baldwin was fretting badly. Uther was a changed animal, and while his injuries had healed already, his heart would not. He ate his food, but when a new noise came, he shivered uncontrollably and tried to hide. If a man knocked at the door, the poor creature would slink away, to conceal himself in any dark hollow.

Baldwin at last managed to limp his way to the walls, leaving the little dog with Lucia. On the walls, with a crutch fashioned from a broken beam at a house, he stared out bleakly.

'Master Baldwin, I'm glad to see you well,' Hob said. 'We were wondering when you would come back.'

'Or whether you would,' Nicholas Hunfrey added.

Baldwin had a feeling of great comradeship up here with them. Anselm and his brother were squatting near the wall playing dice. Nicholas Hunfrey had a half-cooked chicken leg that he was chewing with relish, and others stood taking their ease, idling the day away, while Hob stayed at the parapet, staring out at the Muslims. He ducked quickly as the wall shook, an eruption of thick black smoke rising from a fresh missile. Then he was up again, peering over at the enemy.

'If others had their way, I wouldn't be here now,' Baldwin said. 'What has been happening?'

'They loose arrows at us,' Nicholas said, 'so we loose them back; they run at our walls, we throw rocks, oil, everything at them, and they die or run away. But they're tunnelling, I don't doubt. You can hear them at the rocks below, if you listen carefully.'

'Will the walls survive this onslaught?'

'The men who built this city knew what they were doing,' Hob said. He yawned.

'How *are* the men?' Baldwin asked, gazing at them all.

'We survive. But we need to keep them busy.'

'It's this waiting that drains a man,' Baldwin said. 'If we could get out there and fight, it would be better. We should plan more offensives, like the Templars' attack.'

'Perhaps,' Hob said heavily, 'but we all saw the after-effects of that. The leader over there by the catapult had the Templar bodies brought round in front of the walls where we could see them, and had them beheaded. They were used to decorate the Templar mounts they captured, and were led around the front of their army to the Sultan. We could see the horses being presented to the Sultan himself. We don't need more attacks like that.'

'No,' Baldwin agreed. He clenched a fist and rested it on the parapet before him. 'I just want to know when we are likely to fight! I want to get at the bastards.'

'A siege can last a long time.'

'I once heard that it took a whole year to surrender to King Richard, a hundred years ago,' Baldwin said.

'God forbid!' Hob winced.

*　　*　　*

Buscarel was still very weak when he walked out of the Temple. He looked at the ships in the harbour and leaned on a wall while a bout of shivering overwhelmed him. His condition was not from any injury, but a result of the two fevers he had suffered. Leaving the undercroft, he felt as weak as a kitten, and the play of the sun on his face was as delicious as the caress of a beautiful woman.

A rock crashed into the buildings behind him, and he turned with a start. A house only a block or two up from the Venetian quarter suddenly crumbled before his eyes, the outer wall dissolving into dried mud and masonry. It woke him from his reverie. If the missiles could reach him here, then surely his own house would be in danger.

Hobbling, he made his way up into the Genoese quarter, until he came to his own road, to his own house. He must have come the wrong way, he told himself. This wasn't his road. This wasn't where his house had stood.

But it was.

There was nothing left. Where once there had been a tall, strong property, with space for his family, now there was a void, one of many, in which masonry and timbers lay in haphazard piles. He stepped forward, two, three paces, and stood staring in disbelief. His throat swelled; he tried to swallow, but the lump was too big. There was a vast emptiness within him, as if someone had reached in and plucked out his heart.

'Cecilia,' he managed hoarsely. Where was she? Where was his family?

'Cecilia?' he shouted, and then he screamed her name, again and again, his voice swallowed up in the cacophony of the battle.

CHAPTER SEVENTY-SEVEN

Acre was sombre that morning. Despair was like a blanket, smothering hope throughout the city as Baldwin and Ivo walked to the walls. The Hospital was keen to launch another night attack. Baldwin suspected that they wanted to show their age-old rivals at the Temple how a midnight raid should be conducted. They gathered a force of some two hundred and fifty men, with fifteen knights and the rest made up of well-armed sergeants and men-at-arms, and on a moonless night, they issued from St Anthony's Gate, formed into battle order, and set off for the towering mass of al-Mansour.

Their attempt was doomed from the first. The Muslims had learned from the abortive attack of the Templars, and before the Hospitallers had crossed half the distance, a series of fires were lighted and the army roused. For a brief space, those on the walls saw the Hospitallers' weapons glinting in the fire-light, and then they charged – a glorious, determined gallop across the plain that began as a disciplined band of warriors, but soon degenerated into a simple race for the Muslim lines, and as they went Baldwin saw the sharp gleams and flashes as bodkin arrows plummeted down.

Horses plunged headfirst into the sand as arrows struck. Baldwin saw a knight grasping at an arrow in his throat, both hands desperately scrabbling for it before he tumbled from the saddle. Men fell on all sides, and the horses were driven mad with pain. One lost direction, and rode parallel with the city walls, between defender and attacker, his rider holding on for dear life, while more and more arrows were loosed at them, until a merciful shot drove into the horse's skull and the rider broke his neck in the fall.

The Marshal led his men on, while his companions overtook him and went on to slam individually into the line of spears set into the sands. Horses were impaled. Baldwin saw a rider, thrown by a reluctant beast, hurled onto a spear, where he wriggled, his screams carrying clearly back to the city. Two Muslims stood by him, but did nothing to stop his agony. He took a long time to die, while his companions tried to hack their way past the outer perimeter and in towards their objective.

Baldwin saw the swords rising and descending, the forward surge of the men and horses, their falling back, only to regroup and move forward again, and yet there was nothing the gallant Hospitallers could do against the numbers forming against them. As they struggled to make headway, more and more Muslims were augmenting the force opposing them, and eventually the men of the Hospital had to withdraw. The Marshal called his men back, the standard-bearer turning and taking the lead, but even now the Hospital must endure the trial of a long ride under constant assault from the archers and slingers, and even two mangonels which were brought into action. One bolt passed through two riders and then slammed into a horse, killing all three outright. And then it was over. The men reached St Anthony's Gate, and passed inside again.

Now, staring out at the plain, all the bodies could be seen clearly in the daylight. No one moved to take them away. It was as though the Muslims were taunting the men of Acre by leaving them to rot in the sun.

'Everyone knows,' Edgar said. He had joined Baldwin that morning and now stood peering over the parapet with an expression of resolution on his face.

'About the Hospitallers?'

'No, about our chances of survival. If Temple and Hospital cannot force a way through, then we are all held here. And with a hundred or more catapults working day and night, the walls will fail.' His tone was reflective, but matter-of-fact.

Baldwin nodded. 'We need a miracle,' he said.

'Let me in,' Buscarel said as the grille opened. A short time later, he was inside the familiar, cool entranceway to Lady Maria's house.

'Buscarel. I thought you were dead,' she said coolly.

'Your man found me.'

'Your house. Yes. I heard it was gone,' she said.

She snapped her fingers and her bottler appeared with a tray which held chilled wine and goblets of fine glass. He set the tray down on a table, and poured. As he did so, there was a crash from somewhere nearby, and he nearly upset the tray. Buscarel did not need to look to know his face was twitching. The fellow had enjoyed ruling over the slaves and servants in the house, but now the enemy was near, his nerves were frayed. Buscarel didn't care. He didn't care about anything.

'What do you want with me?' he demanded.

He had been camping in the main room of his ruined house

when Lady Maria's henchman had seen him and asked him to come here. Buscarel had nowhere else to go. He had salvaged a few shreds of cloth from another house up the road, and had used this to create a shelter and some shade from the sun – but apart from that, he had done nothing since discovering the house, merely spent his time squatting, watching the piles of rubble as though he half-expected to see his wife rise from them at any moment. It was futile to dig amongst the ruins; a man from further up the road had told him that his family had all been inside when the house was struck, and no one had come out alive.

Buscarel should have gone to the walls, to carry on fighting, but he couldn't. He was still enfeebled after his fevers and instead had remained there with the shattered remnants of his life. He had lost the will to do anything.

'I would like you to come and live here with me,' Lady Maria said.

'Why?'

She pulled a face. 'I have no guards. They have been taken to the walls, and I must have someone here to protect me and my house.'

'You think I can protect you against the Muslims? Lady, when they arrive, we'll *all* die.'

'I am not worried about *them*,' she said impatiently. 'It's the mob that scares me.' The bottler served the wine and walked off with his tray. 'I know enough of the Sultan and his court to know the right men to speak with,' she went on. 'You can leave all that to me. All you need do is protect me and my house. Do that, and you and I will be safe.'

'Safe?' he laughed hoarsely. 'No one is safe here!'

'Will you do this? Protect me, please!'

'Very well. I have nothing else to do,' he said. And nothing mattered anyway. Not any more.

CHAPTER SEVENTY-EIGHT

Later that same day, it seemed as if God had answered the prayers of the people in the city, for a little after noon, cries went up all over the city.

'The King! The King's here!'

Edgar had remained on the walls, while Baldwin and Hob went to help a team of Pisan engineers near the Patriarch's Tower, helping to piece together an even more massive catapult than those which Hob had already built. Hob's eyes blazed with an ungodly light when he was working on these machines of death, and Baldwin clapped him on the back and joked, 'You will kill more Muslims with your catapult than I will with a sword and twenty men behind me!'

Hob nodded grimly. 'I hope so.'

At that moment, a man on the wall above turned and bellowed, 'Look! Ships! Christ Jesus, I've never seen so many ships!'

Hob and Baldwin exchanged a look and walked down the roadway towards the harbour for a better view. Baldwin stopped, mouth wide. 'Good God!'

'Aye. They'll help,' Hob said.

From the port itself all the way to the horizon was a mass of shipping. Baldwin's delighted eyes ran over them, trying to count. 'How many are there?'

'The way they're rolling, I doubt even a shepherd could count that little lot,' Hob grunted.

Baldwin reached thirty great cogs, but then gave up. Herding them were galleys of war, with Venetian or Pisan flags flying cheerily in the wind. Men and arms: hope for the people of the city!

But it was the flag on the ship quickly approaching the shore that made Baldwin's heart race: the sky-blue background and five gold crosses of the Kingdom of Jerusalem.

That night was a festive occasion like no other Baldwin had attended in the city.

There was a feast, which had originally been intended to be held in the castle's yard, but bearing in mind the proximity of the catapults, it was agreed that they should move further from the city walls. Instead, King Hugh II of Jerusalem ordered that tables be set out before the Temple, and here the notables of the city gathered, including secular knights and merchants wearing their finest silks. With the press of people in the yard, it was a miracle anyone could sit. If a missile *had* landed in their midst, it would have wiped out most of the commanders of the city, Baldwin thought. The Commune was present, as were the Grand Masters of the Orders, Otto de Grandison, the leaders of the Venetians and the Pisans, amongst others, and all were determined to demonstrate that they were unconcerned by their position.

Ivo was invited, and he brought a reluctant Baldwin along with him. Baldwin would have been happier to remain behind with Lucia, and leave this task to Edgar. More and more men had turned to theft and violence in recent days, and although those caught trying to cut a man's purse or stealing into a house at night were invariably hanged, some still used any opportunity that presented itself. Still, with Edgar and Pietro in the house, Baldwin told himself, there could be few women as safe as Lucia.

When Baldwin and his master entered the court, the young man felt as if he had been transported back to Acre's heyday. He had never seen such a feast, even when he was living back in England. Beneath flags bearing the royal symbols were set out spiced dishes of many kinds that Baldwin did not recognise. Many were coloured into a variety of hues, and he wondered what might be in them. Glad to leave Ivo at his table, he walked over to where servants stood, watching the festivities. As he glanced about him, he saw Buscarel, standing in a corner.

'I wondered if you would be here,' he said as Baldwin approached.

'I thought you were dead!'

'So did I. I was found by a fisherman and brought back. The Templars looked after me.'

'You were unwell?'

Buscarel shrugged. 'I lived.'

'You are not recovered – I can see that. You should be resting.'

'I don't want to rest. My family . . . they are all dead. A stone.'

'I am sorry.'

'While I lay in the Temple, recovering, a rock tore down my house with my family inside. I wish I'd been with them.' There was a world of despair in his tone.

Baldwin could say nothing. Any enmity between them was done, and he could empathise with a man who had lost so much.

'Why are you here?' he asked eventually.

'Without me, my Lady Maria would lack a guard tonight.'

'Maria?' Baldwin repeated, and then risked a quick glance around the tables. There, up at the top of a middle table, he saw the familiar green clothing, and as she turned her head, he saw her features once more. 'Why are you here with *her*?'

Buscarel looked over to his mistress, and shrugged. 'She has no one. Why should I not help her?'

'I see.' Baldwin had little sympathy for the woman who had threatened him and his lover.

'She reckons she will be safe when the Muslims get in, but I think I will kill her when they do.'

Baldwin nodded slowly. It would save her from rape or slavery. Either was not to be borne.

'With these ships, perhaps we will fight them off,' he said.

'There are not enough men. What, another thousand, two thousand? To what avail are such numbers when they have hundreds of thousands?'

'She might take a berth on a ship leaving here,' Baldwin said.

'Perhaps,' Buscarel muttered.

'Shipman, are you well?' To him, the man looked broken.

'I'm alive – what more can a man ask?'

'So many have died,' Baldwin said solemnly.

'And more will yet. I will kill as many Muslims as I can for revenge. Oh, when will the bastards break in!'

Baldwin nodded, but he could not help a feeling of elation to see the King of Jerusalem here. It seemed to show that God was on their side again – that He was holding them in His hands and defending them. If the banners of Jerusalem were here, in Acre, it meant that He was here too. And He wouldn't wish to see His kingdom on Earth lost to heathens.

'And what of your Lady over there?' Baldwin asked. 'Is she still devoted to the city?'

'Lady Maria is devoted to herself,' Buscarel said coldly. 'Not to the city.'

It was hard for Baldwin to recall that this man had beaten him, that he had robbed him of his father's ring. He felt the last vestiges of anger and bitterness leave him as he saw the deep sorrow in the Genoese's eyes. Buscarel had remained when all his countrymen had sailed to safety, he reminded himself.

Buscarel's eyes fell, and he began to walk off, but Baldwin called him. 'Master Buscarel?'

'Yes?'

'God be with you, my friend.'

CHAPTER SEVENTY-NINE

Baldwin settled back on his bench as the feast progressed, but he couldn't help but think that such a profligate use of food was foolish. All these dishes had been brought with the King when he landed, and now it was being squandered. There was a part of him that understood the importance of such celebrations, demonstrating to the populace that life would continue, and that they should not be downhearted, but while his heart understood such reasoning, his brain told him that they should be husbanding their reserves.

But perhaps they knew there was no point, he thought. What if they already accepted that the city must fall? No, that was ridiculous. For one thing, the King would hardly want to come and risk his life if he thought there was no possibility of success.

There came a bellow, and the King's steward stood at the front of the King's table with a staff, which he ceremoniously slammed into the ground.

'What's that for?' Baldwin said, looking at Ivo.

His friend sucked a piece of meat from his teeth. 'How should I know?'

Baldwin watched as a succession of young men were called to the table. Some few he recognised. One he was sure had been with Sir Otto's men, and had ridden on the night of the attack on the catapult. Others were unknown to him.

And then his own name was called.

He looked at Ivo.

'Go and find out,' Ivo said, answering his unspoken question. There was a gleam in his eye.

'You are Baldwin de Furnshill?' the King asked when Baldwin stood before him.

'Yes, Sire.' Baldwin could feel his belly dissolving with nervousness to be standing before all the great men here.

King Henry stood and held out his hands. 'My Lords, knights and friends, people of Acre, we are here to celebrate our arrival today with this feast. We all know that our city's future is resting on a knife-edge. To fail will mean disaster. Because if we fail, Outremer will lose her last great city. But we will not fail!'

There was a loud cheer, and the pounding of fists on table-tops. Baldwin felt proud to be here, but a cynical part of his mind questioned whether there would be feasting and cheer in another fortnight.

'There have been many deeds of bravery in the last weeks. I am honoured to recognise the individual courage of these young gentlemen here, and I should like to reward them. From the defence of the walls to the outstanding courage of those who rode to the great catapult, these men deserve their recognition.'

Baldwin felt his mouth fall open.

'Kneel, gentlemen!'

Baldwin knelt, but the rest of the ceremony went by in a blur.

There was the brief lecture from the King, about how a knight should be courteous, bold, hardy, generous and debonair, but to a foe, ferocious and determined. He should protect the poor and weak, and uphold God's law. There was more in a similar vein, and then the Patriarch came and blessed them and their swords, and they were each given the *collée* – a light blow from the Patriarch's hand to remind them of their oaths and responsibilities.

Soon, he was walking back to his seat.

'Sir Baldwin.'

He almost didn't turn. It would take him time to become used to his new title, he thought. 'Sir Jacques?'

'Well done, my friend. Well done indeed.'

'But I've done little more than any other.'

'It was the way you saved the Marshal of the Temple on the night of the attack. He was impressed.'

'That was kind of him.'

'He thought you merited it,' Sir Jacques said. He rested his fist on Baldwin's shoulder. 'I am sure he was right, my friend.'

When Baldwin and Ivo entered the house, they knew at once that something was wrong. Edgar was standing in the garden, and Lucia was nowhere to be seen as Sir Jacques closed the door behind them.

Baldwin did not know Edgar well, and the expression on his face was not one to inspire trust. Edgar shuffled and looked away as soon as Baldwin entered. It was the kind of look Baldwin would expect to see on a felon.

Edgar mumbled, 'I am very sorry, Baldwin.'

'Where is she?'

'Who – Lucia? She is with him.'

'What?'

Ivo put his hand on Baldwin's wrist and pointed.

It was at that moment that Baldwin saw the hole in the rear of the house. A stone had smashed through the north-eastern corner of Ivo's house and demolished the whole of that section. Baldwin stared, and then was running to his chamber.

She was in his room. Uther was lying on his scrap of cloth as usual, but now his wide, anxious eyes were still. There was no answering thud of his tail as Baldwin walked in.

Lucia stood and stepped back from Uther, as a slave would, trying to become invisible.

'No, please, Lucia,' he said, and held out his hands to her. She put her arms around him, but it was no comfort as he stared down at the dog's body. 'You poor brute,' he muttered. 'You never had much of a life, did you?'

And then he realised he was weeping as he buried his face in Lucia's shoulder.

CHAPTER EIGHTY

The days following the arrival of King Henry were happy ones, Baldwin thought afterwards. Whereas before, all had begun to give up any hope of the city's survival, suddenly there was renewed optimism. The sea could bring them reinforcements along with food, and the sight of the bright blue robes of the King's guards and his footsoldiers gave a fillip to all those who had already endured a month of siege.

It was not merely the sight of new warriors walking about the city, men with clean clothing who were not bandaged and foul with lice, it was the confidence that they radiated, and the ideas that they brought.

King Henry's first proposal was that an embassy should be sent to the Sultan.

'It will not hurt us to ask whether the Sultan has a legitimate grievance for breaking his peace treaty. We can investigate whether there is any restitution the city can offer, while also delaying further offensives,' he said.

That at least had been the hope.

Baldwin heard of the failure when he spoke with Sir Jacques. That morning, Baldwin and his men were stood down from the walls, while newcomers from King Hugh's entourage took their places. They were nothing loath. Baldwin stretched his legs walking about the city, and when he returned, he found Sir Jacques talking to Ivo.

'The King sent Guillaume de Canfran, a Templar, and Guillaume de Villiers to speak with the Sultan,' Sir Jacques said. His face was still twisted where the gauntlet had hit him two weeks before, but his smile was still there. 'And they did as they were bid. De Villiers is a mild-mannered fellow, but de Canfran is, I fear, one of the old breed, who learned no humility when a child. His arrogance must have been difficult to curb. Not that it mattered.'

'What happened?' Baldwin asked.

'They reached the tent and waited. The Sultan demanded to know whether they had brought him the keys to the city, and they said that they couldn't, and when they asked whether he would accept redress for any imagined grievance, he reminded them that it was their people who had murdered Muslims in the market during the riots. When they asked what he wanted, he said that his father had said he wanted the city, not the people. Just as he had said to the Templars last year. So, there you have it. A pleasant chat all round, I think. Almost convivial.'

'Really?' Baldwin said.

'Baldwin, you need to learn about sarcasm, lad,' Ivo grunted.

Sir Jacques' twisted smile grew. 'There was an unfortunate incident. While they were talking, the Muslim artillery was continuing to fire their weapons at us. One of our catapults retaliated, and flung a stone that landed near the tent where they were speaking. It sent the Sultan into a rage, and he had men grasp the shoulders of the two Guillaumes and force them to their knees while he drew his sword to despatch them. It was only the intervention of one of his men that saved their lives.'

The three men fell into a gloomy silence. It was clear that there would be no further negotiations. Baldwin thought he had never see Sir Jacques so sunk in gloom, and Ivo sat scowling at the mazer in his hand as though searching for the future in the wine's depths.

'Well, at least we know where we stand,' Baldwin said.

'Aye,' Ivo breathed. 'On the brink of Hell.'

CHAPTER EIGHTY-ONE

Baldwin was dozing when the shout came. His first, groggy thought was that the enemy had managed to break in through the walls, but as he snapped his eyes open, he saw that the fellows on his section of wall were not alarmed.

'What is it?'

'They want tinder and combustibles in the barbican,' Hob said. There was a deflated look about him, like a punctured pig's bladder.

'Why?'

'They're going to burn it. The barbican's too weakened, and the Muslims are tunnelling underneath it,' Hob said.

Baldwin clambered to his feet and stared at the tower projecting from the middle of the outer wall. 'Are you sure?' He could see the men running along the walls even now, carrying bundles of faggots, and already there were wisps and streamers of smoke escaping from the top of the tower. 'Christ's bones, they have lit it already,' he breathed.

'Aye.' Hob stirred himself. 'It's a good strategic decision. If the enemy's already tunnelled beneath, better to evacuate before it collapses. Now all those men can be withdrawn safely, and used in the city itself.'

Baldwin looked at the tower, and then at Hob. The barbican had been built to protect the walls here at this point. If deserted, the defences of the city were all the weaker. But the other men of the vintaine were standing about and listening. Baldwin held Hob's serious gaze.

'Yes,' he lied. 'We'll be safer now.'

But their illusory safety was short-lived.

Baldwin and his men were called to move nearer to the Tower of King Henry II on the same afternoon, and stood to with their weapons ready on the outer enceinte as the last men left the Tower of King Hugh. Smoke was billowing, with yellow-orange flames spurting from the roof, and Baldwin felt a mood of resignation amongst the men of his vintaine. There was no glory in this, any more than there had been in the wild charge of the Hospitallers that night. Baldwin himself still felt that their efforts were not in vain. With such a committed defence, and with their control of the sea, the Muslims must realise they must fail. God wouldn't allow them to win.

But his exhaustion was eroding even his optimism.

Only a short time after they had reached the tower, the enemy catapults began a heavy assault. From the tower, Baldwin could see the men scurrying at the feet of their huge machines like flies crawling over carrion. It was a picture that sickened him, but then he had to duck as the fresh bombardment began to strike.

The Muslims were aiming directly at the walls now. The number of arrows being fired was reduced, probably because they were saving them for the actual onslaught, when it finally came.

'Shit my breeches!' Hob swore as a missile crashed into the wall just below the battlements, and Baldwin and he were thrown to their knees.

The entire wall was rocking and bucking beneath them. They could feel it, all the men in the vintaine, a rippling that shivered along the stones with each new impact. Baldwin could imagine the immense slabs of masonry being pushed inwards with the force of these blows, the rocks crumbling as they were slammed together, until the whole wall was a fluid rampart of broken rocks, gravel and sand. After a month of this bombardment, it was a miracle that any of the stones remained whole.

Another tremendous hammer-blow struck the wall, and suddenly a gush of flame roared up. As Baldwin climbed back to his feet, a foul black slime flew into the air, and then fell onto three men from his vintaine near to his side. It ignited instantly with a loud whoosh, and the three began to scream in agony as they were burned alive. Baldwin could do nothing for them. He only prayed that they would die quickly.

Arrows flew past, but he paid them little heed. The terror of the attacks was diminished with every fresh horror. He sat on the wall beside Hob, and rested. Too many nights with little sleep, too much living with constant fear, had eroded his capacity for feeling. He looked up when Hob rose to peer over the walls, and wondered why he bothered. Standing was not worth the effort. All a man could see was the teeming thousands of their enemies.

Baldwin closed his eyes, lay his head against the wall, and dreamed of England. England, with the cool mists rising from her rivers. The warming sun gradually burning through, throwing long shadows, setting the tree-trunks a-shimmer in her golden light. And the leaves would all be that delicious pale green, almost translucent. England in the spring was a wonderful place.

There was a man up near the tower, and as Baldwin glanced over, a mangonel bolt caught him directly in the breast, and he was thrown back with such force that the bolt penetrated the wall behind him, pinning him there like a doll, his arms and legs moving feebly, his head set at a foolish angle. Baldwin watched as he died, his mouth opening and shutting for some minutes without making a sound.

All around him, men were dying. The walls were assaulted with rocks and fire pots, each hurled with all the ferocity the besiegers could manage, and inside the city of Acre men were crushed, burned, pierced and broken. Their bodies formed mounds down by the gates already, and yet more were being carried away every hour to sit and recover at the Temple or at some other makeshift place of healing. It was all pointless, he thought. Soon they must be eradicated. It was impossible to survive this.

There was a roar, and Baldwin looked quickly up and down the lines of the walls, wondering whether this was a cheer of delight from defenders or enemy.

'It's going,' Hob said quietly.

Baldwin stared at him uncomprehendingly for a moment, then rose and peered over the wall. In front of him, the enclosed wall that led to the Tower of King Hugh was still standing, but the tower itself was gradually collapsing. Baldwin thought at first that it looked as though a missile had struck off the top, along with a section of masonry, but now he saw that the catapults had ceased their endless battery, and the gynours were themselves staring at the damage they had inflicted.

455

The tower shuddered like a dandelion in the breeze, and then a greyish mist rose. It was paler than the smoke from the fires within, and as it climbed, it seemed to accelerate upwards. Baldwin felt almost dizzy to see it, and then he realised that as the pale smoke left the tower, it hung there, in mid-air. In reality, the tower was shrinking away from the mist, collapsing in upon itself.

In another moment, there was no tower, only the harsh rumble of all the rocks rolling and bouncing away from their foundations, and the mist became a thick cloud of acrid stone-dust that clogged Baldwin's lungs and made his eyes water. It was like breathing in lime dust. It coated his throat and nostrils until he felt he must choke.

Looking over the wall again, he was astonished to see that there really was nothing left of the tower. The connecting walk-way and wall was thrust out like a finger towards the ruins.

And now that finger of rock itself became the target of the catapults. They slammed into the wall, two, three, four at a time – some from the north, some from the south. Those that missed, hummed over Baldwin's head, to crash into the high walls behind him. Many thudded into the wall below. One jarred his head, throwing him bodily forward from the wall against which he leaned.

All he wanted was to sleep. He closed his eyes, and for a time he knew no more.

CHAPTER EIGHTY-TWO

In only a week the outer walls were lost.

It began with the Tower of King Hugh. With ever more fire-power concentrated on the narrow point of the walls, the stonework could not survive. Daily, as Baldwin peered over the walls at the enemy, he saw more cats and siege shields erected, protecting the miners who were even now trying to undermine all the city's defences. No matter how many were crushed by the Christian catapults' rocks or arrows, always more appeared to take their places. The Sultan had an uncountable number of men from which to draw upon, and he spent them recklessly, apparently caring nothing for those who were left broken and wailing on the bloody sands.

Not that the Christians were capable of hurling too many stones. All the hoardings were broken or burned away, and with them much of the protection for the catapults had also gone. Only three catapults remained which could continue any form of barrage: one on a castle tower behind St Anthony's Gate, one behind the German Tower, and a last one in the Templar's sector, behind the St Lazarus Tower. These three kept up a sporadic bombardment, but their impact was negligible in the face of so many enemies.

After the collapse of King Hugh's Tower, the next to fall was the Tower of the English, two days later. It succumbed slowly and majestically, as if reluctantly giving up the battle. Only one day later, the Tower of the Countess de Blois slumped, the outer walls crumpling, and tearing down a mass of stonework from the walls at either side as it went. With these gone, the defence of the outer walls became ever more precarious.

On 15 May, Baldwin was back at his post on the outer wall with his men near the Tower of St Nicholas. Here, too, the walls were beginning to crumble. As had happened with the first sections to fall, as soon as their objective was realised, the Muslims moved their artillery and began to hurl missiles at the nearer targets. As one tower disappeared in a grey haze, the gynours would already be at their crow-bars and ropes, pulling the devices around to point at the next. There was no need to devastate the city with more fire-pots or stones, since the people of Acre were already demoralised enough.

That was the last day before the real storm struck them. Because late on that morning, suddenly the outer wall of the King's Tower gave a tremendous shudder – and disappeared. With that lost, there was little to hold the enemy at bay.

Baldwin and his men raced to the tower. They ran and ducked over the rubble on the walkways, along the drawbridge towards the tower, and when they reached it, Baldwin and Hob stood with shock, staring out where the front wall should have been. There was nothing, not even a firm floor on which to stand. No defence could hold this, not while the Muslims kept throwing rocks and pouring in arrows.

Pulling his men out to the protection of the remaining wall, Baldwin went with Anselm from one body to another in the devastated chamber, seeing if any were alive. One lad was still breathing, and they dragged the masonry from his crushed legs to haul him to the Temple, but as the last rock was lifted, he gave a long, shuddering sigh, and was dead.

Baldwin stared down at him. The victim was younger than Baldwin himself, and handsome, with fair hair and blue eyes. He could have been a northern man, or German. Just another wasted life. For a moment, Baldwin was overwhelmed by a sense of the futility of this defence, and felt a tear start.

'What shall we do?' Hob called from the doorway.

Wiping at his face, Baldwin glanced through the gap in the tower's wall. He could see more stones being hurled at the tower. One crashed into the upper levels, and he sprang back before a pair of beams holding up the roof fell into the room. 'Get out!' he screamed, but it was too late.

Anselm was beneath one, and even though he tried to dart away, the beam threw him to the floor, and Baldwin saw him look up as a massive weight of timber fell upon him, crushing him entirely.

Baldwin gave a cry, and would have run to him, but Hob caught him and pulled him to the doorway. 'No! We can't lose you as well, sir. He's dead – there's no good will come of pulling a corpse from there. Leave him!'

Baldwin found himself on the walkway again, his arms gripped by Hob and Thomas. The latter was weeping without cease. 'Thomas, I'm sorry!'

'He was a good man,' Thomas sobbed, 'but he wouldn't want you to die to pull him out. Leave him, Vinten'ry. There's nothing we can do for him now.'

'He's right,' Hob said.

Baldwin felt his arms released, and fell to his knees. He could see in through the door from here, and one boot of Anselm's was still visible. Just discernible behind it was a dark pool of liquid, and Baldwin bent his head in despair, his hands on his face.

He was a failure. He had wanted to come here to protect the city, yet it was being torn down around him. His woman would be left to the savages as they poured into the city, and all his men would die. What was the point of his being here?

'Sir?' Thomas said.

Thomas, the son of a peasant from somewhere in England, had lost his brother, and yet was more controlled than him.

Baldwin stood, and gazed about him. None of them would escape the city, but they could help others to do so. The women, the children – perhaps the more elderly men too. That was his duty now, to hold the walls until all those who could, had escaped.

And then sell his own life as dearly as possible.

'We can't do anything while they keep this up', he said decisively. 'When it gets dark, they may leave it alone. But we'll have to come back then to defend it in case of night attack.'

Hob nodded, but without enthusiasm. The thought of a night assault was not appealing to any of them. Baldwin didn't care. He knew his death was approaching. It was merely a case of how long he could survive beforehand.

CHAPTER EIGHTY-THREE

It was soon after dawn that the shouts came from the men on the tower-tops. Baldwin and Hob had rested outside the tower, below the battlements, while one man stood guard at all times through the night. Hearing the bellows from above, Baldwin stood and peered up, covering his eyes, and saw the men on the Tower of King Henry shouting and waving their arms. Someone began to ring a bell in alarm, and Baldwin stared at the enemy only to see the lines of infantry moving.

'They're coming!'

Hob was at his side, and staring out from narrowed eyes at the Sultan's ranks walking forwards at a shuffling pace. 'This is it, then,' he said.

In answer, Baldwin took his hand, and the two stared into each other's eyes for a moment. Hob had a bloodshot eye where a stone splinter had hit his brow, and Baldwin knew that his own face was streaked with soot and blood, but both managed a faint grin before drawing apart and unsheathing their swords.

The night had not been restful. Throughout, a steady

scattering of missiles had kept on slamming into the walls, making them feel as solid as a ship on a stormy sea. Baldwin's legs had a constant trembling, as though he was nervous or panicked, but it was the ripples of concussion against the wall. In his exhausted state the occasional gouts of flame from Greek firepots were strangely beautiful and relaxing in comparison. He rather liked the way that the flames occasionally burst skywards, throwing the whole wall into stark relief.

'Here they come!' Hob called.

Baldwin watched them with resolution. The enemy had built many towers high enough to reach over the city's walls, but they remained in the background. This was no all-out assault, then. It was to be a concentrated effort on one or two sections of the walls of Acre.

As he watched, Baldwin saw Mameluk warriors running forward, in pairs, gripping heavy scaling ladders between them. 'Archers! Archers!' he shouted, and himself made his way into the tower. He stepped around the masonry where Anselm's body lay, praying to his dead companion.

The first of the Muslims was almost at the tower when a pair of clothyard arrows slammed into his upper body, and Baldwin saw him thrown back, kicking like a struck rabbit. It gave Baldwin a savage delight. The man behind him tried to pick up the ladder on his own, but a bolt from a crossbow appeared in his forehead, and he was jolted back, unmoving. In almost no time, there were forty fresh bodies lying dead a short way from the tower, their ladders scattered all about them. It was now that the Muslims chose to exercise more restraint.

Only a few feet from the tower was the cat which had protected the miners while working at the foundations of the tower. Now this was laboriously turned and brought to bear on the tower again. While men erected fascines behind to protect the men running to the cat, others could stand inside it, and use it as a protective corridor. Soon a ladder appeared at the wall, and Baldwin and Hob ran at it, shoving it away from the wall, but it did not overbalance; instead, it swung back to clatter against the stonework. Already, two men were starting up it at a rush. Baldwin yanked at the ladder, until it fell away to the side, and the men fell onto the ground beneath. One began to scream and wail, but Baldwin was on to the next already.

'Hob, Hob, throw rubble!' he bellowed, and heaved a large rock at the first ladder. He saw it strike a man on the head, and he fell, taking two more with him. Others rushed to the ladder, but Baldwin rolled a large rock to it, and it was massive enough to break several rungs, rendering that ladder useless. Another appeared, and Hob and Thomas were at it already, letting loose another stone. That killed a man at the ladder's base, but two more were on it already, and now there were two more ladders. Another ladder, another bearded face, and Baldwin drew his sword, stabbing.

There was no means to fight off so many. All they could hope for was to delay them. As soon as one ladder was knocked away, two more sprang up. And all the while arrows clattered tinnily about the rocks. A member of Baldwin's vintaine gave a cry, and Baldwin grabbed for him just too late. The fellow toppled and plummeted head-first. Two more were hit in the leg or arm, and had to be helped away. Hob had an arrow pass so close to his face, it sliced through the fleshy part of his ear. This lent fury to his defence, and as a Muslim reached the floor, Hob swung his sword at the man's head so hard that it clove his skull in two.

Baldwin fought unthinkingly. His arm moved with a mechanical determination – swing, stab, parry – and each time a man appeared at the top of a ladder, he did his best to kill him before he could get off and climb into the room, cutting a man's arm off, or his hand, or stabbing quickly in between the rungs, into a face or breast, anywhere to bring him down . . . but although reinforcements were soon with them, the battle was unequal. A pair of men somehow climbed to the top of the tower, and stood above, dropping stones onto their heads. Arrows did not cease, and before noon it was plain that they could do no more.

'Back! Back to the walls!' Baldwin roared, shoving the nearest and cutting at another. 'Fly from here, quickly!'

Hob was at his side as the rest of the men withdrew, and Baldwin and he fought side-by-side, hacking and slashing, until they could leap through the door and lock it, using baulks of timber from the smashed hoardings to block the doorway.

'And so it begins,' Baldwin gasped.

All about the walls, where the Muslims had constructed their huge towers, men stared out anxiously.

Ungainly, lumbering things, the towers were now drawn forward. Each rested upon a row of logs, which must be collected from the rear as the tower passed over them, and set down before it, while the men behind and inside the towers could shove it onwards. They would not move on the sandy plain else. Screams and bellows could be heard from within as the men were urged on, and the damp skins from freshly killed oxen deterred fire-arrows from setting them ablaze.

There was a catapult still on the castle's tower behind St Anthony's Gate, and this kept up a regular barrage against the foe. One lucky shot slammed into an approaching tower, and shattered it to tinder, the men inside hurled outside, shreds of skin thrown in all directions, but one good hit could not detract from the overwhelming force to which the city was now exposed.

Baldwin watched as they reached nearer and nearer. 'They'll not get here tonight,' he said.

'No. It'll be an attack in the morning, I reckon,' Hob answered. 'They will want their towers in position, ready.'

Baldwin nodded. 'See to it that the men get their food ration tonight. They'll need it. And plenty of wine, too. To fight like lions, they'll need to have fed and drunk and slept.'

'Yes.'

'Hob?'

'Sir?'

'You get some sleep too.'

'What of you?'

Baldwin looked out. 'I'll keep the first watch.'

This was the day that would decide the fate of the city, Baldwin thought. The drums started as dawn threw a salmon-pink glow over the plain. Shouts could be heard, and then, while Baldwin blearily stared out over the flat lands before the city, he saw the Muslim army standing to. A massive, long line of men separated into cohorts, the sun sparkling on each wicked spear-point. As he watched, he heard the muezzins calling them to prayer, and the whole line sank to the ground, performing their obeisance, the ritual given a solemn significance on this day of all days.

Glancing at the men standing along the walls, Baldwin saw they were all, like him, tired out. But their eyes gleamed with an unnatural fire at the sight of their enemy. And then there was a shout from one side of the wall, over towards the Temple's ward, and the blast of a horn. Looking up at the wall behind him, Baldwin saw that Sir Otto was on the Accursed Tower, that which stood in the very point of the inner wall. The knight drew his sword and lifted it high, so that it caught the light from the sun, and Baldwin clearly heard his voice cry out: *'Courage, my friends! You are Christian! We fight for God, for Jesus, and His saints! Be brave!'*

Baldwin's heart was comforted by Sir Otto's words. He turned to face the hordes with a renewed determination.

'He doesn't have to face 'em from this close,' a man grumbled from along the line.

Hob shouted, 'Shut up there! By Christ's bones, I'll have your arse in gaol if I hear another word.'

Baldwin grinned to himself. There was no silencing an English peasant, crusader or not. The English fought because they believed in something, not because of foolish heroics.

'I'll be dead before you can get me there, Hob. You too, most like,' the man retaliated.

Today, they would fight for what? he wondered. For Outremer? For their lords here in the city? For business and trade? No, for none of those.

'You can say what you want about Sir Otto,' he told his men, 'but he's right. We're here to protect our souls, not the city. We're here because this is God's last city in His Holy Land. Don't forget that. If we fail, God fails. We fight for your souls, and those of your families.'

The hecklers were silenced, but whether it was Baldwin's brief speech or the sight of the enemy facing them, Baldwin didn't know or care. He too was staring back at the Muslims, and now he heard a scream bellowed from their ranks. There was a deafening roar from all the men, and the Muslims began to march.

Behind them, Baldwin saw the long arms of the catapults rise lazily, and their missiles rose yet again as the enemy broke into a run.

'Archers! Loose!'

From behind Baldwin, the ranks of archers on the walls let fly their arrows. Over the cacophony of stamping feet, shouting, rocks crashing into the walls, Baldwin could hear them hissing through the sky, two thousand at a time. As soon as the first flight was gone, the second was off, and he could see the Muslims falling before their terrible impact, but there were not enough arrows in the city to stop this army.

A crunch.

Baldwin felt his teeth slam together. There was an emptiness in his belly, and he looked about him, dazed. He was on his back, and Hob was beside him, shaking his head, a great rivulet of blood running from a gash in his brow, while Nicholas Hunfrey sat back at the wall, staring at his stomach. His trunk had been opened from his groin to his breast, and he had his hands clamped there, trying to hold himself together.

There was a vast gap in the battlements a yard away. A rock had exploded into it, tearing it apart and flinging slabs and splinters of masonry into the men behind. Baldwin could see broken and bloody bodies lying scattered. His eye took in their faces, and he recognised many as the men from his vintaine. Only he, Hob, and Thomas remained whole. The rest were dying – or dead. The remains of another vintaine was nearby, their sergeant dead.

Baldwin gradually became aware of sounds once more, but his legs were like jelly.

Men came to help them, but Nicholas refused to be moved. He whimpered and moaned, but wouldn't rise. There were drums, booming away in the distance, screams and roars, and then Baldwin saw a ladder at the wall where the hole had formed. Enemy soldiers began to appear. An arrow took the first, and then Hob was up, his sword snapped a foot from the hilt, and hacking at the men trying to force their way up.

Another man joined him, and then Baldwin saw Nicholas, with an axe, hack at the foot of another Muslim. More men, and Baldwin climbed to his feet, and picked up his sword. It was bent, and he stared at it uncomprehendingly for a moment, before joining Hob.

Below the wall, the ground was black with Muslims. It was almost impossible to see the sand between them, there were so many. Ladders kept being slammed against the wall, and now and again a grapnel hook was thrown. One caught a defender, and as the rope was pulled, the barb pinned him against the wall, his flesh ripped apart by that cruel hook while he shrieked.

The Muslims were on the wall further to the right, near the German Order, but even as Baldwin glanced that way, they were hurled back by a rush from the knights. To the left of the ruined tower, he saw more running up ladders, and there was the sound of axes on the door holding them in. He wanted to reinforce it, but even as he had the idea, the first blows to penetrate the timbers began to show. They couldn't hold this section any more. He bellowed at Hob and the others, and even as he rammed his sword into the face of a man appearing up the ladder again, he saw an axe flash at Thomas, and Thomas's eyes widened as he slumped back, his breast gaping.

'Back!' Baldwin bellowed at the other troops, pulling Hob towards the Tower of St Nicholas. 'Back, all of you!'

It was stamp and slash the whole way. As they relinquished their section of wall, more and more Muslims appeared on the walkway, screaming in delight at their success, while Baldwin and Hob hacked and dodged, parried and stabbed, all the way to the Tower. There, at last, they managed to dart in and slam the door shut, a pair of bars dropped into place to hold it.

Hob was panting, his face a reddened mask. The gash had opened his brow to the bone. Inside the tower, there were few who were unharmed. A sudden crash announced the arrival of Muslims with a ram.

'Supports!' Baldwin yelled, and baulks of timber were brought up and jammed against the door.

The men leaned against them, and with each splintering thrust of the ram, felt themselves jerked in sympathy with the door, but somehow it was holding.

Baldwin prayed it would continue to do so.

CHAPTER EIGHTY-FOUR

Edgar and Ivo were at the ruins of the English Tower when they saw King Henry's taken. Suddenly the enemy were everywhere on the walls, and Ivo took a bow from a man nearby and began to loose his own arrows, taking careful aim and wasting not a shot. More bowmen from the inner walls were plying their trade, too, and the Muslims who reached the walls paid for it.

Alas! It was not only that section of wall that was in danger. When Ivo felt a tap on his shoulder and turned to look the other way, he saw that an all-out assault was being launched on the gate. Where the Tower of the Countess de Blois had stood, now the Muslims were clambering up the rubble and beginning to attack the gatehouse itself. More and more men were scaling the walls, helped by their towers and more ladders, and the defenders were hard-pressed.

So this, Ivo thought, was how Tripoli fell at last.

'We should leave,' Edgar said calmly.

Ivo shot him a look. 'Get a move on!' he bellowed,

wondering whether this Edgar could ever show alarm. He always seemed so collected.

They reached the inner walls just in time to escape being trapped by a second party of Muslims who had managed to come around behind them. That was when Edgar and Ivo realised that Baldwin and his men were still in the tower.

Baldwin and Hob went together to the roof. There had been a catapult here, and its ravaged timbers lay broken beneath the rock that had demolished it. Peering over the wall, they saw a group of eight Muslims with a heavy timber, running along the walkway and ramming it into the door. They could feel the collision through their feet.

'Help me,' Baldwin snarled, turning to the catapult. In amongst its remains were the pieces of masonry which it had used as missiles. Now, the two began to roll one of the heavy lumps of stone towards the edge of the tower. With a heave, they managed to lift it to the battlement, and rested it there. The Muslims had retreated, and now they came on again, pelting over the walkway and onto the timbers of the entranceway to the tower. As they did so, Baldwin and Hob thrust at their rock. It fell, and Baldwin heard the screams and cries as it struck the men below, but then there was a terrible cracking sound, and when they peered over, they saw that the rock had crashed through the timbers of the drawbridge to the tower. There was little chance now that the enemy would break into their tower.

Baldwin flinched as an arrow pinged off the stone near his head, and stared down into the gap between the two lines of wall. 'Hob, we have to retreat. They're in behind us.'

Hob scratched his ear. 'I think we're too late.'

'Perhaps so,' Baldwin agreed. He cast an eye about him. Thousands of their enemy stood bunched up before them on the plains, and there was a thin sprinkling behind them. He looked up at the inner walls, and saw Sir Otto high on his tower, but then there was a bellow from the Tower of the Legate, and he saw a party of Christians making a sortie from the Tower's gates.

'Quickly!' he shouted, running down the ladder to the main chamber in the tower. 'We can make it to the inner line.'

Hob scowled. 'If we do, we lose all the outer walls. Shouldn't we remain here and contest every section?'

'If we do, we'll die. We can't hold them off. All they need do is keep battering us with their catapults, and we'll be buried in the towers. Better that we go now, and can join in the last fights.'

'Aye. Very well, Vintenary.'

There was shouting outside now. Baldwin went to the door that led out towards the Legate's Tower. Sliding open the bar, and drawing the bolts, he peered out cautiously. There were only Christians here. He pushed the door wide and bellowed at the men to evacuate the tower. There were steps further along, and he pushed and cajoled his men along the wall towards them. As he went, a ladder appeared at the parapet, and he thrust with his sword at the man who appeared. It was satisfying to hear his howl of pain as he slid down again.

The stairs were clear, and they ran down them, heedless of the risks of falling. At the bottom, Baldwin took a quick look about him. There were small groups of Muslims fighting with members of the city's guard further along, and he ran at them, Hob in his wake. The sight of so many reinforcements was enough to persuade the first group to flee, and the Christians joined Baldwin and his men, rushing to support the next group, but in a moment it was clear that they would be stranded if they remained. Baldwin heard a shout from the wall above, and saw Edgar high overhead.

'I think you'll find a postern-gate down here,' Edgar called, jabbing a finger down below him. 'It would be sensible to use it.'

Baldwin took a quick look behind him at the growing number of Muslims, and bawled to Hob and the others to follow him. They pulled back, arrows from the walls covering their retreat, and when the last of them slipped in, Baldwin himself followed. He shoved the three bolts across, then dragged the bar across and stepped out of the way as men ran up with timbers and propped them against it. No one would get through there in a hurry, hopefully.

'Master Baldwin, I think your men would be appreciated at the gatehouse,' Edgar said.

Ivo was already inside the second line of walls when the assault began in earnest.

Until now, the enemy had concentrated their efforts on winning the towers and the remains of the wall at the outer ring, but now they brought up a ram and more men to attempt the gates. Two tall storming towers were rolled laboriously over the rough ground, their high platforms full of archers, who rained a storm of arrows on the poor fellows who stood at the gatehouse itself. More arrows plunged into the enemy towers themselves from two sides, and for a time it seemed as though the men on them must all die, but such hopes were short-lived. The attackers reached the gate, the drawbridge fell, and once inside, the enemy rushed, shrieking their unholy war cries, into the groups of defenders.

Ivo saw the black-clad hordes overwhelm the men, and the spirited defence was gradually silenced. The Muslims had the outer gates, and their men opened them to the army outside. Soon, like a plague of locusts, the warriors gained the space between the walls.

Ivo stared down at the men in the gap, but then he saw that more men were approaching the gate, and these had a ram with them. They ran it at the gates, heedless of the arrows and rocks that rained upon them, berserk in their desire to be first to break into the city. He wanted to go and join the men on the gatehouse, but he could see that already there was little enough space for the men who were there.

As he watched, the cat was brought into the space between the inner and outer defences, and drawn over the heads of those at the ram. Arrows served no purpose now, but the heavier rocks did smash their way through the thick wooden roofing beneath the skins. A few tried fire arrows, hoping that the skins would have dried out by now, but they made little impression. The thunderous clamour of the men yelling inside the cat rose like the screeching and yabbering of demons, and the noise was enough to make Ivo's heart quail. He glanced about him at the remains of his command, and saw too many men with faces drawn and petrified. It was enough to unman the noblest and bravest.

A shout, and a cracking – and he realised that the gates were beginning to break already. Madness! They should have lasted much longer!

If he was to die, Ivo decided, he would die with a sword in his hands, bellowing his defiance at his enemies. He would not go meekly into death. His poor Rachel deserved better. He had a sudden memory of her smiling at him, their son beside her, and the vision was like a dagger in his heart.

'To me! To me, my vintaine!' he roared, and ran for the ladder. He and his men would guard that gate until none was left standing. He ran along the road, until he was outside the gateway, and here he found many of the city folk, all prepared with their lances under their arms and butted against the paving, staring at the gate as it moved and creaked under the onslaught.

'Here! To me!' he shouted again, and found that Edgar and Baldwin were already with him. 'How did you get here?' he demanded, but before they could answer, there was a crash from the gates, and the ram pierced the timbers.

Ivo leaped forward as the ram was withdrawn, but it was clear that the men could not hold the gates. Their enemy was too powerful. Looking about him, he saw the last remains of the timbers Baldwin had stored there all those weeks before. 'Baldwin, Edgar! Fetch those timbers, get logs, carts, anything, to barricade this area. They'll break the gates now, so we need a new line of defence!' he roared.

As the ram was withdrawn, bolts and arrows flew in. Archers fired back. The screams of the injured rose to Heaven, but there was no diminution in the attack, and then the first men began to hack at the hole in the gates, axes flashing wildly.

Ivo stared, appalled, but could do nothing to stop them. He felt pathetic, old and useless. And then he heard a joyous sound that would remain with him for the rest of his days. The brilliant, clear calls of military command, and when he glanced over his shoulder, he saw the gallant figure of Marshal Matthew de Clermont from the Hospital, and the Grand Master of the Temple, Guillaume de Beaujeu.

Guillaume saw Ivo and smiled broadly. 'All those horses you bought, and never time to use 'em, eh?' he called, and then there was another order, and the knights with him and the Marshal drew into ranks. They marched before the citizens, and planted their own lances firmly, while Guillaume de Beaujeu stood with the Marshal, Hospitallers and Templars together.

At the sound of a crack from the gate, de Beaujeu snapped a command. Two Templar sergeants ran forward with spears, and shoved them through the gap. A shriek came from the other side, and the two bellowed back. Instantly, as they stood aside, two archers fired into the gap again, but as soon as they did so, a flurry of arrows flew through, and one of the archers was struck and fell.

The Marshal of the Hospital muttered under his breath. Ivo heard another creaking, groaning complaint from the timbers.

'More supports!' he called, and to his relief, he saw that the makeshift barricades were rising steadily behind him, as more lumber was brought to shore up the gates. Men were hurrying all over, ignoring the dangers of arrows from the other side of the gates, but then there came screams and cries from over the gates as the guards were attacked by more Muslims.

Ivo saw the Marshal and two sergeants running up the stairs, and soon afterwards the bodies of three Muslims were hurled from the top, and men set about them, ensuring that they were dead. Meanwhile the shouting and screams continued, and Ivo went to the roof as well, bringing the remnants of his vintaine with him. There he found a scene of horror.

Christians lay slumped, some with arrows in them, while spread over the flooring there were more bodies. Limbs hacked from them lay all about. As he reached the top of the steps, he saw another Muslim being dropped unceremoniously over the battlements by two weary-looking men.

The ladders which had conveyed the men to the top were mostly thrown down, but one remained, and Ivo saw this being thrown over by a Templar sergeant. As the man turned, he recognised Roger Flor.

'Didn't expect to see me up here, eh?' Roger Flor said breathlessly.

'To be truthful, no,' Ivo said, but as he spoke, there came a sonorous thudding as the Muslims beat their drums for another assault.

'We all have to do our part,' Roger said. He looked tired and tense, but so did everyone else.

Ivo peered down at the men below. He had a good view of the front gatehouse, as well as the plains beyond, and was surprised to see that the attacking forces were standing back. There could be only one reason for that, and he bawled out a warning as he saw the catapults beginning to move and sway, their deadly missiles despatched.

Moments later, the mournful whirring he recognised so well came over the breeze, and with the others he ducked as rocks slammed into the gatehouse in front of them. The parapets were broken down, and a couple of shards of stone were flung at Ivo himself, one slashing a long cut in the tunic over his back, but fortunately not reaching his flesh. Then there was a second massive blow that seemed to hit his heart, and a great rock hammered into the gatehouse's wall, sending a shock through the whole structure. All was noise: the enormous jolting crashes as rocks impacted, the screams of the injured and dying, the whine and tinkle of arrows that hit the walls and bounced aside . . . it was Hell itself, here on Earth.

When the outer walls began to shiver, all knew that the gate could not last long. The floor was already bucking from the constant assault, and as the walls began to move, there was an urgent rush to the stairs. Ivo was there, and Roger Flor, as the turret on the north side collapsed in a rumble of tortured stone.

Ivo was well away, but he saw someone nearer the walls suddenly jerk, and pitch forward. With a horrible premonition, he ran to the man and rolled him over. It was Pietro, and the old man stared up at him. 'Eh? Am I dead?'

'You old fool!' Ivo hissed, and began to drag him away. 'What are you doing here? You're too old, in Christ's name! They come and find you here, they'll think we've run out of men, and have to throw all the old cretins at them. Come on!'

'Leave me, Master. Leave me!'

'Oh, shut up. You think it's easy to find a cantankerous old git like you? Who'll I argue with if you're not there?' Ivo demanded. At the line of barricades, he saw two youths. 'You! Please, protect this old fellow. He has been hurt.'

Even as the lads took hold of Pietro, a fresh roar of battle cries came from outside the walls.

'They come!' the Grand Master bellowed. 'Knights, to the front; sergeants, prepare! The Sultan's minions think to take our city and us! I say, "Never!" They will not take this gate nor this city while there remains a whole Christian man here! What say you? Will you give her up?'

There was a ragged denial, and the Grand Master looked about the people with satisfaction. But then there were four massive blows to the gatehouse, and two more rocks missed and went humming past, one pelting into the barricade and leaving a bloody smudge where a man had been standing a moment before.

Ivo grasped his sword more tightly. This was what he had come to this land for all those years before. To fight, and to kill the enemies of his Prince. The enemies of his faith. Perhaps he would die here today. Well, if he were to do so, he thought, pulling his little wooden cross from his chemise and kissing it fervently, he would be glad to die and see Rachel and Peter once more.

CHAPTER EIGHTY-FIVE

The gatehouse collapsed all of a sudden. The gates moved apart slightly, there was a crack like a plate of steel hit with a maul . . . and a moment later, a cloud of fine dust arose and the gatehouse was – gone! Only a mass of rubble remained, with here and there the timbers of the roof jutting up, as if a forest had been burned, leaving only bare trunks.

Guillaume de Beaujeu lifted his sword. 'Templars! Lances and spears: kill as many as you can! Remain shoulder to shoulder; if they want to reach us, they will die first!'

'Men of the Hospital! No quarter! No quarter!' yelled the Marshal. 'Acre! God is with us! God is on our side! You fight for Christ and the saints! Sell your lives dearly!'

And Ivo smiled, and lifted his sword as he heard the roars of the Muslims running across the plain to the ramp of rubble where the gates had been, and shouted, 'For my Prince, my King! For England! For Rachel and for Peter!' and began to charge in the wake of the Templars up the rampart, and stood at the top, behind the knights, waiting for the clash of arms.

For Baldwin, as the rubble fell and the cloud of greyish dust wafted away, there was a sense of relief. At last, the battle for the survival of the city was real. There was no more pretence: fighting remotely, waging war by straining catapults and bows. This was real fighting. He kissed the cross of his sword, eyes closed, and then scrambled and clambered up the rubble to the top. Only a few feet away, he saw Ivo, and in the moments they had left, Baldwin smiled at him. Ivo returned his grin, a wildness in his eyes, but then he clapped Baldwin on the back, and the two turned to face their enemy.

The arrows failed to strike them because the outer gatehouse remained intact. It was only as the Muslims came in beneath it that they could loose off their bolts and arrows, and already the men of Acre had gathered together a strong force of Pisan archers, who stood on the surviving walls at either side and kept up a withering flank attack. Sir Otto sent some of his English archers in support, who managed a faster rate of discharge. Soon many bodies lay beneath the gatehouse, and the way past was so narrow that the Muslims could only approach by clambering over the bodies of their comrades. Yet still they came.

Baldwin saw the first ranks of the Temple almost overwhelmed. The Hospitallers turned to their aid, and a shoving, heaving mêlée ensued, with the two Orders bound together, hacking, stabbing and thrusting, and then Baldwin saw Edgar throw himself in from the right flank, as he had when Baldwin was fighting in the alley for Lucia. Seeing more Muslims rushing up near Edgar, Baldwin ran to his side to help keep them back.

His entire consciousness was concentrated on avoiding weapons while trying to kill the men clambering up the rampart. A spear jabbed his flank, and he grabbed it, pulling hard, and bringing his blade down on the man's exposed wrist. A horrible jarring, and the spear was released. He turned it on his enemies, left-handed, over his head, thrusting downwards – and caught a Muslim's face, then stabbed at another. It sank in, and the spear was plucked from his fist. He grabbed his sword again, the bent blade gleaming weirdly as it caught the light.

It was dark before they could stop. As night began to fall, the Muslims fell back, called by blasts of trumpets, and relinquished the rampart but not the outer walls. Those were manned, and the old outer gate blocked with three mantelets. They had guards on duty all night.

Baldwin fell to his backside as soon as the last enemy ran. He was so weary he could not even weep or praise God for their delivery; for this was a delivery of sorts. They had held back the vast army today, and who could tell what the morrow might bring? For now, all Baldwin wanted was a chance to rest his head – just for an hour or two, without interruption. It had been so long since he had been able to sleep without being woken.

'Baldwin?'

He looked up to see Ivo holding out some bread and a pottle of water.

'Too tired,' he mumbled.

'You need to eat, boy. You haven't eaten or drunk all day,' Ivo said wearily. He looked about him at the destruction. 'You'll need it for the morning.'

Pietro and Lucia had cowered in the house listening to the battle raging.

'I cannot bear it any longer,' Lucia burst out.

'Mistress, you can't do anything,' Pietro said. He had a gauze bandage wrapped about his head, but his scowl spoke of the pain he still felt from that blow. 'A rock, and I was too slow to dodge it,' he said again bitterly. It had been his constant refrain since waking late in the afternoon.

'You stay here,' she said with determination. 'I am going to find out what is happening. I cannot stay here while Baldwin fights for me!'

'Eh? You think it'll help him to see you?' Pietro said.

'Yes,' she snapped, and was gone before he could rise to his feet or admonish her further.

The streets came as a shock. Rocks lay strewn, and dead buildings stood black and charred against the sky. It made her feel as though she was walking through a city of the dead. Shouting came to her, and the sounds of fighting: the clash of weapons, screams and cries of pain, and over all the sounds of splintering wood and rock.

Turning the corner near the castle, she saw before her the barricades blocking the street, and men struggling fiercely at the top of the rampart of rubble where the gatehouse had once stood. She could do nothing but stand and stare as the men fought, every so often one of them losing his footing and sliding down the ramp, sometimes rising immediately, but often remaining on the ground. She saw a man at the top who collapsed, falling back instantly to lie with an arrow jutting obscenely from his face.

Pietro was right. There was nothing she could do here. It was stupid to think she could help. She was a woman, and the thought of fighting like this, in a pack, shoulder to shoulder with other men, was appalling. She wanted to turn and flee, but something held her rooted to the spot. Why on earth had she come back with Baldwin? If she had remained at the farm, she might have been assaulted again, but even rape was better than this. If only she was strong enough to wield a sword or axe herself, and could join those men up there, bravely keeping the enemy at bay.

'Mistress?' A woman was at her side, peering at her. She was a well-to-do lady, with greying hair under her wimple, and her face was pale, like a woman who had never worked in the open air.

'Yes?'

'There are holes in the walls, and fresh cracks appearing. They must be filled, and our men cannot do it. They needs must rest tonight, not toil. It is work that we can help with.'

'Yes, of course,' Lucia said eagerly. 'I would do anything to help!'

'I know. It's the waiting, isn't it? Being incapable of doing anything while our men fight and . . . and die.' The woman had a catch in her voice, and Lucia guessed what was going through her mind.

It was the same as had passed through her own mind every few moments of the last day: was her man still alive, or had he died hours before?

Baldwin came to in the middle of the night, not because of any alarm he could discern. And then he felt a pain in his leg.

He was sitting with his back to the city's inner wall, and there was a stiffness in his neck and torso. His right shoulder and forearm were a mass of strained and tortured muscles, not ripped or broken, but simply over-weary. Never before had he wielded a weapon for so long a time. He stretched his hand, staring at it as he did so, marvelling at the way that the tendons stood out, how the fingers curled and uncurled. So many men

483

today had lost their hands. He had been fortunate. There was a scratch, literally, on his neck, he was bruised badly under his left armpit where a spear had caught his mail, and his foot hurt where it had been stamped on three times in the previous day's efforts.

There was also a soreness in his thigh. His wound had more or less healed, but with the efforts of the last days, it was aching constantly.

Men were resting all about him. He felt that he could have been lying in a mass grave. Men lay curled up, or sprawled on their backs; some men huddled up while others lay sobbing, some moaning. One was calling for his mother. Most, however, were snoring. Even the terror of invasion could not keep them awake any longer. Baldwin glanced over them all. Hundreds of men, some in the colours of the Kingdom of Jerusalem, some English archers from Sir Otto's force, mingled with the brown tunics of Templars, and one knight.

He stared more closely. That was not a Templar, it was Sir Jacques d'Ivry.

The older man had his twisted smile still from his injury, but at least he was smiling, and as Baldwin watched, he opened an eye. 'So, my friend, you are not asleep either?' he whispered.

'I couldn't,' Baldwin said. 'How did you know?'

'I felt someone else was awake.' The older man rolled over onto his backside with a grunt and bent at the hips, stretching himself, before standing. 'I think it is time to check our defences.'

'I will join you.' Baldwin was not fully refreshed from his sleep, but he reckoned he would be unlikely to get more rest tonight. In any case, he was sure that soon he would die, and to squander even one precious moment in sleep seemed a crime.

There was a heaviness in the air as the two walked away from the sleeping men and up to the wall. There, Sir Jacques leaned on the remnants of the parapet and stared out at the Muslim camp.

'They're dancing and singing again,' Baldwin said.

It was so much like being at home, he thought. The sounds of cymbals and tambours, a reedy piping, all were reminiscent of a village party back in Devon, and he was suddenly oppressed by a sense of loneliness. This land was so strange, so malevolent. 'You know, you once said to me that if I came to understand God's purpose here, I would understand the country and the people. I don't think I ever shall.'

Sir Jacques turned to him and smiled. 'Perhaps you've come to understand more than most pilgrims do when arriving here, then. There is no secret, my friend. The Holy Land is holy because we hold it as such.'

He crouched and scraped his hand over the stones of the walkway. 'Look! All this stone has become sand from our tramping feet, but it is what the land here is made of. If you walk over it, you find more and more sand everywhere. But the people, my friend, they are resilient. They have been attacked and lost their lands to so many enemies over the centuries. Christ did all He could for them, but when He ascended, the Romans still held the land. And then others took it from them. This land, it is nothing without the people. You must remember that.'

'And now the Muslims want to take it.'

'And they may succeed. But God will not forget it. He has greater plans, perhaps. When peace truly does reign over the world, perhaps it will start here. Right here, in Acre. Or in Jerusalem. Would that not be a wonderful day? The day that all fighting and wars were stopped, because all accepted the one God as their own?'

'Perhaps,' Baldwin said. 'But too many have died already in defending this city. How long before we can have peace?'

Sir Jacques shook his head. 'Perhaps you and I shall not see it. Perhaps it will come soon after the Christians have left this land. Perhaps that is God's plan, to see all Christians forced from here so that our brothers in England, in Normandy, in Angoulême, in Lombardy and Tuscany and the Holy Roman Empire, will all rise up to come and regain the whole of the Holy Land. A holy host coming to retake Acre, Tripoli, Bethlehem, Jerusalem – all the lands which once Jesus looked out upon. Now *that* would be a wonderful plan.'

'After we are dead.'

'Ah, well, that is the risk with great schemes,' Sir Jacques said lightly. He was looking out over the enemy camps. 'It would require a large force to take on all these fellows.'

Baldwin was about to agree, when he saw women at the base of the wall and the rampart. 'What are they doing?'

'Did you not know? While we rested, the women have been filling in the holes in the walls. Is it not a joy to see them join in our efforts?'

Baldwin nodded, a lump in his throat, as he watched the lines of women. They walked with wicker baskets on their backs, or cradling stones, and went with quiet dignity to the wall, where they set their stones down, rebuilding the walls, filling in the rampart where the gatehouse had stood. Already there was a row three deep and two high along much of the rampart. Others were setting their stones between the baskets.

Then he saw her.

'Lucia!'

Lucia set the basket down and stood straight as she made her way down the rampart, her back muscles complaining. She heard him, but didn't turn immediately. Not until he was at her side.

'Lucia, please, stop.'

'I must get on,' she said.

'Are you all right? Where's Pietro? Isn't he here?'

'No, we are working on our own. We do what must be done for the city,' she said.

'I wish I could take you away from this place. I want to be with you,' he said miserably.

She put her hand on his cheek. 'Baldwin, I am happy here. I am free. You have shown me affection, and there is nothing more I could have asked for.'

'I wanted more.'

'I know, but I am a slave. I have learned never to want. Slaves don't receive what they want, only what others see fit to give,' she said, a trace of hardness in her voice.

There was a call from the walls. Baldwin put his own hand over hers, and she saw that there were tears in his eyes.

'Lucia, I love you,' he whispered.

'I know,' she said, gently removing her hand.

He watched as she walked away along the street with the other women, past the barricades and into the city. It felt as though his heart was going with her.

CHAPTER EIGHTY-SIX

Lucia overheard two women talking about the rent in the wall nearer the castle as she passed on the way to collect another basket.

'It needs something to fill it, but we won't be able to use large enough stones. We need something else.'

'I know where there are hurdles and timbers,' she said.

'Where?'

'My Lady Maria lives not far from here. She has many fixings, if her house is undamaged.'

'Take us there.'

Lucia was soon walking down the familiar paths and lanes. There, that was where Philip Mainboeuf had lived. She supposed he must be dead now. The poor man didn't deserve such an ending. This was the place where she had seen those first bodies on the day of the riots; this, the fork where she had taken the wrong turn in her fluster. And this, this was the door she knew so well.

She knocked tentatively on the timbers, but the older woman

with her rapped sharply. It was a long time before the little grille slid open and the bottler stared out. 'You!'

'Open the door,' Lucia said calmly.

'I'll do better than that!' The door was drawn wide, and the bottler reached out for her wrist. 'An escaped slave? You deserve another good whipping, you devil. You nearly killed my Lady's favourite stud at her farm, didn't you? As it is, he's no good except for rutting and heavy pulling now. He's like Samson, destroyed by you, his very own Delilah.'

'Let go of me,' she said clearly.

'I'll take you to your favourite room, shall I, you bitch!'

She stood her ground, and when he pulled, she took out her little knife and stuck it very deliberately in his hand. He gave a sharp cry and let go, and she held it out, showing it to him. 'See this? A good Damascus blade, Bottler. And I will use it. I am no slave now. I am working to save this city.'

Leading the way, she took the women through to the garden and out to the fencing beyond. There, they pulled and tugged at the hurdles and took them away, while the bottler watched, eyes narrow with hatred, clasping his injured hand. Lucia walked past him without looking.

'Lucia! I would speak with you.'

'Lady Maria.'

Her lady was still much the same as ever. She had drawn on a great shawl of green silk over a simple shift, and stood at the door to her bedchamber eyeing Lucia.

'What do you want, Lady?'

'You are a cocksure little sparrow, to come in here after all you've done!'

'What have I done?'

MICHAEL JECKS

'You betrayed your mistress. Even now you whore your body with your Frank lover, against all the laws of his faith and yours. And you tried to kill my Kurd.'

'He *raped* me!'

Lady Maria's contempt was poisonous. 'He couldn't. He was commanded to sire a puppy on you.'

'You are *evil*!'

'Me? I saved your life. You should have been executed for blinding my Kurd, but I allowed you to live.'

'Why?' Lucia asked. She feared the answer.

'So that your lover would suffer. How much more satisfying to know that he craved you. If you were dead, he would find another slut; with you alive, but kept from his reach, he would remain in torment.'

'You failed!'

'We will see. When the city is back to normal, I will have you denounced by the Commune, and then you'll be taken away – and this time no one will rescue you!'

Lucia looked at her, and then, with a feeling of release she had never before experienced, she laughed. Not a shy, anxious laugh in the presence of her mistress, but the steady, strong laugh of a woman with nothing to fear.

'You laugh at me?' Lady Maria shrieked, and clubbed her fist to strike. Lucia said nothing, but her eyes held enough threat. Lady Maria let her hand fall.

'You really think the city will ever return to normal, my Lady? This city is finished, and you too. If you stay here, you will die, but if you leave you leave with my curse. I swear you will take nothing with you. All you possess will be lost!'

Lady Maria fell back, whey-faced, as if bitten by a viper, and Lucia left then, without satisfaction, but glad. There was an ending in that confrontation, and she felt as though her old life was eradicated once and for all as she made her way with the other women, back to the walls.

'Buscarel!' Lady Maria shouted.

'Yes?'

'You were here, but you did nothing to help!'

Buscarel looked at the bottler, who still clutched his stabbed hand. 'You want me to wage war on the women who work to save the city?'

She was furious. 'I told you I wanted you here to guard me and my property, and at the first opportunity you failed!'

'If you don't want me here, I can leave.'

'You are here to protect my things,' she said. He looked at her – damn him! – as though she was nothing more than a poor widow. She was a woman of authority in this city!

'Lady, I will protect you from attack, if you want. But I won't hurt those who are doing all they can to protect the city.'

'Then go! Go and die on the walls with the other fools! Don't you realise I'm offering you the chance to survive? With me, you could live.'

'We'll all die. Maybe some few will make it to ships, but most will die.' His expression changed. 'Why would you think yourself safe?'

'I have friends in the Sultan's camp, Buscarel!'

'Do you really believe that? What, do you expect that when a hundred thousand men arrive in these streets, they'll make an exception because you tell them you know their general?'

'Stop that!' she screamed. 'You think you can laugh at me? I hold the power of life and death, and—'

'Woman, you don't understand anything, do you? You have no friends in the Sultan's camp. When his men come here, they will break down your door and steal everything they can carry.

You, they will rape and kill. Then they'll set fire to this place. Your "friends" in the Sultan's camp will never even know you were here.'

There was a weary conviction in his voice, but she refused to believe him. No! He didn't know the Sultan. She had spent so much time making alliances with the men of Qalawun's court. After her faithful service, his son would want to reward her. He would ensure she lived.

As Buscarel turned and walked from the room, she opened her mouth to call him back – but then closed it. Perhaps he was right. It would not hurt her to ensure that there was an escape, if need be. She could gather her choicest jewels, her money. A woman like her would be bound to find space on a ship.

She nodded to herself, and then gave a shudder.

It was not pleasant to reflect that all her advice and assistance might have led to the destruction of Acre without even the advantage of protecting her own position and lands. In fact, it made her want to weep.

CHAPTER EIGHTY-SEVEN

The fighting began as soon as the muezzins had finished their calls, when the enemy launched themselves at the gatehouse again. Their catapults were aiming beyond them now, and Baldwin was glad of that, except that every time he saw a projectile flying overhead, he worried that it might be hurtling towards Lucia.

He had found a new sword, with a straight, true blade, and while it lacked the balance of his other, it was at least firm enough in the grip to give him confidence that it would not shatter or bend too easily.

Flat breads were brought to all the men at the gate as dawn gleamed on the horizon, and when it was full daylight, they had all been fed and filled with watered wine, and stood at the ramparts, which had been reinforced with baskets full of rock, interspersed with palliasses and individual rocks.

Baldwin and Ivo were in the second rank at the rampart of wickerwork baskets and rocks. This new obstruction might hold the enemy for a little. The Templars and Sir Jacques took the front line, over to the left, armed with spears and lances; the Hospital and some German Order knights held the right. There would be no need for lance-armed knights on horseback today. All weapons were needed here at the front.

Their first warning was a rock that whirred through the air and beat against the wall with an enormous crash. A second stone filled with Greek fire came just after, and hit the walls behind the English Tower. Baldwin saw the foul black smoke, the gout of flame, the twisting, shrieking bodies of men encased in fire who ran and leaped from the walls to end their agonies. More rocks. He saw them strike, from the yellowish clouds that rose from the walls on either side, then more yellow-orange bursts, and one that came much closer, a pot of fire that slammed into the ground behind the barricades. Men immediately ran to it, dousing the fires before the barricades could catch light and be ruined, and while they were there a second struck, showering the men with burning pitch and oil. They ran about, deranged, screaming hoarsely until a sergeant mercifully despatched them.

At that moment, Sir Jacques turned and smiled at Baldwin, and that small act settled the young man's fears. For he did have fear, and he was not alone. Beside him, a pock-faced man he recognised from the market, muttered a constant stream of invective as they waited, while farther along the line a trio were praying and kissing their rosaries. Over on the right he could see Edgar and Ivo, and next to them a stern-faced Pietro with a bandage about his head.

Then the clash of arms began.

A solid mass of Muslims, running full tilt, swords gleaming and spear-points ready, pelted up the rampart, screaming their hatred and rage . . . and the impact of their bodies thundering into the wicker wall was terrifying; their mad determination inhuman. They sprang onto the wall, slashing down at the Christian line. More came on, packed so tightly that on the rampart it was like being faced by a herd of oxen.

Some were instantly impaled on the Templar spears, but were forced on by the crush of men behind, until their moving jaws were almost close enough to bite the defenders. Others hurled themselves on their dying bodies, treading them underfoot to bring down the spears, and then stabbing with their own. A man in front of Baldwin gave a hideous shriek and fell, and Baldwin saw that the spear had entered the eyehole of his helmet. He scrabbled with his gloves for the shaft to pull it free, but another Muslim sprang to him and hacked with his curved blade. A Templar thrust with his sword and that man fell, but another spear slid over the Templar's coat of plates and under his chin, and he too was slain.

As the sun rose in the sky, so the battle continued, until the wicker baskets were reduced to threads of twigs and their contents were spilled – and yet the onslaught carried on, with the enemy thrusting and stabbing. All day long Baldwin and the others were pushed back, only to force their way forward again, their numbers reducing, more men filling the gaps, and they stumbled on the bodies of the dead and injured, and they fought, while their arms weakened and their necks ached, and the constant belabouring of axes, swords, spears made their heads ring and bruised every limb. They fought at first with anger and defiance, then with savage determination, and finally they fought without hope or thought, but only a mechanical obstinacy.

There was no possibility of surrender, nor retreat; there could be no terms. Their enemy was determined to wipe them out. This city would be laid waste, the population utterly destroyed.

A flight of arrows flocked overhead, then sliced into the men behind. Screams and shrieks came to Baldwin's ears, but only as a background. It was like the waves to a shipman. They could be heard as a rumble and crash behind, but the shipman was more focused on the wind in canvas and cordage. In like manner, the sounds of men dying was overwhelmed by the roaring of his breath in the enclosed space of Baldwin's helmet, the deafening clang of weapon against weapon.

A spear caught his left shoulder, high, under his collar-bone. The mail snagged the point, and he felt it puncture his flesh, but he pulled his shoulder back, and jerked it down, and the spear went over him. Another spear raked along his right forearm, under his sleeve, and he felt his skin sliced by the razor-edge, all the way to his elbow. Not deep, but it would sting.

About the middle of the day, with the full heat of the sun bearing down on defender and foe alike, the two forces parted for a space. Baldwin and much of his line was removed and fresher men installed, while they were allowed to sit, ungrip their weapons, drink water. Baldwin pulled off his helmet and tipped a ladle of water over his head. It felt as though his temples must explode into flame like the fire-pots the enemy hurled at the city, he was so hot. He could not drink for a space. His throat was so parched, his lips cracked and sore, and he could barely lift his arm with a ladle of water.

'My love.'

He looked up to see Lucia. She and other women were going from man to man with food and buckets of water. She knelt before him, and brought the ladle to his lips. 'My love,' she repeated. 'Oh, I wish I could help you! You look so lost.'

'Don't worry about me.' He managed a smile. 'I am not dead yet.'

'I wish I had spent more time with you.'

'Perhaps we will escape. I could take you home and show you to my brother. That would make him jealous.'

'You tease me.'

'No. No, I would never do that.'

He stared at her, drinking in her beauty like water. Just now, knowing that he must surely be close to death and would never see her again, she had never looked so painfully lovely. Her wonderful eyes, her regular bones, her clear complexion, all contributed to her perfection. If he could, he would die with her face in his mind, he resolved. The Blessed Virgin Mary Herself could not be so peerless.

There was a shout, then the rattle of arrows clattering on the stones. 'Quick! Go!' he said, pulling his helmet back on and rising with an effort. He drew his sword, but when he glanced back, she was still there, dread upon her face.

'Damn their black souls to Hell,' he muttered. 'I shall not die here! Lucia, run – go away. Back to the house. I will see you there!'

She nodded, and was gone.

The first roaring charge knocked the first line back three feet, and Baldwin and the remaining lines must form behind and shove, heaving and sweating, to recover that yard. Baldwin felt a rip in his left shoulder, and glanced down fearfully, thinking he had been stabbed, but it must have been a muscle tearing. There was no injury visible, no weapon nearby.

A loud bellowed command, and the men began to push, more piling in behind, their weight adding to that of the line, and gradually they started to succeed. There was a shout, a sudden command, and Baldwin felt more men, fresher, eager, behind him. Looking back, he found himself staring into the face of Guillaume de Beaujeu.

'Come! You think to let these sons of the Devil push you around? Like a boy in the stable-yard? Push, my friends, push! Heave for all you are worth! Are you Christians? Then prove it! *PUSH*!'

Baldwin could feel the line advancing. Step by dogged step, they climbed to the top of the rampart once more and then they were over the top, where the wicker baskets had been trampled, and could stand waiting for the enemy to group again and charge. But now, when Baldwin looked up, the sky was darkening in the west, and he realised with a vague surprise that the enemy was pulling back now that night was drawing in.

Someone gave a shout of triumph, but Baldwin could not join in. All he felt was utter bone-deep weariness. He watched while the others all waved their weapons, some derisively, most with exhausted gratitude, and the women reappeared, bearing fresh containers full of rocks and rubble, while men began to sift through the bodies, seeing if any of the injured could be saved.

Baldwin suddenly saw Ivo and Pietro with bent heads over at the far side of the breach, kneeling beside someone lying on the ground.

He knew it before he saw the face.

Sir Jacques d'Ivry was dead.

Lucia saw him as soon as he walked in through the door. He stood there a moment, his helmet in the crook of his arm, and she went to him. 'Are you hurt?'

'No. Sir Jacques is dead.'

'Oh!' She placed her hand against his heart, face torn. 'He was always so kind to me.'

'To all. He loved one woman, and when she was taken from

him, he joined his Order in order to serve her as much as God, I think.'

Baldwin closed his eyes and shuddered. The sword at his waist was a painful burden that threatened to pull him to the ground. His left forearm had a deep scratch, but that, the slash to his thigh and barked knuckles were his only wounds. The men in the front ranks had been far less lucky.

'He fell. I think he carried on for too long, but he wouldn't have admitted it.'

The door opened and Pietro and Ivo entered, one after the other. As Ivo collapsed onto his bench, he began: 'Hoi, Pietro, go and . . .' He stopped, and stared at Pietro.

His bottler blinked slowly. The bandage about his head was stained and grimy.

'Sweet Jesus, you look in a right old state,' Ivo said wonderingly.

'Which isn't surprising, after the last days,' Pietro said with a trace of his old asperity.

'True. Come – sit here. I'll fetch you some wine.'

'Eh? No, you can't. It's *my* place to serve *you*.'

Ivo rocked forward to bring himself to his feet again. 'Ach, this old body is too used to easy cushions as it is. Pietro, I *command* you as my servant to sit there.'

He walked off and before long had returned with a tray of cups and two of his largest jugs, filled with wine.

'This is the last of the wine from Beirut,' Ivo said sadly, pouring. 'I don't think I need worry about keeping it.'

'I am sorry about Sir Jacques,' Baldwin said hesitantly. He was shrugging off his coat, and Lucia hissed and muttered under her breath at the blood. She washed his wounds and cleaned them with damp towelling, while Baldwin sat, wincing.

'I knew him a long time,' Ivo told him. 'He and I came here with the Prince many years ago. His woman and mine, they were friends, and then she got that damned disease, and went to the convent. He felt the need to serve as she did. He never seemed to regret it.'

'He was a good man,' Baldwin said.

'Aye. One of the best.' Ivo nodded glumly to himself and then lifted his cup in a silent toast. Sir Jacques had been his oldest friend.

Pietro was almost asleep, head nodding. Ivo looked at him with great sadness. You poor old whoreson, you're too old for this. Same as I am, he thought.

'We won't survive this onslaught for long,' Baldwin said. 'They must break through before too long.'

'They will, I think,' Ivo said. He rubbed a hand over his face. 'Well, I won't save my bleeding wine for a bleeding Muslim soldier to guzzle after he's killed me. Drink up, boy! Drink up, Edgar. Lucia, you need a drink too. We drink to Acre, to my friend Jacques, to my wife Rachel, my son Peter, and all the others who've died in this damned land. And once we have been kicked out, I pray that no other Christian army ever comes here again, for God has forsaken it – and us,' he finished viciously. He dashed away the tears as he took more wine.

Baldwin and Lucia drank their wine with him, but left soon afterwards, going to Baldwin's room where they made love as though it would be their last time.

And so it was.

CHAPTER EIGHTY-EIGHT

Abu al-Fida had stood at his machine's side all that long day. Al-Mansour was performing with exemplary reliability. They had used seven slings, and had had to replace the beam arm a week ago, but apart from that, nothing had gone wrong.

He watched the final shot loaded, the beam arm straining and creaking under the weight pulling at one end, and nodded to the gynour at the pin. The gynour yanked at his rope, the pin slipped out, and the arm rose, the leather sling scraping the rock along the channel, and up. The sling's upper loop came away, and the projectile was launched. In the gathering darkness, he lost sight of it in an instant. He thought he could discern it at the uppermost point of its trajectory, but then it disappeared from view again. There was only the flat-sounding crump as it landed.

It did not matter. They had hurled many rocks at the city today, and he had seen the result: the collapse at the gates, the destruction of the final towers nearby, the immense faults showing in the walls themselves. Acre must soon be theirs.

'Emir, the Sultan asks that you join him.'

Abu al-Fida nodded perfunctorily to the bowing messenger and called for his horse. If the Sultan wanted him, he had better hurry.

Sitting on his horse and cantering from the army of Hama all about the northern edge of the plain until he came to the Sultan's pavilion, gave al-Fida a measure of just how enormous the force was that Sultan al-Ashraf had accumulated for this holy task. There were men from all over the Sultan's lands, even a few from the wild Nubian plains west of Cairo. Terrifying men, with their black features and fierce glares.

He dropped from his horse at the entrance to the Sultan's pavilion, passed his sword to the men standing guard, and bowed low just inside the doorway.

'I am glad to see you here, Emir. Your catapult is serving us well.'

'We are pleased to serve you.'

'And the memory of your son.'

'Of course.' Abu al-Fida looked up at that. He would not bow to any man in his sorrow for the loss of Usmar.

He did not like this new Sultan. His father had been a hard man, determined and dangerous. This, his son, was already blooded in deceit and politics. He had killed off those whom he felt had threatened him. Even the mention of Usmar sounded to Abu al-Fida like a threat, as though his determination to avenge his son was to be doubted.

The Sultan eyed him narrowly. 'Tomorrow, you will increase your rate of discharge at dawn.'

'We do not have many more missiles,' Abu al-Fida objected. 'If we send them too speedily, we must exhaust our resources. We have been throwing them every day for over a month.'

'I know, Emir. However, there will be little need for you to maintain your firing for too much longer.'

'You will storm tomorrow?'

'Early, yes. By nightfall we shall own the city.'

'Then may I respectfully ask that I join the storming parties?'

Sultan al-Ashraf stared at him with a bemused expression. 'You realise the danger? The Franks have many men still. The storming parties will suffer terrible losses.'

Abu al-Fida looked at him with a steady eye. 'I do not care. If I can help win the wall, I will be content.'

Baldwin, Ivo and the others were at the gates again the next morning an hour before dawn. Edgar and Pietro stood near, while Baldwin and Ivo arranged the last of their vintaines into a group. Hob was still alive, but had a gash under his right eye from a spear. It was still bleeding, but he grinned with the other side of his face. 'Looks good, eh, Master? The girls in London will all want a piece of me when they see this!'

'I am sure that will make a pleasant change for you. It improves your looks greatly,' Baldwin joked weakly.

Lucia had also come to the front.

'I can help,' she said. 'We women will bring stones to fill in holes in the ramparts. We can throw stones, too.'

'It's dangerous.'

'More dangerous than sitting at home and waiting for them to come? I'd prefer to die at the gate, near you, than alone.'

They were arrayed in the third row, Baldwin on the far left next to Ivo, and Edgar and Pietro on the right. Before them were some few Knights Hospitaller and two Templars, for it was clear that this was one of the weakest parts of the wall. During the night, women and others had slaved over the barricades, and now at the top of the rampart was a thick line of baskets, palliasses, a trolley and a cart, with stones and rubble filling in all the gaps.

'They are coming!'

Baldwin glanced up at the man high on the Accursed Tower as he set his helmet on his head. The sentries atop had the best view of the enemy. Baldwin gripped his spear more tightly, and shifted his feet.

And then he heard it: the steady tramp of thousands upon thousands of feet, the brazen blaring of trumpets and the nightmare din of hundreds of kettledrums all being pounded at once.

''Ware the missiles!' came a bellow, and suddenly the air was full of the hammer-blows of rocks as they slammed into the walls, splinters cracking off and hissing through the air. Baldwin saw one run along a man's neck, cutting bone and sinew at the same time, and the man collapsed like a pole-axed ox. A rock touched the top of the inner parapet, bursting pieces of mortar and stone in all directions, then ploughed into a line of men hurrying to the front. All were crushed. A leg remained where a man had stood only a moment before.

Another struck the tower at full tilt, and Baldwin saw it wobble, a vast crack opening in the side, and as he stared, the tower seemed to rotate. Another hit would bring it down, he thought, but then there was a crash, and he found himself staring through his eye-slots, up at the blue sky overhead.

He was hot, and wanted to pull off his helmet and breathe clean air, but he couldn't. There was a weight on him, and when he managed to lift his head and look, he saw a man lying over him. All around were more men, most crushed. Slivers of stone lay all about, and as Ivo came and hauled the body from him, Baldwin saw another projectile slam into the Accursed Tower.

It tilted, and as he was helped to his feet, the outer wall seemed to fold in upon itself, and the top of the tower began to move. A crease appeared, as if the tower was made of a mere fabric – and then it tumbled. He could see the sentries at the top, clinging to the parapets, as though that would save them, another man leaping, falling perhaps eighty feet onto the loose rubble.

More rocks: thundering into the walls near the tower, and then the arrows began to fall. Lancing down in great swathes, rattling like a child's toy on the stones all about. But their impact, when they hit men, was deadly.

'Get up!' Ivo was bellowing at him. Baldwin stood, still dazed, and as he did so, an arrow struck the side of his helmet, and bounced away. 'Shit!'

'Aye, well, get used to it!' Ivo snapped.

The line had been demolished by the impact of the rock. The remains of Ivo's men were huddled in a group, Hob among them. A splinter had opened his groin, and his blood had washed the stones around him.

'Look after these arses, Master,' he managed, but then his eyes fixed on something far, far away that Baldwin could not see.

There were shrieks and sobbings all along the line of men, but then came a warning shout, and men were pointing out over the walls.

'Form again!' Baldwin yelled. 'Here they come!'

They had waited since before dawn, and as he heard the first cries of the muezzin calling them to prayer, Abu al-Fida dropped to his knees and bent his head to the ground.

The process of the ritual was enough to calm his nerves. Any alarm at the thought of the battle was washed away, and he found himself viewing a scene in his mind's eye of how Paradise must look. It would be blue and clean, always. There would never be any yellow colours, he decided. Yellow and ochre were the colours of sand, of heat, of thirst. Paradise would have no reminders of such things. He would be thirty-three once more, and he would recline on a couch inlaid with precious stones, while his house would be built of bricks of gold and silver. Servants would place foods before him that were so delicious, he would eat and never wish to stop.

But he *would* stop, when his darling Aisha came to him. His lovely wife would kiss him and respect him. And they would again know that perfect happiness from their love-making. And he would see his son once more.

It was a beautiful scene in his mind. A picture that a man might hold on to for the rest of his days.

A trumpet sounded, and then he was marching with his men. There was no time now for foolish reflections. This was a time for stern duty.

There were three hundred camels arrayed behind the army, and as he turned to his men and ordered them forward, the kettledrums began to pound. There were two per camel, and their rhythm was a solemn call to arms, to death. But today Abu al-Fida felt more alive than he had in the whole of the last year. Today would bring about the end of the Franks in his land. Once they were gone, he could die happily.

The trumpets and drums continued, and as he marched the hundreds of yards to the walls, he heard the first of the rocks humming and whooshing through the air. So many, they seemed to hit with one enormous concussion that threatened to shake the earth itself.

And then he recalled the scenes from that other siege so many years ago, and his heart quailed within him.

A man on his left disappeared, and glancing down his line, he saw others toppling, or screaming and shouting as arrows found them. So many arrows were falling, it was like walking in the rains and trying to avoid each drop. He set his face, breathing in deeply, thinking that if he was to be hit and killed, better to get the business done.

'Run!' he shouted.

They were at the first, outer walls now, and there, before them, was the ruin of the city gate, a rampart of rubble paved with Muslim bodies.

CHAPTER EIGHTY-NINE

Stumbling, Baldwin allowed Edgar and Ivo to pull him away from the bodies and to the barricades behind. This second line of defence would have to withstand the onslaught, if the Mameluks managed to breach the first line on top of the rampart, and just now, with so many dead and dying, Baldwin found it hard to see how they could survive.

He was ready before the first white-turbaned Emir appeared at the rampart, urging on his regiment with an eager, high-pitched command. An English arrow ended his cry. Others with their black turbans were already at the barricades, and spears and swords flashed. Baldwin lurched to his feet, and as he did so, felt much better. Snatching up a spear, he ran at the lines, shoving his weapon in between other men . . . and thus began the heaving, sweating, jabbing and killing once more.

Encased in his helment, he could see little, only the backs of the men in front, and occasionally some of the enemy, teeth bared in their bearded faces, as they hurled abuse and tried to push into the city.

A man leaped onto the spears hafts, balancing like a tight-rope walker, and there began to lay about him with his sword at the heads and hands of the Christians, but a Templar cut off his feet at the ankles. Another copied him, and managed to stab a Hospitaller in the vulnerable spot where his mail shirt met his helmet before he too was dispatched.

Baldwin felt his feet sliding on the loose rubble and stones. The whole line was moving back, and then he heard the enemy roaring as they realised they were succeeding. Men called for help. Some matrons who had been filling baskets with rubble hurled rocks.

A bellow, and Baldwin felt impelled by its urgency to glance up, and when he did, he saw the Muslims had taken the Accursed Tower. They were all over the walls, their banners flying, and he saw black and white turbans, while still more streamed up ladders.

'Ivo! Ivo, they've got the tower!'

'We can't do anything about that . . . have to stay here. Hold hard there, you worms! Have to hope someone can get . . . them reinforcements.'

Baldwin knew he was right, but it was hard to concentrate on this area, knowing that Muslims were running behind them into the city. It would only take three or four men at their rear to throw their line into terrible defeat.

With a surge, the Muslims began to win the shoving contest. The Christian line was forced back, legs struggling to keep their ground. Baldwin saw a sword rise and hack, and the man in front of him was gone. Suddenly a sword flashed at him, and he had to drop his spear before it took off his hand at the wrist, and he drew his own sword instead.

In an instant, the whole line had collapsed into a series of hand-to-hand combats. Baldwin saw Ivo over to his left, Edgar

509

beyond him, while all about them was a circle of screaming and yelling men, their weapons glinting.

He was hard-pressed. A blade nicked his thigh, another his knee – then a man edged in closer, and Baldwin could feel that this was no amateur, but a practised swordsman. He forced Baldwin back, and would have killed him, had Edgar not turned, hacked once, and the man's neck was broken. He fell, and Baldwin moved forward again, thankful for Edgar's joy in battle.

'Back! Back to the second line!' Ivo shouted, and they all broke away and pelted for their second line of defence.

The timbers piled here were meagre, but at least offered some resistance to the Muslims, who tried to clamber to the top, only to meet a vintaine of spear-men, who stabbed and prodded them back. Baldwin fell to the ground with profound relief, rolling over to see how the battle was progressing.

Pietro was wildly swinging his blade, Ivo beside him with his more effective, economical parrying and stabbing, but then, at last, they were saved. Baldwin heard a bellow from behind and as he turned, he saw six mounted Templar knights. They came at the gallop, spears lowered. Baldwin scarce had time to bolt, and Ivo and Pietro threw themselves to the side as the massive horses pounded to the barricades, and sailed over them. They landed on their enemy, and some more were pierced by Templar spears, and the horses began to kick and bite even as the knights on their backs threw aside their spears and used swords, axes or maces to lay about them. Arrows rained down about them, but by some miracle, the men and their horses were unhurt.

Ivo was already up behind them as the last Muslim fell back warily up the slope, watching the Templars. One spurred to the rampart, pushing him and the others back, while his brothers dismounted and stood in line. A troop of Templar sergeants and squires joined them, and all set off up the ramp, to stand at the top. Rocks and arrows were cast at them, but men were already scurrying about setting baskets back in place and refilling the gaps between.

Pietro and Edgar were near Baldwin, both panting, and he stood with them. For a while, no one spoke, merely gathering their resources for the next fight.

Then: 'We need to help there,' Edgar said, nodding towards the Accursed Tower.

'Someone else must go,' Baldwin said. 'We are too few already.'

'The Templars should help us then. Or the Hospitallers,' Edgar insisted. 'If the enemy are allowed to hold the tower, we will soon be fighting them behind us as well as before.'

There was sense in what he said. Baldwin cast about, looking for someone who could be sent. Just then, a large force of English and men of the King of Jerusalem's forces came at the run, and while the King's men took up positions behind the Templars, the English went to the walls at either side and nocked arrows to their bows, ready.

Baldwin waited until he saw the archers bend their bows, and then set off up the rampart again, but this time the Muslims were there in still greater force; they scaled the walls, appearing at the inner battlements, and ran along, stabbing the archers and throwing them from their positions. To his dismay, Baldwin found that he and the others were now caught between the Mameluks in the gateway, and those who had come up behind them.

'We cannot hold this!' Ivo cried despairingly. 'We have to pull back!'

'We can't leave the gate!' Baldwin shouted.

But they had to. Nothing remained for them to hold. The gates had gone, the barricades were crushed or knocked aside, and Baldwin found himself forced back with the others, towards the Accursed Tower.

Baldwin, Ivo and Pietro were thrust further and further back, and Edgar was a short way away, with two Templar sergeants, who fought like berserkers. They were all soon pushed from the main gates, and thence back towards the castle.

Staring about him, Baldwin recognised where they were. At the castle, there was a gateway – the original gateway to the city, he assumed, before the second space had been added to incorporate Montmusart. He had little hope they could hold the gate here, because now that the Accursed Tower had fallen, the city's defences were lost. But still, there was the second series of gates at the second wall that kept Montmusart separate from the old city, and if it were possible to recover the Accursed Tower, the city could perhaps pull back and hold this second line.

It was a possibility. A cause for a last desperate hope. He shouted this to the others, and saw Ivo nod. Then, as they retreated through the gates, Baldwin bellowed and charged. Edgar and the two others saw his plan, and they too roared and redoubled their efforts, and their sudden change in tactic made the forward line of Muslims hesitate. Only for a moment, but that was enough. The four men turned and pelted through the swiftly closing gates, and the bars were slid across before they had drawn breath.

Baldwin grinned at Edgar and clapped him on the back. 'That was a good job!'

'But not enough,' Edgar said, staring at the Tower's remains.

Ivo snorted. 'Aye, we should go there and see if we can help.'

There was already a steady thudding on the gates. Baldwin looked at them. 'What about that?'

'If they're into the city up there, this gate won't save us,' Ivo said harshly.

They left some men at the gate, and ran to the corner of the walls. Here, they soon saw, all was desperate. The Muslims had a firm toehold, and there were hand-to-hand struggles all over. A trio of Christians stood at the entrance to one alley, while Sir Otto's men were still on the walls, fighting to regain the tower.

Taking a deep breath, Baldwin pelted into the flank of the men before him. With Pietro, Edgar and Ivo, he managed to clear a small space, and the four did push the Muslims back a little, but then the weight of their enemies began to tell again.

That was when they heard the rallying cry of the Temple. Guillaume de Beaujeu appeared at the head of a strong force of Templars and Hospitallers. He and Matthew de Clermont of the Hospital joined forces and ran at the Muslims like men possessed. Their swords and their maces whirled, and their enemies fell back, terrified by their fanatical strength. With his sword held high, Guillaume de Beaujeu shouted out an order, and the men of the Temple closed up about him, the Hospitallers rallying to their banner, before they started to push and hack their way towards the tower.

Seeing them, Sir Otto's archers loosed off arrow after arrow, and Baldwin and the others joined in, redoubling their own efforts in the mad attempt to reach the tower.

They had nearly reached it, when the disaster happened. As Sir Guillaume lifted his sword to point to another objective, a Muslim archer saw his target. He loosed his bolt, and it sped straight and true, striking Sir Guillaume in the armpit.

Baldwin saw him thrown sideways by the impact, and thought at first he had tripped. It was only as the Templars

513

formed a protective ring about him that he guessed at the truth. He saw men pick up their Commander and hurry him away, while he grimaced.

'No! Don't leave us all here!' Baldwin heard somebody shout.

Sir Guillaume stared around, and there was wildness in his features as he cried out, 'Gentlemen, I can do no more! I am dead! Look, see the wound!'

Although the men fought with no less determination, without the Grand Master they knew that the battle must slip through their fingers. Matthew de Clermont escorted de Beaujeu to the Temple, while the remainder of the Hospitallers and Templars resorted to hand-to-hand fighting to hold the enemy to the line near the tower.

'To the Temple! To the Temple!' Baldwin heard, and felt himself caught up in the general movement back along the roads. The Templars did not lessen their efforts, but held the Muslims at bay while the rest of the city folk withdrew in good order. With the walls lost, now Sir Otto's men were vacating them, and hurrying to join the retreat.

Baldwin was swept along with them all, but even as he retreated, he wondered where his Lucia was, and prayed that she might be safe.

CHAPTER NINETY

He was alive, but Abu al-Fida felt sickened.

His own men had performed miraculously well, climbing the rampart to the city with only a small number killed, but here in the streets was where the worst danger would lurk. He knew the potential for traps.

They made their way to the inner gate, but it was barred against them. Men at the walls overhead pelted them with rocks and arrows, causing a number of injuries. Abu al-Fida sent a party along the wall to see if there might be a second entrance that could be more easily taken while he organised his men here to assault the gates. They found a heavy timber and six of his men ran with it, one falling dead from an arrow as they crashed into the gates. Pulling back, another man taking his place, they ran again – and again the wood held. A third, a fourth, and there were six of his men dead now. It was frustrating, and he chafed to be thwarted by such a small force.

Five of his men had gone to find ladders, and now they returned. The walls were high, but the men had courage and faith. They set up the first ones, and while archers beneath kept the walls clear, the first men set off up the rungs. The first was hit by an arrow, and he fell into the second, who almost tumbled from the ladder, but managed to keep his grip, and moved still more urgently up the remaining rungs.

Abu al-Fida waited impatiently. Three more of his men fell from the walls while trying to reach the parapet, but then there were shouts of glee, and the bodies of some Franks were thrown from the battlements while his men gloried in the victory that Allah was giving them. They were proving their faith in Him and He was rewarding them.

The gates opened, and they pelted in. The streets here were narrow and tangled, but they could hear the clamour of the fighting. Abu al-Fida led his men at the run towards the rear of the Accursed Tower.

The scene that met his eyes was one of carnage. Franks, Muslims, all lay together in untidy piles, body heaped upon body.

And then he heard the snapped orders, and he saw the Templars behind him, preparing their charge.

Ivo was more weary than ever before. His city was in ruins. He hurried through streets in which he had once strolled. In the past he had come here to curse traders who had bartered too crudely. One of them, he saw now, cowering in a doorway, hands over his head, wide, petrified eyes staring wildly.

It was at the western edge of the Pisan quarter that he spotted Lucia. 'Here, Lucia, here!' he bellowed, but it was Edgar who darted from the line of men, caught her about the waist, and drew her back to his place.

Muslims harried them along the north and eastern edges of their formation. Templars and Hospitallers were fighting with great valour, but they could not hold back the enormous numbers of their enemies without aid. One fell, then another, and soon there were all too few remaining. Baldwin joined them, protecting their left flank as best he could, but he was tired after so many days of struggle.

It was a relief when another Hospitaller ran to the line and pulled Baldwin out of his way, setting about the men ranged against him with eagerness unabated. Baldwin realised it was Matthew de Clermont.

'Men of the Temple, I salute you! Your Grand Master has died, and is in Heaven, where we shall soon all join him! Praise be to God! We die in His service!'

With each word, his sword leaped, and three times he stabbed or cut a Muslim. His companions fought with a steady silence, men of the Hospital fighting with those of the Temple.

Seeing Lucia, Baldwin ran to her.

'What now?' she pleaded, staring up at him. 'Don't let them catch me, please, I beg.'

'I won't,' Baldwin stated, but as he spoke there was a screamed command, and he turned to see more Muslims pouring out from an alley. They must have come through Montmusart to get here, he realised, but then he and Edgar were hard at it again.

The Muslims managed to separate the groups from each other. The Orders remained fighting desperately at their front, while the enemy attacked the main body of men from the rear. Baldwin pushed Lucia behind him, but then Edgar called to him.

'The alley there looks clear. I can see to the sea.'

Baldwin looked, and sure enough, Edgar was right. There were no Muslims along here yet. Even as he had the thought, he saw two of Sir Otto's men passing along it, and made his decision.

'Come with me!'

He set off, gripping Lucia's wrist in his hand, past alleys and lanes, always continuing towards the water. Down there, he thought, was the harbour, and it must be possible to get to a ship. If no one else could be saved, he could at least place Lucia on a ship and see her free.

Lady Maria stood at the harbour, jostled by the common folk, silent and bitter.

Her life was ruined. Her lovely house had been struck by two rocks today, and was devastated. She could not return to Lydda, nor to her little farms, where her olives and pomegranates grew. Instead, here she was, preparing to leave her city and her land forever. Because she would never be safe, returning here. She had come to appreciate that.

A necklace of gold was about her neck, while at her ears were her two best emeralds. Other precious stones and jewellery were held in a small box, the more valuable pieces held next to her breast in a soft purse.

But there were not enough ships to rescue everyone. Although the Venetians and Genoese had many vessels, some in the harbour, more lying off out to sea, the hubbub of the citizens at the quays was deafening. Some ships were already leaving, the number of people on board straining the boundaries of safety. Some smaller craft were being rowed out, but even as she watched, she saw one struck by a galley, and it was broken to pieces in an instant, and simply disappeared. The passengers were there one moment, and in the next, gone.

Lady Maria stared at the screaming throng.

Buscarel gripped her elbow. 'Come with me,' he said, and began to barge through.

The scenes were heart-rending. She saw a young woman tearing at her garments as she pleaded with an obdurate ship-man to let her children aboard. A family of merchants whom she knew vaguely were begging a rough-looking Piedmontese for passage, and everywhere women were wailing, wretched and despairing as they watched ships leave the port.

'Hoi! You!' Buscarel bawled in a voice loud enough to reach the forecastle from the afterdeck in a gale. 'I have someone to come on board.'

Lady Maria found herself pushed up the gangplank of an enormous Templar craft. Its very size was gratifying, for every-one knew that vessels sailed at the mercy of the seas: if larger, she must surely be safer. Others were imploring an enormous Nubian, but he allowed no one to pass him or his unsheathed sword.

At the deck, a tall, swarthy man turned and eyed her unsym-pathetically. It was Roger Flor. 'You want a berth, Master Buscarel? I may be able to find you a menial function, I suppose.'

'Do you have space for a woman?' Buscarel asked.

Lady Maria did not know Roger Flor, but she recognised his cross. He was a Templar! Oh, she felt the relief like wine in her blood. The Templars had many faults, including their arro-gance, but they were at least Christian, and would not desert a woman like her.

'We may have space for certain cargoes, yes,' Roger Flor said. He was stowing a rope, and now he left it in a coil, and wandered over the deck to give her a careful scrutiny. 'You have a good dress, madame. I like that colour. Is it silk. Yes? Good. It'll fetch a good price. What's in the box there?'

'My jewels,' she said.

'Good. Give them to me.'

'They're all I have.'

'And now you don't,' he said, holding out his hand.

She had a moment's hesitation. Then a catapult's rock smacked into the sea. The people near the quayside were drenched, and a woman dropped her baby. The child bounced on the hard stone edging, and tumbled into the water. The mother shrieked, and two men grabbed her to stop her following it. A man jumped in, but with swaddling bands wrapped all about it, the baby had no chance of floating or swimming. The man dived three times, desperately searching, but did not find it. He finally climbed out, and the woman collapsed at the water's side.

That stone decided her. 'You want how much?'

He looked at her, and he wore a seraphic smile. 'Everything you have, madame. I will not be choosy.'

She looked at Buscarel, but before he could speak, Roger Flor beckoned a sailor. 'Bernat here doesn't like customers arguing about the fee. If you don't want to pay, that's fine. I'll be gone before the Muslims get here. There are many other ladies and their gentlemen who have been here and asked my price. They wanted to go away and think about it too. But remember this, madame. When my ship is full, I sail, and if you arrive here even one second after the ropes are slipped, you are one second too late to live!'

Buscarel pushed her slightly. 'Go. You have nothing to hold you back here. Find a new life, my Lady.'

'Well, Buscarel? Are you coming too?' Roger enquired. 'What will *your* price be? Perhaps I will allow you to go half-way, and then cast you overboard? That would be fun.'

'You hold a grudge against me, when I enriched you by a ship?' Buscarel said. He shrugged.

'Well, come on, then. I can't take you if you don't climb aboard.'

'No,' Buscarel said.

Lady Maria had made her way over the gangplank onto the ship, and stood anxiously holding on to a stanchion as the vessel rocked gently.

'Your man doesn't want to come too, eh?'

'His wife and children are all dead. He stays to kill Muslims.'

'You'll fight them on the land, then? Good luck to you, ship-man. You'll find them that way,' Roger added, pointing sarcastically.

Lady Maria watched Buscarel before he was swallowed up by the people at the quay as they barged forward, hands held out, pleading.

Roger Flor smiled, but his answer was the same to all. 'You want your life? Then give me all you have: your jewels, your money, your gold and silver. Nothing less will do.'

She turned away from the weeping, pleading crowd, and made her way to the side of the ship, sitting uncomfortably on the planking of the decks.

'Oh, *and* I'll have that purse under your dress, madame,' Roger Flor said as he passed her a short while later.

'That is all I have!'

'No. You don't. As I said before – it's mine.'

Baldwin finally reached the harbour by the simple expedient of using the pommel and hilt of his sword to force a way through the crowds.

He could feel the citizens' panic. If only they had believed the Templars all those weeks ago, when Guillaume de Beau-jeu had warned them of their fate. But no, the people had smugly accused him of cowardice and of feathering the Templar nest. Now their stupidity was coming back to haunt them all.

'My love, please,' Lucia said. 'You must come with me.'

'I cannot,' he said.

They had reached the harbour, and as they stared along the ships, Baldwin gave a little gasp of relief. '*He*'ll help us!'

'Who?'

He dragged her after him, excited by the sight of Roger Flor, but before they could reach his ship, he heard shouting, and a squad of Hospitaller Knights came out from an alley. They carried a wounded comrade on a ladder, and Baldwin groaned to see that it was their Grand Master, Guillaume de Villiers. The latter was demanding that they take him back, protesting that he did not wish to sail from here, but none of his men listened to him. They strode to a Venetian ship and curtly demanded that their Grand Master be transported away from here. When the shipmaster tried to haggle over a price, a sword-blade appeared a scant inch from his nose.

But now there were desperate cries from further up the quay, and as Baldwin stared over the heads of the people nearest, he saw a contingent of blue-clad men with gold crosses on their breasts march to a ship. More came down the hill, clad in the same blue tunics of the Kingdom of Jerusalem, and then, in their midst Baldwin saw the King and Amalric. They said nothing as the populace spat and jeered, crying out at the betrayal.

'Cowards! Cowards! You are supposed to fight and protect your people, it's your duty to stay!'

There was no response, other than waved weapons. The King and his brother looked neither to the right nor the left as they boarded ship.

They were not alone. Sir Otto was not long after them, and he and Jean de Grailly commandeered all the ships in the harbour for their men.

Baldwin stared with incomprehension. Surely the warriors should remain, and allow all the unarmed people to escape. That was the duty of the Bellatores – to serve the priesthood and protect the poor. If they would not do their duty, who would?

He saw Roger Flor once more, and made his decision. Half-dragging Lucia with him, he reached the stern-post and rudder, and called to the Templar: 'Will you take my woman, Roger? Please?'

'You coming with us?' Roger cried in response. 'That's good, old friend. We'll make our fortune with this voyage. Do you have any idea how much we'll make? All the richest people in the city are giving us everything. And later, we can take another ship, and we'll become the wealthiest men in the whole of the Mediterranean.'

'I can't come – I must stay. But please, take my woman.'

'Her?' Roger gave her a cool, appraising look. 'She doesn't look like she has any money, Baldwin. How will she pay?'

Baldwin felt his mouth fall open. 'Please, for me?'

'No, my friend. You, I could use. Especially in a fight. Her? No!'

Lucia grabbed his hand and wouldn't let go. Baldwin considered leaping into the ship and killing Flor there and then. It was because of that raid, he saw. It was there in Flor's eyes. He wanted another felon like himself, and if Baldwin were not capable of his work, he would not take Baldwin's woman.

'I won't go without you, Baldwin,' Lucia said.

He saw where she pointed. There, in the stern, was a group of people, and some distance away, sitting with her back to the hull, was Lady Maria.

'I would prefer to die here with you than go somewhere with her,' Lucia said.

Baldwin nodded. They hurried back through the crowd of people to where he had seen Sir Otto – but by the time he reached the ships where the English and French were embarking, there was no sign of him.

'Where is Sir Otto? Sir Otto, where is he?' he shouted, but the guards at the harbourside said nothing. They couldn't. They were standing with polearms held half-staff, while all the frantic men and women surrounding them shouted, screamed, cajoled.

'Come away, Baldwin, please,' Lucia begged, and at last, baffled and miserable, he returned up the road whence they had arrived.

He was distraught. 'How can I get you away? I have to make sure you're safe!'

'Where would I go without you? What should I do? I am happier here.'

'No, I have to—'

'Baldwin. If we are to die, let us die together.'

The decision tore at him. He would do anything to make her safe and happy, but God had chosen a different fate for them.

There was a shout, and the clatter of arms from an alley. People were streaming down it, screaming in terror, and when Baldwin looked up, he saw turbanned heads.

He also saw Edgar and Ivo. They were fighting for their lives.

CHAPTER NINETY-ONE

Ivo shouted to Pietro to move, and they bolted towards the sea. A group of Muslims had encircled them, but with Edgar on their side, the fellows were soon routed. Edgar went through them like a hot knife through butter, shrieking a battle-cry as he wielded a sword and a dagger.

'I've never seen a man like him,' Pietro said with awe as Edgar drove off the last of them. He was like a man possessed.

Ivo grunted, and the two hurried after him.

They were almost at the harbour when disaster struck. At the crossroads there came a scream from the alley on their left, and a flurry of arrows shafted past, the nearest almost grazing Ivo's nose. He jerked his head back, and gave a loud, 'Phew,' then realised that Edgar was at the opposite side of the junction from them.

'Edgar, carry on!' he said. The sea was visible from here.

'What of you?'

'We have to take another route.'

Edgar looked at him, and gave a slow nod. 'God be with you, my friends.'

'Aye. Well, godspeed. Be careful!'

They watched as Edgar trotted off.

'What now, eh?' Pietro asked.

'Well, we could try to run through that space. If we are missed by the arrows, we can join him,' Ivo said.

'And if not? We'll be punctured like my lady's pin-cushion and will bleed our last there on the roadway. So, perhaps we should find another way to the sea.'

'You know as well as I that there is none.'

'Aye.'

Pietro looked up at him from beetling brows. 'So this is it?'

Ivo was about to suggest that they might run to the Temple, when he saw behind them a fresh mass of Muslim troops. They saw him at the same time, and with wild shrieks, swords held high, they began to advance the alley.

'Ballocks!' Pietro spat.

He and Ivo exchanged a look. Then, roaring with their fear, the pair bolted. A desultory clattering told them arrows had been fired, but they were neither of them harmed. Ahead was a bend in the lane, and they hurried along it, but then there was a shout, and they slowed.

It was Edgar. He crouched at the next alley's entrance. 'I thought you were going the other way?'

'We were,' Ivo agreed. 'Some Muslims dissuaded us.'

'I see. There's a bowman up there,' Edgar said, pointing up the alley. 'We may be able to rush over, before he can fire. What do you think?'

'It's better than waiting and knowing we'll die here.'

'That was my thought, too.'

Edgar gave the two a grin, and then launched himself over the gap. He almost made it, but as he reached the wall, there was a solid sound, like a knife cutting into a cabbage, and he gave a cry, turning and falling; an arrow was protruding from his left arm, pinning his arm to his back. Snarling, he took his sword and hacked the shaft away, then drew his arm free from the stump with a grimace of pain.

Peering round the corner, Ivo saw a solitary bowman fumbling with an arrow. Bellowing his rage, Ivo raced up the alley to get at him, closely followed by Pietro. The wide-eyed Muslim drew his bow and launched an arrow that hissed past his ear. Then Ivo was on him, and when his sword hacked into the man's neck, he fell, wriggling and moaning quietly.

'Sweet Jesus, how many more are there?' Ivo panted, and was about to make his way back to Edgar when he almost tripped over Pietro.

The old man had taken the arrow meant for Ivo. It had hit his brow, and he was so close, it had sunk in deeply.

'Old friend,' Ivo muttered, and felt the tears spring. 'I'm sorry it was you, not me.'

There was no answer. Ivo wiped at his tears and patted Pietro's face, then stood, sighed, and ran off. He made his way back to Edgar, and helped him along the roadway some yards, but they could hear the booted feet of the Muslims pursuing them.

'We have to fight,' Edgar hissed through his pain.

'Can you?'

'I fight better than I die,' Edgar snapped.

They stopped there, and as the enemy approached, Edgar lifted his arms with that familiar war cry. The Muslims were nothing loath, and the two soon found themselves beset in an unequal fight. Edgar was tiring, and Ivo could see that the arrow's shaft was a sore irritation. He was almost ready to accept defeat – when Baldwin appeared.

His silent entrance was a surprise to their enemies. His eyes fixed with a ferocious determination, he wielded his blade with a savagery that drove back the nearer Muslims. A moment later Buscarel arrived, fighting with a cool precision that saw two men killed in the first moments.

But even their fighting skills could not check so many. They were driven back towards the harbour, and Baldwin saw that Edgar was slowing as he went. 'Ivo, Buscarel, Edgar's losing too much blood.'

'No, Master,' he gasped. 'I am just a little over-tired, that is all. I need a draught of good English ale.'

And then came a familiar bellow, and the tramp of many boots. It was the English, with Sir Otto himself leading them.

Baldwin and the others retreated while the English troops kept the enemy at bay.

'Sir,' Baldwin said. 'I was never so glad to see a man.'

'I can imagine it,' Sir Otto said. As he spoke, one of his men fell back, a horrible tear in his throat. 'God's blood, save us,' he muttered as the fellow collapsed on the ground. 'Your woman told us of your peril.'

'I thank you sincerely. I wanted to ask you, would you take her with you?'

'I should like to, but my men come first. I have to have all of them embarked before I can think of passengers,' Sir Otto said.

'I understand.'

Make your way to the ship, then,' Sir Otto said, and Baldwin put his arm around Edgar and helped him down the alley.

They passed many bodies on their way, mostly women and children. 'Have the Muslims been here already?' Baldwin wondered.

'Look at them. There are no stab wounds or arrows to be seen, are there?' Ivo grunted. 'These were killed in the rush to the harbour. They were trampled to death, poor sods.'

'Sweet Mother of God,' Baldwin murmured.

He found Lucia at the entrance. She gave a little gasp on seeing them, and flew up the alley to them.

'I found the ship and wouldn't go until I'd spoken to the knight,' she said breathlessly. 'He was very kind.'

'He will take us away from here,' Baldwin said. He had a great feeling of relief at the thought.

Several Venetian galleys had already slipped their moorings and had taken their cargo of English soldiers with them out to the open seas. The harbour was still filled with the wailing, distraught women and children from the city, who pleaded with the shipmasters and others to take them to safety, offering money, lands – one woman even baring her body in her desperation for rescue – but the shipmen could offer nothing.

There were many small craft and rowing boats, and all were being commandeered. As Baldwin watched, he saw the Patriarch being helped down the steps to a little rowing boat. He had blood on his white coat, and looked very feeble. Seeing the people at the harbour, he burst into tears at their distress, Baldwin saw, and beckoned to those nearest. Three women and their children clambered aboard the vessel, and then another, while the men rowing expressed their anxiety. No more were permitted, but as Baldwin watched, they rowed away from the harbour and out towards the open sea past the Tower of Flies.

There was a shout from the farther side of the harbour, and over the heads of the waiting people, he saw black and white turbans begin to rush in among the crowds. 'Sweet Jesus!' he groaned, and drew his sword again.

Glancing back at the sea, he saw that the rowing boat had gone. The first wave had sunk her. All were lost.

*　　*　　*

Abu al-Fida hurried with his men to the harbour, while his comrades hacked their way to the Hospital and the Temple. He thought it likely he could cut off attempts by the citizens to escape. The Sultan would want as many slaves as possible, after all. He had not expected so many people, however. As he and the men pelted down the alleys and lanes into the harbour, he was confronted by a vast crowd. The only warriors he could see were already on the ships that were pulling away from the quay.

'Take them!' he shouted, and his men sprang forward like greyhounds after a desert hare. He was glad to see that they were capturing the women and children, and keeping them back, like sheep to be held penned. All the Christian men were ruthlessly cut down. The screams and wails of the women were hideous, but Abu al-Fida's heart was stone. His Usmar had been as deserving of pity and sympathy, but these people had killed him. It was the fathers of these children, the husbands of these wives, who had stabbed Usmar in the streets back there in the roadway.

Yet he could not help but feel sickened. Blood sprayed as the blades hacked at men and boys and old women.

He turned and saw a small group of Franks at an alleyway – two men fighting furiously, a third with an injury, but also wielding his sword with great skill. His men had passed around them, so they were cut off from the next group: a force of knights. He could see their Commander, a bold, imposing man, who charged with his men into Abu al-Fida's company. They were rolled back, several cut down, while the knights held a barrier, and behind them, men-at-arms and archers hurried to the ships.

The action was brief. As soon as the last warrior was on the ship, the knights turned and climbed aboard as well, and the ship was pushed off, archers sending flights of arrows at Abu al-Fida's men to keep them back. The galley's oars were lifted, a drum began to beat, and the ships started to make their way out of the narrow entrance to the harbour.

He turned his gaze back to the three at the alley. One was familiar. And then he remembered: a young Frank who had expressed sympathy and sorrow at the death of his son.

No matter. He was a Frank.

'Catch them,' Abu al-Fida said, pointing to the trio.

Baldwin saw the Emir's pointing finger, and felt a cold certainty that this was the end of their bid for freedom.

'Up this alley,' he shouted, and all pelted up the hill. It was the Venetian quarter, Baldwin remembered. Buscarel glanced at him as they came to a fork, pointing to the left hand. 'We must get to the Temple,' he panted. 'It's our only hope.'

Edgar was labouring badly with the arrowhead still in his flank and back.

'How is it?' Baldwin asked.

'I do not know,' Edgar answered honestly. 'It is sore, but so it ought to be.'

Ivo took a quick look. 'I think it has lodged in the bone, which is good. If it were to have entered his lung, he would be dead already. But if it's in the marrow, and poison gets in . . .'

Edgar said with grim humour, 'I don't think you need worry about a lingering death, not when . . .' He didn't have to finish his words. The first Muslims were closing in, and there was no time to waste.

Buscarel took the next left. A man and woman shouted down from a window, begging to go with them, but Baldwin and the others could not stop. However, the Muslims paused to kill the man, Baldwin saw when he shot a look over his shoulder. He feared that the woman would be raped, but his feelings were blunted today. Too many had already died for him to grieve over one more atrocity.

There was a very slight downhill gradient, which Baldwin found a huge relief, but he knew full well that he was running along the fourth side of a square. Unknown to him, this was the direction from which the arrow had been fired at Edgar. Still, there was no sign of Muslims yet. He hoped that they were already engaged in robbing houses. He didn't want to think what they might be doing to the occupants.

Their luck held. In a short while, they were close to the Temple. Muslim soldiers were fighting a group of Templars to the north of the square, and while the gates were almost closed, there was daylight visible, and before it another unit of Templar sergeants, weapons at the ready.

'Quick!' Baldwin pushed Lucia ahead of him before taking Edgar's hand and helping him over the last few yards. Ivo remained with him, his sword out, warily observing the alleys behind them as they went.

Arrows, more arrows, and then screams as the Muslims pelted from the alley after them. But already the squad from the gates had seen Baldwin and the others and had come out to cover their retreat.

Once inside the gate, Baldwin fell to his knees and bent his head to the ground, giving thanks to God for his unexpected survival.

CHAPTER NINETY-TWO

The aftermath, as Abu al-Fida had expected, was appalling.

His men, drunk with lust and greed, went through all the houses. The Venetians had already emptied their warehouses of all valuables, but there were still servants and children to be taken. Thousands of women and children were captured and led away to the slave pens outside the city. No men were spared: all those found were immediately put to the sword. So were the old women who would have little value as slaves. Besides, they wouldn't survive the journey back to Cairo's markets. It was kinder to kill them here.

Men walked the streets laden with the possessions of the people of Acre. Every house they entered was more splendid than the last, and often, when a woman was discovered there, they would make their use of her before bringing her to the pens.

It was the way of war, Abu al-Fida reflected. In this way were women subjugated. As he had this thought, a woman shrieked nearby.

The city was taken. Only the last remaining fortress had held out – that of the Templars.

Abu al-Fida thought it must soon fall.

Baldwin and Ivo saw to Edgar's wound as best they could.

A Jewish physician who had some experience of such injuries, managed to remove the arrowhead without too much trouble, and then bathed the wound in fragrant water before binding it and advising them to change the bandage each day, if they could.

Edgar looked at it doubtfully after the man had gone. 'You leave it as it is,' he said. He had no trust in the man.

For three days little happened. The catapults were brought closer so that they might send their stones into the Temple, but against the massive walls they could do little in a hurry. Baldwin spent as much time as he could with Lucia, but he had to walk the walls with the Templars and all those who were old enough to bear arms. Lucia was kept safe in a chamber with all the women and children who had been rescued by the Templars.

'How many will have gone to the Hospitallers, do you think?' she asked Baldwin on the third morning.

He shook his head. 'We are all there is, my love.'

'But the Hospital?'

'It fell. There are some sergeants and knights of the Hospital who succeeded in coming here. They said that their buildings were destroyed and all inside were killed. We are all that is left of Acre.'

'That can't be. No, so many cannot be dead.'

There was no answer to that. Baldwin put his arms about her. He wanted her desperately, but not here. Not now.

The women were frantic. Most knew that their husbands

were dead. In addition, many of their children had been taken from them or slain, and these mothers had lost their minds to their horror. They squatted and rocked, moaning or wailing. In the first two days, three of them died. One was a suicide who hanged herself, much to the concern of the Templar priest who came to take her body away, but an older priest told him that suicide while temporarily insane was not a crime.

'God may judge her. But after all this, He will be merciful. So should we be,' he said.

It was on the fifth day that the bombardment ended, and suddenly the Temple was a haven of peace.

Baldwin had been eating in the chamber with the women when the noise ceased, and he hastily bolted the last of his bread and ran for the stairs. It was all too reminiscent of the attacks last week, when the enemy appeared as soon as the stones stopped.

He reached the walls in time to see a white-turbanned messenger on horseback out in the space before the main gates. Sir Pierre de Sevrey stood at the gates. He was younger than the Marshal and the Grand Master had been, and his beard had little silver in it.

'Stop there!' he bellowed, and two archers stood with cross-bows ready beside him.

'My master, the Sultan al-Ashraf Khalil, would spare you further bloodshed. He does not wish for death, only the city. If you will surrender this fortress to him, all the inhabitants will be granted the freedom to leave. Your knights may keep their weapons. Your women and children will be honoured and may go with you.'

'You swear this?' Sir Pierre demanded.

'I so swear,' Abu al-Fida declared, his hand over his heart. 'What is your answer?'

'I will return shortly,' Sir Pierre said, turning from the messenger.

Baldwin saw his gaze going from the Templars on the walls, down to the inner ward of the fortress, where more citizens of Acre stood. A woman could be heard sobbing in the clear evening air.

Sir Pierre looked like a man torn between a keen appreciation of his duty, and the desire to protect his charges: all the women and children.

Ivo sidled up to Baldwin. 'Well, which way will he jump?'

'I don't know.'

'Shit! We can't hang about like this!' Ivo spat over the wall, and barged past Baldwin. 'Sir Pierre?' he said without preamble.

'Yes?'

'You have to trust them. It grieves me to say it, but if you don't, the Christians here will all die. This isn't Safed. What reason would the Sultan have for breaking his word? We aren't numerous enough to be a threat to him.'

Sir Pierre nodded. He drew his sword and stared at the cross for a moment, and then leaned forward and gently kissed it. 'I didn't want it to come to this,' he said, 'but you are right. Our priority must be the women and children.'

He sheathed his sword.

'We accept.'

Baldwin remained on the walls for a little longer. Ivo strode away, his face pale and downcast, and Baldwin was sure that he was thinking of his wife, slain in another city just because the men in charge wouldn't negotiate a peace. Then, when Tripoli fell, all the people inside were slaughtered.

Not that here was much better, he told himself. Out there, beyond the main square, he could see the bodies. Those who had been found in the houses had been beheaded or had their throats cut, and been thrown into the streets. There would be food for the rats for months to come. He turned from the wall and descended the stairs, his heart heavy within him. God had allowed Muslims to take His last city, and that was incomprehensible. He sought to punish everyone, but why? This was no Sodom or Gomorrah. Or was it because the end of the world was approaching? Someone the other day had forecast famine, war and disease before the final days. Well, perhaps. Baldwin would put his faith in God and hope and pray that He had another plan for His people.

At the ward, he strode to where Lucia stayed with other women in a great dining hall. The refugees were filling all the larger chambers, while the two hundred remaining Templars tended to keep to their dorter and the chapel. They were very keen to avoid the women. It was quite touching, Baldwin thought, that even now, in the midst of the disaster that had befallen them, the Templars were determined to stick to their Rule and neither kiss nor even touch a woman. To avoid all temptation, they segregated themselves. Only men like Ivo and Baldwin who had survived the catastrophe in the secular city remained near the women.

Buscarel was in the chamber with the women as he entered, talking to Edgar. The latter's injuries had healed remarkably well.

'Well?' Edgar said.

'We surrender,' Baldwin told them.

Already outside he could hear the gates being opened. There was a flurry of shouts, and Baldwin went to Lucia. 'We will be allowed to leave. There are ships not far away, and we will go to them and sail away.'

'What will happen to me?' she asked.

'You will come with me, of course. We will be married.'

She nodded, but she was thinking of the men outside. They were her people. She had been captured and held as a slave by these foreigners. If she went to England with Baldwin, what would become of her there? It was a strange land, so she had heard, and they worshipped the Christian god, not Allah. It was a terrifying thought, to be cut off from her own kind forever. Perhaps be forced to renounce her faith and take up a new one. That was impossible.

Ivo walked in, his face drawn and anxious.

'You have saved us, Ivo,' Baldwin said.

'I hope so.'

'Can there be any doubt?' Edgar wanted to know.

Buscarel walked to the door and stared into the ward beyond while Ivo spoke.

'I think I have hastened the end. There is a chance that we will be safe now.'

Baldwin laughed. 'Come, Ivo! They said we can all go free.'

'As they did at Safed,' Ivo said.

As Abu al-Fida rode his horse in at the head of the men of Hama, a feeling of great success warmed his heart.

The Temple was a building he had never expected to enter. The symbol of all the arrogance and savagery of the Franks, no Muslim would be permitted to ride under these doors. There was the enormous chapel, round like all the Templars', instead of cross-shaped like the Christians' usual churches. He would take a look at that in a short while. First, he would discuss terms with the Marshal. His banner, he ordered to be taken to the top of the gatehouse, and soon it flew there, a proud declaration of the change of ownership of this great fortress.

A man was at his stirrup. 'I wish to speak with your Marshal or Master,' Abu al-Fida told him.

'There is none. I am called Sir Pierre. I am the most senior knight here, by virtue of my period of service to the Order,' the man said stiffly.

Abu al-Fida nodded, and dropped from his horse. 'We must discuss how to remove you and all the people from this place.'

They walked together along the inner ward, but they had not gone far when the first screams could be heard.

Baldwin was prepared for the arrival of the Muslims, but the Muslims were not ready for the sight of the Christian women.

Later, he would swear that the invaders stopped with honest shock when they saw all the women. A number of them, perhaps twenty or five-and-twenty, simply stood in the doorway and gawped. Perhaps it was because the women here possessed few of the usual garments. More of their flesh was visible than would normally have been the case. And the Muslim men, unused to seeing more than glimpses of eyes above veils, or the hint of the line of a thigh or breast, were astounded. To them, perhaps, it was like walking into a brothel.

Four entered, their eyes round and disbelieving. One began to giggle, in a high tone, while another licked his lips and crossed the floor. A widow stood defiantly, and he reached out with his hand and grasped her breast.

There was a gasp of horror from the other women, and she slapped his face, but that only enraged him, and he tore at the neck of her tunic.

Another man had darted forward to a blonde woman, and was gripping her, trying to kiss her face, while she screamed; the third was still giggling as he ran at a woman with a young son, but he left the mother alone.

539

It was then that Ivo gave a bellow of rage and drew his sword. He attacked the man with the boy, and with one blow he was dead. Edgar kicked a man down, stabbed him, and went to the next. Buscarel slid his sword into the kidneys of the nearest, and Baldwin had his sword ready as a fellow reached for Lucia. He died quickly.

There were many more Muslims, all now screaming their rage and running in, but the Templars who until now had remained away from the women, had heard the hubbub. Thirty or more appeared at the door, and seeing the fight, joined in with gusto until all the Muslims were dead.

Baldwin ran from the chamber, and led the way to the gates, roaring, 'They are attacking the women!'

Abu al-Fida had left his horse with a group of his men at the gates when he heard the shouting. Sir Pierre left him, running to the source of the noise, and Abu al-Fida was alone for a moment. It was then that Baldwin appeared, sword in hand.

When Abu al-Fida saw the blood on his blade, he shouted, 'Treachery! Treachery!' and drew his own sword, parrying Baldwin's weapon and lunging. His blade caught Baldwin's cheek and opened it from below his eye to his jaw. Baldwin was surprised, and jerked back, and in that time the Emir's sword came to his throat.

The two stood silent for a moment, Abu al-Fida recalling that day when he left the city, and a man who showed him sympathy. 'You remember me?' he asked.

'After the riots. You were in the market,' Baldwin said.

'You saved me that day. Today I repay the debt,' Abu al-Fida said. He took his blade away, turned and ran for his horse.

'All retreat!' he shouted when mounted again, and rode to the gates. Templars had killed all his men, and the gates were being closed. It was only by slamming his knee against one closing gate that he managed to escape. Otherwise, he too would have died there. Outside, he heard the bars being slotted into place while he sat on his prancing mount.

Sir Pierre appeared at the top of the gate. 'So, is this how you honour our people? By raping our women?'

'A hothead, perhaps. This is your reason for bad faith? A couple of women complained and you tear up the peace?'

'There is no peace, Muslim. We fight to the death,' Sir Pierre said. 'Your men behaved atrociously.'

'Then you will die!'

'We will *all* die,' Sir Pierre said. A moment later, Abu al-Fida's banner was torn down and hurled into the dirt at his feet. The Templar banner returned. 'Now, go,' Sir Pierre told him. 'If you remain, I will order an archer to fell you.'

CHAPTER NINETY-THREE

That night, under cover of darkness, a galley braved the sea. A small rowing boat was despatched from it, and it landed at a small quay that gave access to the Temple.

Baldwin and Ivo were there, Baldwin nursing his scarred cheek, when the shipman came and discussed evacuation with Sir Pierre.

'How many can you take?' Sir Pierre demanded.

'Thirty, perhaps. No more.'

Sir Pierre nodded. 'There are some essentials that must be saved,' he said. 'We have the Treasury, records, and other important papers. Then I would send Tibaud de Gaudin, our Treasurer, so that these documents can be protected and understood. However, after him we should save as many women and children as we may.'

The selection of the fortunate few was made by lots. The mothers all drew straws, and twenty-two women and children were chosen. They joined the chests and boxes and the glum-looking Treasurer in the boat, and soon were bucketing through the waves towards the Venetian galley that stood a mile or so out to sea.

'Will there be another ship?' Baldwin asked Ivo.

'The *Falcon* should come back, since she is a Templar ship,' Ivo answered, but then he sighed heavily. 'But Roger Flor is no fool. He'll be enjoying himself in the fleshpots of Cyprus rather than coming here for us.'

Baldwin watched the ship. So far away, and yet such a good size. 'Lucia, I am sorry. You should have been on that ship.'

Lucia rested her head on his shoulder. She did not tell him that she had drawn a short straw. She had plucked it from the fist of the Templar sergeant who came around all the women in the chamber, and as she took it, she had seen the woman with the boy next to her. Petrified with fear after the way he had been assaulted by the Muslim, he had clung on to her skirts. In his face there had been utter terror. He knew that if the Muslims came in again, he would suffer rape, and then death. He was only a young lad, not a man. Perhaps ten years old, no more.

She had looked at his mother. Tears ran slowly down the woman's cheeks as she opened her hand and looked at the long straw. Lucia reached down, and replaced it with her own.

'Sir Pierre! Sir Pierre! I would speak with you!'

The braying of the trumpets had announced Abu al-Fida's presence, and now he sat upon a mare while he waited for a response.

It was some little while before a series of heads wearing Templar helmets appeared at the battlements. 'What do you want?'

'Yesterday, hotheads broke the truce. The Sultan offers you his full apology. He is prepared to offer the same terms as yesterday. Free passage for you and those inside the Temple.

Your knights and men can keep your weapons, your women and children can leave. You will all board a ship to go to Cyprus.'

'How can we trust the Sultan's word?'

'The Sultan wishes for no further disturbance. How many more must die? There is no purpose in such an outcome. Better for all that you accept terms and that you all vacate the fortress alive, that our men enter the fortress without fighting. Many thousands are already dead. Do we need to have any more die?'

Sir Pierre looked about him. 'Well?'

Baldwin shook his head. 'It is sensible, is it not? They wish to save their own people. It's easier for them to have us walk from here and sail away, than that they should have to break into yet another strong wall. Assaulting the Temple would cost them dear. They know that.'

'If we walk out of here, they won't let us live,' Ivo said flatly.

'Why do you say that?' Sir Pierre asked.

'They are offended that we killed their men yesterday. In their minds, that is us breaking faith. They don't understand how we could surrender, and then seek to protect our women. They don't think like us. They know it was provocation, and if Christians broke into a Muslim harem, they would be outraged, but for their men to assault ours, that they will consider different. They will seek to capture us all, by guile if they can.'

'I cannot tell whether you are right or wrong,' Sir Pierre said. He stared over the parapet at the massed troops all about. 'But I know this: if we don't agree, we will all die here. There are miners beneath us now. They will be digging out a chamber and burning the supports to force the walls and the Temple to collapse. All the women and children will die if that happens.'

'All roads lead to death,' Buscarel said. He was behind

Baldwin, honing his sword with a lump of stone. 'Some are swifter than others. That is all.'

'I think my own path is clear,' Sir Pierre said. He had been standing with his head bowed. Now he kissed the cross of his sword, then leaned over the battlement to shout at Abu al-Fida. 'I am coming down. I will discuss terms with your Sultan.'

Baldwin and Ivo stood watching as he descended the stairs at a swift but unhurried pace. He pointed to three Templars in the ward, and all formed behind him.

'Open the gates!' he bellowed, and the four men marched out.

'Baldwin?' Ivo said. 'It has been good to be with you for the last year.'

'Perhaps we shall be together longer,' Baldwin smiled. As he did so, there was a shout from outside.

Before the Templars could draw steel, all had been grabbed. Now all were thrust to their knees, and as the garrison watched in horror, each was beheaded.

Ivo looked at Baldwin. 'It won't be long now, my friend.'

There was a ship in the bay, and a rowing boat was approaching swiftly as the last assault was launched.

Baldwin and Ivo remained on the walls, hurling stones at the men clambering up the ladders. There were no enemy turrets as yet, for to bring them through the narrow, winding streets would have been difficult even before the siege. Now that each street and lane had piles of rubble from fallen buildings, it would be a mammoth task. Instead Sultan al-Ashraf depended upon ladders and his overwhelming force.

Thousands were scaling the walls. A massive timber battering ram crashed repeatedly into the gate below. Templars and women ran about the ward, fetching anything that could be used to strengthen the gates and save them from collapse. Baldwin saw Lucia running from the kitchens with a couple of other women, a large beam in their arms. Lucia almost collapsed with the weight, but then they were off again.

Baldwin had enough on his hands already. He beat off a man clambering to the top of a ladder, and thrust it back, but with the weight of men on it, all he succeeded in achieving was to make it move away and then clatter back against the wall. He tried to grab it again, but a man hacked at his hands. His leather gauntlets were no protection against an axe. Instead he stabbed at the fellow's face through the rungs, and felt his blade strike.

A bellow, and when he turned, three Muslims were pelting towards him from another ladder. Baldwin threw himself to the side, shouting, and the archer behind slammed an arrow into the leading man's belly. Baldwin was up for the second, stabbing him in the throat, swinging around with his blade still embedded, and thrusting his sword's cross into the face of the next. The guard's arm broke the man's nose. Baldwin pulled his sword free and stabbed him too. All about him was death. The Muslims were reaching over the walls at all sides. Baldwin hurried down the steps before he was engulfed by the latest waves. In the ward itself, he saw Lucia about to run back to the gates, a pair of planks of wood in her hands. He waved at her. 'No! Go back and lock yourself in with the women! Quickly!'

She stopped, staring at him, and then realised the danger she was in as she saw the black-turbanned men dropping down the walls behind him. He saw her turn and flee, and then he was facing the enemy again. On his left he saw Buscarel standing similarly, and then Edgar, and four sergeants from the Templars. Seven men to guard a narrow front. Now the Muslims were gathering. There was a shout, and they formed into a line of men, shields ready, swords held high, and began to move slowly forward. The Templar nearer Baldwin gave an order, and the sergeants stepped to the guard.

A bellow, and suddenly the Muslims were on them. A sweeping flash and Baldwin was aware only of the swords before him. He must give way, and his feet moved of their own volition, shuffling back, then darting forward when there was an opportunity. A man fell, and then Baldwin felt a stinging cut on his thigh. Luckily a slash, not a stab. He moved again, hacking at an arm, but someone else's blade was under him, and he cut his forearm, and that hurt, but he dare not look down at it.

A rumbling sound came to his ears, and he was sure that the ground was moving, but he kept on fighting. It must be the assault making the flags beneath his feet tremble and shudder. Or God was giving them an earthquake.

'Give me space, boy!' Ivo snarled as he came up from behind and took on three men to Baldwin's right. Edgar was on his left, swinging his blade with gusto, a small smile on his face. He only ever seemed to wake fully when he was fighting, Baldwin thought to himself.

For a space it seemed as though the attackers were losing their momentum. There was an increasing number of men lying, sobbing and wailing, and fewer wanted to launch themselves at the diminished line of Christians.

Then there was a concerted rush. Baldwin caught a glimpse of a Templar falling, and at once he knew they would not hold this place. 'Back! Retreat to the main buildings!' he bellowed.

Edgar nodded, and turned, but as he did so, two arrows hit him. One was high, and passed through the soft flesh beneath his collarbone. It carried on, right through him, and on. The second was lower, and slammed into his thigh. He fell at once, grimacing, and for once his smile was wiped away.

Baldwin bent to help him up, and now the two hobbled together while Buscarel and Ivo and the Templars gave them cover. He would never know how he did it, but he managed at last to throw Edgar in through the door, and then turned to bellow to the others to join him. They ran. The first inside was Buscarel, holding up his forearm, where a long raking cut had sliced through to the bone at his elbow. Ivo was next, miraculously unhurt, and then the Templars arrived en masse. They stood in the doorway, and then sprang back and closed the doors, swinging down the hinged bar and bolting it securely.

'Lucia!' Baldwin said, and grabbed her.

'There is a ship. The injured must go first,' she said, pulling away and staring down at Edgar.

He had fallen to the ground, and now he lay there gritting his teeth against the pain of the two arrow-wounds. 'Do they think me a pin-cushion that they would prick me so?' he groaned.

'You will at least be safe,' Baldwin said. He took up Edgar's arm, pushed his head beneath, and hoisted the man to his feet.

'I'll wait here,' Ivo said. 'We need to hold the door. Get Edgar to the boat, and as many women as you can.'

'I'll be back as soon as possible,' Baldwin said.

He knew the way to the landing-stage from the other night when they had helped the women to the rowing boats. There was a short passage from here that gave out to a small yard, and beyond that lay narrow alley that led to the water.

Baldwin and Edgar got to the alleyway, and slowly negotiated the stairs cut into the rock. With Edgar wincing and sucking in his breath at every step, it was not a fast process. Women and some children were behind them, terrified lest they be too late, and Baldwin waved them on when there was space, letting Edgar rest. Then they were up again, taking the gentle descent, and limping on to the ramp to the boat.

Baldwin handed Edgar to the shipman. 'Godspeed, Edgar of London.'

'Godspeed, Master Devon,' Edgar grinned, his face waxen with pain.

Baldwin turned and began to make his way back, but suddenly he saw the building before him give a dramatic lurch. There was a cloud of smoke, and then a terrifying rumble as if a mountain was collapsing. Before his eyes, the Temple was engulfed in smoke and dust. The wall near him moved, and a stone knocked him from his feet, and he found himself on his rump.

There was shouting, but he could hardly discern anything. The crack had been so loud, his ears were ringing still. He tried to climb to his feet, but an exquisite shaft of agony lanced up from the knee to the top of his head, and looking down, he saw that his foot was twisted at a peculiar angle. His leg must be broken.

He gazed back at the Temple, desperate to return. 'Lucia! Lucia, I'm coming!'

Ivo and Buscarel held the door with the Templars. A pair of sergeants and a knight joined them as the timbers creaked and moved. The Muslims had found a beam from somewhere, probably the pile of timbers that had been holding the gates shut, and now were assailing the doors with reckless abandon.

'We should open the doors when they least expect it,' Ivo muttered. 'Let the bastards run in, and we cut their legs off when they're in, then lock the doors again.'

'I think I'd prefer to keep the door shut,' Buscarel said.

Ivo nodded. Then he sniffed the air and frowned.

At the farther side of the room, Lucia could smell it too. There was a reek of burning rising from the floor. She knew what that meant as well as Ivo.

There was a last shattering crash, and the doors were flung wide. They could hold the Muslims at bay no longer. Lucia sobbed, but refused to shriek. She saw the men almost falling over themselves to get inside – black-turbanned warriors, one Emir with his white turban. He and the others had drawn swords. She saw Buscarel hacked to pieces at the door, and then a man was running at her, a Muslim with one eye, and in the flash of a moment she saw the Kurd again. The man of her nightmares.

That was when she screamed.

Ivo heard her, and span about to see the man pawing at her. He roared with rage, and ran, slamming into him. More Muslims were pouring into the chamber, and Ivo stared at them, then at Lucia.

'Girl, go with God,' he said, and plunged his sword into her heart just before the first blow fell on him.

Only a few moments later, as two thousand Muslim warriors ran through the Temple, chasing women and children before them, whooping and shrieking with triumph, the floors gave way. The Sultan's miners had done their job too well. As the timbers beneath burned, the Temple shuddered, and when the Muslim army entered, there was nothing to support their weight.

With a thunderous roar, like the sea pounding against rock, the whole Temple collapsed. The roof fell in on to the people inside, and the entire edifice tumbled into the caverns dug out beneath.

No one survived.

EPILOGUE

30 May 1291

He woke again to the creaking of the ship, alongside the sounds of men vomiting and women weeping. His leg was giving him a deal of pain, and he wished he could rise, go to the upper deck and see where he was.

'Master Baldwin?'

'Edgar?'

'What happened to you?'

'I broke my leg.'

'And the Temple?'

Baldwin recalled that hideous sight: the collapsing building, the smoke and dust. For a moment he could remember the first view he had had of Acre – the city of gold rising over the seas, a place of elegance and culture. It seemed inconceivable that it could have disappeared in a matter of days. In place of the city of gold was a city of the dead.

And he remembered the slow smile on Sir Jacques' face, his kindness and gentle humour; Ivo, his good companion, the man who had rescued him on arrival and given him a home; Ivo's irascible bottler, Pietro; Buscarel, the man who had been Baldwin's enemy and who became his friend; Hob, and the other men of his vintaine.

And he thought of Lucia. The woman whom he loved.

'The Temple's gone. It's all gone. The city, the people, everything,' he said, and closed his eyes against the tears that trickled from them, running stickily into his temples. He rolled with the ship, keeping his sobs at bay, thinking life could not hold anything for him that could replace all he had lost.

'I'd like to kill that bastard,' Edgar said after a while in a musing tone.

'The Sultan?'

'No. He was doing what he had to. No, I meant Roger Flor, taking the ship and all the women. I'd bet he took all their money, too. I wonder what happened to that bastard. Where has he gone?'

Roger Flor at that moment was sitting in a tavern.

Cyprus was an island he appreciated, and rarely more than now. He had a purse full of money, he had a ship, and he had enjoyed the affections of three ladies on the journey here. A man needed such diversions.

'So, do we sail for France?' Bernat asked.

'France . . . Yes, we could,' Roger Flor said pensively.

'We could go to the Temple. We do have a ship.'

'Oh yes, we have a ship,' Roger Flor agreed, and poured himself more wine. 'We have a ship, and the ability to sail anywhere. Now that the Muslims have control of all the ports and harbours off the Holy Land, there are ships full of valuables sailing from Cairo each and every day . . .'

'You want to turn pirate?'

'No. I want to turn *rich*.'

Bernat stared, and gradually a smile broke out over his features. 'I'm in too.'

Roger Flor grinned back and passed a cup to him, filling it.

'A toast,' Roger Flor said. 'To the men of the Temple. They can survive in future without my aid.'